The Nymph & the Lamp

THOMAS H. RADDALL

NIMBUS
PUBLISHING
—— NIMBUS.CA ——

Nimbus Publishing Limited
PO Box 9166
Halifax, NS, B3K 5M8
(902) 455-4286

Nimbus Publishing is based in Kjipuktuk, Mi'kma'ki, the traditional territory of the Mi'kmaq People.

Cover painting: *Sable Island Seals and a Dark Sea*, © Briana Corr Scott
Cover design: Whitney Moran
Printed and bound in Canada
NB1746

Library and Archives Canada Cataloguing in Publication

Title: The nymph & the lamp / Thomas H. Raddall.
Other titles: Nymph and the lamp
Names: Raddall, Thomas H., 1903-1994, author.
Description: "The classic work of Atlantic fiction." | Previously published in 2006. First published: Toronto : McClelland & Stewart, 1950.
Identifiers: Canadiana 20230591086 | ISBN 9781774713006 (softcover)
Subjects: LCGFT: Novels.
Classification: LCC PS8535.A27 N8 2024 | DDC C813/.54—dc23

Nimbus Publishing acknowledges the financial support for its publishing activities from the Government of Canada, the Canada Council for the Arts, and from the Province of Nova Scotia. We are pleased to work in partnership with the Province of Nova Scotia to develop and promote our creative industries for the benefit of all Nova Scotians.

CHAPTER 1

When the *Lord Elgin* set Carney ashore at Packet Harbor he was already a legend on the coast. He was one of the small group of telegraphers who had manned the first Canadian wireless stations in the days when Marconi's invention was brand-new and regarded by most people as a species of black magic. For years he had served in lonely outposts, chiefly on Marina Island, a sandy speck in the North Atlantic eighty miles from the nearest land. It was a desolate place, the scene of many wrecks, and regarded with equal dread by passing shipmasters and the young men of the coastal radio service. Three or four times a year a government ship called with stores and mail for the lightkeepers, the lifesaving crew and the staff of the small wireless station, and then left them to their thoughts.

Among the wireless operators Marina was rated the worst station in the service, and there was an unwritten law that twelve months' service there entitled a man to a fortnight's holiday in civilization and then a more congenial post somewhere on the mainland. For a decade Carney had watched his juniors come and go. From the moment they landed in grim resignation at his station they counted the days and talked of the time when they could go "ashore," as if Marina were some sort of Flying Dutchman forever breasting the long seas rolling down from Newfoundland but never getting anywhere. Most of them were young, and all were convinced that a year on the island was all that a man could stand without losing his wits. Carney's clear and untroubled mind after all his time on Marina they put down to a freak of nature.

In the service he was regarded as a fixture. In the wireless cabins of grubby Cape Breton colliers, in the smart varnish-reeking radio rooms of liners out of Halifax, in weatherbeaten stations from the butt of Nova Scotia to the peak of Labrador, men spoke of him as "Carney you know,

Carney of Marina," as if he were part of the place like one of the wild ponies on the dunes.

Men who had served at Marina wore that service afterwards like a badge of fortitude. They spoke of it with a wry pride, and their tales of the island and of Carney passed by word of mouth, by letter, and by dot-and-dash gossip from Cape Sable to Cape Chidley. Even inland, on the Great Lakes, young fresh-water radio operators had visions of a giant with a yellow beard and mild blue eyes, a sort of latter-day Robinson Crusoe who lived with two Man Fridays and a morose male cook on the most desolate of desert islands and was content to call it home.

They said that he had gone to sea as a boy and sailed before the mast in square-rigged ships; that he had helped Marconi to fly the kite that picked up the first wireless message across the Atlantic; that he had been in the Arctic with Peary and Bob Bartlett; that he was ill-educated and yet a kind of genius with gasoline engines, dynamos and the mysterious tangle of switches, wires, dials and knobs that made up the world's greatest miracle.

They vowed that he swam like a seal and rode the wild ponies of Marina like a Cossack; that he was the most fearless boatman in a place where the surf had to be seen to be believed; that on stormy days and nights he liked to stride along the beach with his yellow hair blowing in the wind, shouting lines from Byron at the top of his wonderful voice; that he was fifty or sixty and looked no more than thirty-five; that he had been crossed in love in his youth and had never spoken to a woman since.

Some of this was false, some garbled, and some true. The last was a fable. In the year 1920, when Carney left Marina for his first holiday in years, he was just forty-six; and he spoke to the island women as he spoke to their men, in a pleasant voice that did not distinguish between one and the other, as if they were all made sexless by the barren life they lived. His manner was at once friendly and remote, as if he were separated from the other folk of the island by the mysterious spaces of the ether in which for so many years he had lived and worked and thought.

Young operators in the solitude of Marina found this manner irritating. It was outrageous that Carney should not feel as bereft, as restless and as bored as they. He seemed inhuman. The only women on the island were the wives of lightkeepers and lifesavers, too busy mothering broods of children to notice Carney much. They found him "queer," and, pressed for an explanation, said that he seemed like a man in a dream. It was perhaps the best description of Carney; at least it could be understood.

In the early days radio work had a dreamlike quality that grew upon a man. As late as 1910, when Carney went to Marina, there was nothing to do but sit for hours with a pair of heavy old-fashioned phones clasped on his head, listening intently in a void. Sometimes for the benefit of new operators who took the modern traffic as a matter of course he liked to recall those days.

"Only a few ships were fitted, you know, before the *Titanic* went down. The shipowners considered it a fad. It cost a lot of money and it didn't work very well. Aboard ship you were a bit of a joke, a fellow wearing an officer's uniform who sailed the sea in a chair, sitting in a cubbyhole and playing with knobs and electric sparks. That was what they called you, Sparks, and they grinned and told you how useless you were, you and your silly box of tricks. Oh, it was hard to keep your faith in it, sometimes. You'd sit, watch after watch, hearing nothing but static, and every half-hour solemnly cracking off CQ-CQ-CQ with your spark—like yelling 'Hey, Mac!' down a drainpipe in the dark. If you got a reply it gave you quite a start. Your fingers would tremble on the key. You'd muddle your dots and dashes a bit. You felt like one of those old prophets in a desert somewhere, talking to Jehovah."

Carney had been at the Marina key when the *Titanic* struck ice and went down like a punctured can. He talked about that a good deal. The *Titanic* affair had made a tremendous change. After that Sparks got a grudging respect aboard ship, he was even a hero for a time. Before the fuss died down governments had passed laws, and shipowners had to install the mysterious apparatus whether they liked it or not. By 1914 the sea air was alive with dot-and-dash talk. Then came the German war and there fell another silence, weird and different, prickling with the strain of all those taut men listening about the sea; a silence so intense that it hurt, relieved now and then by some ship, attacked and desperate, flicking a scrabble of letters and figures across the void; or a shore station, solemn and purposeful like the voice of God, pouring out a stream of mysterious cipher and stopping with the final click of a water tap shut off.

Carney had taken the war years as calmly as he took the sinking of the *Titanic*. There had been some danger. The island, naked and remote, especially the wireless station with its mast thrust into the sky, offered an easy mark for the German submarine gunners. But nothing happened. Bits of ship wreckage came ashore: sometimes a boat or a ship's raft splintered with bullets, and now and then a sodden ruin of flesh and bone rolling drunkenly in the surf with a lifebelt still knotted about its breast.

Supplies and mails were irregular. The regular system of reliefs collapsed from a chronic shortage of trained men. There were weeks and months when the island crew existed on short rations and what was worse, no news. They seemed abandoned and forgotten, and the strain of their incessant vigil in that evil silence put their nerves on edge. They squabbled over petty matters. Sometimes they tore at each other with fists and claws in sudden explosions of violence that cleared the air of the station for a time. There was one who went queer and began to see beautiful women beckoning over the dunes on moonlit nights, and they had to watch him with care until the supply steamer came and Carney packed him off to Halifax.

But now the war was two years past. The phones buzzed with sea gossip again, musical now in the improved modern manner, dots and dashes on every note from the high canary warble of the German ships to the deep drones of Halifax and Cape Sable and the clear wailing voice of Cape Race. Even Marina's hoarse bass had been changed to a shrill treble. ("They've made a eunuch of us," operator Skane had grumbled.) But of course these were trivial things compared with what was happening "ashore." The war had thrust radio forward a good twenty years. The wireless telephone had appeared, and now in one or two American cities there was a strange new business called "broadcasting" that promised literally to set the world by the ears.

In fact the world that Carney had last seen in 1910 had changed beyond his imagination and far beyond the bits and pieces of news that reached Marina in old Halifax papers and the operators' letters. He could not grasp the magnitude of the war, which had been for him chiefly a silence. He measured the struggle in Europe in terms of the Boer War, a romantic affair below the Equator that had been the chief excitement of his youth.

The world's change did not strike Carney at once. The *Lord Elgin* had taken him off the island in the course of her regular round of the outposts, and now she set him down at the first port on the mainland and went on about her work. The land was as he remembered it, the gray stone face of the coast, the crown of somber woods, and between the forest and the sea the fishermen's sheds and cottages clinging to the rock like weathered wooden barnacles. It was a hot May day and he smelled the warm air from the forest as he stepped out of the ship's boat. By Jingo! For ten years his nostrils had known nothing but the salt wind blowing over Marina, where nothing grew higher than the tough dune grass. Trees—you missed the trees! Often you dreamed of trees, the pleasure of their shade, the way they rustled in the wind, and the smell of them, especially the smell of pines. It was something to smell pines again. He was glad he had come.

With an ancient suitcase in each of his big hands he walked up the rickety wharf, sniffing the westerly breeze with the enjoyment of a boy approaching a bakeshop. The local idlers stared. Packet Harbor was not a regular port of call for anything bigger than a lobster smack, and a visitor like Carney might have come from the moon. He was not quite the giant of the operators' fables but he stood six feet and had the chest and shoulders of a wrestler. The island cook had cut his hair and trimmed his beard in the close-clipped mode of Edward the Seventh, which was the accepted mode of British seamen when Carney went to Marina. That King Edward and his beard had been dead for years did not occur to Carney, and the knowledge would not have troubled him if it had. He had never shaved in his life.

He was clad in the faded blue serge suit that he had taken to the island ten years before. He had preserved it all this time with care, hanging it out occasionally to air; and the sight of these sober garments dancing obscenely in the breeze never failed to send his junior operators into fits of laughter. Imagine Carney in a rig like that! His island costume was a gray flannel shirt and a pair of duffel trousers tucked into heavy leather sea boots. He seldom wore a coat except in storms, and then it was a brown canvas thing lined with sheepskin that he had bought long ago at a trading post on the Labrador. He never wore a hat.

The cook had washed and ironed his small stock of white shirts and starched his half-dozen collars. An old mackintosh was slung over his shoulder. A pair of new shoes, ordered by mail last year, gleamed in the hot sunshine and creaked at every step. He felt quite well dressed. After all there shouldn't be anything strange, in Nova Scotia anyhow, about a man coming from the seaward a little too big for his clothes, and his clothes a bit out of style. It was not until he had boarded a train, and the train had put him down in the city, that he noticed people staring.

Carney stared himself. Everybody looked queer, especially the women—skirts up to their knees and hats down over their ears. Most of them seemed to have cut off their hair. Some of them looked like young men. What the deuce! Even the streets looked queer. All these motorcars! On his way to Marina in 1910 he had counted six on a Halifax street and thought it marvelous. Now they were everywhere, dodging among the horse traffic, blowing horns, giving off a great stink of gasoline. Even the people on foot seemed to be in a new and frantic hurry. Young women rushed about with anxious faces as if their lives depended on getting in or out of the shops in the least possible time.

They brushed past Carney trailing exotic scents like a swift procession of flowers. And their faces were like flowers, the kind you saw in florists' shops, very pretty and unreal and very much alike. He recalled something Skane had said, about women painting themselves like Indians since war began in '14. Skane said things like that, of course. He disliked women and you took what he said about them with a grain of salt. Yet here they were, painted right enough. He thought how in 1910 a painted woman was said to be "fast." Now they were all fast—going like mad, in fact. What had happened? Was it the war? Or was this "progress"?

He was bewildered. After all, ten years was not a long time. It had gone by very quickly now that he looked back on it. It seemed only yesterday that he was driving down to the waterfront in a horse-cab, on his way to the ship for Marina, and pleased as Punch with his first post as chief operator. He remembered the hack rattling down George Street, the steady clip-clop of the cabby's nag, the first sight of masts above the shops and sheds, and the reek of codfish drying on the flat roofs of the warehouses. Everything then had seemed decent and fixed in its pattern. Women in big hats, with masses of piled hair, with puffed shoulders, and skirts that came down to the toes; women without legs, almost without feet, moving along like images on wheels, towed by invisible cords. And men in bowlers, in waistcoats with large and drooping watch chains, in wrinkled trousers with a comfortable look about them; men with big mustaches, with handsome beards. He looked about him now. Not a mustache anywhere except those comic clipped things under the young chaps' noses. And where were all the beards?

The wireless office was in a street near the wharves, where he had left it. Something unchanged anyhow! He approached the door with the air of a man coming home. It had always been more like a men's club than an office. The Superintendent, a fat red-haired man, and his clerk, both former operators, had faced each other over a big oak desk whose edge was scored by their heels in leisure moments, and charred by neglected cigarettes. Operators from ships in the port had drifted in and out, filling the air with smoke and tales. Now and then a chap looked in for mail or to pick up travel-money on his way from one shore station to another, joshing with the seagoing "ops" about the joys of life at Cape Race or the Lurcher Shoal or some other Godforsaken corner of the coast. It was a kind of cult, speaking a language of its own that had to do with keys and phones and sparks and aerials; a band of men, most of them young, set apart from the rest of mankind by a curious knowledge, and having about them an air of the sea and of something else, not easy to define.

In those days ops were comparatively few, and most of the shore-station chaps you knew. You shouted their names and punched them in the ribs, as if you were all a band of wandering brothers who came together now and then for old times' sake. Everyone talked at once, the names of ships and ports and capes and islands flew back and forth, and the Superintendent put up his heels and lit another cigarette and enjoyed the racket. Aboard ship you were Sparks, a young lubber playing with dangerous and weird devices. On far coastal stations, where the only neighbors were Eskimos or fishing folk, you were a lucky devil who got fifty or sixty dollars a month for sitting in front of a magic box. But here in this room above the Halifax docks you were a god who talked across the world and knew your worth.

Carney's anticipation faded as he stepped inside the door. He found himself in a severe little anteroom stinking of fresh paint. Half a dozen hardwood chairs were arranged along the wall like those of a dentist's waiting room. Through an open door he could see two young women typing busily, and beyond them another door with frosted glass bearing the words Superintendent, Atlantic Division. Two youngsters of nineteen or twenty, in merchant marine uniforms with twined golden cords on the cuffs, sat with a resigned air in the row of chairs. They inspected Carney for a moment and turned their eyes away.

One of the girls came to the doorway and inspected Carney with care. He did not look like an operator. Operators were cheerful youngsters, usually in uniform, and inclined to be flip if you gave them the slightest encouragement. The present Superintendent had impressed that upon his typists. It had taken him some time to clear out the old easygoing atmosphere and put the office on what he called a proper business footing. The old days were gone. There were so many operators now, and so many more important things than personnel. "Find out what they want," he had told the girls, "and get them out as quickly as you can."

The big man in the shabby clothes was obviously different. His thick blond hair, his crisp beard, his calm blue gaze, the slow instinctive gesture towards his forehead as she approached, his whole fish-out-of-water attitude set him apart from the young men on the chairs. She summed him up as a tramp skipper wanting to sign on an operator, or perhaps to inquire about a wireless set.

"Yes," she said, lifting her brows. She was a tall girl, rather pale, with tortoise-shell glasses. Her brown skirt was neat but too long to be fashionable, and she wore a cool white blouse. Her dark hair was done up in, a thick bun at the back of her head. The young ops on the chairs ignored her. Their eyes were focused on the other girl, whose shorn blond head caught the afternoon sun and whose silken legs, generously displayed through the open door, they regarded with a frank and cheerful lust.

"The Superintendent," Carney murmured in his deep voice. "Is he in?"

"Mr. Hurd's rather busy. Is there something I can do?"

He hesitated. He pictured the mysterious Hurd engaged in matters of importance to which the affairs of Matthew Carney were as dust. The whole atmosphere of the place, including this young woman with her strictly business air, made him feel an interloper.

"My name's Carney," he said awkwardly, but in that rich musical tone. "I'm from Marina—Marina Island, that is. I've come ashore on leave and I was told to report here."

"Oh!" she gave him another long glance and turned away, walking past the blond girl, and rapped on the glass of the inner door. She stepped inside and reappeared almost instantly saying briskly, "Go right in, Mr. Carney, please."

Carney passed inside and found a slim neat-featured man of thirty rising behind a glass-topped desk and thrusting out a hand. Carney had never seen him before. Mr. Hurd wore pince-nez, which added a note of cleverness to an otherwise undistinguished face. His gleaming black hair was neatly brushed and there was a carnation in his buttonhole. There was a touch of the sea about him, faint and remote, as if it had not lasted long and as if a good deal of office air had intervened. He had the look of a man who for years had enjoyed good meals, steam heat, a soft bed and the embraces of a satisfactory wife. At this moment his eyes were curious but his smile was like the sun.

"Carney? Carney of Marina? Well, well! At last we get a look at you!" They shook hands. The Superintendent waved him to a chair.

"This is an occasion, Carney! You know, you're rather famous. The operators tell all sorts of tales." And seeing Carney's uplifted brows, "Well, you know, they talk of Marina as if it were the last place God made. And of course they're a foot-loose lot. Any man who's stayed in one place for ten years is a phenomenon. Anyone who's stayed that long on Marina is, well, a kind of monstrosity. Nonsense, of course. They haven't a sense of duty nowadays, not like the old-timers; not like you. Why, you're a pioneer, one of the originals. Is it true that you helped Marconi fly his kite in Newfoundland?"

"Yes. What's queer about that?"

"Nothing at all. It's magnificent! You're—you're one of the great few. Everybody on the Canadian coast has heard of you. Everybody knows your hand at the key on Marina. Everybody talks about 'Carney of Marina.' Do you mean to say you don't know that?"

Carney regarded him seriously. "There must be other chaps who've stayed in one place a long time. Nothing wonderful in that. When I went to Marina I'd planned to ask for relief in a year or two, but the time went by. Then the war came, all the young chaps off to the navy or the army or some other excitement; somebody had to stay, so I stayed. Foot-loose? I used to be that but I got over it. Went to sea as a boy and got it out of my system. I wouldn't have asked for leave now if it wasn't a bit important—one or two things I've put off too long."

"Of course," Hurd murmured, all solicitude. Men like Carney were hard to find. Life on the shore station was lonely and monotonous and the new generation of operators wanted nothing of that sort. Young, feckless, no thought for tomorrow—the war, no doubt—all for the blue water and the far ports of the world, the taste of strange drinks and the tingle of foreign women. When you hinted at a job up the coast they said, "I got through the war alive, why bury myself now?" And off they went, cap on one ear, flashing gold braid and brass buttons like admirals, and winking at the girls.

"I'm going back of course," Carney said.

"Ah! Good! Meanwhile a run about the mainland won't do you any harm, old man. Look after your business, whatever it is, and then take a holiday—you've earned it. The *Elgin* won't be going back to Marina till the end of August, so you've three months clear. Have a good time. Anything you want? Money?"

Carney shook his head. "My pay's been banked all this time, you know. Nothing I want really, thanks."

"What about the station? You left Skane in charge, eh? A queer sort, but a good man, I think. I sent young Sargent down to take the empty watch, and he'll stay the full year."

"Yes, I talked to him on the beach, when he got out of the boat. Seemed a nice young chap. Stick it all right, once he gets used to it. Of course he'll find it's not like life aboard ship. MacGillivray's year is up in July. He'll want to come away when I go back."

"I suppose so. And what about the station?"

"All right. Did you send down the paint I asked for? The sand wipes it off the buildings, blowing about in the winter gales, but I like to keep the place smart and shipshape. The radio traffic's falling off a bit but it still keeps us busy. All the liners seem to be full up with people sending messages, especially the westbound. Emigrants pouring out to the States, the French boats, the Italian boats, all those, popping stuff at us by the hour as soon as they come into range—'Meet me Ellis Island with fifty dollars'—that sort of thing. Keeps us on the jump, copying the stuff and then buzzing it on to the mainland. Hard on the engine, running it day and night for such long spells. We ought to have another for a stand-by." As he said this, Carney's look was anxious.

"Um! I'll think that over. Everything's in short supply, you appreciate that. Terrific demand. Things are moving fast since the war, I tell you. All these new ships to fit, all the old ones wanting new gear. Gad! A few years ago you had to sell the very idea to shipowners and masters. Now they come yelling for direction-finders, radio-telephones, every newfangled thing under the sun, as if we could pull it out of a hat."

When Carney went out, the tall typist came in with some papers, and Hurd said whimsically, "Well, that's the famous Carney—Carney of Marina. You know, we all think of radio as something born yesterday, and there's old Carney to prove we're wrong. Of course, those first ops weren't youngsters like the kind we get today. Some were sailors, some were railway telegraphers attracted by something new. Carney actually had been to sea in square-rigged ships, fancy that! Still wears a beard, and looks like something out of a China clipper."

The girl put the paper down for him to sign. "He doesn't seem awfully old. His eyes are like a boy's."

Hurd scratched his name at the foot of a letter and picked up the next. "Carney's forty-six. That's old, in this game."

"He looks younger," she insisted. "Because he's big and healthy, I suppose. I'd have said he was in the middle thirties without the beard, of course. There's something about him, I can't think of the word. Innocent? That seems absurd. And..."

"And what?"

"And rather attractive."

"You're joking!"

The girl pressed her lips together. "Not at all. Will you sign the duplicate of this one, please, it's for the marine insurance people. I fancy most women would see something interesting in a man like that, in spite of those awful clothes."

"Ah, that's because he's lived on a desert island for years. Women never understand how a man in good health can get along without 'em, and what they don't understand makes 'em curious." Hurd smiled over the pen as he said it. Miss Jardine was an excellent secretary, serious and businesslike. He liked to tease her now and then. It gave him a chance to exercise his wit, and he enjoyed seeing her pursed lips and the mild indignation in the gray eyes behind the glasses.

She made no answer. She was looking out of the window at the row of masts showing above the rooftops of Water Street.

"Well," he said crisply, "there's the lot, signed. I'll see one of those young ship ops now. Send in the chap from the *Stella Maris*. Oh, and Miss Jardine..."

"Yes?"

"Make a note of that chap Skane—the one Carney left in charge at Marina. He's been there two years or more and seems to like the life. A good operator, too. Another Carney in a few more years. We need men like that."

"I'll put a special card in the personnel file." Miss Jardine took the letters and went out.

CHAPTER 2

It would have puzzled Hurd to know that with two or three months of leisure, with several thousand dollars in the Bank of Nova Scotia, and with all the pleasures of civilization at his hand, Carney could think of little but his birthplace in a remote fishing village in Newfoundland. It was an odd sentiment; for there was nothing to be sentimental about. At seventeen his mother had been seduced by a glib straw-haired Norwegian from a barque loading dried fish for Pernambuco. She never saw the man again, and Carney was brought up under his mother's name in the little outport, where such accidents were not uncommon. When she married later it was natural that young Matt should be sent to an orphanage in Saint John's. He had run away from the place at fourteen and shipped as mess boy in a sealing steamer. From that time he had known nothing but the sea and a queer variety of ports in Newfoundland and Nova Scotia, in Labrador, Spain, Italy and South America, seen chiefly in barques and schooners engaged in the salt fish trade.

At twenty-five he had tired of the sea and found a job on the Newfoundland railways. This had led to a post as agent at a small station in the interior, where he used to lie awake on winter nights wondering what was to become of him. The pay was barely enough to cover his board and clothing, and the prospect of advancement had no more substance than the frost that gleamed so white on the nails protruding through the roof above his head.

Then, by one of those accidents that make the comedy of life—a train delayed in his station by a snowstorm—he had met a man engaged in the strange new business of wireless telegraphy. The man was looking for a few telegraphers, and Carney's years at sea had given him a knowledge of the rigger's craft, very useful to a man engaged in setting up masts and aerials about the coast. So Carney's life was changed by a whirl of snow out of Labrador; and the change had led him through the years to various bleak places on the Canadian east coast, and finally to Marina.

The orphanage had taught him to read and write. In the first years of his new profession he had sent for books on electrical theory and studied them with dogged persistence in the long dull watches of the night. Up to a point he had learned a good deal, much more than the average operator of his time. But there was a limit. The new invention grew too fast. It became technical beyond his grasp. The higher mathematics were involved and they towered above his head like a mountain range whose peaks were lost in the clouds.

In the course of his duties he had acquired a knack with the simple inductance coils, transformers, condensers and other apparatus of the early days, and with the gasoline engines that supplied the power. He fell back on this knowledge at last, and rested content with what the orphanage (with marvelous foresight) had termed the station to which it had pleased God to call him.

The technical books he had thrown aside. Thereafter his reading was confined to the more romantic sorts of prose, and especially to verse, which he admired. In the course of time and solitude he came to regard such people as Wordsworth and Lord Byron in the light of gods, immensely more important than Signor Marconi, a heresy that would have shocked his superiors; and he liked to get away by himself, walking for miles along the barren shore of Marina, shouting aloud the lines that stirred him. Of all the operators' yarns this at least was true.

And it must have been this, the music in other men's words, the romance of memory on which they chiefly played, and a craving to be touched even faintly by its magic, as poets were, that led him now towards the place where he was born. He took a train to North Sydney and crossed over to Port-aux-Basques in the small mail steamer. It was a pleasure to hear the idiom of Newfoundland again, not from the lips of some wanderer but on every side, in its own habitat, murmuring or shouting the trivial things of life like the voice of the land itself.

All was familiar. Even the railway seemed untouched by time. Nothing had been changed, not even the battered rolling stock. He sat back in a shabby chair and smiled as the train lurched off across the wilderness towards Saint John's. When the conductor, walking like a seaman in a gale, came through the cars calling out each station in his flat singsong the very names seemed like music. Codroy, Fishels, Bay of Islands, Deer Lake—by Jingo, where else in the world could you find names with a sound like that; or Horse Chops, say, or Heart's Content or Topsails or Come-By-Chance or Joe Batt's Arm?

Rain was falling when the train rattled past the little way station where he had spent that stranded year so far from the sea. He pressed his nose against the streaming pane, as eager for a sight of it as on that day, long ago, when he had come there delighted with the prospect of life in the heart of the land. Nothing was altered; the small red shack beside the rails, the sodden bits of washing hanging limp on a cord at the back, the wisp of chimney smoke, and even (in a blurred glimpse of a bored face bent over a telegraph key) what might have been the ghost of himself. Then it was gone, and once more there was only the barren landscape, with the telegraph poles staggering past and the wires swooping up and down in the rain. *I might have stayed. I might have been there yet*, he thought piously.

He spent a month in Saint John's, wandering about the dusty streets and looking down on the blue harbor in the bowl of rocky hills. Once or twice he found himself before the orphanage, trying to make up his mind to go in; but he turned away. No! Nothing to remember there except the bewilderment of a small boy suddenly alone in the midst of strangers, the dreary daylight hours, the weeping in the dark, the slowly fading vision of a familiar young woman-creature, kindly in a placid way, who had called him Matty and let him run wild like the young goats on the hill.

The law of gravity is not on the books in the Saint John's courthouse but it governs all that city's life, and it carried Carney, as it carries everyone, towards the docks. There he found company, boarding ships with a bottle of smuggled Saint Pierre rum for a talisman, and swapping tales of old voyages to the seal-ice and to Spain. Or he sat alone against a bollard at a wharf's end, sucking slowly on his pipe, with his eyes closed against the dazzle on the water. There was a reek of old blubber where the sealers docked in spring. He sniffed it luxuriously, and like a Chinaman at opium was filled with pictures of his youth.

First there were pictures of a voyage to the ice fields, his maiden embrace of the sea. It was all very clear; the sealers swarming over the ship's side, running over the ice like an invasion of gesticulating ants, shouting, striking with their clubs at glistening dark forms that writhed away, and paused, and then were still. The busy flash of knives, the limp bloody masses of pelt and blubber dragged to the ship and hoisted aboard. The long dim cavern in the 'tween decks where at each day's end officers and crew and seal hunters ate in relays at a common board; the thick reek mingled of food and wet wool, of sweat, of tobacco, of seal blood and fat; the white teeth grinning in rows of gaunt unshaven faces, half lost, like ghosts in the overpowering murk; the voices shouting for more food, more tea, and he, the mess boy, rushing about with mugs and plates and heavy steaming pots.

And one final vision photographed in every detail on a memory boyish and virgin: the stark beauty of the ice pack, all white fire in the sunshine of a March afternoon, patched with scarlet where the seals had died, veined by the blue water of the leads, silent as death under the spring sky, and fading away astern with one last blink on the horizon as if at an unspeakable outrage.

But there were other pictures. The old barque—what was her name, *Cassandra*?—with her patched sails and rotten timbers, her bowsprit steeved so high that his nose was level with the foreyard when he stood on the jib boom's end. Ah yes, *Cassandra* and that voyage to the Azores; the boats discharging salt fish to the shore, the foreign houses white in the sun, the cathedral and the convent bells that rang all day long, the jabber of Portuguese, the women all dressed like nuns, the smatch of new wine from the vineyards on the mountainside. By Jingo, it was all new then, and wonderful. It was something to be young, to go to sea, to suffer, to smile, to sweat with labor and to sweat with fear, to wonder how long the old hooker would last in the seas that ran and the winds that blew; and then to find over the curve of the wet world a place like Fayal, waiting all this time for you. Just for you.

And yet, not quite. Not all for young Matt Carney of the yellow hair, nineteen and shy and tongue-tied and amazed. He remembered the soft air of an evening, stars on the water, lights in the town, a sound of oars and the giggling voices of women. And then the wine, the laughing drunken sailors, the scrape of the fiddle, the dancing on the foredeck, the scuffling and the laughter and the tumbling in the bunks. Matt liked the taste of wine but would not swill the stuff; something within had rebelled at making a fool of Matthew Carney. And so it was with the women. Excited by the fo'c'sle tales he had dreamed of women, of their soft white flesh, and of conquest, with all the healthy instinct of nineteen, parched by the monkhood of the sea. But in the presence of women all those fine pictures fled. Some men are made for the full feast of life and they have the glib tongue and the bold eye and the bold sure hand. And then there are the Carneys, the tall shy men, the awkward and aloof ones for whom life only passes by. Matt Carney could not bring himself to touch, much less make love to a woman. His shipmates marveled. For women of the easy kind, the lusty kind, the ardent and the impudent, came to Matt Carney in port after port, drawn to his clean strength like flies to honey. And he fled. The other kind, the "nice" ones, the virtuous women, serene and aloof, were beyond his clumsy tongue—beyond his reach. And so as the years and the voyages rolled by Carney had withdrawn into himself, too clean to wallow, too bashful and too proud to beg, until at last he had a shell that nothing could break down. For years he had not thought about a woman except that vague creature of his childhood in the village up the coast.

At the end of a month the interest of Saint John's grew thin; the old sea pictures faded, and suddenly the harbor smells offended him. It was time for what he had come to regard as the supreme experience of his life. He took passage in a grubby little steamer for the north shore, and stood at the rail for hours in a cold wind blowing down from Greenland, watching the slow procession of rugged islands and the grim gray face of the coast. In a long swell out of the northeast the packet-steamer wallowed with the energy of a dog in grass, flinging up her nose and plunging deeply, and giving first one flank and then the other to the green sweep of the sea.

From time to time a deck hand, a grinning unwashed youth, in a checkered shirt and greasy cap, stopped on his errands about the ship to point out some feature of the land. Carney answered him a little testily. What did the young fool think he was, a tourist of some sort? "Look here," he wanted to say, "I knew this coast before you were born, from Belle Isle to Port aux Basques, round by the east. When I was your age I'd been to Spain and Italy, and down to Barbados and Brazil—in schooners and square-riggers, mind, none of your stinking steam tubs—and before that I'd been out to the sea-ice five seasons with the swilers. And you tell *me* that's the Horse Chops!"

But he said nothing, of course. The habit of silence had fallen on him once again after those eager conversations in the fo'c'sles of Saint John's. His face was unmoved as the sailor chattered and the miles went past. His blue gaze rested on the passing scene with an immense gravity, as if all this were some solemn tale read before, but whose climax he had forgotten and was trying to recall.

He slept in a cabin redolent of unwashed passengers coming down from Labrador in the years gone by. There was a scurry of rats behind the bulkhead. When he switched out the light a host of cockroaches emerged from the ancient woodwork and ran about the cabin ceiling, dropping on the floor with the persistent tap of a leaky roof in rain. He smiled in the darkness. Like the sealers, that! Life hadn't changed much, up here at any rate. And tomorrow...ah, tomorrow! He felt a glow of excitement in his big frame, lying in the unclean bunk.

On the next afternoon the ship crept into a steep nook of the coast. She put ashore Carney and his baggage, disgorged a few packages of small freight, and then departed with a single absurd shriek that fled along the cliffs. Carney picked up his suitcases and trudged up the stony street like a man in a trance. By Jingo, it was here all right! Fishing stages clinging like a wooden growth to the face of the rock; small gray houses with curled and weatherbeaten shingles perched amongst the rocks, each chimney with a blue wisp of wood-smoke, each dooryard with its nets spread out to dry, its brushwood flakes covered with split fish, its heap of firewood sawed and split, its beaten path to the village street.

Here was the church, and there the rickety schoolhouse, the village shop, the post office sign that traveled across the street whenever the government changed, the nimble goats with their silly gray faces, the ragged children playing, the women dragging buckets from the wells, the old men with brown withere-dapple faces smoking in the sunshine—it was like a photograph, lost for years in the bottom of a ditty box, and suddenly held to the light.

Outside the shop he put his burdens down. A small bell swung and jingled when he opened the door, and a young woman appeared through an inner doorway and stepped behind the counter.

"I'm looking for a Carney woman," he said, in the idiom of the coast, "who married a man from up-along, Betts Cove way. He came this way to fish, thirty-five or thirty-six years ago."

The woman sucked in her lips. "That's a long time—'fore I was born. I'll have to ask Pa." She opened the inner door and cried Carney's errand to a presence within. A voice replied, old and thin, quavering indistinguishable words.

"I dunno," the woman cried again. "He's a big man with a beard off the boat." Again the distant whisper, trembling, halting, going on again. She turned to Carney with an apologetic smile.

"He says she's gone—dead, years and years ago. She marrit a man Lewis from up-along, and died in childbed the next spring."

For a full minute he was stunned, a bearded statue towering in the midst of the shop. Then, "I...I see. And Lewis?"

"Lewis, he went away after she died and got some longshore work in Saint John's. Never came back here. Marrit again, 'slikely."

Another long silence, broken only by the tick of the old alarm clock on the wall.

"The Carney girl—would there be any of her folk hereabouts?"

The woman echoed this through the doorway. Again the old voice like a whisper from the grave itself.

"He says there's none. Her folk died long ago. She was a fine upstandin' gel, he remembers that. Her folk were big people, quiet like. Never had much to say. No Carneys left here now. That's all he knows. 'Course, he's gettin' old now and forgetful-like."

"Yes, of course." Carney turned away quickly lest she see his tears. All the charm of his romantic journey had vanished with that final whisper through the door. He thought of all the years in ships, in dismal waterfront boardinghouses, in isolated radio shacks about the coast, where at growing intervals he had promised himself to go back, to seek out his mother and see her face. He had conjured visions of finding her in poverty and alone, of stepping through the doorway like a prince out of a fairy tale, flinging down money and crying, "I'm Matthew—I'm your son!" And all that time she had been dead, thrust away and forgotten in some patch of soil amongst the rocks!

So end the dreams of so many of the waifs, the gypsies of the sea, who never find time to write letters, who hug to themselves a notion that some day they will return, and never do, or who come back like Carney and perceive that life has played a trick upon them after all.

Carney looked past the village to the harsh cliffs and the windy sea, with a sudden anger, as if they were responsible for the cheat. God! All that time in lonely places, doing the job faithfully, lost in a round of days that came and passed and turned up as tomorrows like the nags of a shabby merry-go-round—and what had he got to show for it? Money in a bank at Halifax—too much for his wants, and a smirking compliment from that fellow in the office!

The suitcases were at his feet. He sank upon them in the village street like a traveler in a railway station, thankful for one familiar object in a vast confusion. The urchins paused in their play and stared, and from behind the tobacco advertisements in her window the woman of the shop peered at him curiously. They saw the stranger throw up his head and laugh, his big shoulders shaking, as if he had come upon an enormous joke in the dust of the street. The children drew away, as if he were accursed. And so he was.

CHAPTER 3

A man accursed must find something to occupy or to dull his mind. For Carney the usual ways were closed. His pride of soul refused the indignity of drunkenness. Women were out of the question. Work was weeks and miles away. Movement and change were his only resources, and he spent a great part of the next two months in coastal packets, in trains, in strange hotels, with the air of a somnambulist. He remembered little of it afterwards. Quebec was a hill and an accent. Montreal a rush of faces, trams and motorcars, Toronto a hot desert of brick and stone.

Towards the end of August he found himself back in Halifax, not quite sure how he got there, making his way towards the waterfront with the instinct of a stranded fish. For a long time he stood on a pier, sniffing the harbor air, and with a summer rain beating on his face. He found a room in a small hotel near the railway station and walked about looking at the shop windows. At noon he dropped into a seat in a small restaurant near the docks and saw across the tablecloth a young woman whose face was vaguely familiar.

She acknowledged his presence with a flick of gray eyes and busied herself with her meal. In all innocence Carney uttered the glib greeting of the men he most despised.

"Haven't I seen you before somewhere?"

She looked up and said straitly, "Of course. In the wireless office. You came in to see Mr. Hurd."

"Ah! You're the young lady with the glasses. I didn't know you without them."

"I only wear them at my work."

"It makes a difference."

Another gray look, suspicious, this. But there was no guile in his bronzed face. She said quickly, "I can see quite as well without them. They're just for easing the strain of my work—all that typing. At least, that's what the optometrist told me. They always sell you a pair of glasses, whether you need them or not."

"You look better without them."

He said it with no desire to please but as he would have remarked, for the sake of polite conversation, that the sky was blue or the breeze a little cool for August. The girl stirred her tea and considered him as he talked to the waiter. The wrinkles at Carney's eye corners gave him the look of a man who has laughed a good deal in his life, but there was nothing of the jester about him. The sun, she surmised, beating up from the sea and those bare sands at Marina. She pictured him on a lonely beach, squinting against the glare. He turned to her again.

"Can you tell me when the boat leaves for my station?"

"Next week—Thursday, I think. Are you sorry to be going back?"

"No. When I came ashore I felt like a kid out of school. But things didn't turn out the way I expected. I daresay I've been too long away from all this. Everything's changed. I feel like the fellow in the book, Rip Van What's-his-name. It came to me suddenly, in a hotel somewhere, Toronto, I think, that Marina was the only place that had meaning for me. Sounds funny, doesn't it?"

"I think it sounds rather sad. Tell me about your island—why is it called Marina?"

"Well, that's a Spanish word for sailor. The story goes that in early times a Spanish explorer came upon the island and found a wreck and a lot of dead seamen flung up the beach. So he marked it Isla de Marinas on his map. Our people dropped the 's,' that's all."

"What sort of place is it?"

"Just a lot of sand, shaped like a half moon. Not a stone big enough to throw at a bird. Sand all stretched out in beaches and tossed up in heaps and partly covered with dune grass. Little ponds of fresh water in the hollows, and a rim of turf and reeds and cranberry vines. Wild strawberries, beach peas, a few low bushes of wild rose, blackberry and blueberry and so on. Nothing higher than your hips."

"No trees?"

"None. Even the bushes only grow in the deepest hollows, where there's shelter. We get the force of every wind that blows. In winter sometimes the sand's like a blast out of a shotgun. Twenty years ago a Deputy Minister of Marine sent down a lot of trees to be planted. Some kind of tree that grows in sandy places on the coast of France. Thought they'd take root and stop the drift of the dunes, make shelter for the wild ponies, make the island show up better from the seaward, all that. Well, they didn't last a year. The ponies took the plantation—five thousand saplings, fancy that—for a new kind of forage. Gnawed off all the bark they could reach, and the sandstorms did the rest. The whole thing was dead by spring and buried in the fall. God may make trees, but the Devil made Marina—and he writes the rules out there."

"You make it sound very wild and terrible," Miss Jardine said.

"It's wild, anyhow. Mind you, it's all right in summer when the wind's warm and the sea behaves. Miles of the finest kind of sand, pony rides, good swimming in the lagoon, surf bathing everywhere else—if you could tow the whole jingbang down off New York somewhere or Boston, say, you'd make a fortune just renting bathing suits and beach umbrellas. But you can't. You can't even sink the thing and get rid of it. That's the devil of it."

She smiled at him over an uplifted teacup. "You seem to have a great respect for the Devil."

Carney grinned. "Well, he's clever, you've got to admit. And he works hard at his trade. Who but Old Nick would have thought of shoveling up twenty-odd miles of sand, right out there in the North Atlantic ship lane, where it's got no right to be? There's no other way to account for it, in spite of what they say about the Gulf Stream, and the Labrador Drift, and the Saint Lawrence Current, and the silt of ages and the rest of it. Pooh! The Devil, I say. And look at the beggar's patience! He had to wait for Columbus to discover America before the thing began to pay. But after that—phew! Do you know what sailors used to call it—what the newspapers still call it? The graveyard of the Atlantic!"

Carney could not remember when he had talked so much to a woman. It was a relief to talk to anyone after all that mute wandering in strange towns and cities, caught like a chip in a flood of indifferent and even hostile faces. And it was easy to run on about the one thing he knew well, especially to someone who at least knew what he was talking about. He offered her a glance of apology and found her looking at him curiously, as if she had taken him too carelessly at first and now found him of interest.

"Go on," she said.

"The only people there are on the government establishment lightkeepers, the lifesaving crew, the wireless operators, and a number of wives and children. About forty or fifty in all. We're all there to beat the Devil, so to speak. Everybody has a job to do or a watch to keep, so we don't see much of each other except when the steamer comes and we all get together at the west end of the island to pick up our stores and mail. That's three or four times a year. There's a telephone line, of course. The stations are scattered along the whole length of the island and there's a lighthouse at each end."

"How do you get back and forth?"

"Ride, mostly. The lifesavers catch a few wild ponies and break 'em in for riding, hauling the supply wagons, the lifeboat carriage and so on. Everybody rides on Marina. The kids can stick on a pony's back almost before they can walk."

The waiter brought his order, a platter of fried potatoes and codfish cheeks, and Carney attacked it with vigor. The girl watched him, amused.

"You know," he said cheerfully, "they serve what they call fish inland, but they mess it up in fancy ways and it tastes like nothing that ever swam in God's good water. I went into a place that advertised 'Sea Food' somewhere, and asked the girl if they had tongues-and-sounds, or fried cheeks, say, like this—and she looked at me as if I'd asked for something out of the garbage can."

"But Marina," she persisted. "You said it had a meaning for you. What?"

He frowned at his plate. "It's hard to put in words. Maybe it hasn't a meaning at all. Maybe it's just the only place where I feel at home, because the people out there are the only friends I have. For weeks I've been knocking about eastern Canada like a lost soul, from city to city. Everybody scrambling—what for, I wonder? You'd think the world was going to end tomorrow and all hands had to get another dollar before the last trump stops the works. Everyone shoving someone else, and eyeing each other like a lot of sulky sled dogs on the Labrador, ready to snap at the first wrong move. Well, we're not perfect on Marina. A few people thrown together on a sand bar, little jealousies, squabbles made up out of nothing, for a bit of excitement more than anything else—something to do. But on the whole we take life quietly. Clothes don't mean much. Money's nothing. You see? Nothing to shove each other for. Anyhow, you can't go in for petty meanness on a place like that. God gets too good a chance to look at you."

Miss Jardine pushed out her lips. "I don't think I'd like that. It sounds like a fly under a microscope."

"That's because you've always lived indoors, in this kind of madhouse."

"Wrong! I was born on a farm, and before I came to the city I taught in country schools for several years."

"Why did you leave?" He was astonished.

"Ambition, Mr. Carney, just ambition. I wanted to earn a lot of money and wear smart clothes and go to theaters and dine in those wonderful places I'd seen in the movies on Saturday nights." She looked about the drab little restaurant and her gaze came back to Carney, rueful and amused.

"And did you find them?" Carney said.

"For the past seven years I've worked at a typewriter for sixty or seventy dollars a month. I've a bedroom over a small restaurant, very much like this one. I can't afford the kind of clothes I used to dream about. My notion of a good time nowadays is to take the tram to Point Pleasant on a fine Sunday afternoon, and sit on my favorite bench under the trees behind the old Point battery, where I can watch the steamers going in and out of the harbor, and the yachts slipping into Northwest Arm."

"Why don't you go back to the country?"

A pause. "I couldn't," she said slowly. "Teaching's the only living there, and that's not much. Besides, I wouldn't want to. I've got used to the city now."

"What do your folk think about it?"

"They're dead."

"I'm sorry."

Miss Jardine shrugged. She opened her handbag and thrust a coin under the saucer. "I must get back to the office. Shall I tell Mr. Hurd you're in town and ready to go back to Marina? He likes to have everything tidy."

"I'll report to him tomorrow." Carney jumped to his feet politely as she stood up and adjusted her hat. She gave him a nod and walked over to the cashier. Then she was gone.

For two days Carney roamed about the port. He bought a new pipe for Skane, cigarettes for young Sargent, a blood-and-thunder novel for the cook. He sat for hours in the Public Gardens, feeding peanuts to the greedy pigeons. He reported dutifully to Hurd, who greeted him with the same effusiveness, as if he were the one reliable man in the whole division, and promised "action" (whatever that meant) on his request for a new stand-by engine.

The tall typist was not at her desk and he came away with a vague feeling of disappointment. She did not appear in the restaurant. He wondered if she were ill. On Sunday afternoon, when the city was stifling and deserted in the summer heat, he took the tram to Point Pleasant and in a spirit of idle curiosity made his way to the old battery. And there she was, on a red bench under the pines, on the slope above the carriage road. It stood by itself and was approached by a path through the trees. As he drew near he saw that a book lay open on her lap, but the shell-rimmed glasses dangled from the finger tips of a hand laid across her knee. She was gazing towards the east, where the harbor mouth glittered through the trees. She looked cool in a white dress with short sleeves. A white hat, a fragile thing of net and wire, very wide in the brim, lay on the bench beside her; the sea breeze had blown some of her brown hair out of its pins. She did not hear his approach on the brown carpet under the trees and dropped the glasses, startled, when he spoke.

"I was afraid you were ill," he said gravely. "I didn't see you in the office." She picked up the glasses, flushing. "I'd probably gone out for the mail."

"You haven't been in the restaurant since."

"I don't eat there very often. I usually get my meals in the cafe below my lodgings—it's only a little way uptown."

Carney paused uncertainly. The breeze rumpled his bare head. One lock fell across his brown forehead like a handful of hemp, lifting and falling with the stir of air.

"Won't you sit down?" she said, diffidently.

He sat carefully, with the broad white hat between them, and fumbled in a pocket. "Mind if I smoke?"

Miss Jardine shook her head. Her eyes were fixed once more upon the water. He lit his pipe and regarded the scene, clasping one knee in his big hands. It was a peaceful spot. He had seen it before and he admired her choice. The bench stood on a small rise above the road, well shaded by the kind of trees he loved. Below, on the farther side of the road, sat the squat bulk of a fort built in Victoria's time, and now abandoned. It was surrounded by a tall fence of red iron pickets, each running up to a forbidding point. Inside he could see the crumbling stone casements. The grass on the rampart was long and unkempt, and weeds rose knee-high from the chinks in the small flagged court behind. He remembered seeing soldiers there, smart young Tommies in striped trousers and tight red jackets and pillbox caps, back in the days of the Imperial garrison. That was in '93—no, '92. He was eighteen, ashore for a stroll after a voyage in a malaria-ridden brigantine from Demerara. Jingo! How time flew!

The young woman held her pensive attitude, silent, absorbed, as if he were not there. He had a guilty feeling that she did not want him there.

"Look here, Miss. I'm sorry. I shouldn't have done this." He started up, but she turned quickly, saying, "Please don't go. I didn't mean to be rude. I was just thinking."

"Barging in like this, when I don't even know your name!"

"Do sit down, Mr. Carney. I'm the 'J' you see at the bottom of Mr. Hurd's letters. My name is Isabel Jardine."

He resumed his seat, but with a dubious air.

"This may sound strange," she murmured. "I was thinking of you."

"Me!"

"Well, I was looking at the sea and trying to picture Marina. You seem to like it but I've heard what the operators say. It's always seemed to me a lonely and awful sort of place. I suppose that's why it came into my mind. I've felt rather blue, the past few days."

"I don't quite like the sound of that," Carney said defensively. "When I think of Marina, I'm happy."

She was staring towards the sea again. "Ah, but I'm not like you," she said impulsively. "I can't accept the way things are, not so calmly anyhow. You said you'd found a meaning in Marina. I can't find a meaning in anything. It's not just those silly notions I told you about. Every country girl dreams of a wonderful life in the city. And if she goes she usually finds herself working in an office or a shop, sleeping in a cheap room, scrimping on clothes and meals, and after a few years wondering what it's all about."

"Oh, but look here," he protested. "You're young. The best of your life's in front of you. You mustn't talk like that." The words came easily. He had said them before, in the same Dutch-uncle tones, to young operators fed-up with his island, with the radio service, with existence. That was the trouble with being young; you saw yourself as the victim of a tragedy whenever things got dull.

"How old do you think I am?" Miss Jardine said.

He pondered, turning the pipe in his fingers and regarding her averted face. "I'm not much good at guessing. I'd say, well, somewhere between twenty and twenty-five."

She gave him a swift glance and looked away. "You don't know anything about women do you? In another year I'll be thirty."

"That's young."

"Not to a woman. You wouldn't understand."

He was mystified; but something in her attitude, the closed eyes, the melancholy set of her mouth, the bent shoulders, the hands lying palm upward on her lap with the slender fingers half opened as if in appeal to a destiny against which she had no defense, gave him a pang. His simple soul, which could bear his own woes with philosophy, was touched by this sadness of Miss Jardine's. In Hurd's office she had seemed so cool and efficient, so perfect an illustration of the modern young businesswoman he had read about in magazines, that the change in her confounded him. The sea breeze freshened and made a pleasant swish in the pines. The grass on the old rampart bent and swayed. On the blue background of the harbor reach a small yacht flitted between the tree boles like a swift white moth. A coil of Miss Jardine's hair fell apart and blew across her face in long brown strands, hiding that strangely pitiful mouth. The light stuff of her dress, long and full in a fashion killed by the war, lifted and fell with the gusts, billowing sometimes to her white-stockinged knees. The closed eyelids gave her the look of someone in a trance.

Carney, slowly sucking on his pipe, inspected her profile with puzzled interest. She seemed very young, for all the weight of nine-and-twenty years that she seemed to find so terrible. Her figure had a look of vitality about it, the good long bones and firm flesh of the country-born. Her pallor came obviously from years in offices, in dim little restaurants, in the perpetual shadow of buildings, and too much reading of books in the stuffy air of poorly heated bedrooms.

She startled him by saying, "I suppose you're wondering what's the matter with me?" She had not moved. Her eyes remained closed.

"Yes."

"Do you know any poetry?"

"Quite a bit. Why?"

"Do you know 'The Lady of Shalott'?"

"Who doesn't? That's Tennyson."

"Well, I'm sick of shadows, just like her. Shut up and seeing life go by in a glass—you get awfully tired of it. And the worst part is knowing that it's bound to go on like that, and nothing you can do about it."

"She did something, didn't she—the Lady of Shalott?"

"Ah, but what happened to her? Probably it wasn't Sir Lancelot at all. Probably it was just some ordinary lout on a horse and her imagination did the rest. You couldn't expect her eyesight to be very good after all that weaving by night and day. You see, I know. I broke my spell once. Only I didn't find myself drifting down to Camelot. I just found myself before the mirror again, watching the same old shadows and weaving the same old pattern."

"I'm afraid that's out of my depth," Carney murmured.

Miss Jardine opened her eyes and plucked the hair away from her mouth.

"It's quite simple, really. One of the most hackneyed stories in the world. I suppose every girl hopes to meet Lancelot. But I wasn't good-looking and the kind of knights who came my way weren't up to the Round Table standard. They pawed. Then one day during the war along came Lancelot—bugle, armor, plume and all. At least, he was a young officer in a regiment going overseas. I met him at a YWCA dance. We were both twenty-four. He was quite good-looking and full of ideals, and he liked me because I was serious. We went about a lot together. At the end of two weeks I was in love with him. Utterly, you understand. When he kissed me he could have had anything. But he was honest. He really had ideals. He asked me to promise I'd wait for him, and I promised—of course I promised! I was so happy that I wept as I said it. When his transport sailed I stood at the end of a pier for hours, in a cold wind down the harbor, in squalls of snow, trying to find his face in all that khaki along the ship's rails.

"As soon as he reached England he wrote, and I wrote back. I wrote letters every night, rapturous things, and posted them in the morning on my way to work. He couldn't write so often; the training was hard and sometimes there were weeks on end when he couldn't manage anything more than a scrawl on a bit of paper torn out of his field notebook. But sometimes there were long letters, very enthusiastic, full of army talk, and always a paragraph at the end about his ideals—and me. I read them over and over. When I went to bed I'd take the latest and put it under my pillow. That seemed to bring him near to me, and intimate a little fulfillment of the promise.

"You've heard all this before, I know. You've probably read it in a dozen novels about the war. But it happens. It happened to me. When he crossed the Channel to France his letters were fewer still. That made them all the more precious. He still loved me very much. But his ideals weren't quite the same. The army wasn't the wonderful crusade it seemed at first. After a year in the trenches he began to wonder what the war was for. Then he was wounded at Vimy Ridge. Not very badly, but I was in agony from the time I saw his name in the casualty list until the first letter came. It was written with his left hand, not very much, a few huge pencil scrabbles on a sheet of hospital notepaper, but I found it beautiful. Because it said that my love was the one thing he had found worth living for.

"There were more letters, and each time the scrawl improved. Then it got worse—his arm was healing and he'd begun to use his right hand again, to exercise the cords. And all that time I wrote and wrote. My hours in the office were one long purgatory until I could hurry back to my lodging and see if a letter had come. When I got one my fingers used to tremble. The mere sight of my name in his hand used to send me into ecstasies, as if he'd caressed me in the flesh. No doubt all this sounds schoolgirlish to you. Or is it only dull?"

"No," Carney said. "You're not dull."

"It's just the story of half the women in the world, it seems to me. You love a man and he loves you. You're separated by war or money or something else that's cruel and makes no sense. You eat out your hearts for each other, and in the meantime you pour out your love in envelopes. I won't bore you with any more of that. His wound entitled him, he felt, to a cushy job in a staff office in England. Anyhow, he got one. And he confessed his ideals had taken a battering with the rest of him. The army had taught him a lot about life. His letters went on like that. He didn't put so much into that final paragraph which meant so much to me. And the words weren't quite the same. But I refused to notice any difference. I went on reading his letters and seeing things that weren't there anymore. Then his letters stopped. I never heard from him again.

"You've guessed the rest, of course. He'd met a girl in London, very pretty and daring and amusing, just the sort he needed, just the sort I wasn't. So he married her. I heard about it afterwards from one of his fellow officers on the Pay Corps staff in London. It wasn't unusual in the war. I don't blame him, you understand. You can't live on ideals for long, not when you're young. After a time you've got to have something you can feel in your arms."

She took a handkerchief out of her bag and made swift little dabs at her eye corners, and blew her nose.

"Don't be alarmed, I'm not crying. I got over all that long ago. It's just the wind, and not wearing my glasses. I shouldn't have told you all this. But I haven't talked to anyone in a long time, except on business. You just happened to be the victim."

"I didn't mind," Carney protested. "I like listening to you. I never heard a woman talk like you."

"Nonsense! All women talk—like me!"

Miss Jardine put away the handkerchief. Her fingers went up to her hair, tucking the loose strands away under the pins with swift darting movements fascinating to watch. She put on her hat and slipped the book and glasses into her bag; and she stood up briskly, smoothing her dress.

"I mean the way you talk," Carney said mildly. "Your voice, and the way you say the words. Everybody ought to speak like that."

"Pooh! That's the school ma'am in me. Now I must go. I can catch a tram at the top of the park if I walk quickly. Good-by, Mr. Carney."

"Good-by," he repeated; and then, when her light form was moving swiftly through the trees towards the road, "Miss Jardine!" She stopped and turned, with a surprised look, one hand thrown up to hold the big hat against the wind. Carney walked down to her. The sunlight glinted on his beard and the unkempt yellow hair.

"Look here," he said jerkily. "I'm not one of those brash young ship operators you meet in the office. I'm just a chap from Marina, old enough to know my place, and I'm going back there in a few more days. Would you mind very much if I asked you to have a meal with me, or go to a theater—anything you like? Just for company, you understand. I don't know anybody here."

She was doubtful, he could see. There was a flush in her cheeks that might have been annoyance. She regarded him carefully, with the dress fluttering about her legs.

"I'm not much of a squire," he admitted lamely. "These clothes..."

"They're all right," she broke in, with a faint smile. "Are you sure you aren't just feeling sorry for me? Because I'm quite happy. You mustn't think..."

"I'm simply feeling sorry for myself."

"Well, in that case...all right. Tomorrow afternoon, after work. You may take me to tea and a theater. Nothing expensive. And please don't come to the office for me. Miss Benson wouldn't understand—nor would Mr. Hurd. He has a peculiar sense of humor. I'll meet you by the post office, across from the Boer War monument, at a quarter to six."

Away she went to catch her tram, and Carney watched her out of sight.

CHAPTER 4

Miss Jardine's abode was a lodginghouse in one of the lower streets. It was not to be judged by the outside, and certainly not by the grubby restaurant that occupied the ground floor; for above stairs there was good evidence of soap and scrubbing brush, of frequent moppings and dustings, of morning airings with upflung windows when the lodgers had gone to work.

Like many such establishments in the lower town it occupied two upper floors, a warren of small chambers furnished each with a brass-knobbed iron bedstead, a birchwood chest of drawers, a mirror, a cane-bottomed chair, a strip of carpet and a curtained closet for the hanging of clothes, all worn by the impact of untold lodgers who had come and stayed their days or years and then gone their way in the city's labyrinth.

The wallpaper, once the hectic yellow of a stormy sunrise and clustered with exotic flowers, had faded to a brown desert in which the blossoms had withered and perished and now awaited only a stiff breeze to blow them away. And the once gaudy pattern of the carpets had receded into the battered fabric, where it leered like the face of a trollop worn out by the passage of men and time.

Each floor had a single bathroom, a narrow shrine lit day and night by the glare of a dangling bulb for lack of a window, and the scene of morning and evening devotions by men in undershirts and women in wrappers, each clutching a towel and toiletcase. Its fixtures had a defeated look. Often they surrendered their functions altogether and forced their patrons to invade the hostile territory of the next floor. In each of these cells the scents of toothpaste, shaving soap, bath salts, cosmetics and disinfectants battled with the ammoniac reek of the water closet; and over all a faint but pervading aroma of flesh, male and female, mingled in vulgar intimacy from morn to night.

Nevertheless the air of the house was respectable, an adjective much employed by the landlady, who lived with two teen-age daughters on the second floor. She was, she at times explained, the widow of a sea captain, whose untimely death in a collision off Cape Breton had obliged her to go into the lodginghouse business in the rooms over Feder's Grill. The captain's enlarged and tinted photograph hung in a gilded rococo frame above the parlor mantel, and there were further mementoes of his existence in the shape of conch shells, bits of coral and other curios on the mantelpiece and in the shelves of a whatnot in a corner.

Mrs. Paradee was vigilant and shrewd, as landladies have to be, but she was not the frowsy harridan of the storybooks. She had been a rather striking brunette when young, if a photograph on her piano did not lie, and at the age of forty-two she was still quite handsome in a sharp-featured and full-figured way. This was especially evident on Wednesday and Sunday evenings. On these occasions the daughters, stolid blond-pigtailed girls who attended a school in one of the upper streets, were sent off with tram tickets to spend the evening with a relative in the west end; and Mrs. Paradee had a lingering hot bath in the cell on the second floor, from which she emerged in a bright scarlet wrapper and smelling pleasantly of violets.

Within her apartment she inserted herself into a pink corset trimmed with black lace, pulled on a pair of sheer black stockings, a pink slip and finally a black silk dress. The gown was sleeveless and fashionably short, revealing all of her round white arms and a good deal of her large but not unshapely legs. At the bosom a net of black lace lent the right touch of modesty to a pair of breasts that all but escaped from the foundation garment. Innocent of rouge or lipstick but with lightly powdered arms and bosom, with her dark hair elaborately curled and her black eyes alight with a light that was never bestowed on her lodgers, Mrs. Paradee awaited the coming of a man.

Whether or not he was her lover was a matter known only to Mrs. Paradee and the man. The lodgers speculated much upon the point. Every Wednesday and Sunday, exactly twenty minutes after the departure of the stolid girls towards the tram, a man entered the street door, walked briskly up the flight of stairs to the second floor, and tapped on Mrs. Paradee's door. He was a short and active person with an air of furtive assurance. Not much else was known about him except that he always wore a topcoat and a bowler hat, in the shadow of whose brim there seemed to be a small beaked nose and a pale toothbrush mustache.

He never had to knock twice. The door opened as if by some magic in his touch, and for a moment there was a glimpse of Mrs. Paradee in full array, unsmiling, wordless, but with a strange luster in her sallow face as if some pale and secret fire had leaped up after smoldering for days. The door closed on a murmur of voices, the woman's low and vibrant, not at all like Mrs. Paradee's of the other days, and the man's almost indistinguishable. There followed a silence as profound as death.

After two hours the door opened and the man emerged with the punctuality of a cuckoo from a clock, and the occasional lodger passing upstairs or peering from the upper landing saw the topcoat and bowler slip with the same furtive ease into the street and vanish. But this time there was no sight of Mrs. Paradee. The door closed slowly and mysteriously, there was a faint click of the latch, and then the handle slowly turning as it was released. In another hour, sometimes more, the daughters returned, clattering up the stairs, and the landlady greeted them in her normal voice, asking sharply if they had wiped their feet or merely inquiring after the health of Uncle Harold and Aunt Em.

To the "regulars" this semiweekly phenomenon was an accepted part of the house routine. Transients, like girls from the show at Acker's or vaudeville people from the Strand, seldom stayed long enough to learn the habits of the house, except the musical-chairs routine of the busy bathrooms, at which they became adept. In any case theatrical people were too full of their own affairs to be curious about Mrs. Paradee's. A long experience on the road had given them an instinctive hostility towards landladies, an attitude that Mrs. Paradee returned with interest, and they saw as little of her as they could.

Although she tolerated the late hours and noisy ways of the show girls as part of a game in which she could not make all the rules, Mrs. Paradee gave all her young women lodgers firmly to understand that she would have no nonsense about men in their rooms. On this point she was watchful and adamant. One memorable night a party of show folk had staged an impromptu performance in an upper room, enlivened with whiskey and song, and with a disrobing act by one of the more hilarious girls.

At the height of the affair Mrs. Paradee had walked in with the policeman on the beat, and ordered them all out, bag and baggage, into the street. Miss Jardine well remembered this, because the row took place on her floor, and she had been bold enough to unlock her door and peep along the hall. It was a startling spectacle: Mrs. Paradee a wrathful presence in long dark plaits and the scarlet robe; the cynical policeman; three men and two women screaming insult at the top of their voices; and the cynosure, a slim girl of eighteen or nineteen wearing nothing more than a pair of stockings and fantastic garters, suddenly gone maudlin and weeping on the policeman's shoulder.

The other lodgers had thought the affair disgusting or a tremendous lark, according to their sex and inclinations. Not Miss Jardine. For days she was haunted by the memory of the girl, at once bold and pitiful in the light of the hall bulb; and the whispers and laughter of the "regulars" as the strange little procession went shouting down the stairs at last, sketchily dressed and carrying bags. She wondered what became of that woeful creature. She was tortured by dreams of that tearful face crying appeals to a succession of hard-faced landladies and policemen up and down the town. And sometimes these visions turned to nightmares in which Miss Jardine herself stood naked on the stairs, shrinking under the cold gaze of Mrs. Paradee and the policeman, and hearing the comment of the lodgers in the distance like a twitter of malicious birds. At such times she awoke in a clammy stupor, groping feverishly for things to say or do in this frightful situation and wishing she could die.

But in general life in Mrs. Paradee's establishment was much like life anywhere, a monotony enlivened with occasional excitements that were usually annoying but sometimes droll. In this hive from which the bees departed every morning, most of them not to return until night, Mrs. Paradee was queen absolute. The force of her personality was such that, although the lodgers seldom had more than a passing glimpse of her except when paying their rent, they felt her physical presence everywhere, morning and night, as if the house were haunted by a dozen Mrs. Paradees, all but one invisible. And this uncanny sensation convinced them that she rummaged their belongings, read their letters, fingered their clothes, probed the inmost recesses of suitcases and drawers in search of something illicit—or merely indulging her curiosity, they were never quite sure which.

To some extent it was true, for Mrs. Paradee made a daily round of her menage and she had at least her share of curiosity. But chiefly her rounds were made to keep an eye (and a tongue) on the maid-of-all-work, a lean and silent Negro woman whose angular figure was sometimes to be seen working crablike down the lower stairs, with buckets and scrubbing-brush, towards the end of a day's work. The landlady herself did much of the dusting, a transformed Mrs. Paradee in long smock and bandana; and she was not above pushing a broom with vigor about the floors, for besides a scorn of laziness she had a concern for her figure that would have surprised all but her more intuitive lodgers.

Miss Jardine was afraid of this formidable person but at the same time she recognized in her a pillar of order, which has its virtue for timid single women in the world of lodginghouses. And so she kept her room and the contents of her closet and chest of drawers in a state of rigid neatness, with the unquestioning discipline of a private who knows that all his things must pass muster under the eye of a sergeant major, not for the sergeant major's sake alone, but for the good order of the regiment.

Her window looked upon a small back court, from which an alley led to Water Street. It was a kind of no man's land, shut in by four walls of unpainted shingles and tiers of windows exactly like Miss Jardine's. The court itself was littered with broken glass, most of it flung down by the great Halifax explosion of '17, which had smashed every pane in the lower town; and there were oddments of other kinds, rusty cans, rags, bottles and the shards of tumbled flowerpots, and of course the ash and garbage barrels of the restaurant and other establishments using the court.

In this deep wooden pit, festooned with lines of heavy washing each fine Monday, and given a festive note on other days of the week by long silk stockings and brief wisps of underwear fluttering here and there, in various arrangements, like the dots and dashes of a feminine Morse code, the sunshine never crept lower than Miss Jardine's floor. But there, except in midwinter, it touched her window cheerfully whenever the weather was fine. By standing close to the right-hand side she could see down the alley and catch a glimpse of harbor water on the farther side of Water Street, like a vertical blue pencil stroke between the buildings.

The back court made a small world, cheerful at night, when lights sprang in all the rooms and there were snatches of talk and laughter, the tunes of assorted gramophones, male shouts, mysterious little feminine cries, savory smells from the restaurant kitchen, and a pleasant and general air of release from toil. Few people drew their blinds. The court was a Peeping Tom's paradise. Miss Jardine's blind was invariably drawn; but often when she had undressed for bed, laid aside her book and switched off the light, she paused after running up the blind and gazed across the pit.

By that time most of the windows were dark, or had their shades drawn for the bedtime rites; but here and there, lit in their separate frames like pictures hung without regard to subject, she could see a variety of portraits and tableaux. A young woman, or two sharing a room, undressed and yawned over their bedtime toilette with a careless indifference to eyes across the court. A respectable-looking old gentleman with a clipped white mustache lay on a bed, reading a newspaper and clad in a suit of soiled woolen underwear. On summer nights a stout woman in a nightdress appeared at a window and gazed downward at the back door of the restaurant, scratching herself and smoking a cigarette.

None of these was worth a second glance. But one scene caught and held Miss Jardine's attention. It was always the same, although the actors changed from week to week, and it was not always staged in the same room. A group of men, usually young men in trousers and undershirts, sat about a bed playing cards in a blue haze of tobacco smoke. They were sailors, or perhaps merchant marine officers waiting for a ship, for their arms were tattooed and muscular. Miss Jardine watched them as they flicked the cards and passed a bottle back and forth. There were times when she longed to be a man like one of these, with their reckless faces, their hard bodies, their unconscious attitudes of utter fearlessness. She wondered how many of them had loved women, and what sort, and where, and if they ever thought of them. Probably not. You knew what sailors were. And yet how wonderful to be so free and so utterly sure of everything, from women to the chances of the sea, with that same careless confidence in the next shuffle of the cards, and never a look back!

These visions and speculations perished in winter, when the windows were shut and masked with frost, and all the inmates of the lodginghouses shivered over their tepid radiators and crept early to bed. But worst were rainy Sundays, when there was nowhere to go, nothing to do, and nothing to see but the sordid little court streaming in the downpour of the gutter-spouts. In the gray daylight the windows were blank and lifeless. Now and again a mysterious hand parted the curtains for a moment and flicked them back again in evident disgust, or tossed a cigarette stub into the rain. These were the empty pages in their lives, not to be skipped over as they skipped a dull chapter in the battered books they passed from room to room.

On fine Sundays in spring, summer and autumn the warren was deserted during the daylight hours. Nearly all of the lodgers made their way to the Public Gardens, to Point Pleasant, to the park at Northwest Arm, or sat about the slopes of the Citadel looking over the rooftops at the harbor and the Dartmouth shore. At night they returned with a pleasant air of accomplishment; their rooms seemed no longer cells in a prison from which there was no escape; they took off their shoes and sprawled on their beds and contemplated the familiar walls and furniture with a sense of home and ownership.

When Miss Jardine returned from Point Pleasant she ran lightly up the stairs and entered her room with all the relish of a sailor entering port after a voyage. She felt refreshed. It was nice to get back, and she had a good appetite for tea. She did not look forward to tomorrow's tea with the same relish. Now that she had time to think it over, an evening with the man from Marina seemed rather an ordeal, an act of charity that she must perform with all possible grace. She knew she would feel embarrassed and a little ridiculous, going about the streets with that gentle bearded giant in his suit of shabby reach-me-downs.

The odd thing was that beneath these doubts she felt a tingle of elation, and she wondered why. Because she had a date with a man? Pooh! Besides, Carney wasn't a man in the sense that enabled you to say in the office next morning, with a casual air and if possible a yawn, in the manner of the Benson girl, "I was out with a man again last night. Oh dear!"

Miss Benson was a virtuous girl who nevertheless enjoyed a good time and made full use of her charms in getting what she wanted. Men came to her like wasps to jam. Most of them were wireless operators, good-looking youngsters from the ships, who met her in the office, admired her person, and quite misread the invitation in her eyes. One after another, like suitors of a modern Atalanta, they pursued her through dinners, dances and shows, casting their golden apples in the modern form of flowers, chocolates, stockings, scarves or jewelry, according to their funds and their thirst for conquest. It was a splendid game, and unlike Atalanta, Miss Benson always managed to pick up the apples and win.

If the young men were disappointed they seldom reproached her, and most of them admired her skill. Indeed they talked about it in foreign ports, in distant stations up the coast, in dot-and-dash chat far at sea. With less than five years' experience in the radio world Miss Benson in her own way was almost as famous as Carney was in his. She did not know this, and she would have been indignant if she had; but the knowledge would not have spoiled her amusing and rewarding game for a moment.

Miss Benson in moments of candor described herself as a flirt. The young men had another word. Miss Jardine considered her a heartless fraud. After all the young men were simply healthy animals following natural instincts, and Miss Benson's game was not only dishonest but rather cruel. For her part Miss Benson enjoyed the indignant look of Miss Jardine whenever a new victim came under her spell. She was well aware that this tall pale creature made a perfect foil for her own attractions, and on occasion she felt sorry for her.

Sometimes when dancing with an ardent young officer from one of the ships she would say earnestly, "I wish you'd find a friend for Miss Jardine— you know, the other girl in the office." Usually he had failed to notice the other girl, or at best he would exclaim, "What! The spinster with the glasses?" And she would reply, with the instinctive arithmetic of a woman who does not really like another, "She's only a bit over thirty," or if Miss Jardine had been unusually severe that day, "She's thirty-four, that's not very old," and she would add, "Miss Jardine's really quite clever. She goes to lectures and studies art." The young officer would laugh, and so would she; but in these little exchanges Miss Benson felt that she had discharged an obligation to the plain girl at the other desk.

CHAPTER 5

Carney was early at the meeting place, wearing the reward of a day's search amongst the shops, a suit of light gray flannel, a hat to match, and a new shirt with a smart soft collar and tie, all of which fitted him fairly well. He had even bought a packet of cigarettes. It seemed a futile way to take tobacco, but he stood beside the post office puffing smoke in a determined way and regarding the bronze soldier on the monument across the street.

He recalled the Boer War very well. At one time he had thought of enlisting in a regiment for South Africa. The chap on the monument seemed to him a fool, standing on a boulder and holding a rifle high above his head, a signal that meant "Enemy in sight." A silly thing to do in sight of the Boers, who shot so very straight. Carney's gaze was fixed in a disapproving stare when he heard Miss Jardine's voice at his elbow.

"Here I am, Mr. Carney, fifteen minutes late!" Her face was pink and she seemed a little breathless, as if she had been running. She was wearing her brown skirt and white blouse, with a short brown jacket and a prim little hat.

"Let's walk along this way," she said quickly. She did not offer to take his arm. They joined the stream of office workers pouring along Hollis Street.

"You've got some new clothes," she observed. "I'm sure I wouldn't have known you except for the beard. But that's not true. You're so big. I'd have known you anywhere."

Carney smiled. "Why don't you say I stuck out of the crowd like a brand-new fire engine. That's the way I felt."

She tipped back her head and laughed. "I could see that. You stared so grimly at the monument. But, no joking, that gray suit becomes you. It goes very nicely with that golden beard. With a hat on you look quite distinguished. Really!"

He fell into her mood and they were still talking gaily when she touched his arm and turned in to a teashop. It was a small clean place with electric fans buzzing against the heat of a summer evening, and the waitresses wore short green frocks and looked very cool and fresh.

"They only serve light things here," Miss Jardine said. "Soups and omelettes and sandwiches and things like that. But you can have a steak if you ask for it. And the pastry's very nice."

Across a small table against the wall they smiled at each other.

"Any further news of the *Elgin*?" Carney asked.

"You've got another three days."

"Good!"

"I thought you were anxious to get back."

"So I was. But now that I've bought some new clothes I might as well get a little wear out of them."

"Don't you ever dress up on Marina?"

Carney chuckled. "If the people out there could see me now, they'd think I'd gone potty at last. So would Hurd for that matter. And—I say—he must have been busy today, he kept you so long."

Miss Jardine blushed. "I've a confession to make. I chose the post office because about that time of day all the typists are rushing in and out with the afternoon mail, and nobody'd think it strange if they saw me there. But I couldn't stand outside very well. I slipped in by the George Street door and waited twenty minutes, fiddling with one or two letters and peeping from a window now and again. I wasn't sure I wanted to go through with it—please don't be offended. In the park it seemed all right; but in the office this morning I couldn't help wondering what Mr. Hurd or the Benson girl would think if they saw me with you. And you—you're rather shy. I wasn't even sure you'd come. I wasn't sure about anything."

"I was," Carney said.

"About me?"

"You said you'd come, and here you are."

"Yes. You must think me awfully silly."

"I wouldn't have blamed you if you hadn't shown up."

She gave him a clear gray look and said slowly, "I don't believe you would. You're much too kind. It's a good thing you're going back to your island."

"Why?"

"You'd be disillusioned if you stayed here long."

Carney closed his big fist on the table and opened the fingers slowly, inspecting them with a profound gaze.

"I've lost the only illusion I ever had. That makes me safe."

"Oh? Was it—was it a woman?"

"Yes."

"I see. Was that why you got your leave?"

"Mostly, yes."

"I'm awfully sorry."

"It wasn't quite what you think," Carney said deliberately. "But it came to the same thing in the end. When you've been roving half your life, like me, you invent one place and someone there, to think about, to convince yourself that you've got roots like everybody else. If I'd stayed on Marina and gone on believing that it would have been all right. But I had to go and see—and she was dead."

"After all that time!" Miss Jardine exclaimed. "How sad!"

Carney looked up and was confounded to see tears in her eyes. He condemned himself for a fool. She had been so melancholy in the park that he had planned an evening's entertainment, full of lively talk. And now, this!

"I'm afraid I've given you a wrong impression," he said carefully. "What happened to me was just a notion that came to nothing. It gave me a knock but it's over now. Life on Marina was all right for me because I'd absolutely nothing here ashore. I didn't know it then. Now I do. Let's talk about something else. Here's the waitress. What will you have to eat?"

Miss Jardine picked up the menu. "A salad, please. The salmon salad will be very nice. And some rolls, and tea." A cool young person in a green frock took this down and turned her impersonal glance to Carney. He ordered steak and potatoes and coffee.

"Make the potatoes French fried," Miss Jardine put in. The waitress nodded and swayed away towards the kitchen on a pair of legs straight out of a silk-hosiery advertisement.

"What made you think of that?" Carney asked.

"Because you've got a man cook on your island and you eat your potatoes boiled or not at all. And all that stuff out of tins! I've heard the operators. When they get ashore from Marina they eat nothing for days but greens and steak and French fried potatoes. Why don't you get another cook?"

"He's all right. Beside, they're hard to get."

She dismissed Carney's cook with a gesture. "Well, have you picked a theater? There's a stock company playing at the Academy of Music. And there's a girl-and-music show at Acker's if you want something lively. I haven't seen it but I can testify that the girls are lively enough. Some of them used to stay where I do and they made a frightful racket."

"They probably make a frightful racket on the stage. I'd rather see a movie."

"Ah! That makes it simple. What kind do you like?"

"Anything except those Western things with a lot of chaps galloping about, shooting off pistols and never hitting anything. Like Marina in a nightmare."

Miss Jardine raised her brows. "Oh? I couldn't imagine anything less like your island than a Western movie."

"You'd be surprised. When you step off the beach at Marina on a summer's day you might be in the heart of Arizona, or wherever they film those things. The biggest dunes are by the shore and they shut off the view of the sea in a good many places. You can hear the surf but for all you know it might be a thousand miles away. And there you are, riding a half-wild pony amongst the dunes, with nothing in sight but grass and sand, just like those movie chaps. We even use Western saddles and stirrups, brought all the way from the prairie. You can stick on the ponies better in the kind of going you find out there. In fact, all we lack is the fancy clothes and the pistols—and a villain after the girl, of course."

"And a girl?" Miss Jardine suggested.

"Oh no. We've got a girl. She's only seventeen, the daughter of a man in charge of a small lifesaving station eight miles or so from us. She's the belle of Marina. All the young chaps in the lifeboat crew are crazy about her."

"And surely the wireless operators?"

"Oh, MacGillivray rides down there quite a bit. He likes girls. I don't know about Sargent, the new chap. But Skane—no. Skane dislikes women. If the Queen of Sheba landed on our island one fine afternoon in all her glory, Skane wouldn't turn his head to give her a glance."

"And would you?" Her eyes were merry. She was trying to picture Carney with the Queen of Sheba, and the strange thing was that she could. He seemed to belong in some splendid and barbaric scene, where everything was a little bigger than life size, not like this restaurant, not even like Marina.

"I've always thought it was a bit rude, staring at a lady," Carney parried.

"Don't tell me that you've never turned to look at a pretty woman. A sailor!"

He smiled broadly, revealing his square white teeth. "Oh, I've always liked women, you understand. When I was in my twenties and going to sea it was a pleasure to come in from a voyage and walk about admiring the girls, the way they moved, and the sound of their voices. They were marvelous. You wondered how men in cities could be so casual about them. But I never got any further than that. And I must say I've got along very well."

Miss Jardine laughed. "You stuck out your jaw when you said that! You know, you're not a bit like the creature I expected. The operators always called you a 'character'—meaning something queer, I supposed. But you're not. You're absolutely normal. The rest of us are characters, scrambling after hats and dollars— and seats at the movies. We'll have to hurry to catch the show at the Orpheus. That's the nearest."

Inside the theater, seated together in a warm gloom where the tinkling notes of a piano failed to drown the chatter of the machine, they fell into a mutual silence. The picture was a banal thing with an authentic hero, a patent villain, and a gesticulating young woman with a beautiful chalk-white face who ran about the screen and made a tiresome business of misunderstanding both of them. Miss Jardine was bored, but she was interested and amused to find that Carney was not. She watched him with sidelong glances for the better part of two hours, fanning her face gently with a handkerchief in the exhausted air.

Carney sat forward with a rapt face lit by the glare in which those fantastic creatures moved, clenching his fists when the villain became outrageous, shaking his head when the heroine failed to see how outrageous the fellow was. Miss Jardine smiled. She felt like a maiden aunt who has taken a small boy to the matinee. Once, when the simpering she-ghost got into a predicament that she thoroughly deserved, Carney put out a hand and seized Miss Jardine's wrist with such force that she barely suppressed a cry. But she did not move. Her wrist lay passive in his grasp until, in the same unconscious way, he let it go.

When they emerged into the clean air of the August evening Carney drew in a great breath and blew it out through his bearded lips.

"That's better," he announced with satisfaction.

"But I thought you liked the show?"

"Oh, I did. I didn't like that dark chap, though. By Jingo, I could have knocked his head off. I don't understand why the other chap didn't, there in the first reel. He could see what the fellow was."

"So could the girl, if she had any sense."

"I thought she was rather nice."

"I thought she was an idiot."

He turned and looked at Miss Jardine in surprise.

"But you couldn't expect a girl like that to know anything about a fellow of his sort!"

"I could and I did. Even nice girls are supposed to have some common sense. And he was so obvious. He fairly dripped nastiness. Of course, life's not like that anyhow. The man who looks like a hero usually turns out to be the villain sooner or later; and the really nice man might be anybody, like…" She was going to say "you" but she checked the word on her tongue. She did not mean quite that. Carney was nice, of course, but not in the romantic sense. You looked upon him as you might have regarded a good-natured uncle when you were small and the world seemed full of huge man-creatures, stern, indifferent, and all as old as the hills.

"Like what?" Carney demanded.

"I can't think of the right word. Anyhow, nice men seldom have a cameo profile and I hope they have a lot more sense than our hero. It isn't any good striking attitudes when the lady's making a fool of herself. Frankly I don't think she was worth bothering about, but a good shake right at the start might have helped. What she really wanted was an old-fashioned smacking, country-style."

Carney chaffed, "You're still pretty much the school ma'am, aren't you?"

"Of course I am! I'm pretty much a cat, too. All women are—or didn't you know? Sometimes I'd like to get out on the tiles and howl. It must be fun. You see? I'm the character, not you. Here's where we turn; and you may see me to my lodgings if you like. It isn't far. I live downtown to save tram fares."

They had come to one of those steeply descending Halifax streets that break the long procession of shops with a sudden glimpse of the shipping. There was no moon but the harbor water had a faint shine in the starlight, and a liner with rows of yellow portholes lay framed for a moment between the buildings on her way to sea. Miss Jardine slipped an impulsive hand under Carney's arm.

"How lovely! Don't you ever want to go back to ships? I would, if I were a man." They swung down the street in long strides, due partly to the slope but with a touch of exhilaration, as if the sight of the water in the starlight had set them forth on an adventure. So it seemed to Carney at least. Miss Jardine's light clasp charged his arm with electricity. When they abandoned the slope and turned along the street on which she lived, she attempted to withdraw her hand, but Carney pressed it firmly against his side.

She halted at last at a doorway beside a small cafe. It was a dingy place. Through the glass Carney could see a few late customers sitting at the tables and a bored slattern moving about with plates. The air was hung with cigarette smoke, eddying slowly in the faint draft of a fan somewhere at the back of the room.

"So this is where you eat!" he exclaimed.

"It's better than it looks," Miss Jardine said defensively. "During the day the customers are mostly clerks and typists like me. At this time of night the place is patronized mostly by men wanting a cheap snack and a place to sit and smoke. I live upstairs. The landlady's rather a fearsome creature but the rooms are very clean, and I haven't far to go to the office. When I first came to the city I boarded with a family in the north end. It was very nice, but it cost more than this, and it was a nuisance getting back and forth. I seemed to spend half my time waiting for trams."

She turned towards the side door and put a foot on the step, "I'm sorry I can't invite you in. There's no parlor for the lodgers, and we're not allowed to entertain anyone in our rooms."

Carney had released that captive hand at last, and he stood awkwardly, wondering what he should say next. Miss Jardine solved his problem quickly.

"Well, it's been very nice, all of it, Mr. Carney. It was so kind of you to ask me." She put out a hand and he took it with a boyish eagerness.

"I..." he stammered. "Look here, I suppose it's too much to ask, but couldn't we do this again tomorrow?"

For a moment her fingers lay quiet in his grasp. Then he felt them stiffen and he let the hand go.

"I'm sorry, Mr. Carney. I couldn't, really. I've got things to do."

"What about the next day?"

A silence. Then, in a subdued voice, "I'm sorry."

"I see."

"Good night, Mr. Carney."

"Good night."

She ran up the steps. The door closed with a firm click and left him staring at the withered paint.

CHAPTER 6

Carney killed the time partly with tram rides about the city, getting off as fancy moved; but chiefly he wandered along the docks, where he was at ease talking to sailors and longshoremen, or boarding a ship and striking up an acquaintance with the wireless operator or one of the mates. The city baked and sweated in the August heat, even the harbor seemed to burn with the shimmering blue flame of alcohol. Amid the clatter of cargo winches the stevedores moved listlessly about the slings. Urchins dived and splashed all day from the ends of the wharves. The fetor of Water Street hung in the unmoving air above the docks. From the hills behind Bedford Basin a bush fire sent up a haze of thin brown smoke, and towards sundown there was sometimes a whiff of burning leaves, borne along the water by a stir of the evening air.

On the morning before the *Lord Elgin* was due to sail he took the ferry across the harbor to see about his berth. The familiar ship lay at a wharf on the Dartmouth side, loading stores, mail, and odds and ends of equipment for another round of the outposts. She had a black hull and a slender buff funnel, a pair of very tall masts of the sort deemed necessary for wireless telegraphy in its earlier days, and a heavy iron sheave hanging over the bow for cable repair work. The foredeck was cluttered with red and black buoys, and in a temporary stall on the afterdeck, placidly chewing her cud, stood a Guernsey cow consigned to some post towards the east.

The ship went about the coast like a traveling tinker, tackling every sort of job that had to do with what the *East Coast Pilot* called "all necessary aids to navigation," and doing them very well. Every fisherman knew her slim silhouette and unmistakable masts, and greeted her in passing with a respectful wave of hand, as city dwellers greet the policeman on the beat; and on the lonely lighthouses and wireless stations men and women watched for her as children watch for Santa Claus.

The quartermaster at the gangway grinned and said, "Hello, Mr. Carney! Going back?" Sailors working about the forward winch looked up and waved. The chief engineer, stepping out of his cabin as Carney thrust his big form into the alley, announced, "Well, the wanderer returns!" The captain cried "Come in!" at his knock and grasped his hand and shook it vigorously.

"Ha! Knew you'd be back, Carney. When you came off with us someone said you'd had enough of Marina and were going to retire. I knew better and I said so. And here you are. What do you think of life in civilization?"

Captain O'Dell was a fixture in his ship, a thin gray man of sixty with a haggard face and frosty blue eyes. He had the look of a man ill to the point of death and he had looked that way for twenty years. His spare figure had a curious protuberant paunch that gave him, whenever he walked down the gangway, the appearance of smuggling something ashore under his waistcoat. He had a wife and family but nobody in the ship had ever seen them. He spent most of his time aboard, even when the ship lay at the dock. The *Lord Elgin* and the scattered posts and lighthouses were his life, as Marina Island was Carney's, and he looked at Carney now with understanding in his eyes.

"I've done what I came to do," Carney said quietly, "and I'm glad to be going back. Civilization? You can have it."

"That's what I expected. And you're absolutely right." A dreamy look came into the captain's eyes. "You know, I've sometimes thought of putting in for the job of superintendent on Marina, next time the job comes up. I'm getting a bit rickety for knocking about the coast, 'specially in winter weather. And I can't retire. I couldn't stick life in some stuffy little house in town, waiting for the graveyard to swallow me. Besides, the superannuation pay's too small. I've got a boy in college, and my daughter's separated from her husband, with three youngsters on her hands and eighty dollars a month—when she can collect it—to pay the bills. But of course my wife won't hear of Marina. A city woman—I couldn't expect her to change her whole existence at this time of life."

He fetched a bottle of whiskey from a locker below the berth, and took down glasses and a carafe of water from the rack beside Carney's head. The *Lord Elgin* had been built in the golden age of Victoria, and the captain's cabin was finished with late Victorian notions of seagoing elegance. The panels were of bird's-eye maple, darkened by time, by the penetrating grime of a coal-burning ship, and by the coats of varnish slapped on by unimaginative painters in the long succession of refits.

The broad berth, with its chest of drawers beneath, was of mahogany, and there was a brass rail, polished like gold, to keep the Old Man from falling out of bed ill heavy weather. Above the berth on a small shelf, guarded by a slat of mahogany, a Presbyterian hymn book, a worn *Coast Pilot*, a *Shipmaster's Adviser,* the *Public Speeches and Letters of Joseph Howe* and two or three frayed novels huddled together in snug company.

O'Dell stood the glasses on his desk and tipped the bottle. "The sun's not over the yardarm but a small one won't do us any harm. By noon it'll be too hot to drink anything but water. It may sound strange, but I never could enjoy whiskey properly in hot weather. Say when!"

"When!"

"Well, here's down the hatch!"

"Down the hatch," Carney murmured, and they drank together.

"How do you manage without this stuff on Marina?"

"Whiskey? It doesn't trouble me. I could always take it or leave it anyhow, and when I went to Marina in 1910 I simply left it behind, with a lot of other things I didn't need. It bothers the operators a bit. They usually bring a bottle or two out with them, and when that's gone they talk about old sprees and give themselves a frightful thirst for a time. But on the whole we're teetotalers, and we get along. What about a berth for me?"

O'Dell made an expansive sweep with his glass. "The ship's yours. I've got no passengers except an assistant lightkeeper going up to Saint Paul Rock, unless they send me somebody else at the last minute. That chap Hurd—a bit of a fuss-budget—sent me a chit about your passage several days ago, and I told the steward to give you the best, that cabin off the port alley. You've seen it. Built into the ship for the Deputy Minister of Marine and Fisheries, as if the old chap planned to spend his time knocking about the coast in a thing like this. Rather like mine but in better shape. All plush and mahogany. You'll travel like a blooming swell."

Carney's bearded lips parted in a grin. "The end of a perfect fling!"

O'Dell regarded him curiously. "You make that sound pretty final."

"It is. I've seen all I want of the outside."

"Until the next time," O'Dell suggested.

"No, this is the last time. You'll never see me off Marina again, except for a swim, perhaps."

O'Dell's thin gray brows shot up over the whiskey glass. He took a long swig.

"You don't mean it! Besides, they'll retire you some day. What then?"

"Then I'll build myself a shack among the dunes, a bit to the east of the wireless station where I can hear the spark when the wind's right. I've even got a spot picked out. But I'm good for a lot of service yet, mind you. You might say I'm part of the government inventory."

The thin clang of a brass hand bell sounded along the deck outside.

"Lunch!" Captain O'Dell cried. "Come and eat with us, Carney, and you can tell me all about your holiday."

In the small saloon, already uncomfortable in the forenoon heat despite the open portholes, they found the chief engineer and a young fresh-cheeked third mate leaning against the buffet and talking diffidently, waiting for Captain O'Dell to seat himself. Along one side of the table, and directly under the portholes, extended a long settee padded with red plush. At the head and foot, and along the other side, stood chairs with stout wooden backs and round red-plush seats, each revolving on an iron standard bolted to the deck. The portholes had prim little red curtains to match the upholstery. From the forward bulkhead an electric fan wafted a thin breeze along the table.

They sat, O'Dell at the table head, Carney at his left, and the others in their accustomed places, the chief engineer at O'Dell's right and the third mate lonely towards the farther end, sitting on the settee. The other officers evidently were on leave or errands ashore. A white-jacketed steward bustled about with ice water in a pitcher. When the food appeared, the captain's eyes glistened. That lined gray face, that thin drooped body with its incongruous paunch, the whole being of Captain O'Dell which resembled so much an unburied corpse, had a capacity for food that amounted to gluttony. It was his only vice, and it was famous in the lighthouse service.

With this obsession he had little to say during the course of the meal, and Carney directed his own conversation to the engineer across the table, a heavy red-faced man with drooping mustaches and a shabby uniform. Mr. McIntyre had a glum view of the world which descended on him with especial force whenever the ship was about to sail; but he talked shop with the animation of an expert at his trade, and because Carney had a rough-and-ready knowledge of shipboard machinery they had a common ground. The younger officer sat remote and silent at his food, glancing up the table in wonder at a man who, having once got away from Marina Island, went back there of his own accord.

At the meal's end Captain O'Dell began to converse in the slow vague manner of a man who has eaten heavily and now desires nothing so much as his afternoon nap. The younger officer vanished. The engineer remained politely, glooming over his words with the air of a melancholy walrus. There was another half hour of this, and then Carney took his departure. As he stepped on deck into the muggy heat of the afternoon he cast an instinctive look at the sky.

"Hello! Clouding up fast."

O'Dell inspected the weather from the doorway. "Humph. Rain at last. A lot of it, too, by the look of things."

Carney frowned. It was not quite time for the line gales but you never knew. Sometimes a forerunner blew up out of the West Indies in late August and lashed the Nova Scotia coast for two or three days on end.

"If this is a southeaster coming up, it'll raise a sea on the beach at Marina that won't go down for a week."

"M'yes," O'Dell acknowledged. "Personally I don't think it'll amount to much. We're due for a big rain—the country's parched. May be a bit of wind behind it. If it turns out to be a real southeaster I'll hold up here a day or two. If it's just a stiff blow I'll pull out about sundown tomorrow and run up the coast to Bold Head. Good shelter inside the Head at Packet Harbor, and the shortest run to Marina when the surf goes down. You'd better be aboard by five tomorrow afternoon, Carney, or six at the outside." He waved a delicate white hand and vanished towards his couch.

Carney recrossed the harbor under a sky covered with gray scud drifting in from the eastward. A fitful wind wandered about the streets, whirling up little clouds of dust. When he turned in to the office to say Good-bye to Hurd the first drops of rain were spattering on the sidewalk. Hurd was engaged in a long-distance telephone conversation but he asked Miss Jardine to send Carney in at once. The farewell did not take long. Having arranged for the wireless station stores to be shipped, and for Carney's return, Hurd's neat mind had dismissed Marina for at least three months. As Carney came out he paused at Miss Jardine's desk.

"Well, I'm away, Miss Jardine."

The familiar flush passed over her pale features. She stood up, plucking off the glasses and casting a swift glance into the anteroom, where Miss Benson was being charming to an operator from the French cable-ship in port. She put out a hand and Carney shook it slowly and woodenly and released it. For want of anything else to say she asked, "You're not sailing at once?"

"Oh no, tomorrow evening. I'd thought of sending my gear aboard but I decided I might as well spend my last night ashore."

"It looks like a storm," she murmured.

"Yes. The rain won't matter but if it blows hard the skipper may decide to hold up a day or two. In that case he'll probably phone here and you might let me know. I'm at the Travelers' Arms, a small wooden place down by the railroad station. I don't know the phone number but no doubt it's in the book."

She nodded, and catching up a pencil made a swift scrabble of pothooks in her notebook.

"Let me thank you again..." Carney began.

"Please don't!" Miss Jardine said, with a warning tone.

In the anteroom Miss Benson's voice gave forth the gurgling note that meant another conquest in the making. In the inner office Hurd's voice went on shouting into the telephone. Outside, from the seaward, came a mutter of thunder.

"Good-by," Carney said.

"Good-by, Mr. Carney, and good luck. I'll think of you on your island when the station reports come in."

Her face was still pink and there was a self-conscious smile on her lips. She was thinking, *I might have given him one more evening. It wasn't much to ask, after all.* She raised her eyes to his with a feeling almost of guilt, and saw in his steady gaze only the shy friendliness that made him seem so much like a boy masquerading in a beard. Impulsively she said, "I'm free tonight, if you'd like to take me out."

She was rewarded at once by the gratitude in his face. "That's awfully kind of you, Miss Jardine!"

"Oh, I'm being quite selfish, I assure you. There's nothing so dull as a wet summer evening in lodgings. I'll meet you at Morgan's—you know, the little place where we had tea—at seven. You can give me something to eat and take me to the movies. Here comes Miss Benson. Don't say anything more."

He nodded, with a pleasant feeling of conspiracy, and swung away, putting on his new hat firmly and turning up his collar against the rain.

CHAPTER 7

At five o'clock, when the shops and offices of Halifax emptied their human contents into the streets, the rain was falling heavily. There was no wind. The torrent fell straight down and the big drops covered the pavement with an inch of bouncing water. Caught like everyone else without coat or umbrella, Miss Jardine clutched the thin jacket about her throat and ran. There was a brief haven in the post office, where she drew the afternoon mail from her satchel and tipped the letters into the chute. She waited inside for a time, hoping for a pause in the downpour, but there was none.

A gloomy mass of cloud hung over the city like an immense sponge being squeezed by a maniac giant. The thunder, which at first had sounded from the harbor mouth as if the forts were at gunnery practice, now boomed and rattled over the ceiling with violence, and at intervals the unnatural twilight in the streets was torn apart and a dazzling flash revealed all the scampering figures caught in suspended motion like a photograph.

Reluctantly she stepped into a revolving door whose pace was set by a rush of people eager for shelter, and it thrust her quickly and mercilessly into the storm. As she emerged another flash of lightning splashed the wet walls of Province House with luminous blue paint, and in that moment she saw the Boer War monument and the imperturbable soldier holding his rifle above his head as if to ward off a further blow from the sky. She thought of Carney, then, and smiled. The thunder followed, and she ran towards her lodging, thankful that it was not far.

She was wet to the skin, with her hair dripping and falling out of its pins, when she ran up the stairs to her room. She slipped off the wet garments quickly and put on a silk wrapper. On the stairs and along the halls she could hear the feet of other lodgers running, voices exclaiming over the storm, doors opening and slamming. The thunder had ceased but a deluge still poured from the gutterspouts into the back court.

What I want most, she thought, is a good hot bath. When the last footsteps had retreated down the stairs towards the restaurant, she slipped along the hall. Experience had taught her this propitious time. At the supper hour Mrs. Paradee's indifferent hot water supply was at its best. Soon after, when one or two of the more fastidious lodgers had bathed for an evening out, the taps would run lukewarm and by bedtime the water would be frigid. Also, at this hour when the inmates had emerged from their lairs like some savage tribe in search of food, she had an undisputed possession of the bathroom that enabled her to soap and sponge as much as she pleased, to relax in lazy enjoyment, and to speculate on what she would have for tea.

She returned to her room with that pleasant feeling of wellbeing which is only to be found in the bath. The air in the bedroom was humid and oppressive and she decided not to dress until the last possible moment. She tossed off the wrapper and sat before the mirror brushing her hair. The house now was silent except for a scrape of chairs in Mrs. Paradee's apartment just below her room; but in a few moments she heard a lone tread on the stairs. It sounded like the ponderous step of Mr. Klaus, who was foreman of a wharf on Water Street. The footsteps came slowly along the hall, and halted. Her doorknob rattled. She barely had time to pick up the flimsy wrapper and catch it about herself when the door sprang open.

It was Klaus, with his huge red face and barrel shoulders, swaying as if moved by mysterious gales. He was known to the lodgers as a widower in middle age, a polite and silent creature rarely to be seen except at morning, when he tramped stolidly to work, and at evening when he dined in Feder's Grill after a long day on the waterfront. She knew the man tippled; it was common gossip in that house where everyone knew the other's foibles; but usually he drank quietly in his room and smuggled out his empty bottles with a ponderous air of innocence that made everybody smile. He had been one of the "regulars" long before Miss Jardine's time, and he went in great awe of the gorgon downstairs.

Klaus lurched into the room and shut the door with a slam that echoed through the house. Miss Jardine kept her composure.

"Mr. Klaus," she said quietly, "this is not your room."

He did not seem to hear. Indeed he seemed oblivious of the slim shape standing by the mirror with a hairbrush, inadequate weapon, clutched against its breast. Like most of his stevedores in the summer heat Klaus worked in trousers, singlet and boots, and ordinarily when he returned to his lodgings he resumed the gray flannel shirt, the draggled red tie and the somewhat frayed blue jacket that seemed to be his only other clothes.

Today however he had simply pulled on an oilskin coat against the rain. This he now removed, with violence, as if the thing oppressed him, and he flung it on the floor. He sat heavily on Miss Jardine's bed, propping himself erect with a pair of large tattooed arms. He had lost his hat and the grizzled fringe of hair that so emphasized his baldness had been turned to absurd little wisps by the downpour in the streets. A bottle stuck out of his hip pocket.

"Phoo!" he ejaculated, shaking his head and peering in a vaguely puzzled way at one of Miss Jardine's pencil sketches, framed and hung on the opposite wall. She put down the brush and stepped forward, clasping the wisp of silk about her as if it were armor of some sort.

"Mr. Klaus! Your room's across the hall. Go there, please!"

He turned his head cautiously, as if quick movement gave him pain. His blurred gaze considered her for a moment, looked away, and came back to her with sudden interest.

"How'd you git in here?" he demanded belligerently.

"This is my room. Please get out."

He considered that a moment. Then, flatly, "Out yourself."

Miss Jardine was indignant. She moved on swift white legs to the door and flung it wide, crying imperiously, "Mr. Klaus, for heaven's sake get out before somebody comes!" He did not move. She went to him and put a firm hand on his shoulder, as if by the sheer force of her anger she could hurl this drunken sweating creature out of her presence. The response of Klaus was rude and sudden. He was not accustomed to being hustled, even when sober, and now he arose with a bellow, thrusting out a fist. Fortunately he was in no condition to gauge the distance of Miss Jardine or even to keep his balance. The blow missed her completely and it carried Klaus off his feet. He fell with the force of two hundred and twenty pounds not merely dropped but thrown. His huge body seemed to bounce on the bedroom floor. From his pocket the bottle shot a dark stream over Miss Jardine's worn carpet.

Here was a chance to escape, but escape was far from her mind. She was still more angry than frightened, and all that was stubborn in her Scotch blood resented this intrusion into what was, after all, her home. This was her citadel, the repository of her small possessions, the refuge to which she fled after each day's work, to read, to knit, to practice the sketching lessons she received two evenings a week at the School of Art. She would not give it up to this fuddled animal even for a moment.

It was of no use to cry for help. The whole floor was deserted. In any case she could not call attention to this ridiculous scene. In her sensitive mind already she could hear the titters and sly wit of the lodgers, male and female, who resented her aloofness, her books, her solitary walks, who would regard this spectacle of Bacchus and the prude as a wonderful bit of comic justice, to be retailed with gusto on both floors and over the tables in Feder's Grill. With the fervency of prayer she hoped that no one would come up the stairs until Klaus had regained his senses and his room.

The man was now on hands and knees, swearing softly and thickly. The fall had shaken him. He muttered, "Who left off that hatch?" in a tone of indignant wonder, and Miss Jardine had a hysterical urge to laugh. A stench of raw Demerara rum crept about the room. She went over to him and, this time in a most gingerly way, put a hand on his shoulder.

"Mr. Klaus!"

"Eh!"

"You're in the wrong room."

"So?" He swung his head from side to side like a dazed bull. Her bare feet caught his attention and he inspected them. With some difficulty he raised his head and perceived a pair of shapely marble columns attached to them; but the effort hurt his neck. He returned his attention to her feet.

"That ain't you, Babe?" he said dubiously.

"It's Miss Jardine," she returned impatiently. "Get up, do!" She placed her hand under his arm and pulled. Obediently Klaus heaved himself upward. He came to his feet swaying dangerously and throwing a heavy arm about her shoulders for support. Encouraged, Miss Jardine moved forward, pressing him towards the open door and watching his feet with anxiety, for if he stumbled the whole absurd performance must be repeated. They were in this attitude, approaching the doorway, with Miss Jardine's eyes downcast, watchful and absorbed, when Klaus came to a halt.

"Jeest!" he said.

She glanced at his face and saw the bleared eyes fixed on something in the hall. Swiftly she looked at the doorway. At once she cried in a relieved voice, "Oh, Mrs. Paradee, I'm so glad it's you and no one else. You see..."

"I see," Mrs. Paradee said.

Miss Jardine withdrew her arm. The sodden Klaus tottered and sat down upon the bed.

"Jeest!" he said again.

The landlady's gaze swept past him contemptuously to the overturned chair before the mirror, the scatter of garments just where Miss Jardine had flung them off, the dark stain on the carpet. She sniffed, and turned to examine Miss Jardine from head to foot.

"Well?" she snapped.

Miss Jardine leaned against the wall, astonished, and suddenly afraid. That old nightmare scene in the upper hall flooded into her mind. Her tumbled hair framed a face naturally pale and now the face of a ghost. One hand clutched the thin faded stuff of the wrapper about her person, as if anything could shut out that hard black stare which already had discovered and condemned her nakedness.

"How long," Mrs. Paradee said, "has this been going on?"

"You don't understand," Miss Jardine gasped.

"I'm afraid I do. Klaus, get out!"

The man arose from the bed as if stung, and lurched towards the door. Mrs. Paradee moved aside to let him pass. They heard him go down the hall, fumbling at all the doors.

"He came into my room," Miss Jardine began in a low voice.

"Oh, come, Miss Jardine, that's so old a tale!"

"But it's true! I'd just had a bath, and I was brushing my hair."

Mrs. Paradee tossed her head and uttered a theatrical "Ha!" She had in her fashion a sense of humor. She had found more evil than good in her passage through a flinty world but it had given her a certain amount of cynical amusement along the way. The keeping of a lodginghouse in a seaport city had taught her all she cared to know about men and women, and what she had learned had filled her with contempt. She looked upon her lodgers as a species of animal, not to be loved or hated but simply to be preyed upon in the legitimate way of her trade. Her scorn for mankind was eased by the knowledge that they made tractable lodgers; but for women, by nature messy and deceitful creatures born to trouble, her contempt was supreme.

She had long known that the wharfinger drank, that he was in fact one of those dull beefy animals to whom alcohol is meat and drink and mistress all in one, quite harmless where women were concerned. And while she suspected Miss Jardine of being "deep"—a term that covered most of the sins in her Decalogue— she knew at heart that this cool and remote creature was not the kind to disport with a man like Klaus. Nevertheless the sight of the trembling young woman excited her. The silken wisp drawn so tightly about Miss Jardine betrayed a figure slender but well filled at the breast and hips, and it revealed to the landlady's gaze a pair of comely legs. She had not suspected the typist of such properties, indeed she had always thought of her as a plain and somewhat meager person who wore her clothes unfashionably long to hide the fact.

The sight of this shapely stranger not only excited Mrs. Paradee but aroused in her another emotion. The disdain in her gaze made way for something purely malicious. Like most of her lodgers she had seen in Miss Jardine a superior air that irritated her as much as it amused the others; but chiefly her malice sprang from an incident some months before that Miss Jardine herself had noticed only casually and had long forgotten.

On the occasion of one of those semiweekly evening visitations which so intrigued the lodgers, the man in the bowler, emerging from the Paradee apartment with his customary rush, had all but knocked down the typist on her way upstairs. Miss Jardine had paused and given the man a surprised glance, and over his shoulder she had caught a glimpse of the landlady about to close the door. Their eyes had met, and Miss Jardine had smiled and passed on. It was no more than that. Whether Mrs. Paradee's hair was up or down, how she was clad or if indeed was clad at all, and what sort of look she had on her face in that unguarded moment as she sped her parting guest, the young woman on the landing could not see or at any rate had failed to notice. But in her glance and smile the landlady had fancied every sort of surmise and condemnation. She was infuriated. For weeks she watched the girl's face, seeking a sign of what she knew or suspected or merely imagined. For months she had turned her ear to the fleeting gossip of the stairs and landings, hearing indeed nothing complimentary but nothing to confirm or dispel her doubts.

And now, magically, this superior person cringed before her, caught in a scene of utter disgrace! Mrs. Paradee was inclined to laugh by the sheer justice of the thing; and she was elated to find herself in the familiar roles of witness, prosecutor, judge and executioner, and in a position to return what she had come to regard as a monstrous slight on her own virtue. That the slight was no more tangible than the virtue did not matter a bit. With the wide eyes of a frightened child Miss Jardine beheld a rising menace in the thin line of the mouth, the tense nostrils and the glittering black gaze that confronted her from the doorway.

"Surely you don't think..." she gasped.

"What am I supposed to think? Look at this room! Look at your things, all thrown about. Look at my carpet—ruined! I must say I'm surprised. I hadn't expected such behavior in a respectable-looking person like you."

"Oh, I'll pay for the carpet," Miss Jardine said desperately, "and I'll tidy everything, Mrs. Paradee—only you must believe what I say."

"Young lady, I've been too long in this business not to believe my own eyes. Look at yourself, practically nude. And with a man like Klaus—disgusting!" Mrs. Paradee uttered the word nude with a peculiar drawn-out emphasis that implied the worst.

"But how can you say such a thing! What have I ever done that you should think...why, it's outrageous!"

"Don't take that tone with me. I don't want to be harsh."

"Oh, please!"

"That's better.'"

"Then you do believe me?"

"Not at all. I keep a respectable house and you know my rules. You may keep your room for tonight. In the morning you must get out at once."

"But I'm paid to the end of the week!" the girl cried, catching at straws. The landlady uttered a snort. "What about my carpet? If you're going to make a difficulty like that, you can leave at once." And she added virtuously, "I'm sure I'm only trying to be kind."

Miss Jardine nodded dumbly, turning a slow bewildered look about the bedroom as if to assure herself that all this was really happening. She shuddered. The struggle with Klaus was suddenly remote, it had happened too long ago to matter. She felt defiled, not by the wharfinger's fuddled grasp but by something evil in the hard black eyes that searched her flesh as if the scrap of silk did not exist. She made a picture of despair, and for a moment the woman in the doorway was almost mollified. The moment passed. Mrs. Paradee put a hand to the knob, closed the door quietly and firmly, and passed along the hall and down the stairs.

CHAPTER 8

With the departure of that ominous presence Miss Jardine's first move was to lock the door in frantic haste, as if to shut out every memory of the twenty minutes past. She sat on the bed, still rumpled by the impact of her unwelcome visitor, and put her face in her hands. A mixture of emotions ravaged her. Humiliation, mirth, fright, indignation, all passed over her in waves like the chills and flushes of a fever patient. Eventually she lay full length and wept. Dimly she heard the returning steps of the lodgers, the opening of doors and windows, the familiar evening chatter of voices in the rooms and across the court.

At last she sat up. The tears had dissolved the violence of her feelings and left a dull resentment, not of Klaus, not even of Mrs. Paradee so much as the chance that had made her victim of such an idiotic prank. It was all so preposterous, so like those uneasy dreams in which she found herself assailed by hordes of mice or walking down Hollis Street in nothing but her stockings, that she rose from the pillow trying to convince herself that none of it had taken place.

A glance about the disordered room killed that. She drew her wits together. The urgent thing was to find another place to go. She ran over a mental list of lodgings. At worst she could get a room somewhere in the north end, as she had before. It cost more, and it was a bother, catching trams; but a good many city workers put up with that. It was really much nicer to live where there were trees and bits of lawn. In a few weeks she could forget that she had ever taken the third floor back at Mrs. Paradee's.

It occurred to her that the light in the room was dim, that in fact it was almost night. Suddenly she thought of Carney, waiting for her at the teashop. She sprang up and looked at her watch in the gray reflection of the window. Eight o'clock! How awful! And she thought dismally, I couldn't go out with him tonight. The mere notion of dressing was intolerable. So was the thought of food. She felt exhausted and she wanted nothing but to lie on the bed and if possible to sleep. She stood irresolute at the window, seeing the lights spring up across the court.

Her indifferent gaze flicked from one to another and came to rest on the window where last night the sailors had been playing cards. Two of them were in the room now, under the dangling electric bulb, busy stuffing clothing into cheap suitcases. They were laughing. They paused to punch each other, to engage in a lively wrestle on the bed, a pair of strong figures locked in a furious embrace. Miss Jardine felt a pang of envy. They were clearing off to a ship. Tomorrow whatever memories they had of this place would be lost in the wind outside the harbor heads, and they would be thinking only of the adventures awaiting them somewhere else. She had long ceased to wonder why men went to sea. The marvel was that any stayed ashore. Everybody's in prison, she thought rebelliously, only these men have the key.

Slowly she drew the blind and switched on the light; and still absorbed in her thoughts she began to pluck fresh stockings and underthings from the battered chest of drawers. In another twenty minutes she was walking quickly along the street. The storm had left a delightful freshness in the air. The looming bulk of the upper city and Citadel Hill shut off the last trace of the twilight in the western sky, the street lamps and shop windows glowed, and overhead already the stars were bright. When she turned in to the teashop she fully expected Carney to be gone, but she saw him at once, sitting at a table in a corner and slowly blowing out tobacco smoke. The ash tray on the table held a small mound of cigarette stubs but now his big fist clutched the pipe. There lay the story of his long waiting. She was stung with remorse, but he looked up and sprang to his feet with such a glad smile spreading over his face and crinkling the corners of his eyes that she felt a wave of self-assurance pass over the wreckage of her mind.

"Mr. Carney, I'm always late, aren't I? But this is awful! I really didn't expect to find you here."

"I'd nearly given you up," he confessed. He helped her out of her coat, and she sat down, looking about the shop. There was a scatter of late diners, young couples mostly, lingering over their dessert. She was glad she had put on her best frock, a light flowered thing, and a rather jaunty hat. The hat was old but of a quality that women would recognize as "good." Not many of her things were "good."

"What kept you so long?" he said. "Or is a man supposed to ask?"

"He's not supposed to ask. Anyhow, I couldn't tell you—it's too absurd. It upset me for a time but I feel better now. I could even eat."

"Ah!" He beckoned the waitress who had been watching him so dubiously for the past hour. Miss Jardine did not feel hungry but she felt obliged to order something to accompany the meal of an obviously hungry man. When the food came she pecked at it in a determined way and found, somewhat to her surprise, that she could eat almost with appetite. She led the talk, chattering feverishly about the things they knew, the gossip of the trade, the movements of operators from one station to another, the latest apparatus. ("Did you know the Americans are broadcasting music and things like that? It's quite a fad. People here in the city are fixing up receiving sets with audions and honeycomb coils and condensers and phones.")

The time and the food passed pleasantly. When the coffee came, Carney looked at his pipe and she said at once, "Light up, if you like. And please give me a cigarette if you've any left." He lit a match for her and she drew on the cigarette and exhaled the smoke expertly through her nostrils. It was the first time Miss Jardine had ever smoked in public. She kept a packet of cigarettes in her room and lit one now and then, especially on wet evenings when there was little else to do. She had grown up in a world that regarded the cigarette in female lips as a sure mark of the prostitute. Although the war had changed that with a good many other things she felt it a daring thing to do here in the teashop, where as it chanced not a woman was smoking. But she did not care, indeed she felt a need to dare something for the sake of her ego, and whether it shocked Carney or not.

If he was shocked, or even surprised, he gave no sign. She felt a little piqued. She wondered if it would shock him to tell the tale of that encounter in the bedroom, omitting nothing. There was something impishly funny in the notion of herself sitting here so carefully attired from hat to shoes, talking brightly but decorously to the grave man across the table, when not an hour ago she had been playing an all but naked bacchante to the drunken Klaus. Behind this whimsy however pressed the shadow of her solitude and defenselessness. She wondered, glancing about the room, how many of these young women smiling into the faces of men had the same shadow behind them somewhere, not fully recognized perhaps, not something talked about or even hinted at, but always there. And she smiled and chattered, not so much for Carney as to convince the others that she at least was happy and assured.

Carney was entranced. His acquaintance with women was very limited and of course he had never met one like Isabel Jardine. In the office she was prim and businesslike, in the park she had been moody and mysterious; here she was feverishly alive, she sparkled even when she talked about the new aerial inductance coils or the latest thing in vacuum tubes—as if they were new hats. A sensualist would have said that she talked as if she were beautiful, which of course she was not; and almost any woman could have told him that she talked as if she were frantic, as of course she was.

It did not matter really what she said. He sat immersed in the flow of her voice, seeing in the amber glow of the table lamp the brushed gleam of her hair under the little hat, the flush that came and went in the clear skin, the expressive movements of her lips, the eyes that sedulously avoided his and yet played over his face, his big shoulders and hands as if he, Matthew Carney, were the most interesting creature in the room. He was sorry when at last she looked at her watch and exclaimed that they were too late for the movies, unless he wanted to see half a show.

"What do you suggest?" he asked, helping her into her coat.

"Oh, I don't know. Let's just walk about. It's a lovely night. Wait a minute. There's a band concert in the Public Gardens. We might catch the last bits if we took a tram."

"Let's do that."

In the Gardens a throng of people sat on the lawns or strolled the winding paths in a darkness broken by bright green patches where electric lights shone amongst the trees. The benches about the central bandstand were full and so was the surrounding grass. A hand of the Royal Marines was playing tunes from *Tales of Hoffman,* and their instruments flashed and their red jackets and white helmets made a fine show in the glare of the canopy lights.

Well away from the crowd Miss Jardine and Carney came upon a secluded patch of lawn in the shadow of a giant syringa.

"Let's sit here," she said.

"Won't the ground be damp from the rain?"

"It seems to have dried. The other people don't seem to mind."

"I was thinking of you," Carney said. He had a notion, heard in his youth, that it was dangerous for women to sit on damp grass even for a moment.

She sank down gracefully, tucking her coat skirt beneath her, and Carney sprawled comfortably at her side.

"We don't get so many band concerts now," she murmured. "During the war, when the troops were passing through, and all the navy ships were here, there were bands galore and we had concerts all through the summer, here and at Point Pleasant and on the shore of the Arm. It was quite wonderful. There's something about band music, especially at night, and outdoors under the trees..." She paused.

Instinctively Carney knew that she was thinking of her young officer, the fellow who had treated her so shabbily.

"You still think of him, that army chap, don't you?"

"Yes," she admitted. "Yes, of course. It was the only time I've ever been in love. A woman can't forget that very easily."

The air was soft and warm. It was the sort of night that comes rarely in Nova Scotia after mid-August, when the cool sea winds begin. A dreamy music swayed through the leaves of the shrubbery.

"I don't know much about music, I'm afraid," Carney said. "What sort of tune is that?" He took off his hat and tossed it on the grass.

"It's a barcarolle. Gondoliers—in Venice, you know—are supposed to sing that kind of thing, keeping time with their oars."

"Ah! That's why I like it, I suppose. You could row a dory to that, played a bit slower. On the lagoon at Marina, say, where the water's smooth."

"Lagoon—that sounds very romantic."

Carney laughed. "It's not a bit. No palm trees, not even a bush. Nothing on the shore but sand and salt-grass and wild pony tracks. It's not even a lagoon any more, in the usual sense of the word. Years ago, long before my time, a big storm filled the entrance and turned it into a salt lake eight or nine miles long. In summer the middle part dries up, and then there are two Jakes end-to-end like a pair of sausages. They're only separated from the ocean by a long strip of sand that we call the south bar, running all the way from West Point to Number Three lifesaving station, and the sea beats over that when-ever we get a hard blow from the south'ard. Keeps the lagoon from getting stagnant. We have a dory there, a handy little thing we got from a wrecked fishing schooner, and we sail it on the lagoon, and spear flatfish and eels."

"That must be rather fun."

"I think it is, anyhow. And it's something to do."

Miss Jardine looked about her, thinking how great a contrast it must seem to him, this indecently lush place of grass and flowers and massed leaves, half dark, half garish in the reflected glitter of the bandstand, like a theatrical forest.

"And tomorrow you'll be going back to your desert in the sea!"

"I'd rather talk about something else."

"What, for instance?"

"You."

She turned her head slowly and saw his bearded face turned up to her. And she felt her heart beating in vigorous thumps, after a sort of death that had begun when Mrs. Paradee's steps retreated from that finally closed door. She was tempted to ask what he meant, but she knew, as if in some way quite unknown to Signor Marconi this quiet man prone in the grass were able to communicate his thought without word or gesture in the darkness. It was a miraculous sensation. She felt alive in every part of her flesh, as once before she had tingled when Lancelot first put his khaki arm about her waist. One thing was missing: the delicious warmth that crept over her then and went so quickly to her head. There was no rapture now, not even surprise; only a pleasant awareness of this man, as if some kind of winter had passed and she now felt on her skin the touch of another sun, not so bright as the first, indeed not bright at all, but reassuring for all that.

Not consciously, but by the prompting of an inner voice, cool and rational and fatalistic, she knew that beside her lay a solution to her immediate fears and loneliness. And with a cunning quite foreign to her natural self, in fact in outrage to her virginal instincts, she found herself saying softly, "I wish you'd tell me what you mean...Matthew."

For a few moments he was silent. Then in a low voice, "I don't know how to tell you, Miss Jardine..."

"Please call me Isabel."

"A lovely name that. Isabel—Isabel. What I want to say is ...I'm not a young man, not the sort of chap you ought to have...not the sort who has any right to say anything like this...but I can't help it, you understand? I never felt like this before. Please don't be angry. I'm just a rough chap, no education but what I picked up in books, knocking about at sea and places like Marina. You're young, you're refined—you're everything I'm not. It's a poor sort of bargain to offer, any way you look at it"

"Well...Matthew?"—in that foreign voice.

"I'm wondering if you...if you'd marry me. Don't say no yet. Hear what I have to say, my dear. I'm forty-six, what's called the prime of life—nonsense, of course. The prime of life is seventeen. But I'm healthy anyhow. I've got several thousand dollars saved in the bank. I've had fifteen years' experience in the wireless game, and I know the rigger's trade besides. Means I can walk into Hurd's office tomorrow and tell him I want a job here or I quit the service. Means I'm not asking you to go off to some wild place with me. We'd find a flat in the city somewhere—buy a little bungalow, maybe, out by the Nor'west Arm, with trees and a bit of garden, and a sight of salt water for old times' sake. I wouldn't expect you to love me—not as you'd love some younger man. If you could just like me a little, put up with me, that's enough. I'd ask nothing that you didn't want to give, my dear. I'd like to make that clear. And...and there it is. That's all. That's what I wanted to say."

Now that the thing was out he breathed a long sigh, as if it had required a great physical effort. And Isabel Jardine had a quaint sense of recognition, as if she had known exactly what he would say and how he would say it, even to that great breath at the end. But it did not strike her as odd that she should know at once, without the slightest reflection, how she should answer him. The physical implication of marriage she refused to consider. In any case she knew, even without Carney's saying so, that as his wife she could remain mistress of herself, yielding only what she chose, and when she chose. Timidity is a relative matter and in Carney's presence she felt actually bold. What filled her mind was a picture of the bungalow beside the Northwest Arm, and herself clipping flowers in the garden or busy with housewifery, at peace and secure at last.

She bent over him, putting out a hand to his shoulder, and their lips met. Under her palm she felt a tremor in his big frame. What she had first observed to Hurd, that Carney was, in a single word, innocent, came to her now with force. And she kissed him again with an almost maternal solicitude, as if it were he and not she who needed protection from the world. He did not attempt to rise and take her in his arms, as another man might have done. He did not move, lying on the grass, supported on an elbow, with his face upturned, accepting the touch of her lips and fingers in a kind of wonder, as if they had both fallen under a happy spell that one word or gesture on his part would shatter.

They were aware of music, and now and then a patter of polite applause about the bandstand like the breaking of a sea. Without warning the Marines struck up "God Save the King," and everywhere about the lawns and in the shadows people jumped up and stood in patriotic immobility or scurried off towards the gates to avoid the rush. Carney and Miss Jardine rose and stood together, and as the last notes died away she stooped to brush the grass from her skirts.

"Don't forget your hat," she said.

Carney picked it up but he did not put it on. They walked sedately through the gate and down Spring Garden Road, with her hand tucked inside his arm and pressing it gently from time to time, as if to assure herself and him that they were truly together, and that those tender moments in the shadow of the syringa had really taken place.

They said very little on the way to her lodging. Carney was in a daze. Miss Jardine herself was excited; but her thoughts were very clear and she was aware of a crisis as they sauntered up to the street door at Mrs. Paradee's. She broke a long silence, looking at her watch in the light from Feder's Grill and exclaiming, "Half past eleven! Oh, dear!"

"I shouldn't have kept you out so late," Carney murmured with concern.

"Oh, it's nothing."

They moved on a step or two out of the light. The street was deserted and the tall shabby house had an almost ominous air of brooding over these late wanderers. Miss Jardine took her hand from Carney's arm and faced him with resolution.

"Matthew, I didn't answer your question properly, did I?"

"But I thought you did!"

She uttered a short self-conscious laugh. "Because I kissed you? Well it's true. I couldn't find words to say. Are you happy?"

"You know I am," Carney burst out in his rich tone. "In all my life this is the most wonderful thing that ever happened. And to think it all came by chance just out of meeting you in the office and then in that glorified fish-and-chip shop! I can't believe it's true, even now. I've a feeling that tomorrow morning I'll wake up aboard the steamer, bound for Marina, with nothing but a headache from the skipper's whiskey."

"Then suppose you kiss me again," she said demurely. "Just to prove I'm not something out of a bottle." As his arms went about her she slipped her own around his neck, and he found her mouth warm and alive under his. Then, breathlessly:

"Oh, Matthew, if you only knew!"

"What?"

"How much this means to me. Please hold me closer—closer than that." They stood embraced and silent for a space of minutes.

"Matthew, don't let me go."

"I won't."

"I mean it. I mean don't let me go now tonight."

"But you've got to go to bed sometime, my dear."

"Not in there!" she said rapidly, with a sudden note of hysteria. "Matthew, I can't tell you why, but I can't go in there—not now—not after all that's happened. I didn't think I'd mind, just for one more night, but when we came to the steps and I saw that door again it made my flesh creep. Don't ask me to explain. All I can say is that if I went in there again, even for a minute, I'd lose all my happiness— I'd lose my mind."

"But what about your things?" he said, astonished and disturbed.

"My things! As if things matter when my whole life's been changed! Matthew, do you love me?"

"Of course I do, my dear, but don't you think ..."

"Then take me away with you now. I don't care where. I don't care anything, any more. All I want is to be with you. You're what I need, someone strong, and calm, and kind. And I think you need me, in your way. Perhaps you think I'm queer but I'm really quite nice, Matthew. You've been lonely—so have I. I'll make it up to you, all that long time on that awful island and the other places. You won't regret it, ever."

He was silent, a man in a dream.

"I'm not good-looking," she went on feverishly, "but I think you'll be pleased with me. It's everything or nothing now, Matthew. It's got to be tonight."

She threw back her head, staring anxiously into his face in the half-light from the café window, while her body, closed in his arms, sought in some way apart from words to convey her urgency.

He was profoundly moved. "Tonight," he repeated in a choked voice. "Tonight!"

CHAPTER 9

Miss Jardine awakened slowly, her mind groping for its bearings in a confusion of memories, half dreamed, half real. For a moment or two she was afraid she might open her eyes upon that odious bedroom at Mrs. Paradee's. The first glance reassured her; but at once she was aware of a set of realities much more disturbing than the old. All the courage, all the wild determination, of the night before had gone. Her body felt strangely boneless and relaxed, but her conscience was as taut as a fiddle string and it shrieked one long alarming note. With a swift dismay she summed up the realities; that she was in a strange bed, in a strange room, and with Matthew Carney, a strange man; that she was in fact wearing the jacket of Carney's pajamas for lack of anything else; and that she, an unmarried woman, a "nice" girl in the old-fashioned sense in which she had been reared, had committed if not the most shameful at all events the most vulgar of sins.

She was thankful that Carney slept. She could feel his warmth at her back and hear his deep untroubled breathing. The blind was drawn and flapping slowly in a light breeze through the open window. It stirred the cheap cotton curtains and sent an occasional flash of morning sunlight across the room. There was a sound of engines shunting in the railway yards, whistles, bells, the iron screech of brakes, the booming collision of empty boxcars coming to a halt, and now and then a faint but acrid reek of coal smoke.

She wondered how she could face Carney by daylight, how she could meet his eyes, and what she could say, now that the madness of last night had gone. For she had seduced him, there was no blinking that. Whatever had possessed her? Her face burned on the pillow as she recalled his bashful offer to sleep in a chair and her indignant refusal; her own fingers, trembling but resolute, turning out the light and taking off her clothes; her arms going out to him in a gesture that was at once a surrender and a command; his hesitation, his first shy and blundering caresses, and the final passion that convulsed them both.

Now I know how Eve felt, poor thing. She wondered if this bearded Adam would reproach her as she now reproached her own quenched and lazy flesh. And with every precept of her Presbyterian childhood ringing in her ears she wondered what sort of punishment was in store. For a time she lay sunk in these depressing reveries, so full of guilt. Then, with a surge of rebellion, she felt herself the victim rather than the author of her own and Carney's downfall. It had all begun with that ridiculous scene at Mrs. Paradee's, and it occurred to her in an indignant wonder that if it had not rained that evening, if she had not taken a bath or if Klaus had not taken a drink, her life and Carney's might have gone their separate ways unblemished and unchanged.

From this it was easy and natural to recall the teachings of predestination that had so mystified her childhood. She saw at last a meaning. The meaning was far from comforting but at least it absolved her of deliberate wickedness, and it brought to life her Scotch common sense which argued that nothing past could be undone and that the only thing now was to face the facts and make the best of them. Her life had been thrust upon a new strange course, and if not redemption at least some happiness might be found along the way. Again she thought of the sailors packing merrily for a voyage as if all that had gone before were merely a preparation and a waiting, as if some wonderful promise had been held out to them beyond the sea rim somewhere and nothing else mattered a rap.

She felt the man beside her stir and turn, and knew he was awake. The moment had come. She lay very still with her face to the wall, trying to control her breathing and the slow hard thump of her heart. It was an age before he said quietly:

"Isabel, are you awake?"

"Yes." She did not move.

"Are you all right?"

"Yes."

"I was afraid—you lay so still."

"I'm quite all right."

Silence. Then, hearing him fumble for his watch, "What time is it?"

"Almost nine o'clock. I'll dress and get your breakfast—they don't serve food for the rooms here unless you take it up yourself."

"Don't go," she begged in a muffled voice. "I'm not hungry. And I think we ought to talk."

"Yes?"

She turned on her back, avoiding his eyes and staring at the ceiling.

"Matthew, what about us?"

"Ah! Well, first we'll hunt up a parson and get married."

She had expected that; nevertheless she was relieved to hear him say it. Without conviction but with a certain petulance she said quickly, "I don't want you to marry me just because it's the proper thing to do."

Carney raised himself on an elbow, exposing a broad bare shoulder and a muscular and tattooed upper arm. He gazed down at her with a somber tenderness.

"My dear, it isn't that. Shall I tell you the truth? I want to make fast to you now, while you're still confused and helpless, while you're still in the mood that came upon you last night. I'm afraid you may come out of it and run away."

A tremulous smile disturbed the firm set of her lips, and suddenly she turned and threw herself weeping into his arms. He stroked her hair, calling her his own dear girl, and repeating her name as if the mere sound of it gave him a profound pleasure. He was enraptured to find himself not only her lover but her comforter as well, and the slow trickle of her tears on his skin was an ecstasy. Gradually her sobbing ceased. She lay warm and inert in his arms, exhausted by this passion as she had lain after the other passions of the night.

Her face was pressed against his shoulder, concealed by her disordered hair, and when he attempted to brush the strands aside she murmured, "Don't."

At last she said, "I'm sorry to be such a nuisance. I didn't want to cry. I was going to be so calm and sober about us—about everything. Will you get up and dress now, Matthew, please? Don't bring up my breakfast—I'd rather not eat until I've washed and dressed. Where can I wash?"

"There's a bathroom just along the hall."

"I'll join you downstairs. Leave me a brush and comb, please, and give me half an hour."

"So long?" he said, whimsically.

"My hair's a mess and my face must be frightful. I won't have you see me at my worst."

"Very well. Shall I put up the blind?"

"No."

She turned away as he rose. It did not take him long to dress. He returned from the bathroom and then departed once more. When the door closed she sat up and looked about the room. Carney's small leather dressing-case, purchased in Montreal, lay open on the small table by the bed. On the floor beneath the window lay his old worn suitcases, one closed, one open. The furniture was that of a cheap hotel, not quite so cheap as Mrs. Paradee's but quite as worn, as stark and uncomfortable; the footboard of the wooden bed was scratched as if a regiment of bibulous railwaymen had suffered nightmares in their shoes.

She stepped out of bed and ran up the blind. She went at once to the long mirror fastened on the door, and in the revealing flood of sunlight examined her reflection curiously, half expecting to find herself changed in some way by the experiences of the night. Carney's pajama jacket hung about her in enormous folds, and a smile appeared on the tousled creature in the glass. She flung off that ludicrous garment and saw a familiar figure, unaltered, even untouched. Amazing discovery! Often she had marveled at the poise of young married women, wondering how after intimacies and passions that she could only imagine they managed to retain their nonchalant air. Now she knew; but she was still astonished.

With this revelation past she inspected the figure in the glass more critically. What she saw was comforting. There's one thing, she told herself, you've got a nice bust and waist and very good legs. She surveyed them with the satisfaction of a woman whose physical properties have passed the supreme test, the gratifying of a man.

Turning away from this contemplation she was touched to find that Carney had gathered her things and laid them carefully on the chair. She dressed quickly. As she slipped on the frock she blessed her shopping choice of a stuff that did not rumple easily. In the bathroom mirror she found her lower eyelids swollen, leaving a shadowed fold beneath, a mark of last night's ardors or of the morning's tears, she was not sure which. She bathed her eyes carefully with cold water but the shadows remained. Philosophically she decided that they gave her a new and rather interesting look, and she turned to other matters. It took a long time with Carney's severely masculine brush and comb to smooth her tangled hair, and when she returned to the bedroom she had to hunt carefully over the floor and among the pillows for the scattered pins.

When she walked downstairs she found Carney waiting for her in the small lobby, a place reeking of stale tobacco and furnished with worn black-upholstered chairs and an array of brass spittoons. Two or three framed prints on the walls depicted trains of a bygone day, and there was a large and gaudy calendar devoted almost entirely to a nude young woman knee-deep in a pool. From behind the desk a clerk with oily hair and a lean bilious face gave

Isabel a cool stare. When they were seated in the empty dining room she said at once, "That man at the desk—didn't like the way he looked—at me."

"You mustn't imagine things," Carney said.

"What," she persisted, "did you tell him—last night, I mean, when we came in?"

"Why do you want to know that?"

"Tell me!"

He hesitated and flushed. "Well, it wasn't much. When I went to get my key he asked if the lady was my wife, and I said yes. He asked if you had any baggage and of course you hadn't, so I said no. I said you'd come unexpectedly. After all it was the truth."

"Yes, and then?"

"He said it was customary in cases of that kind to give the clerk five dollars."

"And did you?"

"Of course."

Her eyes were furious. "I feel like a tart!"

"Don't say that."

"I wish you'd punched him on the nose."

"Exactly what I wanted to do at the time, but it would have made a nasty row."

She sprang to her feet. "Please let's go somewhere else, Matthew, I couldn't eat here—I couldn't stay another minute. Everything's spoiled."

He rose unhappily, "I'll get my bags and check out. Wait for me in the lobby." But she would not linger under the cynical gaze of that creature behind the desk.

"I'll wait outside, in the fresh air."

He phoned for a taxi and it drew up at the curb as he came out with his suitcases. They stepped in, and Carney called, "Drive us to a parson somewhere."

"Any choice?" the cabby said.

They looked at each other. "Have you?" Isabel asked.

"None." His eyes were shy and worshipful and she felt another surge of self-confidence.

"Well, so long as you're going to make an honest woman of me, Matthew, I think I'd prefer the Presbyterian kind. There's nothing more respectable. But it seems to me you've got to get a license first, and a ring—I refuse to be a wife without a ring. And what about our breakfast?"

"I hadn't thought of anything," he admitted, with a boyish smile.

"It's a good thing one of us is sensible."

With a rich extravagance they kept the cab waiting outside a restaurant while they consumed a leisurely breakfast, and it took them on their further pilgrimage to Carney's bank and to a jewelry shop. As they entered the shop Isabel determined on something cheap and simple; but she found what everyone finds in jewelry shops, that the cheap things are not simple and the simple things not cheap. Carney wanted to buy the best in the shop at once and without quibbling; but she objected.

"Those white gold things—they're too expensive, and I don't like them anyway. I daresay I'm old-fashioned but it seems to me I'd feel much more respectably married if the ring were plain yellow gold, like my mother's."

The jeweler looked at her naked third finger, "Wouldn't you like a nice engagement ring as well?" he suggested shrewdly, "A nice diamond, now?"

"No."

"Do!" Carney urged. He felt a lover's desire to load her with gifts, and she recognized it with a quick smile that lit her serious face.

"'Rings on her fingers and bells on her toes'? No, Matthew, not for me. Really! I never cared much for jewelry, and it seems silly to wear a ring for an engagement that's only lasted, let me see, twelve hours or so. All I want is a wedding ring, a nice old fashioned yellow one, like that." She pointed.

They came out with the nice gold ring in Matthew's pocket and she kissed him warmly when they got inside the cab.

"You're such a darling, Matthew."

"I wish you'd let me buy the diamond as well."

"You and your diamonds. I'm just a poor working girl."

"And what am I?"

"A big blond monster with a beard. Tell the cabby where to go."

The wedding license was a simple matter. As they turned to leave the bureau Isabel asked the clerk casually if he knew the address of the nearest Presbyterian clergyman. The man gave her a quizzical look.

"Yes. I do. Of course you realize that you can't be married for three days?"

"What!"

"Three days from the date on the license."

"But that's absurd!" Isabel cried.

"No doubt, but it's the law of Nova Scotia."

They came out into the street in a perturbed silence and paused beside the cab.

"Oh well," Isabel said valiantly, "we'll just get a room at a decent hotel. Three days isn't long, and who's to know the difference?"

The cabby looked around and regarded them through the fumes of a cigarette hanging from his lip. "Where now?" he asked. Carney looked at her.

"You'll want to do some shopping, won't you? And we ought to go and see Hurd. We can't just run off without saying anything."

"Couldn't we?" she asked, a little plaintively. "Well—you go, Matthew. He'll be awfully angry, and I'm such a coward." She knew, better than Carney, what sort of thunderbolt the news would be to Hurd. She was even a little amused, foreseeing Hurd's dilemma—whether to upbraid Carney for taking away his secretary, or Miss Jardine for running off with his best outpost operator. But chiefly she thought of the Benson girl. She could see that young woman's smile.

"I won't set foot in the office again," she added vigorously. "It's part of everything I want to forget."

Matthew fingered his blond jaw, staring at the pavement. Her sudden resolve to cut herself away from all her old life mystified him, but it had brought him such a gift that he would not question any part of it.

"My dear," he said slowly, "if you really want to leave everything behind, we shouldn't stay in Halifax. It's not a big city, after all. Every day something or someone would remind you..."

"Yes...Yes, I hadn't thought of that."

"We ought to go somewhere else—Montreal, say. I could get a job there."

She thought with dismay of the little bungalow and the garden beside the Arm. But what he said was true. She had known it ever since she wakened in the bed beside him, when her mind became so crystal clear after the delirious events of the night.

"I've been awfully selfish," she cried. "What do you really want to do?"

"What you wish."

"Ah yes, but you can't go on doing that, Matthew. You'd hate me after a time. Don't you remember what you told me in that restaurant by the docks—that nothing in the cities had any meaning for you now?"

He gave her the shy smile that made him seem so naive and young.

"That was before last night."

"You're dodging my question!"

"If you can put everything behind you, so can I."

"But it's all so different with you, Matthew! You had what you wanted of

life, and I didn't. You were happy and I wasn't. But let's not stand here argu-
ing. Tell the cabby to drive us somewhere."

"Anywhere particular?"

"Yes, Point Pleasant."

The voice of the cabby broke in lazily. "Autos ain't allowed in the park, lady.
On'y hoss-cabs. How about Bedford Basin?"

"No," Isabel said crisply, "I want to ride through the park. Take us to a
livery stable—one that has carriages for hire."

Half an hour later they were bowling sedately through the park gates in
a victoria of somewhat tarnished appearance, but behind a pair of well-kept
bays and with an authentic coach man in muttonchop whiskers and a bowler
hat. Carney could not help chuckling.

"I daresay I'm out of date but this is my idea of luxury. I didn't know any of
these things were left."

"I thought you'd like it. There aren't many. You only see them in the park,
usually with a pair of old ladies taking the seaside air. It is rather nice, isn't
it?" She caught his arm and pressed it to her side. The wheels and the trotting hoofs made a pleasant sound on the gravel and the road wound through
the pine woods in a green twilight pierced by swords of brilliant sunshine.
Presently there was a cool draft in the green tunnel under the trees. The
victoria came briskly down a long slope and emerged beside sea water. They
passed groups of idlers and picnickers sprawling on the grass above the shore,
then a rococo iron bandstand lonely on a small bluff overlooking the water.
Suddenly the old battery was before them.

Isabel ordered the cabby to stop. Carney turned to her, smiling. He found
her facing seaward in that attitude, pensive and somehow sad, in which he
had discovered her before—as if she were alone once more, and as if on that
gleaming expanse she watched once more for the image of Sir Lancelot.
Silently he studied the pale profile so clearly cut against the dark woods of
the farther shore. She was a creature of such quick moods that he was afraid,
recalling how on the very doorstep of her lodgings after that first charming
evening together she had refused to see him again. The weather of her spirit
seemed so changeable, so utterly unpredictable, that he was dismayed. The
thought of losing her now was terrible. It was an age before she spoke.

"Matthew, I had to come here. I've always come here when I wanted to
think, and it seems to me I've been going on impulse ever since yesterday
afternoon."

"Yes?" he said thickly. He was trembling. He wanted to cry out urging her not to think, but an unconquerable honesty held him back. She was still gazing towards the harbor mouth. An old tern schooner with the light breeze barely filling its patched and discolored sails crept slowly down the reach towards Thrum Cap. Farther out, on the horizon, a passing steamer traced a black crayon stroke along the sky. A few gulls, very white and clean against the sea, dipped and tossed on the breeze like scraps of blown confetti. Somewhere a bell buoy clanged dolefully.

"It's strange," she went on in that musing voice. "I suppose it's been in the back of my mind all along—ever since you mentioned a job 'ashore,' and living in Halifax or Montreal. We've both been dreaming nonsense."

"No!"

"Oh yes, Matthew! Listen to me, please! You wanted to give up your post on Marina because you guessed that life in such a place would be unbearable to me. You thought—we both thought that love in a bungalow by the Arm or even a flat in Montreal would be nothing less than heaven. But all the time I knew it couldn't work. It simply couldn't. You'd never be happy, Matthew—please listen—not really happy in what you called a madhouse that day I first talked to you. For it is mad, all of it." She gave her head a backward toss, a gesture that rejected not merely Halifax but the whole frenzied continent. "I found that out yesterday between six o'clock and seven. When I came to you in the teashop I was the complete lunatic—Bedlam could teach me nothing more."

Carney did not try to understand these vague references to Mrs. Paradee's establishment. He knew she had been unhappy there but this harsh, almost strident note in her voice was disturbing; and it hurt him to see the mouth that last night had been so warm and generous twisted now in a wry smile that made another creature of her altogether. He was still under the spell of those miraculous hours which had given him back his youth and fulfilled his early dreams of an enchanting woman given to him alone. He longed to remain enchanted. This change in her was like a change of sky before storm. What was she about to say?

He could read nothing in the averted face. Isabel sat rigid, as if she could not bring herself to utter what she thought. For half an hour she did not move. The horses stamped impatiently. The cabby turned a curious glance from time to time. A party of children wandered up from the shore and stared at his immobile passengers. Suddenly she spoke.

"Matthew, it comes to this. You must go back to Marina."

A silence. Then, "What about you?" he asked painfully.

"Take me with you."

Having said this in a firm voice she closed her eyes, as if to shut out that mirror on the sea; but she remained tense, leaning forward with her face towards the harbor mouth, towards the immense reach of the North Atlantic and that far speck on the face of it which meant home to Carney and was such a mystery to her. For several moments Carney sat dumb, drenched in a warm flow of relief. Slowly she turned to him, and the coachman's sidelong eye beheld the passengers he had taken for father and daughter clasped in a passionate kiss there in the open carriage, in the pouring sunshine of the afternoon. He was astonished, even shocked, and he did not fully recover until the young woman cried something incomprehensible and the bearded blond man turned and shouted up to him "Five dollars if you get us downtown by four o'clock!"

CHAPTER 10

Many times afterward Isabel recalled with laughter that wild dash through the streets of Halifax in the old victoria, the tremendous clatter of hoofs, the whirr and rattle of the wheels, the dogs, the shouts of the cabby, the startled pedestrians and motor-drivers, the derisive small boys, the carriage swaying through the downtown traffic like a barque under full sail in a crowded tideway.

There was little time for shopping. Carney pressed his pocketbook upon her, and with this she made her way swiftly through one of those stores that sell everything from luggage to silk stockings. The dreamy mood was gone. Once more she was the efficient young woman best known to Hurd, casting up a mental list of things required, seeing, pricing, buying, moving on. At last in a taxi laden with parcels and new hand-baggage, and permitting herself a tremor of excitement, she arrived at the ferry wharf where Carney was waiting with his suitcases. On the way over the harbor to Dartmouth she passed him the depleted pocketbook.

"I've been awfully extravagant."

"Pshaw!"

"Matthew, I've never spent so much money at one time in my life. It could have been such fun if there'd been more time going about from shop to shop, trying on dozens of things, and refusing to make up my mind until the very last. Who ever heard of a woman buying a trousseau in an hour? But I've got some nice things—you'll see. And some practical things, of course. It's really a wonderful feeling, darling, starting a new life with every stitch fresh from the shop. I'm so grateful." She caught up his hand and pressed her lips upon it in one of those swift instinctive gestures that so charmed him.

"I went in to see Hurd," he said irrelevantly.

She raised an apprehensive face. "Oh! What did he say?"

"For a time he couldn't say anything, though his mouth was open. He gaped. He stared at me through those pince-nez glasses as if I'd gone completely off my keel. I had to smile—couldn't help it—he looked so like a stranded sculpin. Finally he offered congratulations in a sickly sort of way, and had the Benson girl make out a check for your salary up to the end of the month—very handsome of him when you stop to think of it. Here it is."

She glanced at the check and put it in her purse.

"What did she say—Miss Benson?"

"Not a word."

"She must have thought a lot."

"I daresay."

"What about me—on the ship, I mean. They'll be expecting you alone."

"I asked Hurd to phone Captain O'Dell and tell him I'd be accompanied by my wife. It won't make any difference in the arrangements. I've got a cabin to myself, and O'Dell's used to female passengers, lightkeepers' wives and so on, traveling up and down the coast."

"And what about me at Marina?"

"I sent a wireless message to Skane, the chap I left in charge. He'll see that everything's tidy. MacGillivray's coming off the island this trip—his time is up. Young Sargent's to stay. That'll leave you and me, Skane and Sargent, and of course the cook."

Isabel sank back against the cab cushions. Through the window she caught a glimpse of the battered spiles of the ferry approach, but her mind was far beyond the Dartmouth waterfront.

"You told Hurd we were married?"

"Of course."

"You'd better give me the wedding ring." Carney fumbled in a pocket and produced it. She held out her hand.

"Put it on, please, and kiss me." He obeyed.

"Now give me the license."

"You have it now—you put it in your purse when we came out of the bureau."

She sat up hastily and looked in the purse.

"So I did. I'd forgotten. My mind's in such a whirl."

"By Jingo, I just thought—O'Dell could marry us, couldn't he?"

"Not according to that license man. In two days we'll be on Marina. In any case I wouldn't want that—like crying our affair all over the ship. They'd all think it queer. They'd all wonder why, with the city full of preachers, we didn't think of getting married till the ship was on its way to Marina. I'd much rather let them think you'd met and married me respectably some time during your three months' leave. There are people, the Quakers I think, and people in Scotland somewhere, who marry just by announcing their intention and taking each other. Well, we've got the license to witness our intention—and we've certainly taken each other. My poor strait-laced Matthew, don't look so serious! I'm satisfied—aren't you?"

"You know I am. But I thought women were fussy about such things."

"I'm not 'women,' Matthew Carney. I'm me. Don't ever forget that."

"As if I could!"

Captain O'Dell met them at the gangway, an unusual honor. Hurd's message had astounded him, and now his old friendship for Carney was overlaid by a morbid curiosity. He suspected that the lonely man from Marina had fallen victim to some artful painted creature seeking marriage and respectability, of which she would sicken in a month on his island. He cast a cynical eye upon Isabel as she walked up the gangway; but Carney introduced his wife with such an enormous pride that the captain was touched, and in another moment he was shaking hands with a calm young woman with an erect carriage and a sensitive face, not at all pretty, and innocent of paint. He approved, and at once felt sorry for her. She was so obviously city-bred. He thought of the life on Marina, so simple and primitive and so deadly dull, especially for women, and wondered by what persuasions Carney had induced her to come. And how long would she stay? The *Lord Elgin* called at Marina three or four times a year with stores and mail, and the islanders reckoned time by her appearances. O'Dell gave Carney's bride one trip, or two at best; but he concealed these thoughts with a burst of affability, slapping Carney's shoulder and calling him a sly old dog and a lucky dog, asking Isabel with a cadaverous smile what she saw in the fellow, and shouting in his high voice for a couple of seamen to look after their baggage.

The cabin built for the Deputy Minister of Marine and Fisheries (and never used by that worthy) delighted Isabel. With a schoolgirl's eagerness she exclaimed over the red carpet, the green plush couch, the maple panels, the gilt mirror, the great mahogany berth with its brass-handled drawers below, the water carafe and tumblers secure in their rack, the opulent green curtain sliding on brass rings across the doorway when the door itself stood open for air, the adjoining bathroom, the open ports through which the harbor water cast a dappled sunshine on the bulkhead. She turned to Carney and kissed him with all the enthusiasm of a bride whose husband has secured the bridal suite of, say, the *Mauretania*.

He smiled and left her to unpack, walking out upon the deck with his solid tread to watch the last-minute stores and mail bags coming aboard. When the bell rang for the evening meal he found her freshly arrayed in one of her purchases, a smart yellow frock, and with her mouth full of hairpins, putting the final touches to her coiffure.

"How do you like my dress?" she demanded through the pins.

"Lovely!"

"It's awfully short, do you mind? I feel all legs."

"You look very nice, legs and all."

"It's the fashion," she said, a little self-consciously.

They entered the saloon together and found the officers standing politely at their places about the table. The purser and the young third mate were absent at their duties. The chief officer, a handsome man with curly gray hair and a ruddy, somewhat choleric face, was at the table's foot. The second mate, a pockmarked man of thirty-five, and the other passenger, a fat and cheerful assistant lightkeeper bound for the lonely rock of Saint Paul, were on the settee side. Captain O'Dell asked Isabel to sit at the head of the table on his left, opposite the chief engineer, and placed Carney at the chief officer's right.

The formality of these arrangements, a tribute of which she was quite unconscious, seemed to fit the pattern of that wonderful private cabin and she accepted it as the normal habit of the ship. Carney, familiar with the easygoing air that usually obtained with passengers going to posts about the coast, gave O'Dell a humorous glance. But the captain was devoting himself to Isabel, and in sidelong glances so was every man about the board. The sudden reappearance of the famous Carney with a wife was a phenomenon as startling in its way as the appearance of a bright new satellite beside the Polar Star, and they regarded her with almost the same professional interest.

She was quick to sense it. Their curiosity was a challenge and she accepted it with spirit, chatting vivaciously with O'Dell and the walrus across the table, and from time to time casting a smiling glance to meet Carney's own adoring gaze. He was proud of her in the presence of these men he had known for years and he showed it in his eyes, in his smile, in his absent conversation with the florid man beside him.

The happiest moment came with the dessert, when at a signal from Captain O'Dell the steward passed around with a bottle of champagne smuggled from

Saint Pierre, and they all rose and drank, in the captain's words, "To the new queen of Marina, and long may she reign!" There followed a burst of hand-clapping and demands for a speech. She refused, smiling, and aware that she was blushing hotly as all brides are supposed to do but as well-trained queens are not. Then came demands on Carney, who refused as well, protesting with truth that he was too poor a hand at speechmaking to do the subject justice. There it ended, a pleasant little episode. There were sounds of winches turning on the deck outside, and the voices of longshoremen, and in a few moments O'Dell and his mates gulped the last of their coffee and withdrew to take the ship to sea.

The sun had withdrawn behind the harbor hills. A few clouds high in the west caught the last of the light with a sudden blaze as if afire. In the shadow of Citadel Hill the lower city already was putting on the artificial glitter of its night. In the still air the smoke of its chimneys rose and mingled over steep tiers of rooftops rising from the water, so that all were veiled and mysterious, and in this haze the lights winked like fireflies. Halifax was beautiful then, and Isabel, standing beside Carney on the bridge, felt a momentary pang. Then the memory of that shabby little court behind Mrs. Paradee's establishment rose out of the dusk like an apparition. Again she thought of the sailors packing for sea. *And now I—I too,* she whispered to herself triumphantly. She turned her face toward the bow, and far ahead saw the Mauger's Beach light-house flashing in the twilight, a signpost on the way to adventure.

A procession of familiar things seen from an unfamiliar viewpoint crept past like objects in a dream; the sprawl of oil tanks on the Dartmouth slope, the small hump of George's Island, the long stone breakwater, and then Point Pleasant and its pine woods and the old battery squatting at the tip. She caught Carney's arm.

"See! There's where it all began, Matthew—on the little bench where I was so unhappy, and you came. How wonderful it seems—so much, in such a little time!"

"Some day we'll come back there and sit, for old time's sake."

"That's nice and sentimental, darling. Will you make love to me, too?"

"I'll always make love to you."

A squeeze of his arm. "I've never been beyond this point. What's that out there?"

"Chebucto Head. Where the sea really begins. It'll be a bit rough, I'm afraid. O'Dell's been in touch with Marina by wireless and there's quite a swell breaking on the landing beach."

"What will that mean?"

"He'll take the ship up the coast to Bold Head—the nearest point to our island. From there it's a run of about ninety miles straight out to sea. There's good anchorage inside Bold Head and he'll hold up there until Marina reports decent landing conditions. There's a lot of stuff to put ashore."

"I like the way you say that. Our island!"

"Well, I've always thought of it as mine, somehow. Because I've been there longer than anyone else, I suppose. And now it's ours, of course."

"Of course!"

The ship had begun to dip and sway on a long swell running in past the harbor heads. There remained a smear of light in the western sky but towards the sea all was darkness, and Isabel realized for the first time how thoroughly she was plunging her life into the unknown. She turned for reassurance to the shadowy figures on the bridge; the young helmsman statuesque behind the wheel, with his face gaunt and serious in the faint glow of the compass bowl; the dim shapes of O'Dell, the chief officer and Carney chatting in low tones by the forward screen. But chiefly she sought the comfort of Carney's voice, with its deep and vibrant ring. She gazed at the big figure that had seemed so out of place in the Halifax streets and now was in its proper setting. And she felt now that faint resentment which comes to all women who give themselves utterly and find that a man has other interests in which they cannot join.

Words, phrases, snatches of sea talk came to her in the darkness like murmurs in a foreign tongue. Occasionally someone laughed, and when the voice was Carney's she recognized in it the deep happy tone which she felt belonged to her alone. I'm jealous—how silly! She moved towards him in the heaving darkness, and instinctively he turned away from his companions and came to her, putting an arm about her waist.

"Are you cold? Shall I get you a coat?"

"Oh no, the air's quite warm. And I'm so proud of my sea legs. The water's really quite rough, isn't it? It seems strange, with hardly any wind."

"There's been a southeaster out there," he gestured into the night, "and we're getting the swell it's kicked up." He added casually, "She'll roll worse by and by, when O'Dell hauls up towards Bold Head. She's a tipsy tub when she takes it on the beam."

"That sounds very nautical and ominous."

"Not as bad as it sounds. You really don't mind the motion?"

"I'm enjoying it."

But later, when the *Lord Elgin* began to fulfill Carney's prophecy, her skin felt strangely chilled, as if a cold wind blew. "I think I'll go below—that's the word, isn't it?" And turning to him with a low and intimate voice she added, "Come to me soon.'"

"How soon?" he murmured.

"I'll give you half an hour—that will be quite enough sea talk for one night." He laughed gently, and she caught his hand and pressed it in the darkness.

The cabin looked very snug in the pink glow of the shaded lamp above the couch and she glanced about it with a new approval. Throughout the long day the memory of last night's embraces in the squalid little hotel had oppressed her with a sense of something tainted, and she was anxious to erase it from her own and Matthew's mind. Here in the scrubbed and polished stateroom with its touches of nautical luxury she saw a proper setting for their nuptials, and with the sentimental and theatrical instinct of a healthy young woman at such a moment she prepared to play her part.

The lurching of the ship seemed more violent within doors. The sea legs of which she had been so proud could not prevent her staggering as she undressed. Twice she almost fell. In the bathroom a problem awaited her. Matthew had explained in his offhand way the operation of the short steam hose that heated water in the bath, but she could not remember what he had said. She turned the valve experimentally and was alarmed by a jerk and a loud howl from the hose. A pillar of steam arose like a jinni from the bath and she shut the thing off hastily. Eventually she bathed in cold water, clasping a sponge in one hand and steadying herself against the ship's roll with the other. It was a difficult process. In the white tub the water rushed to and fro like an insane tide, and when she stepped forth at last she was aware of a disagreeable sensation in the pit of her stomach.

From one of the new suitcases she drew forth the most extravagant of her purchases, a black nightgown of a stuff so sheer that it was little more than an illusion. She had felt indecent, buying it under the gaze of so many shoppers, but she had determined on it together with a set of delicate French underwear that a good breath would have blown away. So many of her purchases had been "sensible," and after all she was a newly married woman with a bridegroom to charm out of his wits. That at least had seemed the purpose of the things displayed at the bridal counter in the shop.

She slipped into the illusion and studied it in the glass, moving back to get the full effect. Her first impulse was to take it off at once and cover herself with something more in keeping with her modesty. What would Matthew think? But was a bridegroom supposed to think, or even to be quite conscious? The shop girl had called the gown "bewitching," and surely Matthew was entitled to be bewitched? How pitiful it was, that long barren gap in his life without romance, and how grateful and how naive he had been last night! He worshiped her, there was no doubt of that. But all that had been in the dark. Was it wise here in the lamplight, this bold display of all his idol's charms? Hadn't she given too much already, and too soon?

She debated the matter seriously, with the intuition of women who know that the honeymoon was designed for the creation of charming impressions that will last a husband's lifetime, and bracing herself with increasing desperation against the antics of the ship. And suddenly the ship decided all her doubts and speculations. The queasiness she had felt as she emerged from the bath now spread a clammy malaise through her flesh and sent her stumbling to the couch, where she lay coldly perspiring and gasping for breath in an atmosphere suddenly devoid of oxygen and filled with the stuffy odor of ship's paint.

When the bridegroom came he found a wretched creature ill apparently to the point of death, and clad in a bit of black gossamer whose purpose had been lost. He lifted her into the berth and covered that damply clinging mockery with a blanket. There she lay through the night and most of the next day, staring glassily at the peeling white paint on the deck above, and with clenched teeth fighting back waves of nausea that always won in the end. Gradually her natural pallor assumed the greenish hue that seasickness stamps upon its victims, and at intervals, alarmed at her appearance, Carney with gentle insistence forced a spoonful of brandy between her lips.

Her one shred of hope in this engulfing misery was the anchorage of which Carney had spoken, somewhere ahead. She pictured a harbor where for a few hours at least there would be a respite. Alas for these delusions! The very contrivances of Signor Marconi, with which she and Carney were so familiar, conspired to rob her of a moment's grace. Far out on Marina a watchful patrol on the beach had observed a slackening of the swell, and a bored unshaven man in the wireless station flicked a message across the darkness to the small steamer wallowing slowly up the coast towards Bold Head. O'Dell, aroused from a nap on the chartroom couch, studied the message for a few moments and sent a quartermaster for Carney.

"You know those people," he grumbled, as Carney read a scrawled yellow form in the bright cone under the chartroom lamp. "Always a bit too anxious to get their mail and stuff. 'Sea going down, surf slackening'—ha!—'expect good landing conditions afternoon'—ha!—just the sort of thing that's fetched me out there on many a wild-goose chase afore."

"McBain signed it," Carney observed. "He usually knows what he's talking about."

"Ha! The swell's still running strong here, you can see for yourself."

"From the southeast, yes—Marina way. They'd get the change first."

"You're as bad as the others, Carney. Can't wait to get your feet on that damned heap of sand again, can you?"

"I want to get my wife ashore. She's terribly sick."

"Oh? Oh! Well, all right. But I bet a dollar I'll butt my way out there through a head sea and find I can't land an ounce of stores—have to chuck the mailbags into their surfboat and hump off back to Bold Head where I should have dropped my hook in the first place. Your wife won't thank me for that."

He threw open the door and bellowed an order into the murk of the bridge; and as the *Lord Elgin* swung away towards Marina the unceasing wallow changed to a new discomfort for the unhappy girl in the berth below.

Through all these hours Matthew attended her faithfully, wiping the sweat from her poor face, stroking her cold brow, carrying her limp and unprotesting form to that giddy bathroom as if she were a child, watching even when she lay apparently asleep. All her blissful fancies had fled. All her cherished mysteries had been revealed to his gaze under the worst possible circumstances. She felt herself the victim of a hideous joke no less degrading than that affair at Mrs. Paradee's; and while one part of her mind was grateful for Carney's tenderness, the rest regarded with a sullen resentment his very presence in this utter ruin of her pride.

More than this, with the bitter inconsistency of the sick she considered the whole course of affairs his fault, from the moment when he had spoken to her in the restaurant above the docks. She regretted that she had ever met him and wished fervently that by some stroke of magic all could be undone. Even in those comatose intervals when she appeared to sleep her restless brain went on with the torture, fetching forth the mocking voice of Miss Benson, the malicious smile of Mrs. Paradee, the cynical gaze of Mr. Hurd.

The water in the carafe, the door curtain, the coats on the hooks, the porthole drapes swept back and forth in a tireless dance. The mahogany drawers beneath the berth slid inward a fraction of an inch at each starboard roll, and then back again with a little chorus of dull clicks against the brass securing buttons. Indeed the ship was full of sound—groans, creaks, scrapes, mysterious clangs and knocks, the hiss of water flung over the bow, an occasional running footfall on the deck overhead. As the engines throbbed, hour on hour, carrying her ever farther into a purgatory from which there was no redemption or escape, her Calvinist conscience chanted dismally, *You've been wicked and foolish, and this is the result.* The remorseless engines pounded the refrain, *is the result...is the result...is the result...*on and on through the night, through the chill sea dawn, and far into the next afternoon.

CHAPTER 11

"Well, there it is," O'Dell said, squinting against the glare, "and you can see the surf from here." He passed his binoculars with an indignant thrust, Carney put them up and stared for a long time towards the shore.

"I see," he said deliberately. "Well, I wouldn't say it was bad, Captain. The swell's definitely going down. Send off the light stores first, and by the time you get to the coal and oil and the rest of the heavy stuff there shouldn't be enough surf to matter."

"So you say!" And in a sudden shout forward, "All ready the anchors, Mister?"

"All ready, sir."

"Stand by to let go. Bosun!"

"Aye, sir!"

"Make ready the motorboat."

These distant voices, the reduced clamor of the engines, the changed motion of the ship itself, all came to Isabel with a realization that the longed-for end of this nightmare had come at last. Matthew found her sitting up in the berth and peering at the porthole.

"We're there," he announced cheerfully.

"I can't see anything."

"The island's on the other side—we've just turned the west bar. How do you feel?"

"Horrible."

"Shall I help you dress?"

"No." Her voice was sullen.

"I'll wait for you on deck, then. Don't hurry, my dear. The ship will be here for several hours, and the landing will be better later on."

As the door closed she put her legs over the edge of the berth and slid down carefully. A spasm of giddiness. She locked her teeth and moved towards the bathroom. From the glass above the washstand a ghost stared at her dull-eyed through a tangle of loose hair. There was a gleam of white flesh under rumpled black chiffon. *And like a dying lady, lean and pale, who totters forth wrapped in a gauzy veil.* A satirical smile appeared upon the spectre in the glass. She removed that incongruous garment with a shudder of distaste; and when at last she was washed, combed, dressed and packed for the shore, she opened the porthole and tossed the thing in a tight black ball into the sea.

Her head ached violently and there was still a miserable sensation in her stomach. She made her way to the deck on trembling legs. When Matthew greeted her she answered him curtly and gripped the rail for support. He stretched an arm eagerly towards the shore. There was not much to be seen. The *Lord Elgin* lay a mile off the beach, and far in the sunshine a line of white surf flickered across Isabel's view, extending far towards the east. Behind this a background of low bleache yellow dunes writhed and shimmered in the mirage thrown up by their own heat. A lighthouse stood bold in the sun at the west tip of the island and far towards the east she could see the mirage-twisted pillar of another.

Carney's big finger stabbed the scene. "This is where we'll land—where you see the red watchtower on the dune. It's the only part of the main lifesaving station that shows from seaward. A mile to the left you may be able to make out a tall mast—ours, of course. Four miles to the east of that is Number Two, a beach patrol station, just a man and his wife and a house, shut in by the dunes—all the buildings on Marina are like that except the watchtower and the lighthouses. Shelter, you know. Four miles farther east you come to Number Three—about there, say—another patrol station, chap with a big family, has a garden, grows the biggest potatoes and turnips you ever saw in your life, mixture of sand and pony manure—amazing! Another four or five miles beyond that is Number Four—same story, barring the turnips. Finally there's East Light—the farthest from us. Forty-five men, women and children altogether—all on the government establishment. Not another soul. The kids have never seen a train or a motorcar—for that matter they've never seen a tree. But they saw planes during the war, and of course the wireless station's an old story on Marina now. It's a bit odd when you stop to think of it."

Isabel ignored this talk of trains and turnips. She could see only that low wavering illusion along the horizon, and her mind called up a vision of small dwellings withdrawn one from another amongst the miles of dunes, and in each a little group of humans living secret lives as if afraid of this immensity of sea and sky. Her silence disturbed him. He murmured, "What do you think of it?"

"It's not what I'd expected."

"You're not disappointed?"

"I'd pictured quite big hills of sand, and everybody living together in a sort of village by the shore.
Where is the lagoon?"

"On the other side. The dunes will look bigger when you're on the beach, but of course they're not much. The highest I suppose is about a hundred and fifty feet above sea level. Most of them are much less. Marina's only a glorified sand bar, after all. Hardly a mile wide anywhere, and towards the ends you could pretty well toss a ball from one side to the other."

He laughed and threw out his arms in a gesture that embraced the whole sweep of Marina. "Plenty of room this way, mind you. Two-and-twenty miles!"

"The wrecks you talked about—where are they?"

"Ah, that's what everybody asks. Well, the wooden ships break up very quickly and the sea pitches the wreckage up the beach and into the dunes— especially in the winter storms. The sand soon covers most of it. The iron hulls break up completely too, after a time—you'd be amazed at what the sea can do—and of course all that sinks out of sight. Here and there you'll see an iron stem or stern post sticking up, or a pair of old boilers still fastened to the keel, but that's all. Newspaper chaps come out in the *Elgin* sometimes and the young lifesavers fill them full of yarns about wrecks and all that. They like to swing the lead a bit. Some of their leg pulling gets into the papers and people ashore take it all for cold fact. It makes you wonder about history."

"When are we going ashore?"

"We could go now, if you like. There's still a bit of surf on the beach but it's all right."

"If you have any feeling for me, get me there as quickly as you can."

Her words conveyed exactly what she thought—that she must get her feet on something firm very quickly, or collapse in a wretched heap on the deck under the staring eyes of O'Dell and his crew. But Carney was startled by the cold passion in her voice.

The *Lord Elgin's* launch skittered back and forth towing laden boats as far as the outer shoals, and towing empty ones back to the ship. Carney hailed an island boat just coming alongside. Five men in faded shirts and trousers and rubber sea boots looked up and shouted. Their teeth flashed in the brown faces upturned to the sun. They were young and lean, but they cried up to him "Carney boy!" as if he were one of them; and Matthew answered in kind, singing out nicknames in his strong voice and smiling on them like an older brother returned from the wars. His blue eyes shone.

He belongs to all this, Isabel thought, *he's theirs, not mine.* No jealousy now. The cruel humor of the sea had plucked that away with her other notions and illusions; and now these lively voices confirmed what she had decided in the night. She and Matthew were creatures apart, of different worlds; and already his world had sickened and humiliated her beyond any power of his to redeem. She watched their shallow but broad-beamed surfboat being loaded with what seemed to her a dangerous amount of boxes and packages, and saw with a chill dismay the cargo net go down at last with Carney's shabby suitcases and her own smart things. Matthew took her arm and moved towards the forward deck where the rope ladder hung down the side.

"Now, my dear, hold tight to the ropes as you go down, and feel for each step with your foot. I'll be just below you, so don't be afraid. It's nothing, really." He swung himself over the bulwark. Looking down, Isabel saw the ladder swaying with his weight and the wallow of the ship. It seemed a frightful distance down to the boat and its sunburned crew, rising and falling on the swell as if gripped by some infuriated giant in the depths. Panic seized her. For several moments she could not breathe and the nausea of the past twenty hours was replaced with a surge of utter fear. She clenched her teeth and fought it down. Nothing mattered—nothing but the shore. A sailor helped her over the side. Captain O'Dell, leaning over the bridge screen, saw the young woman descend towards the boat, and caught one glimpse of an upturned face, white and resolute, before she passed from his sight.

In the boat the steersman with a mute gesture offered Carney the long stern oar. He took it and stood with his feet braced, gazing towards the shore and the breakers leaping white in the flat sunshine of the afternoon. His new gray suit, wrinkled by that long vigil on the cabin couch, had an incongruous look beside the rough clothing of the islanders; but his head was bare, the bleached-hemp locks blew about his forehead, and with his clipped beard, his sachem nose, his steady blue eyes oblivious of the sun's blaze on the water, he seemed to Isabel the spirit incarnate of this wilderness.

The launch towed them to the milky backwash of the outer shoals and then swung away. The boatmen slid out their oars. For a time they rowed in silence. Then Carney spoke. "Easy all!" Isabel noticed a new intentness in his eyes, and she sensed in the island men a sudden urgency. They rested with raised oars while Carney kept the boat's stern to the sea with powerful movements of the sweep. What was he waiting for? One, two, three ponderous swells in the endless succession lifted the boat, dropped it, and passed on. The *Lord Elgin* had become a child's toy in the distance, to be seen for a moment as the boat rose to each crest, and lost at once as it sank into the trough. In these deep green valleys, where the boat seemed to be shut in from everything but the sky, Isabel was conscious no longer of sickness or even of fear so much as of a terrible loneliness. The voice within, more insistent than ever, cried *Fool! Fool! Fool!* And something else within her whimpered in self-pity. With a bitter wonder she thought upon the office, the room at Mrs. Paradee's, the meals at Feder's Grill, the old life that had seemed so dull and meaningless and now was like a peaceful dream.

Another swell advanced upon them, overtook them; a rolling hill of green marble veined with white, ponderous, glistening and alive; and as the boat's stern rose and tossed Carney's big figure towards the sky he spoke again.

"Ready all!" And when the bow came up, "Now!" in a ringing shout.

The men dipped their oars and pulled with sudden energy. Perched on the shoulder of the sea the boat rushed on towards the shore. The sound of the breakers, dim at first, soon filled Isabel's ears, and all about her the sea went mad, toppling, bouncing, tossing up in wild white spouts that seemed to have no direction and no purpose except to drown them all. Sitting with white knuckles clenched on the aftermost thwart, with her back towards the rowers and the shore, she fixed her gaze on Carney's impassive face, the one thing known and assured in all this chaos. The length of the boat, the stores and baggage, the straining men at the oars, all were behind her and invisible. There was a peculiar terror in being hurled thus, backward, into oblivion.

An eternity passed. Then, abruptly, she felt the boat's rush checked as if a great hand had seized the keel. Human figures appeared by magic, thigh-deep in the broken sea, grinning, shouting "Carney boy!" grasping the gunwales, dragging the boat from the clutch of the backwash. Carney's stern mouth relaxed. He slid the sweep inboard and, stooping quickly, lifted his wife from the thwart. Operator Skane, turning for a moment from his efforts at the gunwale, saw his chief step into the sea and walk up the beach carrying a tall girl in his arms, like a Viking returning from a far raid with the captive of his choice.

Matthew set her down carefully above tidemark, in the scuffled sand where the stores were being piled. A group of women and children stood there watching. They greeted Carney with quick familiar smiles but their eyes were not for him. At once Isabel felt the concentrated gaze of Marina like the rays of a burning glass. Her trim new boots were planted firmly in the sand but her head still reeled and ached. The island seemed to have no more stability than the *Lord Elgin's* deck. She was glad that Matthew kept his arm about her.

He cried to the women, "Come and meet my wife!" in the joyous tones of a man who has indeed brought home a prize; and they came, slowly, shyly, with what seemed to her an intolerable curiosity in all their faces. They were gaunt and brown like their men, and they wore costumes obviously put away, year in, year out, for these occasions which were the only holidays in their lives. The styles were of prewar days, the heavy stuff of the skirts hung limp and full about their ankles, the jackets had padded shoulders and leg-o'-mutton sleeves, the blouses had high collars of lace stiffened with strips of whalebone, the hats were ludicrous; they belonged to a time that seemed to Isabel as remote as the moon.

For their part the island women stared as if Carney's wife herself had dropped from the moon. She was sharply aware of a modish skirt that barely covered her knees, of the high laced gray-kid boots, and of the curved inches of silken leg so boldly revealed between the boot tops and the skirt. She forgot that only a short time back she had considered the postwar styles ugly and immodest, as well as expensive, and refused to wear them; and now she resented the astonishment of these women for whom the war had been a disturbance in another world whose minds, like their clothes, remained molded in the fashion of 1910.

"My dear, meet the ladies of Marina...Mrs. Jim Kahn of West Light... Mrs. Lermont of Number Two...Mrs. Giswell...Mrs. Nightingale...Mrs. Shelman..." The names were lost at once. Their hands touched hers and fell away, their lips murmured and were still; and having made these polite sounds and gestures they withdrew a little and with one accord turned their stares upon the active figures of their men. The children remained close by, absorbed in contemplation of the strange woman with the face of death; and they followed in a brown troop, leaping about in the sand, wild as hawks, and watching with the bright unwinking eyes of hawks as Matthew, with his arm still about her waist, drew Isabel towards a trampled gap in the dunes. There a pair of shaggy ponies stood harnessed to a buggy.

At this point they were overtaken by a lean blue-jawed man whom Carney greeted cheerfully. "Skane! It's good to see you again! Isabel, my dear, this is

Greg Skane—you know, the chap who's been running the show since I went off to the main." Isabel put out a languid hand, and the newcomer gripped it briefly and turned to answer Carney's eager questions. Isabel had caught a glimpse of Skane in the rush of wet figures about the boat, and now she inspected in profile a rather tall man in sea boots, stained duck trousers, and the shabby and patched jacket of a radio officer in the Canadian merchant marine, with the brass buttons encrusted in verdigris and the entwined gold bands on the cuffs worn down to ragged gilt threads.

He had no cap. His hair blew long and black in the wind. His eyes were of a dark blue, piercing when his gaze was direct. She guessed his age at thirty-five. He looked competent but she disliked him at once. The somewhat gaunt features, from which a heavy growth of beard had been shaved only recently, wore a cynical expression that did not change when he glanced from Matthew to herself. He did not smile, even when greeting his chief, and in his compressed lips she sensed a determination that struck her as rather cruel.

She thought, *He's sorry to see Matthew back.* Her years of intimate acquaintance with radio station politics up and down the seaboard told her that Skane must have hoped to continue permanently as Operator-in-Charge. No doubt it had seemed to him reasonable to suppose that Carney, after his long service on this lonely spot, had gone to the mainland looking for a post in civilization. That was the dream of every outpost O-in-C, even those who had wives to content them in the wilds. And now, instead, Carney had come back, and with a wife of all things! It must have been a blow. But she did not feel sorry for Skane. She felt only the man's hostility, and on a sudden impulse she pressed herself against Matthew's side.

And now MacGillivray appeared, the operator who had "served his time." He was dressed in a dark blue suit, evidently little worn during his service on Marina, and his young face, tanned to a dark leather by twelve months of wind and sunblaze on these barren sands, made a startling contrast with the clean white of his shirt and collar. He shook hands with Carney, ducked his head with an engaging grin at Isabel, and went off, shouting to the boat's crew as if in mortal fear of being left behind. Matthew smiled.

"Like a kid out of school. They're all like that, the young chaps, when they go. Natural, of course. It's something to be young."

He helped Isabel into the buggy seat while Skane stowed and lashed their baggage behind. "I'll stay and check the stores," Skane said. "There's still a lot to come. Vedder will have tea ready for you. I think you'll find everything shipshape."

Matthew took up the reins and drove off along the beach, keeping just above the water where the sand was firm and smooth.

"Where is the road?" Isabel asked.

He chuckled. "There's no road on Marina. Oh, there's a sort of track amongst the dunes from Main Station to our place—a mile or so. But it's rough going. We use the beach all the time, except in high tides or storms. Notice the wheels—those wide iron tires. Keeps 'em from sticking in the sand. All the wagons on Marina have wheels like that."

"I didn't think much of that man Skane."

"He's all right."

"What's the other operator like?"

"Sargent? I only saw him when he landed last spring. Just a kid, nineteen or so."

"And who's Vedder?"

"The cook."

Ahead of the ponies the dark ribbon of wet sand ran on for miles and was lost in the mirage to the east. On the right hand marched a rampart of dunes, a monotony of steep sands, bare on the seaward face, and topped with bunches of pallid green marram grass, waving in the breeze. Here and there a gully opened upon the beach as a lane opens upon a main thoroughfare, and there was a passing glimpse of other dunes whose slopes were covered with that shifting illusory green. On the left hand the North Atlantic stretched away to the horizon, a gleaming blue desert speckled with white where the swells began to break on the shoals.

Above the dunes appeared the topmost section of the radio mast, a white wand held upright by taut wire stays, like a naked umbrella raised to the cloudless sky. Slowly the umbrella grew taller. The mast was revealed as three long wooden spars fastened one upon another like the lower, top and topgallant masts of a ship. And now in each lull of the sea breeze Isabel could hear the pop-pop-pop of a gasoline engine and then the high bugle note of the radio spark in quick staccato bursts. At each of these Matthew threw up his head, listening, smiling a little, and translating the dots and dashes for her benefit. Young Sargent was talking to the *Lord Elgin*, a few common-place phrases flung out into the void, and she wondered at the pleasure in Matthew's face, not realizing that this was for him the very voice of home.

When the mast drew abreast Matthew turned into a gully. The ponies, wiry, half-tamed beasts from the Main Station stables, dragged the buggy at their heels resignedly. The patter of their unshod hoofs sank to a whisper in the dry loose sand. In the hollow of the dunes there was no stir of sea air and the slopes threw off the sun's heat like the walls of an oven. In a minute the ponies shone with sweat. Isabel felt her cheeks burning. The sea had vanished and the murmur of the surf became faint and far. They passed under the island telephone line, a single wire carried over the dunes on a procession of staggering poles.

The gully came to an end and the buggy lurched over a steep dune and there, without warning, lay the wireless station; the tall white mast, which now seemed to touch the sky, a small store-shed and a rectangular bungalow of white clapboards, like a small wooden oasis in a desolation of sand and spire-grass. The island here was narrow, sloping towards the south, and at a distance of perhaps two hundred yards beyond the buildings Isabel saw an expanse of calm water screened from the northerly breeze by the dunes. The heaving face of the ocean lay beyond that, and between the two stretched a bar of sand and a white toss of surf. The sheltered water inside the bar went on towards the east, apparently for miles, disappearing in the haze.

"The lagoon," Matthew said, with a flick of the whip. He pulled up the ponies outside a small porch at the end of the white building and helped Isabel down.

"My dear," he cried, "we're home!"

CHAPTER 12

Isabel had a fear that he was about to sweep her up in his arms and carry her over the threshold, as he had carried her up the beach under the eyes of those staring women and that cynical man Skane; and she forestalled him by stepping quickly through the open doorway. She found herself in a narrow hall from which a series of doors opened right and left. A powder of fine sand lay along the floor. Matthew threw open the first door on the left and revealed a young man sitting in a chair facing the east window, with a pair of phones clasped on his head. Before him a long table ran across the east side of the room, and upon it stood the receiving apparatus, two varnished wooden boxes faced with ebonite and studded with knobs and dials. At his right hand lay the transmitting key with its thick brass shank and round black knob.

There was a black switchboard on the wall at his left with an imposing array of switches and voltmeters and ammeters. A small iron stove and three worn wooden chairs completed the furniture. The wooden floor was bare, and badly worn by heavy boots grinding the all-pervading sand underfoot, so that the knots in the boards stood out like wens. Along the painted wainscot a row of hooks dangled clips of message forms. The upper part of the walls was painted an unimaginative drab. There were two windows, one looking out towards the mast and the other facing north towards the invisible beach and the dunes over which the buggy had just come. It was a room devoid of beauty and of comfort, and to Isabel it reflected faithfully the sterile life of Matthew and the others in this place for all the years. She could scarcely repress a shudder.

The man at the phones sat in a rigid attitude, gazing through the window with alert far-staring eyes as if he could see across the void to the lurching, creaking radio cabin of the ship to which he was listening. But he had seen the buggy draw up at the door, and suddenly, as if satisfied for the moment with that mysterious whisper in the phones, he turned and sprang out of his chair, slipping off one of the earpieces and looking towards the newcomers. Isabel saw that he was very young and shy. He could not have been more than eighteen. He had an oval, rather girlish face, and under the tan a quick flush spread as he met Isabel's eyes. His hair, like Skane's, was badly in need of the scissors. It hung in a brown mop on his neck and across his forehead; but he was freshly shaved. He wore an old navy jersey of heavy wool and a pair of shapeless trousers that once had been part of a naval uniform, and there was a pair of battered leather slippers on his feet.

"Sargent," Matthew said briskly, "I want you to meet my wife." Sargent moved politely towards her, still listening with the other ear to the far-off voice in the air; and Isabel, noting the short length of the phone cord, stepped forward quickly and put out her hand. He shook it bashfully and their hands withdrew.

"Sargent, I'm the happiest man in the world," Carney cried, "and you can see why. And it's going to be a lot better for us all, I tell you, with a woman about the place. Don't let us interrupt your work. I'm just showing Mrs. Carney her new home." He took Isabel's arm and they moved out into the hall. He pointed down the hall. "It ends at a partition, as you see. My—our apartment's on the other side, with a separate entrance. That door on the left, beyond the watch room, is Sargent's bedroom, and the farther one is Skane's. The room on the right, opposite Skane's, is Vedder's—the cook, you know. Next is the operators' bathroom. This one here"—he threw open the door—"is the engine room, as you see."

She peered inside obediently. The place reeked of hot oil. It had a concrete floor and in the midst of it a large single-cylinder gasoline engine whirled a pair of flywheels. From one of these a long slatting belt led her eye to the generator, spinning and whining at the farther end of the room. Along the wall stood a work bench equipped with vises and a scatter of tools, and above the generator there was an array of apparatus that she recognized as radio condensers and tuning coils. She had seen these things by the dozen in the storeroom at Halifax, items that she typed on long forms or mentioned in Hurd's business letters; and from time to time she had seen them sent off to ships or to distant parts of the coast. It was strange to see them in use, especially here in this small sea-desert where Carney of Marina had grown lonely and famous through the years. Outside she heard the steady thudding of the engine exhaust, and through a window she perceived several gasoline drums lying on the sandy slope at a safe distance from the building in case of fire.

Young Sargent, in that barren cell across the hall, began to talk in dots and dashes to the ship that had so engrossed his attention when the Carneys arrived. Isabel, standing on the greasy floor, was startled by a terrific sound as sharp, as deafening as rifle shots, and the little engine room was lit by a rapid succession of bright violet flashes that sprang, like the sound, from the revolving brass spark-studs at the end of the generator shaft. Involuntarily she shrank against Matthew's stalwart form and she was thankful for the arm clasping her in reassurance.

It was no wonder to her now that Matthew had been able to read the messages far down the beach. The sound was frightful, like an enormous and explosive brass trumpet. Electricity in large quantities had always seemed to her an uncomfortable if useful commodity; she had read in the newspapers of people killed by high-voltage wires about the streets; and she wondered how it was possible to stand in this hot little chamber, in the midst of these shattering manifestations, and remain alive. It was clear that Matthew and the others, grown careless with familiarity, were taking desperate chances every day of their lives. Casting dignity aside with Matthew's arm she fled into the hall and covered her ears with her hands. Matthew merely grinned.

"You'll get used to it," he declared calmly. "There's a muffling drum that fits over the spark disc but we leave it off—we have to file the studs clean and adjust the gap every day, sometimes two or three times a day."

"Do you mean to say," she demanded in a voice that sounded thin and strange in her singing ears, "that it goes on like that, day and night?"

"Only when the chap on watch is transmitting."

"But the transmitting goes on day and night—at intervals, I mean?"

"Oh yes. As I say, you'll get used to it."

She did not reply. How could anyone sleep, even exist, with this erratic uproar shattering the silence of the station and of all the dunes within half a mile? And when she thought of days, weeks, months of it, she wondered how any of them kept from going mad. She was glad when Matthew led her outside and they passed along the plank walk to his own apartment at the east side.

As he opened the door she stepped inside with an air of skepticism, expecting the worst. After all, what could you expect of men living this barren life so far from civilization? The long ghastly hours of the voyage had given her an impression of enormous distance, as if she had come to the end of the world. With a quick feminine inquisitiveness she inspected the kitchen, the realm of the still unseen Vedder, a slovenly creature no doubt.

What she saw was somewhat reassuring. The place was clean. The floor had been swept of sand and scrubbed. The boards gleamed bone-white in the sunshine through the uncurtained windows. The wainscoting was newly painted a dark shining brown, and the upper walls with white. A kitchen range stood against the partition wall. It had been freshly blackened and the kettles and pots on the neighboring shelves had been scrubbed to a dull sheen.

"Not many stations are laid out like this, with a separate apartment for the chief operator," Matthew said with pride. "In most of 'em he has a room like the others and the kitchen is simply a living room for all hands. Of course, not being married, it didn't matter much to me—we've all hung about in here, when we were off watch. Vedder grumbles about having to step outdoors to get from the kitchen to his room."

Isabel drew open a cupboard door and saw crockery of a plain indestructible sort ranged in neat rows along the shelves. Another cupboard held tinned food of various kinds and there were bins for flour and potatoes.

"Getting low," he observed. "Always the case, by the time the boat arrives. But tomorrow the wagon will bring up our stores. I wonder where Vedder is?"

There was a coal fire in the stove and a kettle murmured and faintly steamed. On the table stood a teapot, two cups and saucers and a tin of milk with holes punched ready for pouring. Isabel peered into the pot and saw that the invisible cook had put tea in it ready for the hot water.

A worn sofa stood against the farther wall and there were four common wooden chairs of the sort to be found in every fisherman's kitchen. There was a tier of stout shelves, evidently made from ships' planking, holding a great number of worn books whose titles ranged from *Complete Works of Byron* to *Practical Wireless Telegraphy*. She noticed Guerber's *Myths of the Norsemen* and an English translation of the *Heimskringla*; and there were tins of tobacco, boxes of cartridges, playing cards, a pair of binoculars, a bottle of gun oil and other masculine bric-a-brac. A calendar on the back of the door advertised the wares of a marine cordage firm in Dartmouth. Above the kitchen table hung a snapshot of Carney mounted on one of the small island ponies. The frame was curiously contrived of wood cut out in the shape of a starfish, and covered with a glued surface of sand and small shells from the beach. A rusty single barreled shotgun, whose stock had been split and bound with copper wire, stood in one corner, and a double-barreled gun of more modern type gleamed with oil in another. The long bony bill of a swordfish, fitted whimsically with a carved wooden hilt and guard, hung over the stove like a monstrous cutlass.

Above the couch hung a map in a wooden frame. She walked over and looked at it. There lay the island like a slim bean pod in the sea, surrounded by the names of ships neatly printed with a pen, and dates going all the way back to 1804.

"Those are all the known wrecks," Matthew said diffidently. "The life-saving station was established in 1804. Before that the island had been the hangout of all sorts of queer characters, including a gang of wreckers. You'll hear some pretty gruesome legends of those days. The first lifesaving crew included a squad of troops. The equipment was pretty poor in those days and there wasn't much they could do except salvage what they could from the wrecks and gather up the corpses on the beach."

"Where were the dead sailors buried?"

"Usually in the dunes above the spot where they washed ashore. They're everywhere. There are something like three hundred known wrecks and God knows how many others. If you like guessing you can go all the way back to Sir Humphrey Gilbert's *Delight*. You see bones sticking out of the sand quite often."

Isabel glanced out of the kitchen window, at the dunes, at the blue lagoon, at the white flick of surf along the farther side of the bar. She shivered in the warmth of the kitchen. Matthew said quickly, "Of course we don't get many wrecks nowadays. A fishing schooner from time to time, and once in three or four years a steamer off its course in thick weather. Fact is, the day of sail is past. Those ships you see on the map were windjammers mostly, caught on a lee shore and unable to claw off. Steamers can get out of trouble when they see the breakers; and anyhow nowadays when a skipper's in doubt he can get his bearings by radio from the new D.F. stations on the main. What with that, and the improved depth-sounding gear, and of course the island lighthouses and wireless station, Marina's lost its old meaning altogether."

She changed the subject. "This is the living room as well as the kitchen?"

"Yes, and the dining room as well. The chaps will come in here to get their meals."

"It seems rather bare."

"It's all we're supplied. But I'll order some more furniture to come down on the next trip, if you like. And anything else you want. You've only to say the word. Come and see the rest of it."

The bathroom was freshly painted white, and she was relieved to see modern sanitary fixtures, a bath with hot and cold taps, and pipes running off to the kitchen hot-water tank.

"We got these put in during the war when the navy was running the show. Before that things were pretty crude. Here's the bedroom."

Matthew stood aside, and she walked in with an odd flutter in her knees. The nausea had gone, nevertheless she still felt miserable, and the sight of the plain iron bed gave her a longing to shut the door upon Matthew and lie down. A pair of skins on the floor, the soft white coats of young seals killed on the sea ice in the spring, lent the only touch of luxury to the room. There was a plain oak dresser whose mirror had gone dull with damp and time, and in which she could see herself like a ghost and the figure of Matthew looming dimly in the doorway. The window had a blind but no curtains. There was a single chair. And here again were the varnished fir wainscot and the drab paint on the upper walls. The revelation of a bathroom had raised her spirits a little but now her heart sank. It was all so bleak, and the smell of new paint somehow made it worse, like the antiseptic in a sickroom that abolishes germs but at the same time removes all trace of humanity.

"Well?" he asked eagerly.

She did not answer for several awkward moments. Then, in a cold voice, "I wish I'd known, and had a bit more time to shop. I bought some sheets, an eiderdown, one or two other things; but I could have got curtains, a few pictures for the walls, some chintz to cover the furniture—that kind of thing."

"Of course you can order anything you want by the next boat."

"Yes."

The *Lord Elgin* would not return for three months, an eternity. She could not keep the flat note from her voice and did not try. She turned away from him abruptly.

"Matthew, I don't quite know how to say this. I feel awfully unwell but it isn't entirely that. I might as well be frank with you. I was in a hysterical state that night I met you so late—the night of the band concert. I was almost out of my mind. Since then, in that awful berth aboard the ship, I've gone through another nightmare and I'm horribly mixed up. You must give me time to get used to all this—and to you. I've known you so very little, after all."

She paused. Matthew said, "Yes?" quietly.

"Matthew, I want to sleep by myself. Not just tonight but until I feel more settled about everything. Do you mind?"

She continued to gaze out of the window, unwilling to meet his eyes, and she was relieved to hear his deep tone murmuring, "Of course not, my dear. I was going to suggest it," He hesitated, and went on, "Do you remember what I said to you that night when we sat on the grass listening to the band? I said I'd ask nothing that you didn't want to give. I still mean that. And you've given me so much."

For a moment she was ravaged with remorse. The view of the lagoon dissolved in tears. She had to fight down a wild impulse to turn and fling herself into his arms and weep, as she had wept that embarrassing morning in the grubby little railway hotel.

"I wish you'd lie down a bit," Matthew said. "I'll hunt up Vedder and get you some tea and toast. You'll feel better for something to eat."

"Perhaps."

She heard his retreating footsteps and the closing of the outer door. The bed invited her. There was no counterpane and the blankets were coarse gray things, but she was gratified to find sheets underneath. They had been lately washed and aired and the pillows had fresh slips. She took off her hat and shoes, her skirt and jacket, and lay down, covering herself with a blanket. She closed her eyes and longed for sleep, but it would not come. The engine exhaust popped steadily and vagrant gusts of the sea breeze eddying along the lee side of the station brought through the open window a mingled smell of burnt gasoline and the sea. At intervals the transmitter spark rang through the thin partitions like a trumpet and she could hear the continual whirr of the machinery. Amid these sounds her mind was filled with dismal reflections and with speculations on the future, in which there was one melancholy comfort: the past few days had been so fantastic that anything to come must seem commonplace.

The outer door opened and she heard Matthew's step in the kitchen. He was alone. There was a faint rattle of chinaware. After a time she sniffed a faint smell of toast. It occurred to her suddenly that she was hungry. When the bedroom door opened she at first saw nothing but the tray in Matthew's hand, the little mound of buttered toast and the steam rising from the cup of tea. When she glanced at his face she sat up at once.

"Something's wrong. What is it?"

His blue eyes were alight with something she had never seen there. It was anger. He was furious. "Vedder's gone," he said. He came to the bed and placed the tray on her lap. She ignored it.

"What do you mean?"

"He's skipped—bunked—the self-important ass! He waited till Skane went down to the landing place and then packed his bag and sneaked off to Main Station by the shore of the lagoon. I suppose he waited there till he knew the coast was clear and then slipped into one of the boats and went off to the ship."

"But he can't do that, can he?"

"He's done it. Cooks are a law to themselves."

"Didn't he say anything, or even leave a note?"

"He told young Sargent a good deal. That's partly why Sargent was so tongue-tied when we came in. He didn't know how to tell us. Seems that as soon as Skane got my message he put the whole crew to work—himself, MacGillivray, Sargent and the cook—sweeping, scrubbing, painting, polishing—raising hell, as Vedder put it. You understand, we've always kept things clean in a routine sort of way. But in a place like this you're apt to pig it a bit. The sand blows in through every crack. You get fed up, sweeping. You wear as few clothes as possible because the less you wear the less you have to wash. You have to do your own washing and you hate it, so you slop through it as quickly as you can. Once the warm weather comes you practically live in an old pair of trousers or bathing drawers, like a lot of savages. It's a fine free life in a way but of course it wouldn't do with a woman about. That was the point, I gather.

"Apart from that Vedder, like all cooks, the kind we get out here at any rate, always acted as if he was doing us a favor just by being here. We had to treat him carefully, praise his cooking, all that. I was boss of the station of course but the kitchen was Vedder's show and he never let us forget it for a minute. He even hinted to me more than once that we should swap bedrooms so he could live 'closer to his work.' Well, when I sent word that you were coming I don't suppose Skane liked it any better than Vedder. Skane's an odd sort and doesn't like women. But he determined to have everything shipshape, and when Vedder objected to painting the kitchen Skane clipped him on the jaw and told him to get busy or by God he'd beat the tar out of him. So Vedder got busy.

"But whenever he had a private word with Sargent he cursed Skane and me and 'the damned woman' and said he wasn't going to put up with any of us, once the ship came. And so he's gone off. I could wireless O'Dell to kick him ashore but that wouldn't do any good. I'm sorry, Isabel. I hadn't meant to tell you all this but I'm angry and talking more than I should. There's nothing to worry about. I'll get one of the lifesaving chaps at Main Station to come up and rustle the grub for us till we can get another cook on the next boat."

"It seems to me Skane wasn't very diplomatic," Isabel said primly. She picked up a piece of toast and munched it with an appetite that an hour ago would have been incredible. She put sugar and tinned milk in the tea, stirred it quickly and lifted the cup to her lips. Delicious!

"Oh, Skane's got a black temper when he's aroused and he's rather quick with it. Not that I blame him in this case. Skane knew I'd want things tidy and there wasn't any time for diplomacy. Is your tea all right? Shall I get you some more toast?"

"The tea's lovely. I'll make myself some more toast by and by. I'm feeling better."

"I'm glad to hear that. Is there anything more I can do? I've got to get back to the landing and help Skane. We're supposed to handle our own supplies on the beach and it's quite a chore for one man."

"I shall be quite all right. You go and do whatever you have to do."

"I'll see about a chap to do the cooking and send him up."

Matthew turned away. When he reached the kitchen door Isabel called after him. "Matthew! Wait a minute." She put the tray aside and sprang off the bed. They met in the bedroom doorway.

"Matthew, please don't bother about a cook. I can do as well as any man you'd pick up at Main Station, I'm sure of that."

"Oh now, look here my dear, as I said before, I don't want you..."

"Oh, don't be silly, Matthew! I must have something to do—I can't sit and twiddle my thumbs all day. Besides, ever since you told me about a cook I've hated the notion of a strange man pottering about the kitchen in my own apartment. He'd have felt embarrassed and so should I. I think Vedder was quite right— about the 'damned woman,' I mean. I'd have said the same in his place."

"What!" He looked at her aghast.

"I'm determined! Aside from anything else it will give me some income of my own. Isn't there an allowance of fifty dollars a month for the cook?"

"Oh yes, but look here..."

"Then I want the allowance. You must notify the office. Don't tell me it's irregular, for I know that on some other stations the wife of the O-in-C does the cooking and collects the money. It's a very sensible arrangement. Please don't say any more against it."

Matthew regarded her steadily for a time and then nodded with the resignation of a long-married man, a gesture so absurd in view of the facts that

Isabel was tempted to laugh. Away he went, and in a few moments she heard the slap of the reins and the faint grind of wheels in sand as he drove off towards the landing place. She moved into the kitchen, poured another cup of tea and made several pieces of toast. The food gave a physical satisfaction that somewhat eased the torture of her mind. Her thoughts remained confused and unhappy, but in her new responsibility there was something clear to think about and she welcomed it.

A notion occurred to her and she searched the cupboards and the kitchen drawers and at last found exactly what her intuition had suggested, a much-thumbed cook book, the secret bible of the departed Vedder. She glanced at the cheap clock on the wall and saw that in another hour young Sargent would expect his dinner. Matthew and Skane would get theirs at Main Station. She examined the small stock of tins in the food locker and the rest was so easy that she was absurdly gratified. At twelve noon, promptly, she went along the plank walk and called to Sargent through the open window that his dinner was ready. And when he told her, shyly, that he could not leave the phones she brought the dinner to him on the very tray that Matthew had carried to the bedroom. With this accomplished she returned to the kitchen and ate a good meal herself. She had not swallowed a morsel, apart from the tea and toast, since that merry dinner on board the *Lord Elgin* just before leaving Halifax, and now that the seasickness had gone she felt starved.

Finally, satisfied, she rummaged in her handbag for a cigarette and lay upon the bed, blowing out smoke slowly towards the ceiling. The racket of the transmitter had subsided for a time, indeed Sargent had stopped the engine itself in order to save gasoline. The sea wind made a whispering sound in the sparse blades of the dune-grass outside her window. She had a strange sense of peace after storm. Now that it was settled that she should have a room of her own it seemed possible to resurrect a little of her old life. She saw the bedroom as another little citadel in which she could cherish her integrity, as she had so long regarded the room at Mrs. Paradee's. There was a mail-order catalogue in the kitchen. On the next boat she would get the things necessary to soften the harsh lines of the walls and furniture, to make the bedroom a sort of nest to which she could retire and be Isabel Jardine as distinct from Mrs. Matthew Carney, the wife of the O-in-C. She ground out the cigarette butt in one of the quahaug shells that served as ash trays in every room of the station, and in another moment fell asleep.

CHAPTER 13

Within a week the station had settled into its new routine like the sand on the dunes after a flurry of wind from an unexpected quarter. As most of the food came in tins, even the butter, Isabel found the art of cooking simple. With the aid of Vedder's book, and after a few unfortunate experiments, she managed to bake tolerable bread and biscuits and to achieve an occasional cake or pie. Only the boxes of dried codfish and salt herrings baffled her. The author of the cook book apparently had been above such lowly fare, and it was Matthew who showed her how to prepare chowder, and salt codfish fried with pork scraps or shredded and mixed with mashed potato and fried in cakes, and the simple dish of boiled salt herring and potatoes that he so strangely loved. He told her once, "I used to say, after I got away to sea, that herring-and-potatoes drove me away from Newfoundland; but it wasn't true, and there's been many a time since when I'd have given a day's pay just for a dish of 'em."

Each evening she made up his bed on the kitchen couch, and in the morning before the operators came in to breakfast she whisked the bedding out of sight. She felt entirely justified in her resolve to sleep alone but she had a dread that the operators would find out. She foresaw Skane smirking over it with young Sargent, uttering quips about the finicky bride and the unbedded groom; and to preserve the guilty secret further she put on, in their presence, a solicitude for Matthew's every want that pleased but rather puzzled him. He accepted her wifely smiles and touches at the meal table with a fond air, and sometimes when she had been especially charming, and after the others had gone, he turned to her with an air of naive expectancy that embarrassed her. But her embarrassment gave way before the cold indignation that had possessed her ever since that fatal night at sea. At his slightest advance the deceptive vivacity fled from her face, her eyes became the cool gray of a clouded sea, and she turned away briskly to some household task or reminded him in a casual voice that the coal-box wanted filling or that the hot water tap leaked or that something else must be done.

Commonly in stations where the chief operator had a wife he chose day watches for himself, as was his right, leaving the others to divide the night between them. But Carney insisted on the old routine they had followed when they were bachelors all. He had always regarded the custom of married O-in-C's as "a bit of swank" and would have none of it. Thus every third day he took the dreary "graveyard watch" from midnight to eight o'clock in the morning, and Isabel had the apartment to herself. After midnight the radio traffic subsided, and by three in the morning the operator of the watch was able to leave the phones and perform his other duty, filling the station water tank with monotonous strokes of a tall hand pump in the engine room.

Sometimes Isabel heard this at night, and she was astonished to learn from Matthew that all their water came from a pipe and filter thrust deep in the sand beneath the station.

"It's rain water, really. The dunes sop up rain like a big sponge and it settles down to sea level and sits on top of the salt-water table. That's why, wherever there's a deep hollow amongst the dunes, you find a fresh-water pond. The water's a bit brackish, of course, but you get used to it. Soap won't lather properly in it so we keep a rain-water butt under the eave-spout for washing our clothes."

"The water you pump—it must come very slowly, through the sand like that. How long does it take to fill the tank each night?"

"Depends on what's been used during the day. An hour or two, usually."

"Why don't they let you have a motor pump of some kind?"

Matthew grinned. "That's what Skane says, especially after a long session at the pump on a hot night. The engine heats the place like a Turkish bath, even in winter. It's quite hard work. In summer we strip to the skin."

"You should have told me before. I use so much water. I've been running a bath full every night."

"It doesn't matter."'

She frowned. "It must matter to the one who does the pumping."

"My dear, don't give it a thought."

But she did. Thenceforth she was more careful with the taps, and when she bathed it was on Matthew's night at the pump, lest the others find her passion for cleanliness a nuisance. The comparative calm of the graveyard watch, filling most of the night, was for Isabel a blessed chance to sleep. In spite of Matthew's assurance she could not get used to the great electric spark. The steady chugging of the engine was not so bad, indeed after a time it had a soporific effect and often she was able to enjoy an afternoon nap. The uproar of the transmitter was another thing, especially at night. Frequently she was startled out of a deep sleep by the sudden crash of the spark. She sat up in the bed quivering at each terrific ripple of dots and dashes as if under the strokes of a whip.

Worst were the brief intervals of silence, and the waiting, knowing that in a few moments, in two minutes, or an eternity of ten, the man listening at the phones would slip a hand to the key and release once more that scream-ing giant in the engine room. Always she found it impossible to get back to sleep, even when she heard the final blasting *dit-dit-dit da-dit-da,* the signal SK which meant the end of each transmission and which she soon came to recognize. With jangled nerves she sat on the edge of the bed, smoking ciga-rette after cigarette; or she lit the oil lamp and tried to read one of Matthew's old books. Far on towards morning she fell back as if drugged, and awakened to find the lamp still burning in daylight, or gone out and giving off a stink of burnt wick.

One night after such an awakening, and feeling an intolerable restlessness, she thrust her bare feet into slippers, threw a coat over her shoulders and stole along the boardwalk. The dunes were shrouded in a thick fog and the lamps of the watch room put forth bright fingers, one stabbing the gloom towards the north beach, where she could hear the steady booming of the surf, and the other picking out the white butt of the mast. At the north window she paused. Matthew sat in profile with the phones over his lank hair, staring past the receiving apparatus towards the mast with the curious intent gaze of a wireless operator at work. He wore no jacket, his shirt was open at the throat and his sleeves were rolled as if he had just been wrestling with the engine or the water pump.

In the mellow glow of the kerosene lamps at each end of the long table his bearded face was stern and alert, his strong figure sat erect with a pencil in the fingers, an image of watchfulness, of faith and duty. For the first time, curiously, she saw the romance of his profession. She was aware that a shore station watched over and controlled the sea radio traffic within its range, in the case of Marina an area of thousands of square miles; and she saw him now, the lone man in this remote outpost of the continent, listening, considering, weighing the voice of some ship far out in the enormous Atlantic. His right hand dropped the pencil and went to the key. Across the hall the whirling spark disc uttered a succession of maniacal screams. She pictured the engine room windows lit with a blinding blue flash at each outcry, and the operator on the distant ship, a young man in blue and brass and twisted gold braid, listening in his turn for the far high bugle note that was for him not merely the voice of Marina but that of Canada itself.

She thought of going in, of chatting with Matthew for a time, until she felt more restful and could sleep; but on second thought she turned away. She had no business there, especially attired like this. The boardwalk on this side passed the bedroom windows of Skane and Sargent, both open and both set so low that the men often stepped out upon the walk when coming to meals. What if one of them were wakeful and saw her there? What on earth would he think? She fled back to her bed feeling chilled but strangely elated, as if she had discovered a new freedom that still remained to be explored.

After this, in the warm September nights when she wakened and was restless, she stole out to enjoy the dark. It was exciting. Matthew had described the islanders as a superstitious people, and he related with gusto their tales of drowned women, naked or clad in a wet shift, walking about the dunes with hair hanging long and dank about their shoulders; of sailors in queer costumes visiting each other's graves; of a rider on a great white horse, quite unlike the island ponies, who roamed the island singing songs in French. Isabel had no fear of the dark herself and she found something comic in picturing what would happen if one of those credulous men, returning late from a visit to Number Two, say, and letting his pony seek its own way in the dark, should chance to see her pale form gliding about the wireless station.

If Matthew was at the key, that shatterer of sleep, she went along the north side of the station, past the cook's vacant room, past the operators' bathroom and the engine room, and spied upon him with the mischievous feeling of a child peering over the banisters after being sent to bed. There was an odd fascination in watching him at work, so utterly unconscious of her presence. With the final crashing "SK" he put off the phones and walked across the hall to shut off the engine. She heard it wheezing to a stop amid the faint slapping of the generator belt, and then he was back again, putting on the phones, marking something on the long yellow log sheet with his enormous childish scrawl. He turned once more to his book or his game of solitaire, placing the cards carefully with his big fingers, or shuffling them anew with the immense deliberation of a man who has a long dull night to kill.

He never seemed inclined to read in their apartment, preferring to sit and watch her at the household tasks, to talk with her when she was in a mood for talk, and when she was not to pull on his sea boots and disappear over the dunes towards the north beach for a walk, or down to the lagoon for a swim. The pleasure of reading he reserved for the lonely watches of the night, and then always the book appeared to be something immensely technical, with intricate diagrams, for it required the aid of an old-fashioned magnifying glass clutched in his right fist. He turned the pages slowly, taking up the glass once more with the quaint air of a bearded scientist searching for diminutive molds amongst the leaves.

On wakeful nights when Matthew was not on watch but lay sleeping on his couch, breathing with the sighs of some huge and gentle animal, she stole past him and went down to the shore of the lagoon. Fog was rare in these early autumn nights. Often there were fine displays of the northern lights, marching along the horizon like the shouldered spears of an army, or waving like a gigantic luminous flag in a mysterious breeze. Usually the sky was afire with stars, as she had never seen stars before except in small glimpses through the orchard trees as a child on the farm. Between the rooftops of the city they had always been dimmed by smoke and the upflung glare of the streets.

Here the sky had no limit but the round edge of the sea, it was enormous, and she found a joy in being alone beneath it with the cool hands of the night caressing her skin. Matthew kept a dory at the lagoon shore. She sat on one of the thwarts, putting back her hands to grasp the gunwales, and tilting her face to that intricate display. A few of the groups she knew from her school-teaching days: the Milky Way, of course, and Castor and Pollux, the Pleiades, the Square of Pegasus, and the Big Dipper with its pointers toward the Polar Star. The rest were nameless, a sackful of diamonds spilled over the roof of the world as once she had seen gems strewn with an artful careless-ness upon black velvet in a jeweler's window.

On windless nights the lagoon like a sheet of black glass reflected the glit-ter of all this wealth, so that there were two skies, one overhead and one at her feet, divided by the thin black line of the south bar. At such times the prolonged stargazing gave her a dizzy sensation of suspension between two worlds, to neither of which she belonged. And how true! she thought. The regret for the old life which had come to her so sharply in those seasick hours aboard the *Lord Elgin* had dimmed since in the remembered shadow of Mrs. Paradee. The new life had a certain novelty but she knew it could not last. Soon the weather must turn cold and there would follow months of imprisonment in the narrow confines of the station with the three men. She writhed when she thought of that. And always a melancholy voice emerged from its recess in her mind and asked, What is the end to be? She did not know, and thrust it back. When she asked herself, What do I want? there was no answer.

After six weeks all sense of novelty was gone, and there was nothing to take its place. Matthew's efforts to amuse her, his invitations to ride on pony-back, to sail down the lagoon in the dory for a bathe, to picnic beside one of the small ponds in the dunes east of the radio shack, or to pick a winter's supply of cranberries in the hollows there, she turned away with excuses or merely a shrug. She was prepared to be bored and at times it seemed that she was determined to be bored, like those discontented ladies in Russian novels whom she had once so heartily despised. The operators were no longer strangers. Even her dislike for Skane had lost its pungency. She heard without interest their laconic conversations at the meal table or in the instrument room where, when Matthew had the evening watch from six to twelve, she sat knitting or pretending to read.

In the apartment, in reply to her listless questions, Matthew had told her the story of their lives, his own with the rest; and it seemed to her, watching them, listening to their talk, that all they had in common with each other or with her was a mutual imprisonment.

Skane's Christian name was Gregory and he came from a small seaport in Cape Breton where his father, a Methodist parson widowed in Skane's child-hood, now lived in retirement. Skane had got into a scrape at college and gone off to sea as a wireless operator. The roving life suited him. He liked the sea and he had liked the sprees ashore. He could drink his shipmates under the bar and walk away whistling. He had that lean vitality which defies the aftereffects of alcohol and which is irresistible to women. There had been a good many women, it appeared. ("Does he brag about them?" Isabel had asked contemptuously, and Matthew had replied, "Never. I've heard it from chaps who'd sailed with him.")

Skane had served through the war in the merchant marine, and had been torpedoed twice. The second time was a bad one, adrift in a boat for many days, and no one left alive but himself and a messroom boy. After that he was transferred to shore service, in fact he had applied for a post at Marina; and now at thirty-four he was beginning to be an old Marina hand. A good man, a little too short-spoken to be popular with the island folk, but a reliable operator, and satisfied to stay, resigned to the life at any rate, not like the young chaps—not like Sargent, say.

And Sargent? Sargent had no story. Just a kid, a nice kid from Halifax. He was only eighteen and he'd been to sea for three years, enough to get a bit of experience; and then, because he was smart at the phones and could do thirty words a minute on that stiff old-fashioned key, and Hurd was short of men and Marina needed a relief operator, Jim Sargent had been plucked from a collier in dry dock and sent out here. Hated it, of course. Anxious to get away to sea. Only natural. Counting the days and weeks to the time when he could go, like all the young chaps—like MacGillivray, remember?

She remembered, and Matthew's repeated "only natural" irritated her. I'm young too, she thought rebelliously. It was all very well for Matthew and Skane. Skane was only a few years older than herself but then he was not "natural," it seemed. She watched him as they talked of the autumn duck-shooting, now before them. The first flocks had arrived from the north and soon the ponds and the shallow coves of the lagoon would be black with birds. There were decoys in the store-shed, all carved out of pine ship-timber found along the beach, and during the summer Skane and Sargent had repainted them. A fresh supply of ammunition had come on the boat. Sargent looked forward to the hunting with enthusiasm. Skane on the other hand talked of it quietly, with a calm precision, as if duck-hunting were something to be done, and done properly, as he might have talked of rigging new aerial wires or repacking the engine's oil pump.

Carney, presiding over the discussion, leaned back in the chair with the phones on his head, one earpiece slipped off to take in the talk. He threw in a remark from time to time, sucking slowly on his pipe and blowing out thin streams of smoke through his bearded lips. He had been a keen gunner all his days on Marina but Isabel learned that lately he had lost much of his interest. It was, he chaffed, a good way to kill time but it was rough on the ducks. Isabel was appalled to learn that the men of Marina slew ducks by thousands every fall and winter, of which only a few score came to the table.

"You get fed up with eating wild fowl after a time," Matthew explained. "At first it's a relief from canned stuff and you eat a lot. But after that you'll take tinned meat or codfish chowder any time. By the end of November you're leaving most of the shot birds where they drop."

"What a frightful thing!"

She saw Skane's black eyebrows lift. He shot her one of those penetrating dark-blue glances which seemed to her so resolute and so cruel.

"After all, they're as thick as gulls, Mrs. Carney—and you've seen the gulls?"

"Would you shoot gulls for the fun of it?" she returned indignantly.

The three men looked at each other whimsically. "No," Skane said, "but of course the lifesavers do. They've usually got a gun across the saddle when they ride their patrols and they bang away at anything that strikes their fancy." He spoke as if that were "natural."

Young Sargent said, "One or two of 'em knock over a wild pony now and then—for the fun of it."

"You're joking!"

"It's true," Matthew said with a mild resignation "You find quite a few dead ponies among the dunes each year—especially in the spring. The old ones and the sick are bound to die in the winter weather. But now and again you see one with a bullet hole."

Isabel gasped. What sort of place was this, where men indulged such savage whims? And again she had that vision of small stations isolated among the dunes, where men and women lived bored to the edge of insanity in the midst of the inscrutable sea. No wonder they were superstitious! She had heard Matthew's tales with amusement. They seemed to her incredible. But now she could believe the worst. What seemed incredible now was Matthew's firm assertion that the lifesavers, ignorant and superstitious though they were, and cruel in their diversions, could be courageous in manning the lifeboat, hospitable in their homes and barracks, and diligent and watchful in their patrols about the island, even in the most bitter winter weather. It was fantastic.

She thought upon these things when, awakened by the remorseless spark at night, and with rain and flung sand beating on her bedroom window under the thrust of the autumn gales, she lay sleepless in her bed. It was impossible to go forth on one of those nocturnal prowls that relieved such wakefulness with a touch of adventure. She stirred, turning hopelessly from side to side, caught up in the squirrel-cage of her thoughts; and when at last they were exhausted, when she could think no more and still could not sleep, she summoned up memories of Matthew and that night in the hotel.

Those pictures came back strongly and warmly now, and the hideous disillusionment of the night in the ship had lost its sting. She was in a dilemma entirely of her own making. Having drawn an invisible but rigid screen about herself, all mixed up somehow with her pride, she could not bring herself to throw it down or even to withdraw it, bit by bit. As night succeeded night, in the long sleepless hours, lonely, hearing the slash of the storm along the walls and roof, she began to wish fervently that Matthew were more like the other islanders, forceful, even cruel in the satisfaction of his whims and desires. Time and again in the small hours, weary, the prey of longings insistent like hunger that melted away her resolution and all thought of pride, yet knowing that morning would bring pride and resolution back again, she started at every creak of the floor, at each rattle of her bedroom door, hoping to see a new Matthew, aroused and fierce, determined on taking what now she was so ready to give.

She gave herself up to these fancies. She knew the very words she would say; the surprise, the protest, the modest indignation, all whispered because the partitions were so thin; and all the while her shameless flesh accepting the invasion like a town stormed in the dark and thankful for a long siege ended. But he did not come; and as the hours drew on she hated him for his continence as she despised her own flesh for its wants. At first light, with the gray stain on her windowpanes, the yearnings passed in a final whimper, and then came cold reality and all the silly pride back again. Matthew stirred in the kitchen. She heard him splashing at the washbasin. She rose and dressed and got his breakfast with the brisk impersonality of a waitress in a restaurant.

CHAPTER 14

October brought the wild fowl from the north, and frequently the gray skies and wild gales from the southeast. The surf on the beaches, never still, now reached a violence that Isabel found thrilling and terrible. It was weird to sit in the watch room, to hear a great sea break on the invisible north beach, and to see the oil quiver in the glass bowls of the lamps. She had supposed that nothing short of an earthquake could shake a heap of sand. Towards the south from the rain-swept windows she watched the beat of the Atlantic on the bar, that narrow defense of the lagoon. Great waves in ranks like grayclad regiments marched up from the south, moving with a ponderous discipline to the foot of the beach, where they broke their ranks and sprang as if determined to smash this puny barrier once and for all. Each flung into the air a wall of spray stained yellow by the torn sand, and then with a snarl of backwash withdrew to make way for the next. Along the whole length of Marina these assaults filled the air with the boom of a cannonade.

Isabel's mind reeled when she thought how many thousands of tons of water fell in each of these attacks, striking upon the island with the force of the great winds. She wondered how it survived. The winds alone were terrible. When rain was absent and the storm blew from east or west it whirled up clouds of sand and swept them along the island like the storms of a Sahara. It was impossible to venture out when they were at their worst, for a man could scarcely breathe, and the blast of sand in the face was not to be borne.

Then they were all besieged, seeing nothing but blown sand like smoke outside the panes, hearing the vicious sweep of it along the clapboards, and the banshee crying of the aerial wires and stays. Even the wild ponies, those tough and shaggy beasts whose origin nobody knew, inured by generations of exposure to all the elements, withdrew in small herds to the deepest hollows and huddled motionless for hours with their heads together and tails to the storm.

When the winds abated the waves raged on, sometimes for days. Occasionally when a high sea made the beaches impassable they saw a lone patrol, mounted on one of the half-tamed ponies from the stable at Main Station, riding slowly past the radio station, usually with a shotgun or rifle held across the pommel of the saddle. On fine days often there were two or three riders together, and then from the small ponds hidden in the dunes to the eastward came the sound of shots. Sometimes the riders halted at the station, hitched their ponies to the porch posts and stamped into the watch room for a word with Carney and the others. With Isabel they were diffident and uneasy and if she were present they did not stay long. They seemed to her a half wild lot, like the ponies they rode.

Whenever Matthew had the graveyard watch, Skane and Sargent set off with their guns, each carrying half a dozen decoys slung in a bag of old fish-net on his back. They were gone before daylight, following the shore of the lagoon towards the east. Isabel, stirring in her bed, heard them depart, and heard too the whistle of wind and the flick of rain that seemed so satisfactory for duck-hunting. After a time, as the east was lit with a yellow and angry sunrise, their shots came down the wind, and when they returned there were limp and draggled wild fowl among the decoys in the bags. The men stood outside to leeward, plucking the birds and letting the feathers scatter on the wind, and they singed off the finer stuff with a poker heated red-hot in the watch room stove.

Most of the birds were black duck. To Isabel they had a fishy reek and taste that defied the arts of her cook book. She would not eat a morsel. The men devoured the roast duck with gusto at first; but as the days went on, the gusto slackened, as Matthew had foretold. The gunners brought back less and less of their spoil, and at last none at all. But the hunting went on, and hearing the dull crack of guns toward the east Isabel revolted at the waste. She cried once at Matthew, "What a crime! A cruel senseless crime!"

"There's no law against shooting on Marina."

"Then it's a crime in the face of nature and I'm glad you don't go in for it."

"You mustn't give me credit for a virtue I haven't got. I just got tired of it."

"Then why doesn't Skane get tired of it?"

"It's something to do."

She sniffed. "Must a man have something to do?"

"Most men, yes. You'll understand when you've been here a time."

"What about women?"

He was making a pencil note on the log sheet with that abstract air she had come to recognize in the operator on watch, with his body in the room and his mind five hundred miles away.

"Women? Oh, they stick pretty close to the houses, I guess. Most of them have youngsters, of course-gives 'em lots to do."

"And the children—what do they do?"

Matthew knitted his brows. "Nothing much. Amuse themselves. Most of 'em learn to ride a pony as soon as they can walk almost, and they gallop about the dunes and beaches. The boys soon learn to shoot ducks."

"What happens when the children grow up?"

"Well, the girls usually marry island men, or they go off to visit relatives on the main, and marry there. The chief ambition of the boys is to get a job in the lifeboat crew at Main Station. There's usually a vacancy. The pay hasn't been changed since the time of Victoria—thirty-five dollars a month and found—and chaps with ambition push off to Halifax or go to sea. The crews are a mixed lot nowadays. Chaps who come to take jobs in the lifesaving crew on Marina are apt to be a poor lot—fellows from the city attracted by the novelty of the thing, or ne'er-do-wells from the fishing villages on the main who want nothing but a lazy life. As I've said, a wreck is a rare thing nowadays, and except in winter weather a beach patrol's just a pleasant ride."

"I should think they'd be bored to death."

"I daresay they are. The single men sit about the crew house most of the time, yarning and playing cards. In the fall there's gunning, of course. They brew a drink called barley beer—wicked stuff. They've had some famous brawls. What a lot of questions!"

"I've got to have something to do," Isabel said tartly. "What do the others do, the married men at Number Two, Three and Four? There's only one life-boat, you say."

"Their job's to ride the beaches in thick weather. The idea's to make sure that every yard of the shore, on both sides of the island, is looked over once a day—especially in winter. A long time ago, before the beach patrols were set up, a barque was wrecked on the south side of the island, miles from Main Station and the lighthouses. It was snowing and bitter cold, and about a dozen of the crew got ashore. They headed for West Light—they must have seen it through the snow—but they were soaked and played out and they didn't make it. The island people knew nothing of the wreck till daylight, and then they found the bodies scattered here and there along the south bar. One poor devil had actually reached the lifeboat station. They found him frozen stiff almost at the doorstep. Well, after that the other stations were set up; a man and his wife and family every few miles, to provide a thorough patrol and also a refuge for shipwrecked chaps who might land nearby."

"I should have thought," Isabel said gravely, "there'd be a school of some sort for the children."

"I believe they had one, years ago, down at the east end. But it was difficult getting teachers to come to Marina at the pay they offered, and eventually the whole thing fell through. You can't expect things like that on Marina, we're too far from anywhere. School, doctor, church—all that kind of thing we have to get along without."

"What happens when somebody's ill? When a woman has a baby, say?"

He stirred uneasily. "Usually she goes off to the mainland on the first boat before her time is due. Some don't, of course. Mrs. Giswell, at Number Three, has five children, all born right there."

"Who looked after her?"

"Mrs. Nightingale rode down from Number Four, except for the last one."

"And who then?"

"Giswell himself. He turned up at Main Station next day on pony-back, after some medicine. Cheerful as a cricket and proud as Punch."

"Humph!"

Isabel picked up her knitting and withdrew. In the bedroom she lay down and lit a cigarette. She was irritated by Matthew's unconcern. The more she learned of life on Marina the more it seemed a tale of another time, of a people only lately out of the caves. The presence of the wireless station and the occasional smoke of a liner passing hull-down on the transatlantic run made the situation all the more grotesque.

When, therefore, a day or two later Matthew suggested a visit to Main Station, she refused with the indifference of one who already has seen more than she wishes to remember. He looked embarrassed. "I wish you'd go," he urged. "I wasn't supposed to tell you but it's a sort of party in your honor."

"What on earth do you mean?"

"Mrs. McBain rang up on the phone last night and said that today would be an occasion—the end of your second month on Marina—and she'd like me to bring you down. She wants to meet you—you didn't see her the day we landed, she was at Main Station busy cooking meals for all those people at the beach. She's gone to quite a bit of trouble, baking a lot of fancy stuff, and Jim Kahn's bringing his wife in from West Light, and the Lermonts are riding up from Number Two. Oh yes, and some of the lifeboat crew will be dropping in probably, and Skane's coming down in the evening to give us a bit of music. Do say yes."

He looked so anxious that she had not the heart to refuse. After putting out a supper for Skane and Sargent she bathed and changed, choosing one of the more conservative dresses in her new wardrobe, a plain brown frock with half sleeves and a hem that came to within ten inches of the floor. Matthew put on his gray suit and the smart Halifax hat.

"I'll phone Main Station and get them to send up the ponies and buggy."

"I'd rather walk," Isabel said. "It's only a mile, after all, and I'd like the exercise. I'll put on a pair of walking shoes and carry my slippers in a paper bag."

It was a bright October afternoon with a warm breeze from the southwest. The sea had the dark blue tint of autumn and in the offing a long streak of cloud moved slowly towards the east. They walked along the shore of the lagoon at Matthew's suggestion. The sand there was hard and smooth, with occasional small tangles of dried wrack that crackled underfoot. The bank at their right was low and covered with marram grass and the dunes beyond rose with increasing undulations to form at last a crest that hid the north beach from view. The winds had been light for two days and the surf on the shore had a muffled note. On their left lay the glittering surface of the lagoon, and on the farther side Matthew pointed out a few seals sunning themselves on the bar.

The West Light pointed skyward far ahead. Nearer at hand, on top of the north dune, they could see the red watchtower of Main Station. The small beach birds had departed southward for the winter but the herring gulls remained, and the great black-backed gulls which the islanders called "preachers"; and here and there a few belated terns, known on Marina as "steerns," hovered and dived into the lagoon or flitted overhead uttering the thin harsh cry which seemed to Isabel the very voice of this desolation. Nothing else met the eye but the expanses of sea and sky.

"Where are the wild ponies?" Isabel asked.

"They seldom wander west of the wireless station, the island's too narrow at this end. They're a wary lot. East of us where the island's much wider you'll see 'em in small groups, usually about the fresh-water ponds where the grass grows well and they can drink."

He turned off the lagoon shore along a shallow depression in the dunes and in a few more minutes they came upon a wide circular hollow in which half a dozen wooden buildings lay sheltered like a toy village hidden in a bowl.

"Here we are," Matthew said. "That white house with the wind gauge on the roof is McBain's. He's Superintendent of the island establishment—commonly known as the Governor. Over there's the stable. They keep about a dozen ponies to haul the wagons and for beach patrols and so on. Nearest building to our right is the rocket house. Then there's the boathouse. Next is what they call the Sailors' Home—for shipwrecked crews. Hasn't been used for years. Sheltered a good many in its day. Finally there's the crew house, where the lifeboatmen live, all single chaps, or at any rate chaps without wives on Marina, and of course a cook. The sheds behind are just for stores of various kinds, most of 'em empty. In the old days when they depended on sailing ships they used to keep a year's supplies of all kinds tucked away. The steamer changed that, with everything else."

The house of the Governor was a trim place newly painted in white, with the doors and window frames a dark chocolate brown. Mrs. McBain threw open the door as they came up the steps, and Isabel could see heads peering from the stables and the crew house.

"Come right in!" Mrs. McBain cried. She was a small woman in the sixties, with thin snowy hair done in a tight little bun. Behind her spectacles a pair of small blue eyes regarded Isabel with a mixture of pleasure and curiosity. Her smile was broad and it revealed a pair of ill-fitting false teeth, the upper of which had a disconcerting trick of slipping down whenever she opened her mouth.

Isabel found herself in a small parlor furnished like every village parlor on the mainland from Cape Sable to Cape Breton. It was astonishing to find one transplanted so completely to this remote nook in the sea. The softwood floor was painted brown and dotted with hooked rugs in simple flowered patterns made by the lady herself. There was a black horsehair sofa, a pair of high-backed rocking chairs with antimacassars, and two sedate horsehair armchairs, one of which—evidently the Governor's—had a large brass spittoon beside it.

In a corner stood a varnished pine whatnot of three shelves, laden with chinaware dogs, pigs, shepherds and shepherdesses; two or three full-rigged ships in miniature enclosed in small medicine bottles; a rusty flintlock pistol found somewhere among the dunes, sea shells, a pony's hoof polished and mounted on a small block of varnished wood, a walrus tooth, a lobster claw as big as Matthew's right hand, and some relics of McBain's early seafaring days—an ostrich egg, a sextant, bits of white and scarlet coral, and some pieces of Madras brassware.

Upon the walls hung group photographs showing lifeboat crews of other years, mostly in the 1880's and '90's, strapping men with formidable beards, the heroes who had made Marina famous in the days of sailing ships, when wrecks were many, and when the pick of the manhood on the Nova Scotia coast could be had for thirty-five dollars and found. All of these photographs were held in quaint sand-and-shell-decorated frames like the one that she had noticed on Matthew's wall. Making them seemed to be one of the island hobbies. The room was warmed by a tall black stove whose ornate nickel trim was polished like silverware. The stovepipe ran into the wall above what had been a fireplace, long since covered with lath and plaster and now papered in the twining-roses pattern of the rest of the room.

The mantelpiece was still in place, and above it in large gilt frames hung tinted photographs of Mr. and Mrs. McBain, taken in younger days, enlarged to life size, and wearing that vacant and lifeless expression which only the family photographer of the Victorian age could achieve. In the exact center of the room, standing upon a beautiful circular hooked rug, was the inevitable small round table bearing in lonely significance a huge Bible fastened with brass clasps. One note was strange. In place of the customary small harmonium in a corner with a hymnbook open on its music rack there was a piano, an exquisite thing of rosewood, small and well made, with polished brass candle brackets at each side of the music rack; and the rack itself held a worn collection of Chopin's *Études*.

Mrs. McBain saw Isabel's interest. "My daughter's," she explained. "She took lessons as a girl, when we lived in Halifax and Mr. McBain had a brigantine in the West Indies trade. She got to play quite well. But she marrit a Hudson Bay factor and went off to live in the Ar'tic where you can't take anything much bigger than a fiddle. When my husband got the post here as Governor we thought of selling the piano, but it's a lovely little thing and I couldn't bring myself to part with it. So here 'tis. It was an awful job getting the piano into a boat. The captain of the steamer was quite vexed. But we got it ashore safe and sound, and the lifeboat crew carrit it over the dunes from the beach. I wanted it put on a wagon but I guess they had to show the new Governor's wife how strong they were."

"Were you impressed?" Isabel smiled.

"I was too worrit for fear they'd hurt 'emselves, not to mention my piano. Do you play, Mrs. Carney?"

"No, I wish I could. I love music. So did your daughter, I should say." She pointed to the Chopin on the rack.

"Oh, that! That's Greg Skane's. It's queer stuff. He plays well and it sounds quite nice in a way, but we like it better when he plays the kind of thing our Lizzie used to play—'Over the Waves,' and 'Tenting Tonight,' and 'Juanita' and all that. We'll have a rare old singsong by and by."

McBain came in, a thickset man, very bald, with a round face brown and wrinkled like a potato withered a little in dry storage. A gold tooth gleamed in the forefront of his smile and the rest of his teeth were stained a deep yellow by the tobacco he continually chewed. He was dressed in a boiled shirt and his best blue serge, an evident concession to Mrs. McBain; but nothing had persuaded him to put on a collar or a tie. On introduction he put out the hand of a seaman reared in the days of sail, with short thick fingers bent as if ready at any moment to clap on to a rope. He announced, "Pleased to meet you, Ma'am" in a powerful voice, and grinned and struck Carney a blow with his fist.

"She'll do," he declared.

"You take Matt and his wife out and show 'em round," his wife commanded, "whilst I lay the table and get on with my cooking."

CHAPTER 15

Isabel went forth with the two men submissively but without interest. At the stables they walked into a warm gloom where two cows and eight or ten ponies stood in a range of stalls. Above each pony's stall was a painted board bearing its name. The names seemed to be chiefly those of personages famous during the late war.

"We catch a bunch of ponies every fall," McBain explained. "You'll see— we'll be at it in a fortnight or so, every man on the island, even wireless operators, eh Matt?—it's fun alive, I tell you. We always pick out one or two likely ones to break in for ourselves and the rest we ship off to Hal'fax on the fall boat." He jerked a thumb at a row of saddles hanging from pegs. "You must learn to ride, Ma'am. T'aint hard, and you won't get around much till you do. You'll enjoy it. You take Beatty now, or Marshal Fotch, or Lide-Jarge, all good steady chaps, kind as kittens, and used to women on their backs. Miz McBain, she used to ride that Beatty pony clean to East Light with me some times, afore she got rheumatic a few years back; and I often send Lide-Jarge to the West Light for Miz Kahn to come and have a cup of tea."

"You see?" Matthew turned to her and smiled.

"I'll think about it," she answered, but with so much doubt in her tone that McBain gave his head a shake and passed on to the rocket house.

"Not much to see here," he declared, throwing open the door and pointing out and explaining boxes of rockets, coils of rope, breeches-buoys and Lyle gun. Isabel lent him a polite ear until, her eyes getting used to the dim light of the single window, she saw a row of objects on a shelf at her right shoulder. They were skulls, each the color of old ivory and polished like ivory by the sands in which they had long lain. The shadowed eye sockets regarded her with a concentrated stare and the teeth had that chilling suggestion of a grin which is the final mockery of human existence. She sprang back, startled, and uttering a cry that stopped McBain's drone like a pistol shot.

"They can't bite," he said.

"What are those horrible things doing here?"

McBain turned and spat a brown stream through the doorway, "Oh, the boys see one, now and again, riding their patrols, and bring it in for the collection. Bones, too. There's a big dune east of you people that's always been called Frenchmen's Hill. Few years ago some of the boys took shovels and dug on the top of it. Found a man's shank-bone and foot complete, with a wooden shoe on it. Brought it in—it's here somewhere." He peered into a barrel. "Ah!"

Isabel shrank away. The air of the gloomy little shed had a sudden chill.

"I'd rather not see it, Mr. McBain. Really! Shall we go on and look at the other buildings?"

Outside, she drew in a deep breath of the sunny air. She could not help saying in a shocked voice, "Why couldn't they have left those poor things where they were?" McBain answered indifferently, "Oh, just something to do. I suppose it seemed an idea at the time." She frowned and walked on. But she was no longer bored.

The boathouse proved the most interesting part of Main Station. The interest was not in the pair of surfboats nor the big lifeboat perched on its carriage, ready to be dragged by ponies to any part of the beach, but in an array on the walls. McBain explained that the "boys" had always tried to salvage a "nameboard" from each wreck; and here they were. It was a strange collection. Some were whole bow or stern planks bearing the ship's name in crumbled gilt; some had elaborate scrolls at each end, some were plain; some were merely stenciled letters on part of a boat strake. For variation there were several ships' lifebuoys bearing their name and port.

"I guess," McBain said, "you've seen that map in the wireless station with all the names of the wrecks. Of course there's a lot we don't know about. Marina had a bad name in the old times. Some queer yarns—pirates, wreckers, all that. The lagoon had an entrance, those days, and small vessels could shelter inside. People used to come here from the main, fishermen, sealers, chaps after walrus, and find bodies laying about the beach stripped of everything—women with their fingers cut off to get the rings—all that. 'Course a Marina yarn don't shrink with the telling. You don't know how much to believe. Ghosts, I mean to say. I'm not superstitious myself. Nor's Matt, eh? Your husband walks about the beach at night—you know that, I daresay.

Something very few of my boatmen would do, I tell you. Alone, I mean to say, and afoot."

"How do the women feel about it?"

"Well now you take Miz McBain, Janie, she laughs at the tales. But I notice she don't hanker much to go outdoors after dark. I guess they're all about the same way. When you tease 'em about it they bristle up and say they ain't a bit scared. But they are. This here's the house for shipwrecked fellers—what we call the Sailors' Home. Nothing much to see. Cots, blankets, tables, chairs, all that. We keep it clean and ready but it ain't been used for years. We won't go in. But I want you to look in our own crew house and meet the boys. You'll find 'em a bit shy but you must give 'em a chance to say how-do."

It was a large two-story building newly shingled and not yet repainted. The raw shingles made a sharp contrast with the weather-worn rest of it, especially the old-fashioned windows, whose small square panes were misted as if by a faint breath. Matthew explained that the panes had been roughened and robbed of their glaze by the sandblast of God knew how many winters—the house was the oldest on Marina. McBain threw open the door and they passed along a passage and entered a long room furnished with a trestle table and a number of plain wooden benches and chairs.

A dozen men sprang up and regarded her with the unabashed curiosity of the islanders mingled with that air of faint resentment which is best seen on the faces of troops disturbed in their quarters by an officer making rounds. Isabel achieved a nervous smile, feeling absurdly like visiting royalty. McBain called out their names and each man murmured and ducked his head in her direction. She supposed they had been warned of her visit, for each was clean-shaven and had his hair soaked and combed, and each wore his best trousers and a white shirt open at the throat.

Their ages ran from seventeen to perhaps forty and they were lean and sunburned to the tint of old mahogany. At first glance they were much alike, but as her sensitive gaze ran over the faces she seemed to see the mixed qualities that Matthew had remarked. The island-born, at once bold and shy; the college boy taking out a year to earn expenses; the sailor out of a berth and drawn to Marina by curiosity; the coastal village ne'er-do-wells, the loafer from the Halifax waterfront; and one or two whose faces and fortunes were not to be read, who might have been anything from a preacher dismissed for tippling to an unhappy husband fleeing from a shrew. The wild island life had set its stamp upon them all however; they had behind their boredom an air of coiled energy that could be released in a moment by a call to man the lifeboat, a quarrel, a pony chase, or any sort of mischief to be found between the West Light and the East. It was the note of lurking mischief that impressed her. They were like schoolboys bored with the long summer holidays who sit lethargic in the sunshine and hope for something, anything, to happen.

There was something else about them, something that made her skin feel strange as if she stood unclothed in a hot wind off the sands. As she turned to leave it came to her that the crew house was a little monastery, and she had come into their seclusion, a strange young woman, presumably desirable, and had brought them an awareness of the great lack in their lives. The next thought amused her. She had a vision of Miss Benson. It was a situation that Miss Benson would have loved. But her final reflection was a sober one. All these men, even Matthew and Skane and that shy boy Sargent, were castaways really, condemned to a womanless existence in terms of the most deadly monotony; and this sexual and mental starvation gave them their callous attitude towards all other life (and death) about them, and created the eternal need for "something to do." She seemed to hear the echo of Matthew's voice in that phrase she so detested on the lips of McBain. And again she had that uncomfortable notion of herself as the Eve who had robbed Carney of his innocence, the innocence that alone had made this solitude endurable.

These reveries, which held her silent as they walked back across the grassy hollow to McBain's house, were swept away by the sight of Kahn and his wife riding over the rim of the hollow from the west and pulling up with all the flourish of movie cowboys in the loose sand before the "Governor's" door. The West Light keeper was a brown man of middle size with quick sure movements and a mild clean-shaven face. His wife was more remarkable, a rather lean woman, taller than her husband. Her face, long and yellow, the face of a woman who has lived too much in a kitchen but who sometimes goes out in a hot sun, was lit by a pair of fierce green eyes that gave Isabel the impression of a farm cat gone wild and peering at her from the top rail of a pasture fence.

The woman made an extraordinary appearance, dressed as she was in her best prewar garb, even to a pair of worn high button boots, a whaleboned lace collar and a broad hat trimmed with artificial roses. She sat astride like a man, with her heavy black skirt and cumbrous petticoats tucked above her lean knees. As the pony came half leaping, half sliding down the steep sandbank her long figure rose and sank in the saddle with movements inelegant but utterly assured; and the great hat, secured to her tightly coiled hair with a pair of long jet-headed pins, flapped its brim faithfully at every leap. *There,* thought Isabel ironically, *go I in ten more years.*

There were loud greetings, and while they were all shaking hands the Lermonts appeared in a buggy lurching over the rim of the hollow from the direction of the north beach. Inside the McBain's parlor, with hats and coats off and Isabel's walking shoes exchanged for the slippers, they inspected each other carefully. The Lermonts were younger than the Kahns, who appeared to be about forty. Lermont, whose wife addressed him as Charlie, was a tall fellow in the late twenties with a strong-jawed face and large light gray eyes. Mary Lermont was twenty-five, and although they had been married since she was nineteen they had no children. She was island-born, she told Isabel, one of the Giswells at Number Three. Her figure was that of a well-filled young woman who in a few more years would be inclined to flabbiness. She laughed loudly at trifles, she appeared to have one of those shallow minds that reflect each passing thought like mirrors; but when she smiled at Charlie there was in her heart-shaped face an expression of tenderness that was touching.

Conversation proved much easier than Isabel had expected. She had only to ask a question about some feature of island life and she could relax and hear an answer at great length, compounded of all the voices in the room, but chiefly of Mrs. Kahn's. The lightkeeper's wife talked in a loud voice approaching a scream, and at every statement she leaned forward and thrust her clasped hands down between her knees, giving Isabel the full blaze of those feral eyes. In spite of her sallow features and bony person she gave an impression of great vitality, and it was clear that she was the ruler of West Light. She told a story of several years before when her husband and Joe, his assistant, fell ill with ptomaine poisoning. She had felt ill herself but she was able to get about, and for six consecutive nights she had clambered up the steps of the lighthouse to rewind the mechanism that revolved the great mirrors around the lamp. The weights ran down every three hours and it took five hundred turns of the crank to bring them up to the top again.

"But," cried Isabel, "you have a phone—why didn't you ask Mr. McBain to send someone to help?"

"What!" screamed Mrs. Kahn. "And have one o' those fellers from the crew house messin' about our light?" She threw herself back in the chair and laughed, slapping her knees and sweeping the room with that restless and furious stare. And everybody smiled and nodded, McBain with the rest, as if the notion of anybody but Martha Kahn climbing those endless winding stairs and cranking the heavy weights were too funny for words.

The talk went on in this effortless way. They were eager to tell Isabel all about Marina, and when they moved to the adjoining dining room the flow of gossip continued over the food. Isabel found a keen relish in both. It was wonderful to eat something that she had not cooked herself. The lifesaving establishment did not enjoy the quality and variety of the rations that came to the wireless station. It was one of the reasons why, apart from Carney, the islanders envied and despised the wireless men, who got such high pay and such fat rations and did their work sitting comfortably indoors. Yet the people at Main Station lived well. The cows provided fresh milk and cream and butter. They kept hens and had fresh eggs. From time to time McBain and some of his men went off in a surfboat and caught a supply of codfish and halibut. The dish of the evening was in fact baked halibut, served with a sauce of thick cream and chopped hard-boiled eggs; and it was garnished with potatoes and turnips and parsnips grown on the island, and not brought withered and tasteless in sacks from the mainland as the wireless station's vegetables were. For dessert there was a shortcake, heaped and drowned in a rich flood of wild strawberries, picked and preserved by Mrs. McBain in the summer past.

It was all delicious; and when the company removed once more to the parlor, and Skane appeared, Isabel sat back in her chair with the comfortable feeling of one who has been well fed and is now prepared to accept the evening's entertainment in a benign spirit of tolerance. Skane wore the soiled duck trousers, the sea boots, the worn radio-officer's jacket with the frayed sleeve braid that she had seen him wearing so often. He was shaved and his hair was combed to a thick gleaming fall at the back of his neck; but she was a little indignant that he had made no effort to dress for the party when even McBain had gone to the trouble of a boiled shirt and a carefully pressed suit of Sunday clothes. She felt that Skane owed it to the prestige of the wireless station to make a better appearance on occasions—and surely this was an occasion?

She was surprised to see him falling into animated conversation with the Kahns and Lermonts. She remembered Matthew saying that the island people disliked him, considering him "uppity." On this point she was agreed, for she could not dismiss the feeling that Skane considered himself Carney's mental superior and resented the presence of Carney's wife. And now suddenly he was another creature, entering into the cross-talk with easy energy, sending the ebullient Mrs. Kahn into screams of mirth with some quip about sidesaddles, rallying McBain about the quirks of the island telephone system, telling a good duck-hunting joke on himself. He spoke in the crisp educated voice that set him apart from everyone else on Marina, but in telling an anecdote he slipped easily into the pungent island idiom and used it with effect. Isabel suspected a subtle mockery in this, and felt uncomfortable, glancing about the room to see how the others were taking it; but they seemed to enjoy it, and when she looked again at Skane and met his sea-blue gaze she saw only a man genuinely happy and eager to share his warmth.

This mood was still more apparent when Mrs. McBain demanded a singsong. He went at once to the beautiful little piano and struck up "Old Macdonald Had a Farm." It was now getting dark and McBain lit the kerosene hanging lamp and the candles in the brass brackets of the piano. The company clustered about the pianist and sang with gusto. Skane had a rather good tenor, McBain and Kahn and Lermont sang loudly if somewhat off key, Mrs. Kahn screamed happily, young Mrs. Lermont disclosed a strong sweet voice. Isabel ventured her own light clear tone a little timidly at first; and then encouraged by the general uproar she sang with an assurance that she had not known since her school-teaching days, when she led the morning hymn. And now she heard that sound made famous by the operators' tales all over the coast, Carney's rich baritone ringing above the others and through the room. It was the first time he had sung in her presence.

Skane went on to "Juanita," with young Mrs. Lermont singing the verses and everyone coming in on the chorus, and then to "Old Black Joe," and "In the Evening by the Moonlight." For variation he played a few chanties, and Isabel was amused at the vigor of McBain and Matthew, making appropriate motions with their hands and roaring out the words as if the parlor floor had become a deck and there really were sails to haul.

After an hour they were all hoarse and there was a movement back to the chairs. Skane remained at the piano, smoking a cigarette and turning the worn leaves of Chopin. He put out the cigarette carefully and began to play one of the *études*. Mrs. McBain leaned across to Isabel, whispering, "This is what he really comes for. The rest was just to please us."

"I think it's nice, don't you?"

"Well, yes, in a way; it's lively after a fashion but underneath it's sad-like and makes you want to cry. That's my notion anyhow." Isabel smiled and nodded. It was not a bad description of Chopin.

The Kahns and Lermonts regarded the man at the piano with the faintly bored faces of those for whom the best part of the evening had gone by, and soon the men were looking at their watches. Kahn muttered something about "seeing to the light," as if the faithful Joe were not there to climb the stairs and turn the crank; as if indeed the light were not already sweeping the darkness over the west bar and Joe sitting in the old chair by the kitchen window, smoking stolidly and glancing upward every five minutes or so to see that all was well.

At ten o'clock the Kahns and Lermonts left, shaking hands solemnly all round and calling loud good nights from the doorstep. A gust of cold air blew into the house. Matthew looked at Isabel with the uplifted brows of a husband who expects the wifely signal to go home; but she was sitting relaxed in one of the armchairs and her eyes were closed. Skane was not an accomplished pianist but he played well, as Mrs. McBain had observed. His lean sinewy fingers sprang over the keys and his gaunt jaw in the twin lights of the piano candles was serious and taut. Throughout the uproar of the others' departure he had played on, and he played now in the new silence as if he were the only person in the room.

He had none of the mannerisms of the pianist and there was something oddly familiar in his attitude on the stool, the strong figure tense, the head and shoulders drawn forward, the eyes at once dreamy and alert. It occurred to Isabel that it was the characteristic attitude of all radio men, their hands busy before them, their eyes on something miles beyond the panel of the instrument; and again she had that whimsy that they were not as other men but a separate creation, cursed or gifted with a power of throwing their souls into space.

A sudden crash of keys in discord startled them all, and Skane sprang up from the stool. "Good God, what time is it?"

McBain drew a huge silver watch from his waistcoat. "Half past eleven."

"And I've got the graveyard trick!" Skane turned, pulling on his battered sea-officer's cap, and gave Isabel a gesture that was not so much a bow as a quick jerk of his head and shoulders. Then with a "So long!" to Carney and the McBains he was off, slamming the door and running down the steps.

"Does he always go like that?" Isabel asked, amused.

"Pretty much," Mrs. McBain replied. "Wakes up, like, then he's off."

"He seemed almost human tonight. He's usually glum."

Mrs. McBain pushed up her spectacles and rubbed her eyes. She yawned.

"He's a queer sort. Never seems happy but when he's here, in this room with the piano. Comes down quite often, afternoons or evenings when he's off watch, and plays by the hour. I daresay it's something to do."

Isabel twisted her lips. "Well, we must be getting along ourselves."

"I'll bring round the buggy," McBain said rising.

"No, I'd rather walk, wouldn't you, Matthew?"

Matthew hesitated.

"In the dark?" cried Mrs. McBain.

"Oh, but I love the dark, Mrs. McBain, and so does Matthew. It won't take half an hour, the walking's very good by the lagoon—so hard and smooth, like a pavement. Come on, Matthew!"

Outside she took his arm and they walked slowly. The stars were out, with frosty glitter, and a wind blew keen along the shore, ruffling the dark expanse of the lagoon in small whitecaps. To their left the dunes in the cold light had the look of dead mountains on the moon. Matthew seemed absorbed in her presence and the intimacy of her hand on his arm. He looked straight ahead and stumbled frequently over bits of raffle on the sand. After a long silence Isabel asked idly, "Why didn't Skane wait for us? He must have known we'd be leaving right away?"

"He thought we'd be going back with McBain in the buggy. And he had to catch his watch—I venture he's run the whole way. Skane's as hard as nails."

She laughed. "You're all as hard as nails. None of you know what com-fort is."

The wireless station lights appeared. They could hear the engine and in another few moments a harsh fanfare of the spark.

When they reached the door the wind was blowing a full gale, whipping sand in their faces and harping in the wires overhead. It was a relief to step into the warmth of the apartment, where the kitchen fire still glowed. Matthew struck a match and lit the kitchen lamp, and Isabel noted with gratitude that the operators had washed and put away the dishes after their meal. She went straight to the bedroom, lit the lamp and drew the blind. She undressed quickly. In the bathroom she ran the tub deep and let herself into the hot water with the satisfaction of one who has accomplished a far journey; and she returned to her room taking with her beneath the clinging silk of her dressing gown that pleasant aura of clean flesh, of moist warmth, of scent, which always had been to her the very atmosphere of well-being.

She sat before the mirror brushing her hair when Matthew came, in shirt and trousers, and found her door wide open. He gave an apologetic knock on the jamb.

"Isabel, you forgot to put out my bedding. Just let me have it and I'll make up my berth."

She put the brush aside and rose, turning slowly to face him. Her skin was flushed and to Carney in the mild glow of the lamp she was a vision of beauty.

"I didn't forget, Matthew. I've been an idiot but that's over now."

"I'm afraid I don't understand."

Isabel put up a hand to the lamp and turned it low. Her bare feet on the sealskins carried her like a wraith across the room, and without warning she was before him with her hands upon his shoulders.

"You'll never understand, my poor darling, and I can't explain. I'm not sure I know myself—not really, not anything that makes sense, except that I've been what any man but you would call a damned she-fool—and I'm sorry. Do you love me still?"

He made no answer. He stood trembling and she felt in him a yearning that brought tears to her eyes. She put her mouth to his, and at the quick passionate pressure of his arms she wept, drooping in his embrace as if her bones had fled. In an April storm of tears and kisses he carried her to the bed. Outside, the gale blew on. The building shook; it seemed to blench before the stronger gusts, and the keening in the aerials rose to a witches' chorus as if all the ghosts of Marina had found voice about the mast. It was a fit night for passion. Within the walls, in the warm dusk of the bedroom, their own storm rose and fell, renewed itself in sleep, and wakened to new gusts and further calms. In a tranquil moment she murmured, "Are you happy now, Matthew?"

"Yes."

"Am I nice?"

"You're wonderful."

"Better than the first night?"

"Yes."

"Ah! 'Wives improve with much caressing.' Who said that?"

"I don't know."

"Not your precious Byron, anyway. Recite me some Byron—the bit you like best."

Matthew rolled on his back, smiling at the small ring of light on the ceiling.

"It's shopworn, I suppose, but I've always liked 'Solitude' better than anything. I'm a simple chap and the poetry I like says something I can understand. I know the meaning of:

'There is a rapture on the lonely shore,
There is society where none intrudes
By the deep sea, and music in its roar;
I love not man the less, but Nature more.' "

Isabel's face was pressed against his breast, where his deep tones echoed like an inner voice. "That's like you, darling. I'm afraid I don't know Byron very well. 'There was a sound of revelry by night' and one or two things like that. I'm not sure I like your 'man less' and 'Nature more.' What about woman? What about me?"

"Ah, then you don't know how 'Solitude' begins?"

"Oh yes, I do! And how it ends."

"Well, then..."

"I was joking. Go on."

"All right. Smile if you like. Omar Khayyám said it a bit better for me but Byron's good enough:

'Oh that the desert were my dwelling place,
With one fair spirit for my minister.'"

"Lovely! Are you sure you didn't invent that just for me?"

"I wish I had."

"My Byron with a beard!"

Later, wakeful while Matthew slept with one unconscious arm clasped beneath her breasts as if to insure her captivity, she heard the dreary clanking of the water pump. Skane was at the task they all hated, stripped and sweating in the hot reek of the engine room. She thought of her bath guiltily. The main tank was over the operators' quarters and it was one of the petty embarrassments of her life that they could hear the rush of water whenever she tubbed. But the twinge passed. She drifted into sleep with a faint smile on her lips. There was something entertaining in the notion of Skane, the moody anchorite, sweating an extra half hour at the pump for the pleasure of a woman.

CHAPTER 16

November brought the first snow, a few specks wandering down from a sullen sky and then a brisk fall that covered the dunes and the south bar. Below the dark ceiling the sea moved in sluggish gray folds, and when the sun put down a thin ray through a momentary rift in the clouds the wet foreshore had a hard gray shine like steel. The white skin on the dunes gave Marina the illusion of an Arctic landscape, a range of snow hills sunk to their shoulders in the sea, and by contrast made the lagoon a pool of ink; between the black sheet of the lagoon and the heaving gray mass of the ocean itself the south bar made a thin white stroke like a path of virtue through besetting sins. None of this lasted longer than the first hard blow, for then the familiar sand-devils rose and danced above the dune peaks and swept in clouds along the island, burying all that purity within an hour.

Now there was hard frost in the nights, the ponds in the heart of the island had a skim of ice about their margins and often a complete skin that shrank and vanished under the next day's sun. But now the sun itself was in full retreat towards the south. The mast, the telephone poles, the dead brown tufts of marram on the dunes, all threw long and longer shadows, even at high noon. The hollows where the wild ponies sheltered from storm, where in summer the sun fell like a sword, now lay in a perpetual twilight, and a descent from the sunny crest into their deep shade was like a plunge into a tomb.

The southerly slope of the island in the region of the wireless station gave it the full benefit of the meager sunshine. At sunset the last rays shone at sea level and lay flat against the southern edges of the dunes for a few moments like a fiery fan, and gave them a gilded beauty not to be seen in summer. Then the day was gone; the station building, the store shed, the cluster of oil drums lay in shadow; the last of that golden light crept up the mast and vanished with the finesse of a Hindu rope trick, and the night came on like a wave, vast and black, flooding over the dunes from the east.

Most of the wild fowl had moved on, in their great migration towards the south, and the flocks that had settled like living clouds over the ponds and the quiet reaches of the lagoon were seen and heard no more. The gunners from Main Station ceased their visits. Skane and Sargent themselves gave up after one chilly dawn when they returned with a pair of draggled ducks and a tale of tossing a coin to see who should strip and swim out to retrieve them. Skane had lost the toss, it appeared, and the wind had carried the dead birds far out into the lagoon and given him a long swim in that bleak water. Isabel shuddered.

"Suppose you'd got a cramp?" she demanded.

"One doesn't suppose things like that."

"Surely enough people have been drowned on Marina without you and Sargent taking silly chances like that. Don't you agree, Matthew?"

"He can't," Skane said, grinning. "He's done it too often himself. Eh, Matt? Tell your wife about the bet you took, that you'd go for a swim off the north beach last Christmas."

"I don't believe it!" she cried.

"Well, it's true," Matthew said sheepishly. "And it cost Skane half a pound of tobacco."

"But why? And don't say it was just for something to do!"

"How did you guess?" Skane said.

All Marina awaited now the coming of the *Lord Elgin* with the winter stores and mail. "The Boat" was the unfailing topic in every conversation in kitchens, bedrooms, barns, stables, watch rooms and lighthouses, and on the telephone wire that linked their lives. One wife rang up another and they chattered over items in their well-thumbed mail-order catalogues which must be ordered now by wireless if the parcels were to catch the boat. These conversations were public affairs, for like any farm wife on a party line every woman on Marina ran swiftly to take down her receiver, whatever number had been rung. There she listened, throwing in a comment of her own if she felt inclined, or having satisfied her curiosity replacing the receiver on the hook with all the care and skill of a wire tapper in a tale. This diverting custom was not for Isabel, even had she wished, for the wireless station was not connected with the main island line. A bygone "Governor," wishing to preserve the secrecy of his messages to and from the mainland, had arranged that a private line should connect the radio station with his own home. This exclusive arrangement held. Isabel could chat on the phone with Mrs. McBain and no one else. The main island line, skirting her abode on its drunken and sand-blasted poles, seemed to emphasize the apartness of "those wireless fellers" and that still mysterious creature "Carney's woman."

She and Matthew went often to Main Station now. Usually McBain sent a youth with the pony-buggy to take them there, and usually he brought them home; but sometimes at Isabel's insistence they walked, always by the familiar shore of the lagoon. The people east of Number Two were too far to join these petty social affairs, but the Kahns came always, and usually the Lermonts, and often a few of the lifeboat crew slipped into the parlor and sat regarding Isabel with sidelong eyes and listening to the music and the talk.

At Matthew's insistence Isabel had begun to ride, wearing a pair of trousers and seated on Lide-Jarge, a resigned and steady going beast. Carney rode beside her, watching the pony's footing. When Matthew had a watch to keep on a fine afternoon she rode forth with Sargent and sometimes even Skane. Frequently there was a small cavalcade of three, jogging easily along the north beach for a visit to Number Two, crossing the island by a labyrinth of ravines and ponds where the ponies' hoofs crushed ripe red cranberries underfoot, and returning along the shore of the lagoon.

Sargent rode with the cheerful awkwardness of a sailor a-horseback, but Skane and Carney sat their mounts like centaurs, leaving her on the beach from time to time for a wild gallop over the dunes. On these frolics she gazed after them with the tolerant amusement of a schoolma'am for whom the two biggest boys in the class are showing off, but she had to admire the reckless grace with which they rode. Matthew afoot had no grace at all. At times he was downright clumsy, especially at evening before the lamps were lit, when he blundered about the apartment like a man in a dream. In the saddle he was another creature, quick, sure, and somehow pitiless like Skane, and she discovered an odd mixture of disapproval and sensual pleasure in watching their strong figures, and the mastery they exerted by the grip of their knees and the firm thrust of their hard loins.

Before long she had a chance to see the whole adult male population of Marina displaying its horsemanship, for with the approaching date of the fall boat McBain arranged a pony hunt. Isabel arose and dressed before dawn to give Matthew and Skane their breakfast, and saw them ride off at first light with McBain and his troop towards the east, trailing grotesque long shadows over the dunes. They would pick up Lermont at Number Two and ride along the north beach to the farther end of the island, there to be joined by Giswell and his boys from Number Three, Reuben Nightingale from Four, and Judah Shelman, the keeper of East Light.

They would extend a living line across Marina and then sweep towards the west, driving the wild herds before them with whoops and shouts. At first it would be easy, for the island was narrow at its ends; but there would be some lively work towards the center where the expanse of dunes and gullies thickened to a mile. There were perhaps three hundred wild ponies on Marina, living in small herds, each dominated by a stallion of superior strength and fighting capacity and grazing over a section of grassy dunes and reedy ponds from which it rarely strayed.

All of these would be driven together in the chase, a brown melee of flying hoofs and glistening bodies and long tossing manes, doubling back cunningly along hidden ravines whenever a chance offered. Many would thus escape the roundup, especially in the wide part of the island where McBain's twenty riders were nearly a hundred yards apart.

Soon after noon, watching from the window of the instrument room, Isabel and Sargent saw about two hundred wild ponies frothing at the mouth and rushing over the dunes towards the concealed pen in the hollow before Main Station, with its wide funnel of extended posts and wire. Then appeared the line of riders, confident now in the narrow neck between the north beach and the lagoon, urging their blown mounts with sticks and whips of knotted rope. They plied these vigorously, dashing back and forth as the driven herds, finding themselves in the shrinking tip of their sandy home, tried again and again to break back towards the east.

Skane galloped past on a frothing, wild-eyed pony, giving them a smile and a toss of his whip. Towards the lagoon Matthew and three or four others rode shouting at a cluster of ponies stealing back along the shore. Sargent grinned enviously. Isabel was astonished. She had seen in the course of her rides a few wild ponies moving amongst the ponds to the eastward of the wireless station but she would not have believed that such a number could exist in that apparently empty wilderness. Indeed all of it was fantastic; the active bronzed men in trousers and sea boots, in jerseys and ragged mackinaws, in a quaint variety of hats and caps, like beggars on horseback; the deep saddles and closed stirrups that she could only associate with Western movies;

the yells and whoops which she supposed were an imitation of American cowboys, although none of the men had ever been west of Fundy Bay except by sea; and the spectacle of all this violent life in what until today had been a dead expanse of marram grass and sand.

Most incongruous of all was a slim youth in trousers and mackinaw shirt, with long dark hair flittering about his shoulders, who dashed to head off a pair of ponies breaking back past the wireless station. The ponies turned and fled with the rest towards the trap a mile beyond, and the rider reined up violently at the very edge of the boardwalk, giving Sargent a flashing smile before galloping on.

"Who on earth is that?" Isabel demanded.

"That," Sargent said with pleasure in his voice, "is Giswell's daughter from Number Three."

"Not the belle of the island!"

"Yes."

"Is that the girl you go down to Number Three to see sometimes?"

"Yes." He smiled and reddened. The riders dwindled in the distance towards Main Station. "She seems rather wild."

"She rides awfully well," Sargent said, as if that explained everything.

"Does she always look like that?" Isabel asked, with a quizzical look.

"Pretty much. I mean she usually wears trousers and a man's shirt. But she dresses up very nicely sometimes—even powders her nose. Not for me, of course."

"Oh?" It was fun to tease Sargent, he blushed so readily. "I suppose one of the lifeboatmen?"

"No."

"But they go down to Number Three to see her too, don't they? That's what Matthew told me. It must be very exciting, being the belle for so many men at seventeen."

"I guess so. She's nice to all of us in her way—as if we were just a lot of chums."

"Then who does she powder her nose for?"

"You'd never guess." Sargent had the phones on his head, and he left the window now to make his fifteen-minute entry on the log sheet.

"You're making me curious, Sargent. Who?"

"Skane."

"No!"

"It's the truth, Mrs. Carney. Quaint, isn't it?"

"You don't mean Skane makes love to that—that child??"

"Oh no, not a bit of it. He likes the Giswells and goes down there quite often for a meal and a yarn with them. Swears Number Two's a wonderful place because it's tucked away among the big dunes at the east end of the lagoon where you can't see the wireless station, not even the mast. Sara's the oldest of the Giswell kids. Skane's friendly to her but mostly he plays with the younger ones. He's an odd sort, I suppose you know that."

"Matthew told me Skane disliked women. That's true, isn't it?"

"I wouldn't know. He never mentions 'em, not to me anyway."

"He's not good-looking. What does Sara see in him?"

Sargent grinned. "That's what we'd all like to know. He scarcely gives her a word and yet he's the only man on Marina as far as she's concerned. If you'll forgive me, women are funny."

"That's quite true. Don't you think I'm rather funny myself?"

He blushed again. "Not at all."

He was so young and naive that she could not resist pressing the point.

"Didn't it occur to you and Skane that it was rather odd, Matthew getting himself a wife so suddenly?"

"No," he said, unconvincingly.

"Tell me, Sargent—Jim, may I call you Jim?—what did Skane say?"

"Oh, nothing."

"Tell me!"

"Well, he thought it was a nuisance, that's all. I mean, we'd been living in a free and easy fashion, going about the shack practically naked all summer, in and out of the lagoon like seals. Shaving once a month, or something like that. Letting our hair grow to a mop and then amusing ourselves by cutting it in fancy ways, or clipping it all off, jail fashion. You see what I mean. Skane hated to give that up. It suited him. I suppose it suited all of us for that matter. Well, your coming put an end to all that. And then we wondered what sort of person you'd be."

"And what sort did you find me?"

"Very nice."

"And Skane?"

"He doesn't say. He seems to have got over that jumpy feeling he had after Carney radioed to say he was bringing out a wife. He was rather jealous, I think."

"Heavens! Of me?"

"Well, he and Carney had been very chummy. They were always together, riding, swimming, gunning, sailing. Seemed to have everything in common. Of course they were so much older than MacGillivray and I that I suppose we seemed like infants. When Carney's message came, the message about you, Skane was very upset. He drove us like a madman, scrubbing, painting, burning rubbish. I fancy you've heard about that. He couldn't seem to eat or sleep."

"If Skane didn't like it, why didn't he ask for a transfer?" Isabel demanded. "He could have got one easily enough. He's served here two or three years."

Sargent gave her a quick side glance. "I wondered that myself. But of course if Skane had insisted on leaving, MacGillivray would have had to stay—and Mac was crazy to get off the island after his year. It was that, probably, and a feeling on Skane's part that he'd be letting Carney down if he quit. He's awfully loyal to your husband."

"In spite of Matthew's wife?"

"Skane's got used to you now, I think. He's accepted you as part of Carney, and that makes you all right." Sargent smiled engagingly. "You know, it wasn't much of a life here before. Vedder was an awful slop, now that I stop to think of it. You changed all that. The food—everything's better. You seemed a bit strange at first—sort of cold and standoffish. You're different now. So is Carney somehow. I think we're all different. It's really a good thing you came."

"That," exclaimed Isabel, "is the nicest thing I've heard since I landed on Marina! Now let me tell you something, Jim. When I came here with Matthew I didn't know what the place was like, and when I saw the station, how lonely it was, and so noisy and so bare, I didn't see how I could stick it till the next boat came. Then one day everything looked different. Nothing had changed but my own mind of course but suddenly I was happy. I'm still happy. I have a strange feeling of excitement. I suppose it's because this kind of life is so utterly foreign to everything I'd known before. I feel as if I'd stepped through some sort of looking glass."

Sargent grinned again. "Oh, it's not so bad. I'll be glad to leave, mind you, because I want to get back to sea. I joined this service to see the world, and you can't see much from here. But it could be worse, at that. It could be some frozen hole in the far North where there's nothing but ice and snow for nine or ten months a year. And when I think of those jobs on the Labrador I congratulate myself. Here on Marina at least we get mail and fresh grub several times a year. And here you can move about as much as you like."

"And there's always Sara," she teased.

"Unfortunately there's always Skane."

"I suppose." It was odd how the talk came back to Skane. "Well, if that girl's as mad about him as you say, it's a wonder she doesn't find some excuse to see him here. I would, in her place."

"Oh, she used to come here a lot—all the time. After all it's not far, eight miles each way, and you've seen the way she rides. She knew our watch schedule and when Skane was on duty she'd ride up and hitch her pony to the porch post, and walk into the watch room and sit down, as if she owned the place. Visitors aren't supposed to go in there but nobody cares a hoot about that on Marina, least of all Sara. You see, if she'd come when he was off watch it wouldn't be any good, because he'd be in his room asleep or off somewhere with Carney or me. By coming like that she sort of had him cornered—he couldn't just walk away. And you know the way we can keep radio watch and carry on a conversation with someone in the room at the same time, with one earpiece slipped off. She'd sit and talk to him when he wasn't actually receiving or transmitting messages, and he'd answer in a bored sort of way until he got a call in the phones. Sometimes I think he used to pretend a lot of important phone-listening, just to ignore her. I've heard him say to Carney that he ought to tell the girl to stay away, that there'd be some nasty gossip if she kept it up—a flapper of seventeen hanging about a station with four men. But you know Carney. He just grinned and said he and Vedder were safe from the gossip at any rate."

"And you?"

"Oh, I was right on deck whenever she came. I'd sit in the watch room playing gooseberry. When Skane wouldn't talk to her, she'd talk to me. Sometimes she'd be quite nice to me and of course I lapped it up like a hungry pup. That sounds a bit goofy I suppose but I'm not a blooming hermit like Skane. I like girls and it's something to see and talk to a girl on a place like this."

"Of course it is. But what do her parents think of it—this passion of hers?"

He shifted uneasily. "Seems to me they encourage it. I daresay they consider a wireless operator's rather a catch for Sara—'specially a fellow like Skane, who's content to stay here and not apt to go wandering off to sea, like me."

"But she's only half his age!"

"I don't think that matters much to them or to Sara," Sargent murmured. He added, "It often happens after all," and suddenly looked embarrassed. Isabel saw at once what was in his mind. For a moment she was annoyed.

Nevertheless it was interesting to realize that in the eyes of Marina she herself had made a catch. Poor Matthew!

"Why doesn't Sara come here any more?" she asked composedly.

"She does sometimes, but only when you're not here."

"Oh? Why?"

"She doesn't like you."

"But she's never seen me!"

"She saw you on the beach, the day you landed."

Again that memory of the landing place, the staring women in the outlandish clothes, the air of instinctive hostility. Sara must have been one of those busy trousered figures about the boat.

"Skane still goes to Number Three, doesn't he?"

"Oh yes. So do I. Makes a nice break in the routine. You hike there by the shore of the lagoon. Takes a bit over two hours, walking briskly. You stay for supper—Giswell keeps hens, and you get fresh eggs and sometimes roast chicken—and after supper you sit around the table with the whole family playing cutthroat forty-fives, yelling out the trumps and whacking down the cards. The ace of hearts you play with an extra thump, and of course the jack of trumps you give a better one. But when you play the five of trumps—that's the top card in forty-fives—you shove the card up over your head and bring down your fist from there. You've probably played forty-fives—after all it's practically the national game of Nova Scotia—but here on Marina there's a ritual about playing the big trumps. You've got to make the table jump or it's no fun. The kids love it. Well, ten o'clock's the Giswell bedtime, so you shove off for the wireless station. Giswell lets you have their pet pony, a knowing beast called Sam. It's pitch dark as a rule and you can't see your hand before your face, so you head Sam west along the beach or the shore of the lagoon and let him pick the way. When you get here you simply dismount, tie the stirrups over the saddle, give him a lick and yell 'Home, Sam!' and off he goes for Giswell's stable like a homing pigeon."

"I should think he'd stray off with some of the wild ponies along the way."

"Not Sam—not any pony that's been broken in. Once they've had a taste of oats and chopped hay, and good warm shelter in the winter nights, they never want to go back to the dunes. After all they don't have much work to do. It's a soft life for a pony. I'd feel the same, wouldn't you?"

"I wonder," Isabel said. She returned to her kitchen to prepare the belated dinner. Poor Sargent! She felt not the slightest qualm over the way she had pumped that artless youth, and she had enjoyed his talk and especially that bashful vote of confidence. I must talk to him more, she decided. I've not been curious enough about their comings and goings. That business of Skane and the girl from Number Three for example. It was like Matthew not to have mentioned it. But how strange—and how interesting!

CHAPTER 17

The people who most loudly profess a love of the sea are seldom the ones who live at grips with it. Even romantic young men who go to sea, the Sargents of this world, become in a few years the Skanes who have discovered that all the romance lies ashore, and that every voyage is a travail to be endured between one port and the next. The people of the North Atlantic coasts and islands, where the winds are strong and the waters cold, have no illusions about the sea. It is their enemy. Their lives are fixed in its grasp, they must battle for an existence, each day's survival is a little victory; but like all wars their struggle is in great part a monotony, an eternal waiting for tides to rise, for storm to subside.

So it was with the inhabitants of Marina, entrenched in their barren ravines like a beleaguered garrison, and climbing the ramparts daily now to watch for a sign of relief. At last it came, for even the North Atlantic must grow weary now and then, and pause to catch its breath for the next assault. Matthew sent the message himself, and smiled at a vision of O'Dell grumbling over the familiar SEA GOING DOWN BAROMETER THIRTY WIND LIGHT NW EXPECT GOOD LANDING CONDITIONS MORNING. Anything could happen at this time of year—even the barometer could lie, or change its mind in a moment.

But the weather held. When Isabel walked with Matthew and Sargent to the landing place in the first streaks of sunrise there was barely enough surf to make a splash on the beach. "You could land in a canoe," Carney said. The *Lord Elgin* appeared far out, rounding the tip of the west bar, coming in at half speed and anchoring as usual at a safe mile from the beach. A bleak air out of the northwest searched the beach like a draft in some icy tunnel, and Isabel shivered in spite of her trousers and jerseys and the hooded lammy coat that Carney had found in an empty ship's boat washed up on the south bar during the war.

She admired the fortitude of the island women, dressed in their quaint Edwardian fashions, determinedly feminine and decorous, even to those preposterous hats. She moved among them, shaking hands, murmuring greetings, while Sargent and Matthew hustled with the other men about the boats. Mrs. Kahn was there, shouting right and left in her penetrating voice, and Lermont's wife and the others, less familiar and more constrained in their talk with "Carney's woman." Only Mrs. Giswell was missing; she was sick with a cold and had not been able to face the long drive on the open beach.

Captain O'Dell came ashore in the second boat, muffled in a bridge coat, wearing a black fur cap and mittens, and looking more than ever like an animated corpse. He greeted the men and whacked Carney on the back, and stood for a long time in sober conversation with McBain. Then he passed up the beach to the women, shaking hands with each one and calling them by name very gravely and courteously. Suddenly Isabel knew why they dressed up for these occasions. To them the Department of Marine and Fisheries was a thing all-powerful and remote, to be worshiped afar, the God from whom all blessings flowed; while Captain O'Dell was the Department's prophet, who came three or four times a year to deliver them from want, to hear their supplications and complaints, and to receive their respect, which to Isabel seemed curiously like worship.

In the home port, when the *Lord Elgin* lay dwarfed by the great liners and idle among the busy tramps, O'Dell was as insignificant as his ship. Her errands about the coast were barely noticed by the newspapers except when there was something dramatic to report. Even the folk whose windows looked upon her jetty merely observed that from time to time she disappeared and then, mysteriously, was back again. To the Department, a complex machine that performed its functions all the way from Cape Sable to the Arctic (and had on its payroll no prophet of whatever sort) O'Dell was just another captain in the lighthouse-supply service who got things done very quietly and efficiently; but here and at the other posts along his beat he was the whole Department and he played the role with dignity. He lent a grave attention to the problems of the island men; he chatted with the youngsters, wearing the smile of a patriarch, patting their heads and pulling bars of chocolate from his bridge coat pockets; he addressed himself pleasantly to the women, giving each the impression that her life and interests were of his deepest concern. It was in this manner that he came to Isabel; but there was a glint of curiosity in his sunken blue eyes.

"Well, Mrs. Carney, how does it go?"

"Very well, Captain," she returned calmly.

"D'you know, when I saw you go over the side last summer I felt sorry for you?"

"I felt sorry for myself—then."

"Um! And here you are, looking happy and extremely well, if I may say so. Marina's done you good, by Jove! You're another woman."

"A bit of tan makes a lot of difference," she laughed; but she felt uneasy under that old shrewd gaze. What was he thinking?

She would have been mortified had she known. To O'Dell, long past the passions of youth and able to regard them now with a quizzical eye, Carney's bride had seemed a rather frigid creature in those brief glimpses on the voyage to Marina. In truth he had felt much more sorry for Carney than for her. It couldn't last, he had told himself; and all the way from Halifax on the present trip he had expected a radio message from Marina saying that Mrs. Carney would be a passenger on the return. It seemed the logical end to that midsummer madness, a setting-in of marital cold weather after the brief August heat.

Now he beheld the young woman still cool and self-possessed but changed in some vital way. She looked—he searched his mind for the word. Awakened? Ripened? Experienced? Something like ripened. Three months of marriage had transfigured the pale spinster as three months of sunshine would transfigure a fruit long in the shade. It was in her eyes that he saw the greatest difference. Something had gone, something doubtful and fearful—the virginity, no doubt—and in its place was the look of a woman who has found rapture in the arms of a man and calmly expects the marvel to go on, for ever and ever.

O'Dell did not think of it in quite those words. He said to himself: she's taken to marriage like a duck to water; fine well-set-up gel, probably first-rate in bed; thinks she's married some kind of god and that makes Marina some kind of heaven. She's wrong, of course, but how lucky for Carney! His glance strayed down the beach to Carney's big figure, active as any of the younger men unloading sacks of coal from the boat. By Jove, she might be right at that! Carney *is* some kind of god. And when he thought of the Carney he had known so long, the hard clean man, innocent of women, the bearded eking of Marina with the body of a warrior and the soul of a boy, it came suddenly to O'Dell that this slim gray-eyed young person before him had been given an experience that a lot of other women would have envied or at any rate admired. In the light of this discovery he gave her another shrewd glance, a nod of congratulation and approval, and then passed on for a word with young Mrs. Lermont. Isabel, with her face unaccountably warm, resumed her watch on Matthew and the boats.

With so calm a sea there was none of the excitement she remembered in her own landing on Marina. The boats came and went without incident, the men moved up and down the strand with sacks and boxes, the stores at the beachhead grew in their separate heaps. The business of watching all this was dull and cold. O'Dell, having made his round, pronounced his last benison and withdrew to the warmth of the ship, leaving his purser, a sharp young man with a dissolute face, shivering in a lammy coat, to check the stores.

The sky was naked except for a scarf of gray cloud drawn along the southern horizon, and the cold November sunshine struck from the sea a sparkling blue—not the soft tint of summer but the hard deep Prussian blue that comes with autumn and can change so quickly to gray, almost to black, under the canopy of winter storms. Conversation amongst the women at the beachhead languished for lack of anything new to say. There was in them a quality of stolid endurance now. The sight of the friendly ship, the arrival of fresh stores, the ritual with Captain O'Dell, the novelty of being together after months of isolation in the various stations, all these phenomena had been observed. Patiently now they waited the climax, the distribution of the mail.

Isabel tramped stiffly over the dunes to the sheltered hollow of Main Station and the warmth of Mrs. McBain's blue-painted kitchen.

"Hello," said that busy woman. "Everything ashore?"

"All but the mail." Isabel opened the lammy coat and spread her numb hands to the glow of the stove.

"And you didn't wait for it? My, that's the best part of boat day, getting your letters and papers and parcels."

"It was awfully cold," Isabel said straitly.

"What you want is a nice hot cup o' tea. Pull up a chair to the stove and put your feet in the oven—all my baking's done."

Isabel obeyed. She had not told Mrs. McBain the whole truth. The final chill that drove her from the beach had been a sudden realization that she had nothing more to wait for. She felt a sharp and unexpected envy of the stoic island women, those amazing frumps who had friends over the horizon to write them letters. But when Matthew and Sargent came at last with the wireless station mail she had a surprise, a letter for herself, and from Miss Benson of all people.

"Just a line to say Hello," it ran, "and hope you're getting on all right. You gave us a fine shock. Hurd was *furious*. I thought it rather a lark. You always were a quiet one but frankly I'd never have guessed that you were up to anything like capturing the famous Carney. Like capturing a polar bear. Some day when you come off for a holiday (or to have a baby, or should I mention that?) you must drop in and tell me all about it. I'm dying to know the story as who wouldn't. Young MacGillivray looked in for a minute, said you looked a bit sick when he saw you on the beach but he guessed you were all right. I suppose you know I've got your job. Frankly I don't think it's worth the few extra dollars a week. Hurd's got over his rage now of course and is always telling me how much better Miss Jardine did this or that. Phew! And what a lot of work. The way he dictates! I don't get so much chance to talk to the ops but there's a cute chap on the *Princess Patricia* who's giving me a wonderful rush so I don't have time to mope. Cheerio."

Isabel smiled as she tucked it back into the envelope. She had never liked Miss Benson and had made no secret of it. It was nice of her to write. And the flattery in "capturing the famous Carney," a tribute from an expert, had a fillip of its own. No doubt Miss Benson had her agile tongue in her cheek when she wrote that, but it was warming, it implied a comradeship and conferred a decoration in a single phrase, and it strengthened in Isabel the confidence in her physical attraction that Carney's adoration had aroused in her, and which a year ago would have been so utterly impossible.

The rest of the mail was easily carried. There were two or three official envelopes for Carney, several letters for Skane, and a thick batch of letters and a parcel for Sargent. On the way back to the wireless station they paused to watch the wild ponies being taken off the ship. This job, Matthew explained, had been left to the end because it was important to get the stores ashore before any change in the weather. Also O'Dell did not like carrying these fractious beasts and he was always glad of an excuse to leave them on the beach.

The herd in the wire enclosure looked the worse for a week's confinement. "They mill about and kick and bite each other," Matthew said. "Especially the stallions, who don't like to find their mares mixed up with the other chaps'. And of course they've had nothing to eat since they were caught."

"Isn't there hay in the barn at Main Station?"

"That's for the stable ponies this winter. Anyhow these wild ones are easier to handle when they've been starved a bit."

She sniffed. They watched the operation from the crest of a dune overlooking the enclosure and the beach. A post was driven deep in the sand outside the gate, and to this was fastened a rope with a running noose at the farther end. Giswell, the pony expert, ducked under the fence and threw the noose over the head of a pony near the gate. At once the astonished beast backed away, drawing the rope tight about its neck as if determined on suicide rather than submit to the indignities awaiting it on the beach. The men watched carefully. The pony had reached the uttermost inch of the rope and stood motionless, with its whole weight thrown back, eyes bulging, mouth gaping for air that would not come. In a minute the beast began to sway on its feet. A young lifeboatman slipped inside nimbly and fastened a trip rope to one of the forefeet.

Now the gate was opened and a pair of men led the pony, staggering, drawn by the merciless halter, through a sandy gully to the beach. There it was thrown by a quick jerk on the trip rope. Swiftly Nightingale and a sailor from the *Lord Elgin* pounced upon it, lashing all four feet together with stout line. Now the frightened beast was permitted to breathe. Gasping, helpless, trembling, inert, it was rolled over upon a large wooden handbarrow, picked up bodily by a group of island men, carried down to the water, and slid into the bottom of a surfboat. Three of these bound captives made a load for the boat. The seamen rowed it out to the edge of the shoals, where the motorboat threw them a line and gave them a tow to the ship. The rest was simple. The *Lord Elgin's* derrick lowered a cargo hook and one by one the ponies were swung aboard by the lashings on their feet.

Isabel, watching, hearing Matthew's calm description of these matters, had to clench her teeth to keep from crying out. At last she could stand it no longer.

"How utterly brutal!" Carney and Sargent looked at each other.

"Ah, how can you be so callous!" she cried. "And why must they be sent away? They're perfectly happy here, aren't they?"

"Yes," Carney said ironically, "but you can't convince the kind souls on the main. It's done because from time to time someone ashore gets a notion that the Marina ponies would be better off on the mainland. And as the ponies can be sold for cash that makes the theory perfect. So the orders come, and away the ponies go, forty or fifty at a time—'rescued,' that's the word, 'rescued from their starvation and exposure on Marina.' It's all very humanitarian and wonderful. Well, you've seen the way we have to catch 'em, keep 'em, starve 'em, choke 'em, so they can be handled in surfboats on an open beach. They'll kick and bite, with what strength they've got left, all the way to Halifax, and if O'Dell runs into heavy weather they'll be shaken up like dice in a cup. At Halifax they'll be sold at auction. You can guess what they'll fetch. Nice people sometimes buy one to pull a pony cart for the children. Most of 'em drift into the hands of streets hawkers, small farmers, darkies from Preston— people like that. You must have seen 'em about the marketplace in Halifax on Saturdays, hitched to ramshackle carts, their hides a mass of sores and the ribs all but sticking through. They're tame by that time. All the fight and half the life's been beaten out of 'em. On one of those days before I met you I wandered up to the market and found a number of Marina ponies looking just like that. By Jingo, it made me sick. Not just sick at the stomach but sick all over. It was one of the things that made me sure the mainland was no place for me."

"And yet," Isabel said sharply, "you helped to chase them, you and Skane. Skane gloried in it, I saw his face. And Matthew, I saw yours."

Carney flushed and turned away, muttering something about "Had to be done...McBain had his orders...more hands less work..."

"Besides," Sargent said, "it's nice to have something to do." Isabel shot him a furious glance but his face was innocent. She rolled her eyes to the sky and stalked away from that hateful scene with the two men silent at her heels.

As they came over the last dune before the wireless station they saw a saddled pony hitched to the porch. In a moment a slim figure in trousers and mackinaw shirt came out quickly and rode away towards the east. Carney and Sargent went in by the porch door, Sargent to relieve Skane at the phones, Carney to deliver Skane's letters. Isabel turned along the boardwalk towards the apartment. As she passed the watch room she glanced in and met the gaze of Skane himself. He was standing at the window, hands in pockets, phones on his head, and he was smiling, whether in reminiscence or at herself she could not tell. She seemed to see a certain mockery on his lips. She jerked her head away and went on quickly to her kitchen, where the fire was dead and all was cold. She kindled a new fire and stood with the lammy-coat still about her, awaiting a touch of warmth from the chilled iron of the stove, when Matthew came.

"That girl," she announced in a hard voice. "You ought to stop it. I wondered why she wasn't at the landing place—so must everybody else."

"Oh no!" he protested. "Everybody on Marina, including Pa and Ma Giswell, knows that Sara comes here to see Skane. She's had a case of puppy love ever since she turned fourteen and it hasn't worn off yet, that's all. Nobody takes it seriously, least of all Skane."

"She's not a puppy now. Skane must know that."

"But I tell you he ..."

"You told me he was quite a Lothario when he went to sea. And now, here in this monotony, do you think for one minute ...Matthew, darling, you mustn't judge all men by yourself. As for the girl, she's a half-wild creature with no more moral sense I venture than the ponies on the dunes. Heaven knows I'm broad-minded but after all a thing like that, going on right under my nose..."

Carney took off his old fleece-lined coat and dropped it on a chair. "Look here, my dear, this doesn't sound like you. I can't forbid the girl to come here. How would she feel? And what would her family think?"

"Her family! From all I hear, Matthew, her family live more or less like animals—and so do half these wonderful people of yours! A tribe of savages in Hannel and dungarees! Imagine that grinning man Giswell playing the midwife when their last baby was born! And all that going on in the same small house with the rest of the children, including the precious Sara! What can you expect?"

"You don't understand," Matthew said doggedly. "They're decent people."

She saw that he was not to be moved. He was one of them after all Carney of Marina! She made an elaborate shrug. The stove began to glow. She threw off the coat and rearranged her hair, disordered by the hood. As the kitchen warmed, the cold knot in her emotions seemed to thaw. She asked casually, "Did the mail order come—the things from Eaton's?"

"Yes, McBain will send them up in the wagon tomorrow."

Isabel walked across the room and sat on the arm of his chair. "I'm sorry I spoke so nastily, Matthew—about the Giswell girl, I mean. I was a bit upset and ready to fly up at anything. The cold I suppose, and that revolting business of the ponies. But there was something else. It didn't occur to me until the last moment, when those other women still waited on the beach so patiently, that there'd be no letters for you and me—not real letters, from people who cared for us. Oh, Matthew, how awfully alone we are!"

She said this in a mournful tone that touched him to the heart, putting her head down on his shoulder and staring at the floor.

"We have each other," he said woodenly.

"Oh yes, of course. Last summer I thought it wonderful, leaving the world behind. Now it frightens me sometimes. The world's so indifferent. It doesn't know we exist, and doesn't care. And suppose something happened to you? What ever should I do?"

"You mustn't frighten yourself with fancies."

"Don't you ever worry about something happening to me?"

"What shall I say, after giving you that advice?" he answered smiling.

CHAPTER 18

With the disappearance of O'Dell's faint smoke towards the west the garrison of Marina settled down for a winter's siege. For two months the wet autumn gales had flogged the island. Now came the gales of winter. They blew from the northerly quarters of the world. The prevailing wind was northwest, blowing down from Hudson Bay and over the snowbound forests and the frozen Gulf, a blast that pierced any amount of cloth to the skin, rattled the most securely fastened doors and windows, and covered the eight-mile length of the lagoon from Main Station to Number Three with a rugged crust of ice.

When the wind shifted east of north it fetched a dank breath over the long sea reach from Iceland and brought down snow, in small pellets that rattled on roofs and panes like shot, in thick white flakes that blew day and night, filling the air, hiding the dunes, plastering the windward side of the bunga-low, the store shed and the mast itself, covering the rough ice of the lagoon with a virgin whiteness that glittered and hurt the eyes when at last the sun broke through. Occasionally there was a mild freak of weather. The wind crept around from north through east until the restless little schooner on the vane above the store-shed pointed her bowsprit almost south. Then came rain, in big drops, in cataracts, flooding down the panes, splashing against the clapboard walls with the sweep and hiss of a head sea along the hull of a ship, gushing from eaves spouts, dissolving the snow crust on the dunes, whisking the white blanket from the dark lagoon ice and leaving in its place another lake, another lagoon laid exactly over the first, with the ice between. Rarely was the air still. Between gales a restless breeze played over the dunes, now from this quarter, now from that, and set up in the telephone poles a hum of invisible bees, and drew from the aerial wires a mournful crooning that seemed to Isabel worse than the banshee screaming of the storms.

Then came times when the great silent cold of the Pole reached down and gripped the island and the sea and all was still as death. Then the blood seemed to shrink in the veins as the red alcohol shrank in the thermometer. By day the sky had an odd gray tint. The sun, which had long lost its heat, now lost its last thin brilliance and crept like a pallid moon across the southern arch of the sky. The sea had a viscid surface that gleamed and moved with the waves like the skin of some enormous reptile slowly shuddering with the cold; and because actually the sea was warmer than that Arctic air it gave off wisps of vapor that merged and formed a solid bank towards the horizon.

The dunes had a sharp creak underfoot as if each descending boot crushed invisible mice. The boardwalk crackled. At night the very roof and walls of the station seemed to whimper, and the clapboard nails shrank and lost their hold, letting go with the sound of pistol shots. The beaches became tipped shelves of brown cement with a glaze of ice at the upper edge. The grass on the dunes, brown and lifeless, stood as harsh as thorns. The frosty ropes of the aerial halyards went stiffly up the mast from cleat to spreader like slender rods of wood. The smoke of the chimney rose straight in the air and vanished into that strange sky like the miraculous beanstalk in the fairy tale. The engine exhaust shot forth rings of vapor that looked metallic and solid in the bitter air.

Within the wireless station there was no comfort except close by the stoves. The stove in the watch room furnished the only heat in the operators' quarters and the man on watch had to keep the door closed for his own comfort and the efficiency of his fingers. Their bedrooms were frigid. Skane and Sargent went to their beds muffled like Arctic explorers. A bottle of ink on Sargent's chest of drawers froze solid a week before Christmas and did not thaw fully until the middle of April. Several times the water pipes froze in spite of the heat from the engine room, and had to be thawed with the hot breath of a blowtorch and a poultice of rags sopped in a bucket of hot water from the engine's cooling-tank. The very sea lost its energy in the cold, moving in low swells that flattened and slid up the beaches almost without sound.

But then came another sort of cannonade, the sharp and tremendous *boom* of the thick ice on the lagoon, ripped by frost pressure in the frigid hours of the night. Fortunately these spells of polar weather seldom lasted long. Sometimes the thermometer rose to a point where life was comfortable within twenty-four hours. Sometimes it took two days and nights, but seldom more than that. Then the invisible Gulf Stream exerted its mysterious influence. Then over the whole expanse of frosty dunes and frozen ponds arose an indescribable sound like a long faint sigh of relief. For the duration of that pinching cold the air had been too frigid even to snow, but now snow began to fall in slow large flakes, a welcome sight, and the islanders greeted it as the lost Israelites in the desert must have greeted a fall of manna.

For a time after the departure of the November boat Isabel had occupied herself in decorating the apartment with her mail order purchases, ordered by radio from Halifax and sent down in the care of O'Dell. Now the windows looked decent for the first time in prim white curtains that veiled (though they could not hide) the empty face of the dunes and the cold glare of the lagoon. Now there was a new armchair, and covers of bright chintz over the old one and the worn kitchen couch. There were pictures on the walls; for Matthew a full-rigged ship sailing on a bright blue tropical sea, and for herself a pair of landscapes full of satisfying trees and flowers and vistas of flowing water. She had condemned the map of the island with its fringe of wrecks as too gruesome and taken it down. She had put the littered bookshelves in order. She had painted the kitchen chairs and table a cheerful red, and covered the worn board floor with the sleek bareness of linoleum. On the bed in the inner chamber the gray service blankets had given way to some colorful Hudson's Bay things and a bright blue eiderdown quilt. There was a large new mirror in the bathroom and a glass shelf for Matthew's toilet things.

All of these had given a glow of satisfaction for a time, but soon the novelty wore away. The kitchen was still the kitchen with its inescapable odors of past cooking, its too-familiar array of pots and pans. Like Matthew and the others she spent her idle hours in the watch room, the heart and soul of the station. There was no pleasure to be had outdoors. She had ordered and received some extra clothing, chief among the items a pair of khaki jodhpurs, riding boots, a red duffel jacket and a tam to match. But after a few rides with Matthew and the others in the nipping winds she put these things aside. In the cold blast along the beach her feet had turned to stone in the fine new riding boots and her knees in the taut jodhpurs seemed to freeze.

The men shared her dislike of riding in winter weather. It was a nuisance walking to the stable at Main Station to get the ponies and then returning them again. They went forth each day for exercise, usually singly, and they walked along the lagoon shore where the dunes gave some shelter from the northerly winds. Even then they did not go far, and they came trotting back, redfaced and blowing and making straight for the watch room stove.

There was an end to those cheerful little musicales at McBain's house, although Skane still walked there alone, stayed for a meal, and returned in the howling dark. Occasionally McBain phoned to Carney and offered to drive up with the buggy and fetch him and Isabel down "for tea and a bit of chat." But when Matthew turned to question Isabel she glanced at the fuming dunes and shrugged, and he returned to the instrument offering apologies in his slow voice and murmuring something about "later on, when the weather's improved a bit." In truth they were prisoners all; from end to end of Marina the people stayed close to their stoves, and only the beach patrols ventured forth. They chatted back and forth by telephone, except when the wire blew down—a common occurrence—and each night they peered forth at the beams of the East and West lighthouses to assure themselves that all was well.

The sound of the spark no longer outraged Isabel. She had grown used to it, as Matthew had foretold. Often it wakened her in the night, but now she could turn and burrow into sleep again. She had learned the code. It was not difficult—much easier than shorthand, she pointed out to Matthew. When the days grew short and the evenings intolerably long she fell into the habit of sitting at the instruments with the man on watch. He would plug in an extra pair of phones for her and explain this point or that in the Babel of dots and dashes that filled her ears.

At first the great passenger liners were beyond her grasp. They shrilled away on high notes like operatic sopranos, and at speeds close to thirty words a minute. The smaller liners and the tramps were more companionable, droning along at twenty or so; and frequently there were trawlers, rolling scuppers-under out there somewhere on the Banks and muttering away to each other at a childish ten or fifteen. The trawlers were Isabel's kindergarten class, and after a time she could follow the drift of tramp steamer conversations, watching her companion's pencil for the letters she missed.

She learned to send as well. She cajoled Matthew into rigging a small key and buzzer at the end of the long instrument table, and there she practiced with a diligence that surprised the men and somewhat surprised herself. The others helped her, Matthew with indulgence, Sargent with the pleased but somewhat lofty air of a young man who sees a woman trying to play a man's game; but it was Skane who took the deepest interest. He would sit listening patiently while she spelled out in wobbly Morse whole pages of some stale and tattered magazine, or a chapter from that bible of their craft, the *Handbook of Wireless Telegraphy.*

"Stop!" he would exclaim. "You're clipping your dashes again!" Or, "You muffed those dots, 'h' has four"..."a bit more space between words" ..."try to get a rhythm into it, as if you were tapping a drum, say." Or he would snap, "Keep your wrist *down*."

"But I can make the dots more sharply when I lift my wrist!"

"Sure! But how long could you keep it up on that big key yonder? You'd have telegrapher's cramp in twenty minutes, and then you'd be falling all over your message and the chap at the other end would tell you to get another operator—the way kids in the city jeer at a broken-down car and yell 'Get a horse!' You want to do it all with your fingers. God gave you a wrist too, or didn't you know? Forget your fingers. They're just for holding on to the knob. You've got to use your wrist and to some extent your forearm if you want a steady style."

Matthew, looking on, would smile and say mildly, "After all, Skane, she isn't planning to go up for a ticket." And she would cry, "But I want to learn, Matthew! Greg, show me how to hold my hand again." And Skane would adjust her fingers and press her wrist down to the proper angle, and murmur, "All right. Take it from there—and don't try for speed. That'll come with practice. Just concentrate on sending stuff that the other fellow can read. It's like handwriting. Keep your mind on writing a good hand and forget everything else. Now!"

The whimsical attitude of Matthew and Sargent nettled her. She determined to confound them. She had taken it up merely to pass the time but soon it became an obsession. She discovered that she had a knack for it. The nervous skill of wrists and fingers that for years had rattled a typewriter at top speed could be adapted to a telegraph key.

One day when Matthew and Sargent had gone for a walk along the beach she sat at the instruments with Skane, copying word for word with him the messages of a freighter bound for Boston. There followed a lull in the phones, one of those dull periods that came in every watch, when all the ships and shore stations fell silent together as people sometimes do in a busy room.

"Greg," she begged, "give me another sending test—now, while the others are out." Obediently he slipped aside one of the phones, and she moved to the practice key. Skane stared at his wrist watch.

"Okay, go ahead."

She tapped out a dozen paragraphs of the *Handbook*, working earnestly, with the tip of her tongue caught between her teeth. "Well?" she asked eagerly, looking up.

"An average of sixteen words a minute, I'd say, and perfectly done, all but the 'c' in 'inductance'—you bungled that. But you've come along. Gosh, you really have!"

She flushed with pleasure. "Don't tell the others."

"Why?"

"I'm still not satisfied. What's top speed?"

"About thirty words, on one of these old-pump handle keys anyhow. That's fast, mind you. A hundred and fifty letters a minute. When you're doing that, you're pounding brass and no fooling. Of course you'll find—don't think I'm being superior—you'll find that fifteen words a minute come fairly easily once you've learned the code. Then with a bit of practice you reach twenty. After that every word you add to your speed comes mighty hard. Mind you, twenty's the minimum for a First Class ticket and most ship ops don't go any faster than that. It's different on busy shore stations and on the big liners, where at times you've got a lot of traffic to clear off."

"How fast does Matthew send? I mean when he's not rushed?"

"Usually twenty or less. Nobody ever rushed Matt. He's got an easygoing style, nothing fancy, a good clear fist that anyone could copy all day."

"What about Sargent?"

"Depends on how he feels. He's a smart kid. Likes to rattle it off at thirty when he's working a liner like MKC—that's *Olympic*—where the ops are topnotch. Usually goes along at twenty-five, though. It's much more comfortable if you've got a lot to send."

"And you?"

"About the same."

"You're modest. Matthew says you and a chap named Merton at Cape Race are the crack operators on this coast."

Skane regarded his bony hands and long fingers with the wisps of black hair on their backs. "I can rip it off at thirty, if that's what you mean. But it's only swank to do that when twenty-five or less will handle the traffic. Matt used to say there ought to be a printed motto in every station working ship traffic—*Twenty's Plenty*. When you're young like Sargent you feel the urge to tear it off as fast as you can, and you get a kick out of it when some poor fumbling Sparks aboard a tramp has to ask for a repeat. Gives you a superior feeling; and you repeat at a painful fifteen or twenty, just to show the chap—and anybody else who may be listening—what a patient wonder you are. It's a game called 'roasting' that every operator knows.

"I remember when the first German liner appeared in these waters after the war. We had a young chap here like Sargent, just out of the navy and full of hot steam and ginger. We had a few messages for the German and our boy had a fine time roasting the ears off the German's junior op. The chap kept asking for repeats, and finally our wonder boy cracked off 'Get another op.' That's the ultimate insult in this business, you understand. Well, the German fetched his chief, who turned out to be an old hand at the game. He copied our messages all right and then announced he had some stuff for retransmission to New York. His apparatus was one of those Telefunken outfits that warble like a canary, and he had something like two hundred messages, nearly all in German.

"He screwed down his key to the least possible working gap and he zipped those messages at our hero in bunches of ten, going a blue streak. Clinnett—the wonder boy—was sweating blood inside five minutes. He couldn't use the station typewriter because the signals weren't loud enough, so it was pencil and pad, with a duplicate to be made for every message, a carbon sheet to be whipped into place for each new message, and the completed messages to be torn off and marked with the time of receipt—and all that with the German sailing straight on at about thirty words a minute. I know, because I was here in the room and so was Matt, and we plugged in to hear the German's side of the game. The air was quiet. You could sense dozens of other chaps, ship and shore, listening in—because everyone knew what was up.

"At the end of the fourth or fifth group Clinnett had to ask for a repeat—a signature here, a word or two there. At the end of the seventh he was asking for whole phrases. You could fairly see the German grinning. And then it came, a curt little service message in perfect English, addressed to the O-in-C, Marina, demanding 'Please use capable operator.' There was dead silence in the phones for a moment, and then you could hear ships up and down the coast piping 'Hi-hi-hi'—the signal for a laugh. And the laugh was on us, on Marina, you see. Matt was furious, with Clinnett as much as the Hun."

"What happened?" Isabel asked.

"Matt took over the watch himself, tapping out 'O.I.C. here' in his slow way and telling the Hun to go on with his messages in groups of ten. By that time everyone on the coast had stopped to listen, for they all knew Carney's fist—and they knew what was coming next. A lot of smart ship ops have been fooled by that fist of Matt's. They think they've got a slow chum at the other end of the line and they screw down their keys and try to roast him. Well, Matt's been in this game so long that the code's his native language—he *thinks* in dots and dashes. And nothing bothers him—interference, static, speed— nothing. He can read the stuff by instinct, and faster than any human hand could send it. Everyone on the coast knew that, but the German didn't and away he went like greased lightning with his next ten messages.

"At the end of them Matt gave him 'R' for the lot, and added 'Send faster.' The German zipped off another group; and again Matt said 'Send faster.' The Hun was good, mind you; he was sending as fast as any man could go. But he couldn't keep up that pace. His wrist was getting tired. When he tried to cram on a bit more speed it was fatal. He began to make mistakes, falling all over himself, going back and repeating. Another group, and Matt cracked off, in that same slow fist, mind you, 'Send much faster. Have other traffic to clear.' There was a pause, and the German came on again, going at a terrific rate. But when he got to the third or fourth message in the group he stumbled badly, went back and repeated, zipped on for a bit, and stumbled again.

"At the end of the group it was rather pitiful—like watching a good penman ruin his fist by trying to write too fast. And of course there was nothing the German could do or say about the speed—he was dealing with a shore station, and a shore station in its own official range is practically the Almighty; its word is law. By the time he got to his twelfth group the Hun was stumbling and fumbling, making a stuttering mess of it; and then Matt put an end to it, tapping out in his calm way, slow and merciless like the cold wrath of God, 'Use recognized code or get someone who can.'

"You should have heard the chorus in the phones—every op in the area snickering out 'Hi-hi-hi.' Even Clinnett laughed, standing there beside Matt with a pair of phones plugged in. And then in the silence before the German's junior op came on again, sending at Matt's own rate, a bit over twenty, no more, Matt got out of the chair and motioned Clinnett towards the pencil and the message pads. 'Take over,' he said. 'And after this don't act the damned fool at my key.' Can't you hear him saying that?"

"Yes," Isabel said, "My key, my station, my island—they're all his, really, aren't they? How that would touch his pride! But it all sounds a bit childish, if you'll forgive me—like a lot of little boys showing off and giggling in a crowded room. I thought this was a serious business."

Skane grinned. "It is, most of the time. That's why we like a bit of fun now and then."

"Something to do!"

He glanced at her curiously. "You don't like that expression, do you?"

"No. But I'm beginning to see the point. That's why I want to be able to do twenty-five on that key."

He chuckled, "Anyone would think you intend to take a watch."

"Well, why not? Suppose one of you got sick, or what's more likely, suppose you fell off a pony one of these days and broke your arm?"

Skane slipped the phone over his free ear, listened a moment, and made an entry in the log. "That's happened before—a chap sick, I mean. Happens on every station from time to time. The other two simply stand watch-and-watch—six hours on, six off—till the fellow's better, or till the boat brings a relief operator. It's a bit tough but after all a man might as well be on watch as twiddling his thumbs about the shack."

"It would be awful to depend on a woman for anything important, wouldn't it?" she said scornfully. And then in a persuasive voice, "Let me put it another way. Look at the life you men lead. Sometimes two of you can get away for a walk or a ride or a duck-shoot together; but usually one man's on watch, one's sleeping, and the other's at a loose end. If he goes out, he goes alone. Don't you see what I mean? Each of you lives in a frightful solitude."

"Not Matt."

"Even Matthew. A man wants companionship of his own kind. I see that plainly now. Have you noticed Matthew lately? He's become awfully dull. He goes out for a walk now and then, but never for long. He used to fairly live outdoors—he's told me that; and I know how he used to love walking the beach at night, especially in storms. He never does that any more. I've offered to walk with him but he knows I hate the wind when it's cold. Don't you see, Greg, if I could take a watch now and then, you three could go off together for hours. You could visit Main Station, West Light, Number Two, Number Three—you could see other faces, hear other voices, and apart from all that you could enjoy each other as you've never been able to do before."

She leaned towards him eagerly and put a hand on his arm. For a time Skane did not reply. His hard blue gaze was directed past the receiving apparatus to the window, to the whirl of sand about the butt of the mast.

"And what about you?"

"Oh, I wouldn't matter."

"I'm afraid you would."

"You mean I'd be the lonely one? Ah, but think how important I'd feel—running the show myself! If you only knew how I long to do something that matters."

"You're Carney's wife. Doesn't that matter?"

"Yes, but that's only one part of my life, and his."

"You get our meals. You're the most important person on the station. You should have heard Vedder."

She drew her hand away sharply. "Oh, you're impossible!"

Skane turned. "I didn't mean to be insulting. I was trying to convey—in poorly chosen words, I'm afraid—how much we appreciate your presence here."

"You thought I was a nuisance when I came," she retorted.

"Yes," he admitted. And then, slowly, "May I ask how you know?"

She laughed. "It was written all over you."

He resumed his stare out of the window and she saw his lips tighten.

"I thought Carney had no business to bring you here. I still think that. Don't ask me to explain. And now I hear MSU calling, offering P."

"What's that mean?"

He grimaced. "*Aquitania* with a lot of mushy sentiments, mostly from ladies of the stage and screen, addressed to all the fools and knaves from London to Los Angeles." He settled the message pads before him, placed a pair of sharp pencils beside them, and threw the transmitting switch. In the engine room the trumpet blared, and amid that brazen music Isabel arose and went back to the apartment.

CHAPTER 19

On the afternoon before Christmas, Giswell drove up in his buggy, with young Sara on the seat beside him. He thundered on the apartment door and walked in. Matthew lay on the couch smoking and watching Isabel prepare a plum pudding. The smiling little man, reddened by the cold, threw on the kitchen table a pair of chickens, plucked and cleaned. They had frozen on the journey from Number Three and they fell like blocks of wood.

"There's your Christmas dinner!"

Isabel turned, throwing out floury hands in a gesture of pleasure, and Matthew arose from the couch murmuring thanks.

"How wonderful!" Isabel cried. "I was afraid I'd have to serve tinned meat. Do take off your things and sit down. How's everything at Number Three?"

Giswell took off his wool cap but remained by the door. "Can't stay—the pony's warm from the drive and I don't want to leave him standing long. Besides, I've got to get back. The wind's come east again and there's a smell of snow—a blizzard if I know the signs. Family's well, thank you kindly."

"Where's Sara?" Carney said.

"Oh, Sara, she went around to talk to Skane."

"But Skane's gone to Main Station for an hour at the piano."

"Oh? Well she'll amuse herself with Sargent then. When a gal puts on skirts to drive eight mile on a winter day t'ain't to talk to folks like you and me." He addressed Isabel. "Funny thing, Ma'am, ever since you come these wireless fellers seem to stay close to home. Ain't seen 'em much since fall."

"Is that a compliment?" she asked dubiously.

"Don't know a better!" Giswell roared. "Makes a difference havin' a woman about a place. Once in a long time Miz Giswell she gits a notion to go off on the boat and visit with her relations over on the main. Means she's gone three-four months and we all git restless as bears, wanderin' about for some-thin' to do. Once she gits back we hardly want to stir outside the door. Now you take Matt and Skane and Sargent, aforetime they was always walkin' or ridin' down to see us at Number Three, or to Number Two or Main Station or West Light; now and again one of 'em would take a notion to ride all the way down east to Number Four, or even East Light. Don't see 'em doin' that no more. That's you, Ma'am, nothin' else. Why don't you git Matt or one o' the others to borrow McBain's buggy and drive you down to see us, once in a while? Looks like that's the only way we'll ever git to see anybody from the wireless station now."

"I shall," she promised, "as soon as the weather improves. I'm afraid I've got lazy since the cold weather came. I've not been outside the door for a month, except to go along the boardwalk to the watch room."

Giswell grinned. "Ah, you'll toughen up, Ma'am, by and by. You'll git so you've got to hear the sound of another woman's voice, and the tellyphone won't do. Women likes society. You come and see us, and we'll git Miz Nightingale over from Number Four, and prob'ly Miz Shelman from East Light, and you can all have a wunnerful jabber together, You git on with that puddin', Ma'am. I'll talk to Matt a bit." Isabel returned to her baking and Matthew and Giswell drifted into a typical island conversation—the weather, the thickness of the lagoon ice, the state of the wild ponies, and duck-hunting yarns going back through the years. At length Giswell departed, carrying with him a gift of Carney's tobacco. He went along the boardwalk and rapped on the watch room window, and in a moment his daughter emerged from the porch and climbed into the buggy beside him.

Matthew and Isabel threw open their door and called farewells. The girl favored Carney with a quick dark smile, but when she turned her gaze to Isabel the smile vanished. She gave Carney's woman a slow look up and down, acknowledged her greeting with a nod, and then Giswell flicked the reins and they drove off.

"I don't think that young lady likes me," Isabel said, shutting the door.

"Just shy, don't you think?"

"She's bold enough with Sargent and Skane."

"Ah well, she knows them better; and they're young men. It makes a difference."

"Apparently,'" she rejoined primly, and went on with her cooking.

By Giswell's favor the Christmas dinner was a famous affair of roast chicken with bread and sage stuffing, cranberry sauce, potatoes, turnip and parsnip. For dessert there was mince pie (the mincemeat out of a tin, one of the luxuries enjoyed by the wireless station) and plum pudding with candy sauce. Practice in cookery had developed in Isabel an instinctive skill which she fortified with a careful reading of Vedder's old book whenever something special was in the making.

Skane was on watch when they sat down to eat. Isabel was touched to find that Matthew had ordered and received by the autumn boat a pair of soft bedroom slippers for her, which he now presented. And Sargent had saved out of his parcel from home a box of chocolates which he produced, painstakingly wrapped in tissue and tied with a ribbon he had got from Mrs. McBain. For her part she had received on the boat some skeins of colored wool, and in leisure hours she had knitted a pair of mittens for each of them, red for Matthew, green for Sargent and blue for Skane.

When they had finished their coffee Sargent withdrew for an afternoon walk to Main Station and Carney went along the boardwalk to relieve Skane. Isabel stepped into the bedroom and repowdered her nose, touched her hair here and there, and smoothed the gray silk frock which she reserved for "best" and had put on for the occasion. She came into the kitchen as Skane appeared. He wore the old shabby uniform but she observed that he had got his hair cut and that he was freshly shaved. He greeted her politely, wishing her a merry Christmas, and in an offhand way passed her a package wrapped in tissue. Within she felt something round and hard. She removed the paper swiftly and took forth a photograph of Skane and Matthew in a wooden frame shaped, painted and furnished with beckets of cord to represent a miniature ship's lifebuoy. It was made to be hung by one of the beckets and on the white circumference Skane had painted in neat black letters MARINA ISLAND RADIO, CHRISTMAS, 1920.

"Actually," he informed her, "the picture was taken two years ago. The female creature in the middle used to stick out of the sand down by Main Station. The figurehead of a French barque named *Clélie* that piled up on the east bar forty or fifty years ago. She's rather a good bit of carving, don't you think?"

"She's rather—opulent," Isabel observed. "And she looks as if she'd just taken a bath in her nightie."

"Well," said Skane, busy with his dinner, "wasn't Clélie the Roman girl who swam the Tiber to get away from the Etruscans?"

"I don't know. I'm afraid I never was much good at Roman history."

He smiled. "Same here. By the way, this chicken is awfully good. The only

THE NYMPH AND THE LAMP

reason I remember the tale is because in my student days I was rather interested in French translation, and I got hold of one or two seventeenth-century novels by Mademoiselle de Scudéry, including *Clélie*. Mam'selle was very decorous and her heroes and heroines were a stuffy lot. She used to skitter very carefully about the edges of their love affairs. In *Clélie* I remember she described the River of Inclination winding its way down from the hills and watering the villages of Billets Doux, Petits Soins, and a lot of other rot. Very good picture of Matt, isn't it?"

"It's awfully good of you, too. I shall treasure this. Did you make the frame yourself?"

"Yes. The idea's not very original but I thought it would make a souvenir for your wall. The wood's from a piece of wreck timber I picked up on the beach."

"I'd like to see Clélie. You must show me her some day when we're down that way."

"I'm afraid she's gone. She toppled over in a storm a few months after that picture was taken, and then we got an unusual succession of nor'east winds and a big dune moved over and buried her. Mam'selle de Scudéry could have written a whole novel about that—the Tempest in the Desert, and the millions of grains of sand hustling in to cover poor Clélie's modesty."

They laughed together. "I'm afraid you're a cynic," Isabel said. "Here's your plum pudding—hard sauce by courtesy of Vedder's cook book. I'll have a cup of coffee with you for company. You haven't opened my present."

Skane unwrapped the mittens and looked up. "Just what I wanted!"

"That's what you're supposed to say, anyway. I made the same for all of you. There's one comfort about knitting mittens, you don't have to worry much about size."

"They're very nicely made," he observed handsomely. He stirred his coffee and offered her a cigarette. Isabel took one, and Skane struck a match on his boot and held it for her. As she leaned forward with the cigarette between her lips their eyes met in the curious intimacy of the rite and there was an odd little silence. Something in the quality of Skane's gaze set a pulse beating in her throat. For a moment she forgot the cigarette. That old silly habit of flushing over trifles, over nothing, suddenly possessed her. She was startled and annoyed. The warm blood spread beneath her skin from throat to temples, and there was nothing she could do about it. She fixed her attention on the cigarette. She drew on the thing with several unsteady puffs and turned away murmuring "Thanks," and staring out of the window with a quite false air of interest as if the sight of her own small washing, a few silken things waving gaily in the cold breeze from the sea, were something she had never seen before.

Skane lit his own cigarette and sat back in his chair, regarding her with that unchanged gaze. She wanted to break this uneasy spell, which had come from nowhere, without reason, and was so ridiculous; but she could not find a thing to say. She thought a little wildly: Why doesn't he say something? Anything! His hand reached out to flick a tip of ash into a saucer, and the hand that was so quick and sure at the key in the watch room seemed a little unsteady, as if it had fallen under the same mysterious spell. The ash fell on the tablecloth.

At last she found something to say. It came to her with a vicious brilliance. "Sara Giswell called to see you yesterday, and you were out."

"So Sargent told me."

"You're not very kind to her, are you?"

"I don't know what you mean."

Isabel felt more confident now. She turned, drawing in a strong whiff of smoke and blowing it out through her nostrils, with her head tipped back, regarding Skane beneath the lowered eyelids.

"You know very well what I mean, Greg. The girl's in love with you."

"Who told you that, Sargent?"

"Never mind. Anyhow I've got eyes. And Giswell was complaining yesterday that you never go down there any more."

"You know what the weather's been like."

"The weather was just as bad in the other winters, wasn't it?"

"I suppose so. But the shack was a place to get away from as much as possible in Vedder's day. You've made life here more comfortable. Anyhow, Number Three had become a habit, and a man's habits change like anything else."

"That's unfortunate for Sara. She can't change hers, apparently."

"My dear Mrs. Carney, surely you know Sara's the belle of Marina? She could have any of McBain's crew, or Sargent, say, just by whistling them up."

"But not you!"

"I'm not susceptible—put it that way."

"So I've heard. But I believe you used to be very susceptible once upon a time. May I ask out of sheer curiosity, what made the change?"

Skane drew hard on his cigarette and opened his mouth, letting the fumes drift forth. "That's too long a story to be interesting."

Isabel felt at ease. She had put him on the defensive. It was absurd that she should have become so flustered over nothing more than a glance and a silence like a schoolgirl tête-à-tête for the first time in her life.

"I wish you'd tell me. You've never said anything about your life. You had a rough time in the war, didn't you?"

"No worse than a good many others."

"Go on, please."

Skane drew on the cigarette again, and again let the smoke curl out of his mouth. It took some time. "Well, I'll tell you," he said at last, deliberately. "I used to take life pretty lightly when I went to sea. I served mostly in tramps, wandering from one port to another all over the show—and it was a show then, for a man in his twenties, before the war spoiled everything. The time at sea was rather dull but there was all the life you wanted ashore. There were so many new things to see and taste and feel—everything from Cuban dances to a Japanese tattoo needle. And of course there were girls here and there. That's what you wanted to know, wasn't it?

"Well, I liked women and they seemed to like me. I don't know why; I was no pretty-boy and it couldn't have been my money. A seagoing Sparks in those days was lucky to get fifty or sixty dollars a month. But I'd like to make this clear: the women were only part of it. The fun was in the world. I got as much pleasure out of swinging my fists in a dockside free-for-all as I ever had from a woman. And I've seen a square-rigger under full sail in the evening light that struck me as more beautiful than any woman that ever walked. Oh, it was all very wonderful, I tell you, till I grew up."

"When was that?" she asked.

"When I was getting on towards thirty. Time, wasn't it? I should have known in '16, when my ship was torpedoed ten days out of Mobile with a load of cotton. But there wasn't much to that. We didn't see the sub. The cotton swelled and stopped the hole to some extent, and we kept the old hooker limping on towards England for another day. Then the cotton swelled enough to burst the hatches off and we took to the boats. The sea wasn't bad. We were picked up inside twenty hours anyhow. When we got to Cardiff we had a wonderful spree to celebrate our luck.

"Then I got posted to another tramp and had another year of it, chugging about the North Atlantic, sometimes in convoy, sometimes not. Things were getting pretty grim at sea by the fall of '17. There was still some fun in the world but you didn't get the same kick out of it. Then, two days out of Wabana, Newfoundland, with a cargo of iron ore, we got it. A submarine slammed two torpedoes into the ship and down she went. With an iron ore cargo you haven't a chance. I picked myself up off the wireless cabin floor and started to send out 'Allo'—the 'I am attacked' signal, expecting the mate or somebody else from the bridge to pop in with the ship's position. I was using the emergency set—the ship's dynamo had gone with the rest of the engine room—and it was one of those old ten-inch coil outfits with an open spark, that hadn't the range of a good clear shout.

"The ship gave a lurch and the cabin door swung open and banged against the bulkhead. I looked out and saw the mate and eight or nine chaps in a boat, floating abreast of the deck. She was down to that in four minutes. The mate yelled to me and I walked out, just as I was, in trousers, shirt and jacket, and stepped over the rail into the boat. We just had time to pull clear when down she went. The skipper and the others went with her—nobody'd seen them after the torpedoes exploded.

"We weren't in convoy. We'd been making a lone run of it, keeping radio silence. Those few squawks on the battery set hadn't got anywhere, and even if they had, there was no position. So you get the picture—adrift in the North Atlantic, in November, which is a cold time in these latitudes, and nobody looking for us. There was no hope of making shore. The nearest was Newfoundland, nearly five hundred miles to windward. For two days and nights the wind blew a gale out of the west and it was all we could do to keep before it, with a bit of canvas hoisted forward. There was a big sea running and it pitched the boat up and down. With the shock of the explosions, and then the wild motion of the boat, several of the chaps got sick. The mate had his bridge coat on, and two of the sailors had lammy coats. The rest were like me, in their jackets. The wind went right through to the skin. We were all covered with red ore dust and so was every inch of the boat. We were a weird-looking lot.

"The mate was an old fellow and we made him keep the bridge coat. The lammies we passed about, so that every man could have a bit of time protected from the wind. If you didn't get seasick you could stick it, but if you retched you were done for. The cold went right through you then. Three men died like that, the first night. We shared out their clothes and put the bodies over the side. We took turns at the oars, not that we'd any hope of getting anywhere but just to keep our blood stirring. The sky was open-and-shut, mostly cloud but a flash of sunshine now and then. There was no heat in the sun but you got some cheer out of seeing it. When darkness came you lost that, and then the cold seemed to reach in and grab hold of your heart. On the second night two more men died, and we took off their clothes and rolled them over the gunwale.

"That was the way it went. There was a small tin of water and some emergency food—ship's biscuit and some sort of cocoa stuff pressed into a hard cake. It didn't do us much good. When you're being flung about in a small boat like that you can't sleep, you can't even relax, and you get so weary that you lose all desire to eat. At the end of a week there were three of us left. We had clothing to spare by that time, each of us wearing everything he could cram on, and the rest of it piled on the boat bottom to make a bit of soft lying. The water tin was empty of course. We hadn't strength enough to row. We left all to the sail, steering with an oar and keeping the boat before the wind, whichever way it blew. There was nothing else to do. It rained quite a bit but sometimes there were squalls of snow.

"I told you this was a long yarn, didn't I? I'll skip a lot. On the twelfth day we were sighted and picked up by a Nova Scotia schooner running east for Lisbon with a cargo of salt fish. The messroom boy and I were alive. The other chap had been dead for days, and we were all three huddled together on that ragman's stock of clothing in the bottom of the boat."

Skane paused and lit another cigarette. His hand shook as it held the match. Isabel sat watching him, dumb with pity. The horror was not so much in what he said or in what she was left to guess; it was in the defiant tone of his voice. He told his tale with a sneer, with a look of utter disdain, as if he despised her for calling up this old nightmare out of his past.

"There's not much left to tell, except the point of all this. I was a long time in a Lisbon hospital, and after that in a convalescent home for merchant marine officers in England. By the time I got back to Halifax the war was in its last few months—and I'd had enough of it. I'd had enough of everything, including the sea."

"And women?" Isabel asked.

"And women. Women! You think a lot about women when the sea catches up with you at last, and gives you the full treatment. It doesn't strike you till then what a lot of soft, empty, self seeking creatures they are, and what a fool you've been to have any part of them. You lump women with the smug ship owners, the busy ships handlers, the Victory Loan orators and all the other comfortable shore people who send you off to sea with a smile—and look around for someone else. Oh, it's wonderful how clear you can see after a few days in an open boat."

"So you came to Marina," she said, unperturbed.

"I put in for shore duty, and somebody mentioned a post on Marina. I'd heard of the place, and of Carney—who hadn't? It seemed the kind of place I was looking for. And when I came here and studied Carney for a bit it seemed to me that his was the kind of life I wanted."

Skane arose, picked up the mittens and walked to the door.

Isabel came to her feet swiftly.

"And then I came, and spoiled everything—isn't that what you want to say?"

He turned and gave her that straight look which seemed to pierce the last recess of her mind.

"No," he said evenly. "Let's say you changed everything." And then in a lighter tone, "We've been very serious, haven't we? And after all it's Christmas and we should be merry. Let me tell you something to make you smile. Our shy boy Sargent confessed to me last night, when he was packing up his gift, that he was half in love with you."

He was laughing as he said this, and she felt again that creeping flush.

"Only half?" she said, with a small toss of her head, and turned to clear the table, feeling absurdly hot and indignant. In the clatter of dishes she heard the door slam and Skane's retreating footsteps on the walk.

CHAPTER 20

Giswell's nose for the weather proved very accurate. For a night and a day the blizzard screamed through the wires and scoured roof, walls and windows with blasts of snow. The telephone wires blew down again and McBain's men did not get it repaired until New Year's Day. On that afternoon the box on the wall uttered a cheerful tinkle and Isabel took down the receiver.

"It's for you," she said. Matthew rose from the desk, slipping one of the radio phones aside. Isabel sauntered into the hall. Skane and Sargent had gone for a walk on the lagoon ice. She had never seen their rooms and it seemed a good moment to indulge her curiosity. Sargent's door was open. She stood for a few moments looking in. It was like the cell of a monk. The furniture consisted of a narrow iron bed, a plain wooden chair and a small birchwood chest of drawers. The walls and ceiling were nailed sheets of pressed wood-pulp, painted that awful drab she had found in Carney's bedroom when she came. The softwood floor had been painted brown at some remote time, but the constant scuffing of boots gritty with sand had worn it bare except in the corners. In one corner lay Sargent's sea chest, a stout wooden thing with rope beckets for handles, and his name in large white letters on the top.

A row of hooks held a raincoat, a ragged pair of trousers and the complete uniform of a radio officer in the merchant marine. The uniform was in good condition. She could see that Sargent kept it brushed and its brass buttons polished. A faint smile played over her lips. Here was full proof of his longing to get back to sea. A photograph stood on the chest of drawers; a man and woman in middle age smiled at the camera; Sargent's father and mother beyond doubt. Pinned to the wall above them were several cuttings from magazines, all pictures of young women flaunting their legs in very short skirts or posed with one bent knee in bathing suits.

She went along to Skane's room. The door stood half open and she pushed it wide, feeling like Bluebeard's wife. The room was like Sargent's even to the sea chest in the corner; but here the clippings were of sailing ships and there was no photograph at all. She wondered at the ships, recalling his hatred of the sea; but perhaps these pictures satisfied some memory of a time when he was filled with the romantic illusions that now possessed Sargent. There was something sad about that. A sealskin with the hair worn down to the hide in a great bald patch in the middle lay beside the harsh iron bed. The clothes on the hooks were odds and ends, trousers, jackets, sweaters, a suit of oilskins, all very shabby and worn. Despite these the room had the same look of rigid neatness that she had found in Sargent's, and which she supposed was a result of their training at sea.

She wondered at the absence of a photograph. Surely he kept something to remind him of his people, his friends, if not his women? Guiltily she pulled open the top drawer of the chest of drawers. Nothing there but a dressing-case, a few handkerchiefs clean but wrinkled, just as they had dried after washing, a collar box, two or three black neckties of the sort that sea officers wore with their uniforms, a seaman's sheath knife, and a scatter of the small and exquisite sea shells to be found along the beach which the islanders used in decorating their picture frames.

A lower drawer lay partly open and she could see neatly folded woolen underwear and gray flannel shirts of the sort to be found in the seamen's-supply shops on Water Street. She turned to the sea chest and lifted the lid. There seemed to be nothing but books. She looked at them, one by one. A history of Canada in two volumes; *Tristram Shandy; Plays of Gilbert and Sullivan;* Flecker's poems; *Handbook of Wireless Telegraphy; Care and Maintenance of Radio Telegraph Apparatus; The lngoldsby Legends;* an English-Spanish dictionary. As she plucked at the next she saw exposed a corner of a snapshot album and drew it forth. It was old, apparently a relic of an early enthusiasm for the camera. It must have been laid aside with other souvenirs—probably boxed in the storeroom of the wireless office at Halifax—and reclaimed when he returned from that final tussle with the sea.

The pictures had been taken with a small camera and developed and printed in a slapdash fashion, probably in tin pans borrowed from the galley of a ship. They had faded badly. There were pictures of various ships, all tramp steamers, tied up at dreary-looking docks or at anchor in harbors whose shores were out of focus and not to be recognized. Pictures of men in shabby uniforms, in ill-fitting mufti, leaning against a ship's rail, against a lifeboat on its chocks, on a sun-blazing white road with a background of palms. Views of houses, of gardens, of Spanish looking churches and other buildings in a tropical setting. A few of Skane himself, alone or with one or two others evidently from the same ship, with arms linked or thrown about each other's shoulders. There was one of him in tropical whites, with his cap at a jaunty angle and a lock of black hair drooping across his forehead. He looked very young. He was facing the camera and laughing with the adventurous air that she had noticed so often in the seamen across the court at Mrs. Paradee's. She thought of him now and felt a pang. Was this what happened to them all—did they all become disillusioned and defeated, hiding themselves away from the world, like Skane?

The album was only half full, and among the snapshots there were gaps with traces of paste and wrenched fragments of paper. And there was not a picture of a woman. From first to last, not one. He had torn them out. She uttered a little cluck of disappointment and replaced the album carefully beneath the books. It would have been amusing to see what sort of woman Skane had favored in those days before he lost his illusions. Were they dark, fair, tall or short? Were they "nice" or were they tarts, or women simply unable to resist a handsome young man ashore for a fling? She pictured him in the white uniform, cap on one ear, walking up from the docks in some foreign town with that laughing challenging air.

There was a sound towards the front door. She fled on tiptoe into the hall. Nobody there. The sound again—Matthew moving about the watch room in his slow methodical way. She stepped into the room that had been Vedder's and peered from the window. Skane and Sargent stood on the shore of the lagoon examining the wreck of the dory, which had been lifted into the air like a paper cup by one of the hurricane winds of last autumn. She glanced about the room. It was bare like the others but unswept. A dust of fine sand layover the floor. There was nothing on the bed but the bare mattress. Skane and Sargent had taken the late cook's blankets for extra warmth in this frigid monastery. The only evidence of Vedder was an array of pictures pinned above the bed, and these surprised her. The cook's indignation at her coming, and his flagrant desertion in the face of it, had given her an image of a brooding ascetic. But the clippings he had chosen to adorn his cell were all of women in various stages of undress, and there were two or three postcards marked "Souvenir de Rouen" exhibiting girls with nothing on at all. It amused her to perceive that the cook had come to this far place to dream of women and then fled from the mere approach of reality.

She returned to the watch room and found Matthew adjusting the receiver dials and tapping a finger on the crystal detector. He listened in the phones intently for a moment and scribbled on the pad before him.

"Hello," he said, looking up. "Where've you been?"

"Exploring," she said honestly.

"What did you find?"

"Nothing. The operators' rooms are awfully bleak, aren't they?"

"Yes. Of course, they're used to it. I've put in for a general heating system several times but it doesn't do any good." He added fretfully, "We need a stand-by engine very badly, too. I told Hurd about it when I went to Halifax and he promised to do something but you know what that means. As it is, we have to turn out at all hours, all hands, whenever the engine breaks down, and work like beavers till we get it going again. We've got a stock of spare parts and all that; but it's rather a nightmare knowing the engine may give up the ghost some time when there's urgent stuff on the air—a ship in distress or something like that. It's not right, you know. Hurd doesn't realize."

"What was the telephone call?"

"Eh? Oh! McBain. He wanted us to come down for a party tonight. New Year, you know. Skane's going down to play the piano. But I said I didn't fancy walking back in the dark, and I wouldn't put him to the trouble of driving us home."

"Oh, Matthew, I wish you'd said yes. We could walk back on the lagoon ice, dark or no dark. The weather's clear, there'll be starlight. And it's so long since we had talk with anybody but ourselves."

He stirred uneasily. "We'd get back very late, and I haven't been sleeping well. I'm sorry, Isabel, I really couldn't go. Look here, why don't you go along with Skane?"

"I'd rather go with you."

"I'm afraid that's impossible."

She walked over and sat on the edge of the desk. "Matthew, do you know you're getting awfully strange? You seem unhappy. What on earth's the matter? Giswell says you used to go everywhere, even in winter. Have I made a difference? Is it me?"

He gazed stonily out of the window. "No."

"Then what in Heaven's name is it?"

"Nothing—nothing, my dear. It's just that I don't like to leave the station for long nowadays—the engine, you know. After all I'm the O-in-C, I've got the responsibility."

"Pooh! It's Sargent's watch this evening. If the engine broke down he could phone McBain's and we'd all be back in half an hour."

"Sargent's just a young chap. You don't understand."

She slid from the desk and went to the north window, staring out at the snow on the dunes. Over her shoulder she said in an irritated voice, "No, I don't understand. I don't understand anything. You men are such a secretive lot. For some time now I've had a feeling that you're all keeping something from me. Sometimes I think it's one thing, one guilty secret that you all share. And then sometimes each one of you seems to have his own secret, something that it wouldn't be good for me to know or for the others to suspect. It's all quite mad to me, here in this place where we're all shut up together. Like a lot of petty conspirators in a private lunatic asylum, when we should be making the most of each other, sharing our thoughts, laughing together—crying together if you like. Don't say Pooh or Nonsense, Matthew, as if I were just a silly woman being emotional over nothing. It's here. It's real. I feel it. This mystery! This awful feeling of suspense! As if you'd all done a murder and buried the corpse under the station! Sometimes at night when the wind makes that doleful sound in the wires, when you're on the midnight watch and I'm alone in the apartment and can't sleep—I get frantic. I feel I must get away from it, whatever it is; I want to run out into the wind and keep running on and on over the dunes in the dark, away from that sound, away from all of you!"

She swung about, panting, and with her hands behind, bracing herself against the wall. "Even when I make love, it's not the same. You're not the same. You seem reluctant. Why is that? Why won't you look me in the eyes any more?"

Carney sat in the familiar posture at the instruments, with his big forearms resting on the desk in front of him, his hands within quick reach of the receiver dials and the key. The headbands of the phones enclasped his thick blond locks. His bearded face, with its immovable gaze fixed on the dunes outside, betrayed no emotion whatever. In that sphinx like attitude he seemed to contemplate with an immense fortitude some riddle of the sands.

"I suppose you think I'm just being neurotic!" she cried.

He spoke then. "I'm afraid it's something of that sort," he said carefully, and without shifting his gaze. "I've heard men talk like that. And it always comes in the winter, about now, or in February, when they've been thrown in each other's company for months, shut in by storms for days on end, and there's absolutely nothing to look forward to but the next boat, which may not come till April or May. They begin to suspect each other of slights, insults, petty injustices, all sorts of things. It works a bit worse in a man. Some chaps get high-strung at this work. It's a certain strain on the nerves of course, all this listening, the everlasting effort to catch a thin sound in the distance, or to fix your attention on one particular ship amongst a dozen all clattering away at once; or to pick out a message in cipher, say, when there's a storm in the offing and the static's crashing in your ears. Add all that to the monotony of life on the station and, well, some chaps can't take it. They get on each other's nerves and finally they fly off the handle—usually at each other's throats. I've seen men trying to kill each other with their fists, here in this room. I saw Skane, the first winter he was here, standing where you are now and slugging it out with a wild red-haired chap from up the Gulf."

"Skane?" she said, with a curious tone. "Of course you stopped them."

"Not at all. I knew it had to come, sooner or later. They'd reached the point of not speaking to each other, even at meals. There had to be something to clear the air, and there it was. I was afraid for a moment that they'd upset the stove and set the place afire—that happened here once, years ago. But a chance blow of Skane's knocked the other chap through that window behind you and they finished it outside. They were pretty evenly matched. They beat each other's faces to a pulp—played themselves out."

"And you—the O-in-C didn't do a thing about it?"

"Oh yes. Somebody had to keep watch. I picked the phones off the floor where Skane had flung them and went on with it."

Isabel uttered a small harsh laugh. "That sounds like everything else I've heard about Marina. Savages! Savages! But I'm afraid I can't work off my jitters with a boxing match."

Carney did not answer. The silence was broken by Skane and Sargent, bursting in red-faced and cheerful from their walk along the ice.

"Hello!" Skane said. "You look very serious, you two. Is the secret out?"

Isabel gave him a startled glance. Carney swung sharply in the chair. "Secret, Skane?"

"Then you don't know?" Skane waved a hand. "Behold my star pupil. Yesterday, my dear O-in-C, your wife did a perfect twenty words a minute, for ten minutes by the clock. You've got another op on your staff!"

Carney turned to her slowly with an astonished smile. "Not really?"

"Really!" she said, with indifference. Sargent picked up the scuttle and rattled coals into the stove. He was oblivious of the odd atmosphere into which he and Skane had so suddenly plunged. But Skane had seen the strained look on Isabel's face. He looked away, reflectively. Then, turning swiftly to Carney with a theatrical gesture, "And now, my dear sir, we must teach her one or two technical details about Signor Marconi's marvelous invention, so she can go up for a ticket. Let me introduce Signor Sargenti, a technical expert. Signor Sargenti, kindly give the lady your celebrated lecture on the standard receiving tuner, 1914 model."

"Oh nuts!"

"Go ahead," Carney said.

"Oh, well," Sargent grinned at Isabel. "There was a W.T. instructor at the Halifax Dockyard during the war. He was Royal Navy, a nice bloke who knew his stuff but rather la-de-da. Believe it or not, he wore a monocle." Sargent fished in a drawer for a large iron washer, stuck it in his right eye, and caught up a ramrod from a corner of the room.

"Now yah," he said loudly, arching his back and stabbing the rod towards the tuner panel, "yah weh have the tunah. When weh speak of the tunah weh do not refah to a fish, nor de weh refah to the chappie who goes about tinkering pianos. Weh refah to this verreh impawtant black-paneled aff-yah with all the little knobs and dials and things. Now the tunah ..." Sargent went on with it, posturing, grimacing, rattling off inanities about the crystal detector, the potentiometer, the aerial tuning coils, the condensers, the theory of magnetic waves and the analogy of the stone cast into the pool. It was his favorite performance and he was delighted to see that Mrs. Carney found it droll.

She smiled in a mechanical way at first; but as he went on her smile became a giggle and before long she was leaning against the wall and shaking hilariously. Her voice rose in pitch and volume. Tears ran down her face. At last she was uttering shrieks that rang through the station, and staring with wide wet eyes, not at Sargent, but towards the farther wall at a point near the ceiling.

The comedian paused. "Look here," he said anxiously, "it's not as funny as all that is it?" There was no answer, Carney was rising from the chair and moving towards his wife. Her laughter went on, peal after peal, each spaced by a long sobbing intake of breath.

"It wasn't my idea," Sargent stammered. A hard boot bruised his shin.

"Shall we retire?" murmured Skane's voice icily.

CHAPTER 21

On an afternoon late in February, Isabel sat in the watch room wearing the phones. She was alone. It was a triumph. After all the months of practice, all her hours at the instruments in company with the operator of the watch, and after a whole morning's persuasion, Matthew had consented to let her take a watch. The difficult part had been to convince him that she must take it absolutely alone.

"What!" he had protested. "None of us?"

"None!" Skane had put in swiftly. "Sargent and I are taking a walk to West Light, and you're coming with us. We'll give McBain a hail on the way past Main Station, and we'll be back here for tea."

"But the engine..."

"Damn the engine. It's running sweetly anyhow."

"But sometimes it stops out of sheer cussedness, you know that, Skane. With us it's just a matter of running into the engine room, shoving the flywheel back on compression, and giving the thing a whirl with the crank. But Isabel couldn't do that, she hasn't the strength."

"The engine's going to run," Skane insisted. "If it doesn't she'll simply write 'Bi engine repairs' in the log and wait for us to turn up. After all the station's off the air from time to time for that very good reason—and one more log entry of that sort might be all we need to get that stand-by engine."

"I don't like it," Carney muttered. "Couldn't we just walk down to the beach a bit and come back?"

"No!" Isabel put in firmly.

"Very well," he said reluctantly. And he had gone off between Skane and Sargent, wearing his old khaki duck coat and with his long locks fluttering in the wind, and saying, "I don't like it!" in a futile voice as they climbed the first dune.

It was a sunny day and the breeze was quite mild for February, a foretaste of spring. The men would enjoy their walk despite Matthew's forebodings. In the succession of storms and bitter calms there had been a few days of mild weather, but these had been wet and had given them more anxiety than the cold. During one January night a freezing rain had fallen—the thing they dreaded more than hurricanes or frost. It was what Nova Scotians called a "silver thaw," a condition that covers the world outdoors with a glaze of ice, making a glassy fairyland of woods and parks, coating every branch and twig and glittering in the next day's sunshine like an enormous crystal chandelier.

On Marina there was neither tree nor shrub to make such a show. But there was the enormous man-made tree of the radio mast with its cone of stays and aerials. The stays were stout enough to hold their unusual load; but the slender phosphor bronze wires of the aerial itself acquired in the course of a few hours the thickness of a man's wrist, and they broke from the masthead, falling on the glassy crust of Marina with a clatter that startled the operator on watch and brought the others out of their beds. Nothing could be done until morning, and altogether the station was off the air for twelve hours.

The repair was a matter of difficulty. Ordinarily the aerials were held at the top of the mast by their spreader, a stout wooden spar that could be lowered to the ground by means of a halyard passing through a block lashed at the peak. Now, however, the spreader, bereft of its metallic load, remained at the masthead, frozen and immovable. That meant hoisting a man up to free it, a ticklish business. The halyard of a bosun's chair passed through another block at the masthead. This was free, but there was no means of knowing how good or bad was the lashing of that block after the autumn and winter storms. But the greatest danger was the great pine mast itself, which had suffered a queer white elephantiasis in the night. The rain had drifted in from the east, and the whole easterly cheek of the mast from top to bottom—one hundred and sixty-five feet—was bloated by a growth of ice several inches thick.

They hailed Mings, one of the lifesavers from Main Station, riding patrol up the beach, to give them a hand with the work.

"You see what it means," Carney said, as they took the halyard from its cleat and rigged the bosun's chair. "The sun's out now and that ice is apt to let go in chunks when I knock against it, going up. Means you chaps will have to mind your heads below. And mind you don't let go the rope!"

"We're not hoisting you up there," Skane said bluntly. "You're too big."

"Let me go," Sargent suggested. His grin was nervous as he said it.

The masthead looked an enormous distance in the sky. Skane slipped into the chair.

Isabel, glancing from her kitchen window, was astonished to see him sitting in what appeared to be a child's swing and going slowly up the mast, fending himself off gingerly as he went. She had supposed that the repaired aerials would be hitched onto something at the mast foot and hoisted from there, as the three men were now hoisting Skane. She ran out towards them, concerned by the anxious look on Matthew's upturned face; and as she approached, each footstep plunging through the white crust with the sound of broken glass, he cried, without shifting his attention from the dangling man in the chair, "Isabel? Go back to the walk!"

"But surely I can help you?" she appealed.

"Get away, I say!" There was a harsh note in his voice that she had never heard before. She obeyed dumbly, a little angrily. But as she stood on the boardwalk and watched what followed, her blood went cold. Skane's lean form rose towards the sky in slow jerks, swinging, fending off with hands and feet. Each time he swayed against the mast a piece of the encrusted ice came down. Some of these were small. But from time to time five, ten or more feet of that strange lopsided elephantiasis lost its hold on the round wood, and with no more warning than Skane's quick shout fell like a javelin towards the straining men below.

They could not jump clear. Carney had to snub the halyard on the cleat before they dared move at all, and then they could only shrink away towards the lee side of the mast, still holding hard on that line which seemed so tenuous to Isabel—holding Skane's life by a thread. Each of those falling ice-shapes, so exquisitely molded to the form of the mast, could kill a man. It seemed to Isabel, watching dry-mouthed and trembling from the safety of the walk, that a frightful accident was about to happen and it must involve them all. It was an eternity before they got Skane to the top, and another passed before his voice came floating down like a cry from another world.

"Okay! Lower away on the bridle!"

Down it came with the spreader, that dull wooden thing, so much more important than men's necks or skulls, while Skane remained like a small black spider at the masthead, hung by a bit of gossamer. When they lowered the bosun's chair at last the strain showed in all their faces; but Carney's and Sargent's and Ming's were dripping sweat, while Skane's, nipped by the keen upper air, was almost blue. They laughed and thumped each other with their fists, as men do when they wish to conceal an emotion that has shaken them; and they were astonished when Isabel ran up to them crying incoherent things, flinging her arms about each one in turn and kissing him on the mouth. They chaffed her about it afterwards in their irritating male way, as if there had been nothing really to the job and as if no one but she had given it a moment's concern.

She could smile about that now. In six months she had come to regard them with something of the air of a maiden aunt who is, or at any rate considers herself, responsible for three schoolboy nephews, of various ages, manners and appearance. She had soon acquired this feeling towards Sargent; and it was odd now to think that she had once been afraid of Skane. That savage confession of Skane's had reminded her irresistibly of a dark moody schoolboy who has gone off to a corner to sulk after a whipping. As for Matthew, she had been attracted by the naive small boy in him from the first, from the moment she saw him in Hurd's office. Even as a lover he had been swayed and governed always by her own impulses; and if now, in the strange aloofness that had come upon him with the onset of winter, he seemed less of a lover and more of a recluse, she knew that sexually at least she had become as withdrawn as he. After that ecstasy in the autumn their passion had drifted into a sort of hibernation, as if it were subject to the weather like everything else on Marina.

This feeling of faintly amused indulgence towards the three men was shadowed by the mystery in which they seemed to wrap some part of their thoughts, and which her intuition could not pierce. At first she decided that she was making a puzzle out of nothing more than the instinctive reserve of the human male, even among his fellows. For all their outward camaraderie men were secretive bodies after all. They never fully revealed themselves, even to each other. Matthew had once confessed that in years of intimate contact with all kinds of men he had felt familiar with the minds of only two or three.

But there came days and nights when a black fog fell upon her thoughts and senses, and then it seemed that behind their professional jargon, their casual jokes, their tales of guns and ducks and ponies, there lay something concealed, something that concerned her as much as themselves but that she must find out alone. What was it? They were all living under some kind of spell, presumably evil. She wondered if there were not some truth in that wild quip of hers about a corpse beneath the station. The whole island was a sepulcher. Those skulls and bones in the rocket house! Those creepy tales of the islanders, handed down from one generation to another, and implicitly believed like a faith brought down from the patriarchs! Wasn't that it? Wasn't this queer tension in the wireless station part of an all-pervading supernatural force arising from all those dead people, those sea-slain men and women in the dunes? A mystic pressure from the nameless dead of Marina! Fantastic! And yet the islanders believed in some such force. Some, like the McBains, would not admit it, that was all.

This is the way your mind goes, Isabel told herself. When you come, you don't notice it. During the first winter, during the long nights and the short gray days, during months of hearkening to the wind in the aerials, you begin to feel it. After the second winter you'll believe it. Then you'll be one with the rest of them, a primitive creature in a lost corner of the world, the prey of phantoms, a prisoner of the weather and the sea—and of the dark. Three or four times a year you'll dress up in shabby finery and go down the beach to make your obeisance to O'Dell, to finger some scrap of handwriting from the outside world as if it were a talisman, to regard the other prisoners dressed in clothes like yours, all wearing the same smiling masks, all uttering the same greetings, the same poor gossip, the same little worn-out jokes; and then you'll go back to your hiding-places among the dunes, back to your servitude, to that eternal surveillance by the watchful eyes of the dead.

Oh yes, it was true. True! For a long time Matthew had been immune from all that. His simple mind had been proof against it. He had even preferred to roam about the beaches in the dark; he had loved a storm at night, the turmoil of great seas rolling in, white on black, and breaking and slithering almost to his feet, and the sound of his own rich voice flinging Byron's verses down the wind. No wonder the islanders looked upon him with a certain awe! But now he went no more in the dark. The fall of dusk now closed the prison doors for him as for the Kahns, the Giswells and the rest. Skane still made his lone dark journeys after dreaming at McBain's piano, but it seemed to her that Skane was not immune either. It was just that he was haunted by a different set of ghosts, the shades of that ghastly lifeboat in the winter sea, and nothing here could have much terror for him. As for Sargent, that ingenuous youth had not been long enough on Marina to come under the full spell. He was like herself, a novice in the sepulcher.

With the slow passage of the winter weeks Isabel found herself slipping into these dark moods more often, and they lasted longer. The pattern was always the same; and there was always the same sense of tragedy beside her, all about her, whispering in tones too thin to understand, like some far ship in the phones, calling Marina with signals too faint to be read. At night as she went to draw the blind in the bedroom her own image on the black pane greeted her like another self looking in, and the expression on that other face was always one of sharp anxiety. The shade came down, like a curtain drawn across a picture, and then there was only the lamp and the familiar furniture; but when she arose and dressed in the black winter mornings to prepare breakfast for her men the image was awaiting her at the pane, it appeared at once as the blind went up, and there was the same question on its face.

So the time crawled, as the sun crawled north towards the Line. The men moved about the station like automatons. Their talk was listless. The last magazine had been read to rags, the last fillip wrung out of their battered playing cards. They went on watch with eagerness; it was the one time in the day when each of them became fully alive. With Matthew, with Sargent, but mostly with Skane, as they sat at the instruments, Isabel had come to know that marvelous sensation of release, of flight into another existence, which came by putting on the phones. And because her feminine mind was not hampered by their male self-discipline, the professional boredom with which, instinctively, they masked their interest, she saw more clearly than any of them the romance, the miracle of what they called, almost contemptuously, "pounding brass."

When you put on the phones it was as if your inner self stepped out of the bored and weary flesh and left it sitting in the chair in that barren room. For a space you were part of another world, the real, the actual living world of men and ships and ports, in which Marina was nothing but a sandbar and a trio of call letters in the signal books. Whistling, growling, squealing, moaning, here were the voices of men transmuted through their finger tips, issuing in dots and dashes, speaking twenty languages in one clear universal code, flinging what they had to say across the enormous spaces of the sea.

Here were the Americans with their quenched-spark sets, their high flute notes; and British tramps with their synchronous rotaries, their hoarse baritone whose tune was halfway down the scale; the Canadians and their high wailing rotaries; the curious musical pop-pop-popping of the Germans with their Telefunkens; the French tramps and trawlers bleating like small sheep lost in the green wet pastures of the sea, and their liners crying out in a quick precise tenor to the shore; the harsh scream of the occasional Japs, whose names were all something-*Maru*, jamming the six-hundred-meter wave with their infernal five kilowatt sparks for an hour at a time, oblivious of international regulations; the quick, jerky piping of the Italians; the ringing manly bosun-tones of the Norwegians, the Swedes and Danes.

All these sparks bellowed, cried, muttered or whispered together on the six-hundred-meter wave, the main channel for ship traffic. At night when the darkness increased their range by three, four or five times the uproar was terrific, the sound of a vast swamp on a spring night filled with vociferous frogs. By day the range and the Babel subsided; but there was seldom quiet. Ships talked to each other, or they demanded notice from the shore, crying the attention of New York or Boston or Cape Race or Marina, that outpost which could pluck messages far out of the ocean air and fling them on to the landline at Halifax. To wireless operators on the North Atlantic run these stations, known indifferently by name but intimately by their call signals— NAH, WBF, VCE, VCT—these were the tongues and ears of North America, the listening posts, the speaking trumpets of the continent.

The great liners with their tall masts and powerful transmitters bestrode the ocean, hurling messages now to one side, now the other. These were the prima donnas of the show, with strong clear voices sheering through the boom and trill of the chorus, uttering a few clipped notes here and there, and then bursting forth in long arias addressed to London, Paris or New York. Their voices rang about the wide sea spaces and all the others shrank to a murmur. But when the last cadenza died in a final dot or dash the chorus rose once more, the vast trampnavy, the rabble of the sea, insistent and tumultuous, demanding the notice of each other or of some distant station on the land.

In all this medley there were certain sounds that had special meaning. Your own call signal first; but that was burned into your mind with letters of fire so that, waking or dozing in a dull watch, or reading or writing or pottering with the dials, its merest whisper brought you erect and alert in the chair, reaching out for pencil and message pad. There was CQ, the anonymous call that might mean anybody, the constant "Hey, Mac!" of the groping tramps. There was QST, the general call to all stations, ship and shore, which usually had to do with navigation warnings, icebergs or derelicts in the lanes, and suchlike matters. But most significant was a simple group of dots and dashes that for convenience were written SOS, although it could have been VTB or any combination of letters involving three dots, three dashes and three dots, all run together without pause. This was the magic symbol by which all the frogs in the great sea-swamp could be hushed in a minute. For every operator, even for cynics like Skane and old hands like Carney, that sound never lost its thrill, its quick clutch at the heart.

Usually the cry came from some foundering tramp, one still small voice in the uproar, barely heard by one or two ships on the edge of its range. But those ships spoke quickly, urgently, and were heard by the nearest shore station, the traffic policeman whose voice was law. Then a lonely man at the key of some outpost like Marina sent a trumpet call ringing through Babel like the voice of God, calling QST—"All Stations"—and demanding silence, adding in a swift flicker of dots and dashes "STD BI FOR SOS." Silence fell within his range, and on the edge of it other shore stations took up the cry, and it went up and down the coast. Here and there a small ship-voice, uncomprehending, uttered a call or went on with some petty business; but then a shore station or a nearby ship cut in with a savage QRT—"Shut up!"

When this took place at night, with its enlarged range, the great silence spread like an infection all the way from Labrador to Florida, and you felt in that enormous emptiness hundreds of alert men on the coast and in the ships, listening, waiting, straining to catch the voice of distress. It was magnificent—all the traffic, all the urgent business of that vast reach of sea and seaboard held up and silenced because, somewhere in the darkness, a few men were in peril.

Then out of the void that still small voice again, uttering dots and dashes on a small auxiliary set because the engine room was flooded and the main dynamo dead, crying faintly the name of a ship, sinking, latitude so-and-so, longitude so-and-so. Silence again. Then the shore trumpet ringing out, repeating, flinging over the wet wilderness that brief appeal. And again silence. You could imagine, yes, you could *see* the operators in the ships, talking to the bridge by telephone, or running up there with the figures jotted on a message form; and you could see the officers of the watch, the smart liner-officers in blue and brass, the unkempt mates of tramps, the grim skippers aroused from their berths, the heads together under the chartroom lamps, the stalking legs of brass dividers, the slither of black parallel-rulers, the pencil calculations and jottings; and you could hear the rumbling voices—"Sparks? Here's our position and speed"—"Five hours"—"Twelve hours"—"Sorry, we can't do him any good, we're four hundred miles to the east"—"Heavy sea from the nor'ard here, anyone nearer?"—"Make it by daylight, weather holding"—"What's their wind, can you get their wind? If they take to the boats they'll drift."

Dots-and-dashes in the phones again. Ships reporting position. A stride to the chart on the station wall. Nearest? This one. But he's only a tramp doing seven knots—poor coal, probably. Next one's a tanker doing close to twelve—says he's got a heavy cross-sea on that bearing but can make it. But here's a liner doing twenty, farther off than the others of course, but he could be there in less time. So many hours. Um! Chances are the ship'll be down before that. Case of looking for boats. Head all three of 'em for it, then. That other chap, too, and the Yankee trawler. We can turn 'em back again if the liner does the trick.

Back to the key. The trumpet blaring. Situation thus-and-so. Suggest this, suggest that. ("Never command," Carney would say. "Remember, you control all wireless traffic in your area but you can't command the skippers. By Jingo, nobody commands a skipper but his owners and his conscience—and you've got no time to contact owners when a ship's going under.") From there on you sat silent, hearing the cross-talk of the rescuing ships. When all was working properly you notified the rest of the coast that traffic could be resumed. At once the swamp came back to life, but with one conspicuous spot of calm in the area of the ship in distress. There nobody talked but the ships concerned, and you stood by ready to snap at any ham-handed fool who interfered.

Oh yes, it was wonderful. It was exciting. The blood in your veins, gone sluggish in so much monotony, went tingling through them then. You were alive in every nerve. Whenever you put on the phones you felt the importance of the whole complex system of which your lonely outpost was a part; but when a ship cried distress in your area you became a god seeing the sparrow's fall. You *saw*. The pictures came on some sort of screen in your mind. Imagination? Part of it, perhaps. It was hard to explain, and Carney and Sargent and Skane had tried to explain it and had failed; it was not until Isabel had spent many hours beside them at the phones that she began to see, dimly, what they meant. The pictures came into your mind with the far thin fluting of the distant spark; it was an induced effect, conveyed by the invisible operator's hand on the key precisely as the motions of a pen across paper convey in a way subtle but very real the writer's personality and character and the emotions of the moment.

This eerie sixth sense came to every operator in a degree that varied with his experience and with the sensitiveness of his own mind and emotions. On the coastal stations, where there was a good deal of interstation traffic, each operator became known to the others by his "hand," his style, the color of his personality flung on the mind-screens of the others by the mere contact of his fingers on the transmitting key.

As the forms of her three men dwindled and disappeared over the dunes towards the west, Isabel thought upon these things and wondered if she could ever fully acquire that occult art. At all events, she reflected, adjusting the crystal point, for the next four hours I've got "something to do." As if to prove the matter a bugle sounded in the phones calling Marina. With the ease of practice, almost of habit, she threw the big transmitting switch with her left hand and slipped her right to the key. Stentor in the engine room awakened at her touch and snarled obediently. She smiled, and wondered why she had ever feared the thing. She made her dots and dashes neatly, with that rhythm on which Skane had been so insistent.

She reversed the switch, gave the crystal an expert tap, and picked up a pencil. The small bugle sang in the phones again. She watched the pencil move across the blue message form. It was as Matthew had assured her. "Once you've got the feel of it, you're simply part of the machine. The stuff comes in on the aerials and runs right down to your fingertips."

It was a routine message; an Italian tramp inward bound for Halifax, informing the agents of its estimated arrival date and time, the bunkers and water required; asking about pratique.

She gave a receipt and called Halifax. The spark screamed through the station and over the dunes, *dit-dit-dit-da, da-dit-dadit, dit-dit-dit,* the dots cracking out like musketry, the dashes blaring, an immense all-powerful sound. She exulted in it now. The sensation was marvelous. And when the deep drone of Halifax answered, buzzing a peremptory "K," she rattled off that humdrum message swiftly and expertly like an old hand at the game. Halifax droned "R," and there was a momentary pause. Then, "WO?" A smile played over Isabel's lips. She had half expected that. In the gray building at the harbor mouth, which she had seen blurred in the dusk as the *Lord Elgin* carried her to sea, the operator had detected a strange hand at Marina and was curious. She answered crisply, "C's wife." Another pause. Then the drone again. "Well done." That was music.

CHAPTER 22

March came in, half lamb, half lion, with a strong blustering wind and a warm rain. The back of the winter was broken. True, the nights were still zero-cold at times, and there were snowstorms thicker than any yet seen; but now the gray folds of the winter sky were swept away more frequently, and when the sun broke through it had a warmth that could be felt on the naked cheek. Each clear day the shadow of the mast, like the lean and silent finger of Time, traced a slightly wider quadrant on the sand from morn to night; but each day the shadow itself was shorter. Sargent amused himself by marking the tip of the shadow at noon, whenever it was visible, with a small bit of driftwood thrust into the sand. He began in February and by the Ides of March his irregular line of sticks was like a midget fence that began and ended nowhere. "When it gets *there*," he shouted, kicking a spot in the still virgin sand towards the mast, "I'm off for Halifax. Think of that!" Carney shrugged, knowing how far poor Sargent's sticks had yet to go. Skane's dark face had a tolerant smile. Isabel was filled with nostalgia, not for Halifax but for the countryside.

In the valley where she was born and first taught school the apple trees were still black and bare, and so were all the shrubs and the hardwood trees. There was deep snow still in the spruce forest on the mountainsides and thick ice on the lakes and ponds. But now the south face of every farmhouse would be shining in the sun, and the furrows of the fall plowing glittering where the snow had thawed in the fields, and the wet red soil looking as rich as blood. The brooks would be running bank-full, swollen by the thawing snow on the mountain. Boys and men would be going up the slope to tap the sugar maples. The first robin would be whistling on the pasture rail, and flocks of juncos working over last year's weeds in the fields in quest of seeds, and crows flying in slow squadrons to the pine woods in the last of the sunset light. The roads would be rivers of red mud where the farmers' carts and buggies wallowed and no car could stir at all. In the woods the mayflower was in bud, and in sunny places a few in blossom, and children picking them on the way to school, and teachers like the young Isabel Jardine accepting them and sniffing the fragrance that every Nova Scotian knows to be the finest in the world.

The wild geese would be passing north and sometimes you would hear them from your bedroom window, an urgent and poignant sound far up in the night. Flocks of wild duck would be passing, too, flitting over the valley sky like the shadows of wind on the sea. By the mouths of the rivers small boys would be watching for the run of elvers, and dipping them, and taking them in glass jars to school; and teachers like the young Isabel Jardine would regard the silvery transparent things and seize the moment for a grave lecture on the habits of the Atlantic eel. Now, too, the shad would be going up the Fundy streams to spawn; and all along the coast the lobstermen would be making a daily round of their traps. At Lunenburg the cod fishermen would be setting out in their lovely schooners for the first trip to the Banks. Already some of them had been seen off. West Light, fishing on the Marina Bank or passing on towards Quero or the Grand Bank itself; and Matthew had been moved to say, when told of this, "There goes the last of Sail in our time."

Apart from Sargent's hopeful sticks there was no sign of spring on the face of Marina. The snow had vanished; but the lagoon was still sealed under thick ice, the dunes stretched their brown length east and west without a sign of green, and there were no birds except a hardy flock of herring gulls that had stayed through the winter. When other signs appeared they were a paradox—a flare of northern lights more brilliant than any seen since autumn, and a white invasion from the northwest, a vast ice field that crept over the horizon and came down upon the island under the thrust of a three-day gale. For miles the sea was invisible under this white mask; and when the first floes touched the beach, closing the last gap of open water, the eye was dazzled by the broad sweep of reflected sunlight.

Isabel walked with Matthew and Sargent to West Light and watched this glittering spectacle from the plate-glass windows of the lantern. Along the north beach the weight of the pack thrust its foremost floes up to the edge of the dunes, but there all progress stopped. The floes groaned, squealed, cracked with the report of cannon, but could not budge the brown rampart against which all the fury of the winter seas had been so impotent. The west bar was another matter. The long spit ran out for miles barely submerged, and sinking gradually into deep soundings. Here the floes inshore touched and held, while those in deeper water moved on. The wind, shifting towards the east, began to press the whole field over the bar and around the west end of the island, a whirling movement that sent the big cakes slithering one over another in the shallows, mounting until sometimes a whole floe rose on edge into the air, swayed, buckled and collapsed.

This struggle, made the more violent by the strong set of current around West Point at half-ebb, filled the small world of Marina with a confused and mighty uproar. To Isabel, even in the safety of the lighthouse, clutching Matthew's arm, the spectacle and the sound were frightening. With amazed eyes she watched the ice field piling up in masses like a spilled pack of cards, grinding its own ruins underfoot and pressing on. And again she wondered, as she had wondered through the winter gales, how Marina, made utterly of sand, without a rock, without even a pebble in its composition, could withstand such assaults for even half an hour.

Walking back to the wireless station she exclaimed, "And this is a sign of spring, you say!"

"Well, you see," Matthew said in his slow reasonable way, "the pack ice gathers in the Gulf all winter and then spews out to sea. We get some of it every spring. In three weeks or so the first steamer will pass up the Gulf and dock at Montreal, and the port bigwigs will be down on the dock to present the skipper with a gold-headed cane—they really do, you know."

"And what about the northern lights? They're so much brighter now. Isn't that a sign of colder weather?"

"A sign of change. They always seem brighter at the equinox, in this latitude anyway. Remember them in September?"

She thought of those unhappy nights when, with a coat over her nightdress, she had slipped down to the shore of the lagoon. That seemed ancient now. She wondered at the passage of experience no less than the passage of time. She had not roamed in the dark since the evening party at McBain's, the first time she heard Skane play, and the spell of his music sent her weeping and passionate into Matthew's arms. She had passed some sort of equinox herself that night. The winter had brought an uneasy pause, a brooding sense of coming storm. And now spring lay ahead. According to the almanacs the vernal equinox must bring great gales and rains before one could enjoy the sunshine and the flowers.

She remembered a mild night in September when, awake and restless, she had crept past Matthew's sleeping form on the couch in the kitchen and stepped out into the dark. It was nearly three o'clock in the morning and the night operator had left his phones and gone to the engine room to pump the water tank. Isabel could hear the dreary suck and clank of the pump, and in a whim of curiosity she had turned along the south wall of the station and peered at one of the engine room windows. What she saw was arresting.

The engine room was an uncomfortable place, for it was always very hot, and usually the windows were kept shut lest sand blow in upon the machinery. In one corner stood a tall cylindrical tank, kept full of water, from which the engine's cooling system circulated. The top of the tank was open, and in the short space between it and the ceiling appeared the overflow pipe of the domestic water tank, which stood in the attic above. Thus when the domestic tank had been filled the overflow began to run into the engine room tank. It marked the end of the operator's nightly labor at the pump, for a few strokes more were enough to replace the water evaporated from the cooling-tank during the day.

On this almost windless night, with no sand blowing, Skane had opened the west window to catch the faint stir along the dunes. But the air in the room was stifling for all that, compounded of a hot reek of grease, of lubricating oil, of gasoline, a smell of warm varnish from the dynamo armature and the queer sharp tang of ozone given off by the spark in the course of the day's work. In this stokehold atmosphere Skane stood naked at the pump. Sunburned by those free and easy summer months when they had "all lived like savages," and wet with sweat, his figure shone like polished bronze. The pump handle rose to the height of his breast and he stood with one foot advanced, and with one arm thrusting the handle back and forth.

Isabel's impulse was to retreat in haste, like a modest woman, but she was held by the expression on Skane's face. He faced the cooling-tank, looking up towards the ceiling where, any moment now, the overflow pipe would begin to gush. One lock of drenched black hair lay over his forehead, and the light of the single lamp on the wall fell on his upturned face and revealed the intent, anxious, eager look with which he awaited the end of his slavery. All the tense rhythm of his lean body, unconsciously poised in the attitude of an athlete at some crucial moment, seemed to flow into that ardent face.

In a few moments the water appeared overhead and began to splash into the steaming top of the cooling-tank, a thin stream, bright in the lamplight and pulsing with the movements of the pump. Skane uttered an "Ah!" of satisfaction and thrust the handle away from him in one final stroke, made with a savage force that conveyed all his hatred of the thing. He turned towards the door, and in that moment Isabel fled.

Now, walking silently between Sargent and Matthew, and wondering what the end of winter would bring forth here, where nothing ever really changed except the sky and the clouds that passed across it, she thought of Skane at the pump. There was a symbol in the picture that remained so clearly photographed on her mind. We've all been at some sort of pump, she thought, ever since winter came, and that's the way we'd all look if the masks were off. We're all waiting for something to happen. We're all watching for something to break the spell that binds us. For the thousandth time she asked herself, What is it? And again there was no reply. But now a new question formed itself and remained, insistent, in the undercurrent of her thoughts. When?

CHAPTER 23

Sargent's absurd pegs crept towards the mast. There were mighty winds and sandstorms, there were drenching rains. But in the sunny intervals a benign warmth came upon Marina. On bright afternoons the sand hills shimmered and brought back a phenomenon not seen since the last days of Indian summer. Now in the distance the dunes writhed like the folds of a slowly shaken blanket, and wild ponies wandering over the slopes appeared misshapen and immense, like buffalo. Lifesavers riding their patrols from Main Station or making a visit "down East" became giants mounted upon impossible beasts as they drew away, and then in a moment, in a blink of the harsh light, changed to mere dots or disappeared. Bits of old wreckage along the beach were endowed with a weird life at half a mile, rising, twisting, swelling, shrinking, now resembling houses, now trees, now ships. With the return of spring Marina exchanged its last hold on reality for the fantasy of the mirage.

The ice on lagoon and ponds turned dark and rotten. Long fingers of sand blown over the surface from the nearby dunes now caught the sun and burned into the ice and opened channels of blue water; and one wild night at the last of March a westerly gale wrenched at the veined and rotten sheets, tore them to rags and flung the gray tatters along the shores. The last stranded floes of the sea ice, like the dead of a polar invasion beaten off the beaches, changed in the sun to a queer fibrous mass that collapsed in a heap of crystals at a touch, and then melted clean away. Wild duck appeared in twos and threes, and then in hundreds, drifting like dark rafts on the surface of the lagoon.

And now on sunny afternoons Isabel began to ride again with Matthew or Skane or Sargent, whoever was free to get the ponies from Main Station and amble about the dunes and beaches in her company. One April afternoon she and Skane rode east to Number Two and called on the Lermonts. Their station looked very small and lonely, a house and a shed tucked away in a cup of dunes so neatly and so thoroughly that only the telephone line betrayed its presence. Lermont came out of the shed and took the ponies as they rode into the hollow, and plump Mary Lermont threw open her kitchen door and welcomed them.

"Thought at first it was Sara back again!" she cried. "She was here only a minute ago, didn't you see her?"

"No," they said.

"She must have rode out of sight awful quick. Been down this way every day since the ducks came, with Pa's old seal-rifle, huntin' amongst the ponds. Says you can't git near 'em with a shotgun, they're that wild. Come on in."

They passed into a severe little parlor furnished after the fashion of McBain's, and chatted over cookies and tea. Lermont's face was still the weathered brown of last autumn. Isabel thought of the winter patrols, and the lone man and his pony facing the blast along the beach. In contrast Mary Lermont looked sallow and it seemed to Isabel a little worn, as if the vacuum of months shut in this lonely hole had drained her soul and her complexion in a single process. She had one topic of conversation, the topic of all the island women now—The Boat.

"You heard anythin' about the *Elgin* over the wireless? No? Pretty near time we heard somethin', ain't it? I got my mail order list made up days ago. You got yours made up? There'll be some changes in the hands at Main, three of the lifeboat crew got enough of it this winter—goin' off to Hal'fax. And the lightkeeper's assistant out at East, he's poorly, thinks he'll take a spell ashore. Ma wants Sara to go off, too, to git a bit o' schoolin' for a year or two. Stay at Ma's sister's place at Port Bickerton. Sara won't have it, o' course. Great girl she's gettin'. And wild as a pony, roamin' up and down."

Mary's large blue eyes rolled as she said this, and flicked from Skane to Isabel, and back again. "Ridin' out quite a bit now, ain't you, Miz Carney? Sara says she sees you quite a lot. She's always up West. Don't know why, I'm sure." You do, though, Isabel thought. Skane was putting aside his empty cup and rising.

"I think we'd better be getting along, hadn't we?"

She nodded and rose, brushing crumbs from her jodhpurs and buttoning the bright red coat. There were polite murmurs, and then they were climbing out of the hollow with the Lermonts watching them from the doorway. As they passed over the crest the house and shed vanished with the suddenness of a conjuring trick. They were alone in the wilderness of dunes. To the north, hidden but close at hand, the surf clamored on the beach, and far away on the other hand came the subdued murmur of the south bar. Behind them only the tip of the radio mast could be seen. Before them the telephone poles and wire ran on and vanished in the mirage towards Number Three. They rode for a time without speaking. The saddles creaked, the feet of the ponies whispered in the sand.

"Why doesn't the sand fill up hollows like that?" Isabel asked, to break the silence.

"Like Number Two? Well, if you'd noticed, those dunes around it are well anchored by tufts of marram and creeping stuff like beach pea. The bare dunes, like those over there"—he pointed with his whip—"are the roving kind. A wind from one quarter blowing steadily for days will shift 'em bodily. That's why from time to time the patrolmen find bones and bits of old wreckage that must have been buried for years, centuries perhaps. Look here, let's ride over to Old Two. It's only a couple of miles."

"All right. What's Old Two?"

"The original Number Two. You'll see what happens when a big dune shifts. The house was built in a hollow, secure from the weather, and for years it was all right. Then somehow the wind began to eat under the grass tufts to the east of it. Probably some of the wild ponies had kicked a hole there and given the wind a start. Anyhow the sand began to shift. Not much at a time, you understand. A few tons, perhaps, whenever a gale blew from the east. The chap at Two battled with it for a year building a fence of driftwood to hold it back, and so on. Might as well have tried to fence off the sea at low tide. Then the Governor got alarmed—it was fifty or sixty years ago, before McBain's time, but everyone knows the tale, it's an island classic. The whole island crew had a go at stopping that dune—even tried shoveling it back. Finally they had to give up. The government built another station farther west—that's New Two, where we've just been. They cleared everything out of Old Two and let it go."

Skane led the way past a succession of small ponds edged with reeds and a thin turf covered with cranberry vines. They passed under the telephone line, ducking their heads, and rode up the shoulder of a bare sand hill. Skane reined up, and Isabel, drawing abreast, saw, in a shallow ravine below, the gable end of a roof. There was a glimpse of beach at the mouth of the ravine and a white flash of surf. She regarded the protruding bit of house and laughed. "It looks a bit silly, doesn't it? Like something you'd see in a child's sandbox."

They rode down to it and dismounted. The dune had buried the house all but that end of the roof and the gable, where an empty window frame stared like a square black eye.

"That's the attic window," Skane remarked. "Sargent and I climbed in there one day and went down inside the house—like going down a mine. All the other windows are intact—they'd nailed boards over 'em as the sand rose about the place, hoping I suppose that some day the dune would hump itself east again. Sargent thought it a fine lark. He was like a kid exploring a cave."

"I'd love to see it, Greg," she said impulsively. "Do take me in."

He fastened the ponies to a stout balk of wreck timber and crawled inside the window. Isabel followed, and as she scrambled to her feet Skane lit a match. In its yellow flare she could see a drift of sand along the attic floor, blown through the open window. They passed down a narrow flight of steps and explored four small bedrooms. The walls were covered with a simple flowered paper, stained with damp and peeling away in rotten strips.

"They took out all the furniture when the house was abandoned, of course," Skane said. In the musty atmosphere of the empty rooms, where every floor had a layer of fine sand and all the timbers of the frame were held in the dead grip of the dune itself, Skane's voice had the dull hollow echo of a grotto. The fuzzy radiance of the match threw their shadows across the farther wall, a pair of giant grotesques.

As they passed on down the main stairs to what had been the ground floor Isabel exclaimed, "Now I know what a diver feels like inside a sunken ship! These stairs—they're built like a ship's companionway—so steep and narrow."

She laughed nervously. "I find it a bit eerie. It's so cold and the air has such a wet feel. I wouldn't be surprised to see an octopus or something else slimy and horrible coming out of a corner." She slipped a hand in his arm and kept close to him as he moved about the rooms, plucking matches from his jacket pocket with his free hand and striking them. In the lowermost cavern, dank and chill as a tomb, Skane rattled the knob of the kitchen door. "You know it's quite right what you said about it being like a sunken ship. That's the way it impressed me before. You feel as if you could walk out of this door straight into Davy Jones's locker."

"Don't!"

"Oh, it's quite all right. Sargent and I opened the door out of curiosity, half expecting to see the corpse of a sailor with his hand on the other knob; but there's a heavy storm door beyond, nailed shut from the outside."

"Ugh! Let's go back, please."

"Let's give it a good look while we're here. See that shelf in the corner. That's where they used to stand their water buckets—you can still see the round mark on the paint. They didn't have kitchen pumps in those days—had to get all their water from a small pond, back there towards the south. Sargent and I found an old puncheon sunk flush with the sand at the edge of the pond, where they used to dip their pails."

He wandered about the lower rooms, striking matches, examining walls and ceilings with an interest that Isabel could not feel. She was aware of a chill horror creeping through her flesh. She moved step for step with him. On the wall their shadows were one.

"Those old chaps didn't leave a thing when they cleared out, did they? Not even a picture on the wall. Natural, of course. When you've lived for years with anything, even a simple object like a stool that you could replace in twenty minutes with an ax and a sharp knife, you wouldn't leave it in a place like this to be buried alive."

At these words Isabel quailed. She tried to force calmness into her voice.

"Do let's go, Greg—now! I'm frightened. It's silly but I actually am.'"

"Eh? Oh, nonsense! There's something I want to show you. Sargent and I found a bit of old newspaper somewhere down here. Where did we chuck it? Quaint thing—a Boston paper with a column headed 'Latest News from the War,' and a long account of the battle of Bull Run, July, 1861."

He stepped away from her to look in a corner, holding the match low, and in that moment it went out. The darkness was intense. It was something wet and solid. Isabel stepped forward and groped uncertainly for the comfort of his touch. It was not there. She stretched out her arms. He had vanished. She listened. There was not a sound. She screamed "Greg!"

"Yes?" he said, quite near at hand, but slightly behind her, not where he had been before. "It's so dark—it's horrible! Why don't you strike another match?"

"I'm sorry, I haven't got any more."

She heard him step towards her and she turned and caught hold of his jacket. She clung to him, shuddering and sobbing, "Take me out! Take me out!"

Skane put an arm about her and they groped their way to the main stairs. She could scarcely breathe. It seemed to her that the walls were closing in.

Under the mass of sand, in the sinister darkness of the house, she seemed to feel the cold clutch of Marina itself, the evil sea-monster with its belly full of wrecks and dead men's bones and still unsatisfied. She was almost fainting when at last they emerged in the fresher air of the attic and saw the shaft of sunlight through the empty window frame. In a few more moments they were outside, regarding the patient ponies and the blue V of sea between the dunes.

Isabel leaned against the curled and rotten shingles of the gable as if she dared not trust her legs. Skane's arm was still about her. The draft from the sea blew cold on her damp forehead. It vexed her to think that in a spasm of claustrophobia she had behaved like a nervous child. The fear had gone, but now there was another sensation running swiftly through her nerves. She turned to Skane instinctively, not moved by fear any more but as if those frantic moments in the darkness had released some other emotion that required his presence close to her. She did not try to think what it was. The face she turned to him was the wondering face of a dreamer absorbed in a vision still obscure but of an immeasurable importance, and whose end she must know.

Skane did not speak. His arms clasped her swiftly and his lips found her mouth. Isabel stood in an attitude of utter submission, with eyes closed and hands at her sides. Skane's lips were hard and fierce. All the repressed hunger of his long monkhood on Marina seemed to find expression in the kisses he wrenched from her trembling mouth. At last he paused. She opened her eyes and met his dark blue gaze. There was no hostility in it now, no smiling cynicism, no cool appraisal, none of the things she had seen and hated in the past; only a need that tortured him, and a demand that was not to be denied. Even had she wished to deny, there was nothing in her experience to enable her to cope with it easily and expertly as Miss Benson might have done; and all her cool integrity of other days, the inheritance of a Presbyterian conscience, the very knowledge of good and evil, were submerged and lost in a quick surge of emotion. Her one conscious thought was that the long frustration of the winter months had led in some mysterious way to this encounter and this moment, and now that it had come to crisis she might find relief.

She was aware of a new and urgent caress, and she closed her eyes.

"Not here," she said faintly. "Not in this awful place."

Skane slipped an arm beneath her knees and carried her slowly up the ravine. The murmur of the sea receded. She felt herself carried up a slope and down another that seemed to fall quite steeply under Skane's feet. She opened her eyes for a moment and saw a small pond in a sandy bowl. It was one of the innumerable and nameless ponds from which the wild ponies drank and where they took shelter from storm. The dunes sloped down to it in an almost perfect funnel like the crater of a small volcano, covered with spire-grass and beach pea. The water was shallow and clear and fringed with reeds, and the margin was pitted by the sharp hoofs of wandering ponies. For a distance of perhaps four yards about the rim of it a thin peat had formed in the course of ages, now covered with short grass and cranberry vines and already showing a hint of green. In one place a gleaming disc in the grass revealed the sunken puncheon of which Skane had spoken. It was the former well of Old Two.

The turf by the pond was soft underfoot and Skane set her down carefully upon it. She did not move. She lay relaxed and quiet in the grass, with her face averted and eyes closed, the attitude of one wearied of struggle and submitting herself to the Fates. There was no further word. Everything had been said in the look that passed between them at the gable of Old Two. The afternoon sun fell hot on the grass where they lay. The sea breeze merely stirred the spire-grass on the crater rim. A diminutive sandpiper, one of the spring arrivals, flitted among the reeds and watched them curiously. Isabel was not conscious of her clothing, or of being unclothed. There came a moment when she felt the sun's warmth on her thighs and then she was caught up in Skane's passion and her own wild longing for oblivion.

An hour passed, or it may have been two. Like a man long parched in a desert Skane drank deeply of the spring he had found, relaxed for a time, and drank again. In the toss and quiver of these ecstasies there was nothing to mark the passage of time. Once in a supreme moment with her head flung back, Isabel opened her eyes and saw framed in the blue circle of sky a lone gull, very white and noble in the sunshine, wheeling slowly and then dipping towards the west. Her eyes closed, and after a time Skane saw tears running down her cheeks.

CHAPTER 24

The long-awaited word came. A prosaic flicker of dots and dashes informed Marina that the *Lord Elgin* would sail for the island in about three weeks' time. Along the island telephone wire the bells rang a carillon from morn to night. McBain drove up to the wireless station in his buggy with a list of stores required for the lifesaving stations and the two lighthouses. Carney and Skane went over the needs of the wireless station, and Isabel was called into their conference regarding food supplies. She was cool and competent, and she relieved them of much two-fingered labor by running off a complete list on the station typewriter. Sargent, on the graveyard watch, had a busy night of it; for in addition to a long recital of provisions from barrels of flour to pounds of tea, and every sort of material from drums of gasoline (for the radio engine) to flasks of mercury (for the lighthouse mirror bearings), there were personal shopping lists from all the island wives addressed to friends on the mainland. All of this had to be transmitted on the three-hundred meter wave, and in the small hours of the night, when there was little other traffic.

The blare of the great electric trumpet going on and on kept Isabel awake; and Matthew, who usually slept profoundly, seemed infected with her restlessness. Once he spoke, but she affected not to hear. Into her sleepless ears, accustomed now to the language of dot and dash, the spark dinned an endless chant of nuts and bolts, of beef and bacon, of kerosene for East Light and wool stockings for Mrs. Nightingale at Number Four; a hardware merchant's nightmare, a provision store's whole inventory and a haberdasher's "Spring Staples" list, all rolled into one unending catalogue.

With unwilling vigilance her mind caught every inflection of Sargent's hand, the falter as he turned a page, the occasional blurred dots as, bored by the whole thing, he made a blunder at the key; the slowly growing hoarseness of the spark, as if it were getting tired as well, although she knew that came from the charring of the brass studs of the whirling, flaming disc. She wondered if Skane were awake. She pictured him turning on that hard cot in his room.

She had tried not to think of Skane in Matthew's presence, not from a sense of guilt so much as a fastidious instinct that demanded it. At meal times and when she chatted with the others in the watch room her manner towards Skane was what it had been ever since the autumn, when she lost her fear of him and talked to him as she talked to Sargent, with the air of a friendly young maiden aunt. And Skane with his quick understanding played his part. They seldom addressed each other directly and when they did their eyes were cool and impersonal. Without conscious plan, without any sort of connivance, they reserved all intimacy for the hours by the hidden pond.

Each fine afternoon Isabel rode forth with one and sometimes two of her companions. Matthew had lost his keenness for riding. He seemed to have put aside all the pleasures that once had been his whole life. He was like a hermit whose habits, simple and innocent, have been shattered with his vow of chastity, and who now seeks penance in a revulsion against joy of any sort. Skane was free every third afternoon in the rotation of watches, but the April weather set a limit on their trysts. When, after rainy delays, they made their way to the hollow at Old Two, Skane was avid and impatient, and she gave herself up to him with the quiet, almost devout air of an odalisque who believes that this, for reasons not of her seeking, has been ordained as a mission in life.

Nevertheless she was not prepared to give him what he so greedily wanted without a firm profession of his love for her. After that first silent yielding she was not so easily compliant. Each time they tied the ponies to the log beside Old Two and walked with arms about each other to the pond, she demanded, not so much with words as with her attitude, another assurance for the sake of her pride. It was the instinct of all women since Eve who refuse to be taken for granted, and Skane, swiftly perceiving, wooed her with every art he knew. It was no pretense. He was genuinely mad about her and it was apparent in his every word and gesture. He lived for these moments when, miles from the station, they could throw their masks aside and slip with words and caresses into Elysium.

For her part Isabel sought in his abject and passionate avowals a fleeting comfort against the pangs of doubt. For the shadows were still there. The feeling of impending crisis that had come upon her with the winter dark was not changed by the discovery that Skane was violently in love with her. At first she had thought it was the answer to everything, and she had yielded body and soul with all the fervor of a woman who sees an answer to the ponderous riddle of existence. But the fears were only subdued, the mystery was still there, brooding over all four of them, and the new light of Skane's passion made the old shadow more somber still. Bewildered, she threw herself into his embraces as if the fault were in herself, and as if it might be purged by some new ardor of her flesh; and afterwards, riding back to the station side by side in the silence of spent lovers or of old companions between whom everything has been said, she avoided his glances and fixed her gaze on the distance where the mast made its thin pencil stroke against the sky. The shallow mirror of the pond, in which she had peered to rearrange her hair, had reflected also the tall form of Skane beside her plucking a reed to put between his teeth, and she had a whimsy that they were phantoms both. The radio mast was reality; and as it drew near, climbing steadily towards the zenith, the raptures by the pool receded and were buried like Old Two itself. The sun was always well down the sky when she dismounted outside the apartment door and Skane rode on to return the ponies.

Once Matthew said to her mildly, "You shouldn't ride so far, my dear."

"Do you mind?" she said quickly with a sidelong glance.

"Oh no, but you seem a bit tuckered sometimes. I'll drop a hint to Skane."

She paused in the bathroom doorway and looked back, regarding him more carefully. Carney sat in the big chair with his pipe. He had been amusing himself with patience and the worn cards were scattered over the table. Did he suspect? There was nothing of suspicion in his calm face, wreathed in smoke and contemplating her with a faint smile on the lips. There was only a friendly solicitude and the touch of profound melancholy that had crept into his features during the past four or five months.

"Please don't," she said. "I'm quite all right, and it's wonderful to be out in the sunshine after so many months indoors." She smiled. "You can feel sorry for the pony if you like." She closed the door and a moment later, over the gush of taps, she inspected her features in the glass. The former pallor of her skin had acquired an amber tint on these sunny rides—"a nice genteel tan" as Skane had told her. It was a healthy tint, and if her mouth was a little drawn her eyes were clear, were even bright. There was only the small fold beneath her eyes to betray the ardors of the afternoon, but of course Matthew could not have noticed that. She was reassured. Nevertheless, she thought, a woman would have guessed. As her fingers closed on the knob of the medicine cabinet she was thankful that the nearest woman, shrewd Mrs. McBain, was well out of range towards the west.

Marina now had come alive. The common seals which lived about the island all through the year had moved into the lagoon with the departure of the ice, and on sunny afternoons they could be seen in herds, lazing on the warm sands of the south bar. A number of big hooded seals had drifted to Marina with the great ice pack, and these hung about the island fishing in the surf. These too came ashore to sleep in the sun, and when disturbed by a passing rider they scrambled with swift ungainly movements into the water, digging their fore flippers into the sand and drawing their sleek hinder parts under them for each forward flop.

But the great change was the return of the birds. Immense flocks of terns communed together on the shores of the lagoon and along the south bar. They filled the air with the white flash of their wings and their incessant harsh *tee-arr tee-arr tee-arr*. It fascinated Isabel to watch them from the south window of her kitchen, hurling themselves into the water like stones, with a bright splash and a plunge, and emerging with small fish. They were jealous of their property rights. A rider venturing near their roosting places was assailed and followed by a living cloud of birds, fluttering, crying, darting to within an inch of his head and soaring up again. In another month, Matthew told her, they would be laying their eggs and only a bold man with a long stick would venture into their rookeries. Yet they were careless creatures, they made no nest, simply scooping a shallow basin in the sand and letting the sun do their hatching for them.

Fox sparrows came in a single flight, paused for a day or two to rest and to sound their music through the grass, and then went on towards the north. So it was with the wild ducks, although some of these remained to nest beside the ponds. Flocks of small beach birds skittered along the sands feeding at the lip of the surf, weaving their course as the water shot up the beach. Sandpipers ran among the marram tufts above the shore. Plover rose and settled in small groups like puffs of smoke in rainy weather. There were other species, small shy things with curious cries and songs. Carney knew them all. They filled him with delight.

"Hark!" he would say with sudden enthusiasm. "Do you hear that wee chap in the grass behind the shed? That's a variety of the Savannah Sparrow. And do you know, Marina's the only nesting place of that variety known to man. Makes you think, doesn't it? Makes you realize how old this heap of sand must be, how long ago it must have been kicked up out of the sea, when a distinct subspecies has evolved. That's what makes me laugh when McBain and the others talk about the island washing away—disappearing in another century or so. They see a big storm in the winter tear a bit of the shore away and they measure everything by that. All that happens is that the sea bites a chunk out of it in one place and chucks it up again somewhere else. McBain and his 'washing away'! Nightingale and that yarn he tells everybody about Marina having been a hundred miles long and forty wide in his great-grandfather's time! I've seen a very good chart of Marina made more than a hundred and twenty years ago, with soundings taken and even the biggest dunes marked and named. By Jingo, it shows the island exactly as it is today, except that in those days you could sail a sloop into the lagoon and today you can't. And what about that sparrow?"

His pleasure in the return of the birds and of the broad strong sunshine seemed to lift some of the melancholy from his spirits. One warm April day he even consented to ride with Isabel and Sargent along the shore of the lagoon towards Number Three. They rode close enough to see Giswell's house looming and shrinking in the mirage and then turned back. For variety they rode part way along the dunes. As they reached the crest of a long ridge with the ponies knee-deep in spire-grass they came upon a little comedy in a group of wild ponies grazing in the shallow green valley beyond. Carney reined up to point them out.

"See the stallion—that's the big dark chap with the very long mane. I can't see him clearly from here—the dazzle on the sand—but I'll venture his flanks are well scarred where he's been fighting for his mares. You see some wonderful scraps when a rival comes along."

"What happens to the stallion colts?" asked Sargent, peering under the shade of his hand.

"He kicks 'em out when they come of age, and they wander off along the island looking for a mate. Like that one—see that lone pony in the ravine just below us? There's a rogue stallion from some other herd unless I'm greatly mistaken."

"Is he going to fight?" Sargent demanded, with interest.

"Not by the way he's working. Probably tried it and got a hearty kicking for his enterprise. Watch him now. See how that little mare has wandered away from the rest—down there. That one. In a few more nibbles she'll be out of the old boy's sight. See? Now watch the young stallion—see him working along the ravine. Now! Now he's slipping up to her—see! See how he's nudging her, nipping her with his teeth—shoving her the way he wants her to go. There! Now they're off together along the ravine. By the time the old chap misses her they'll be a mile away and out of sight."

"She seemed to be quite willing," Isabel observed.

"Oh, yes."

"Rather like people, aren't they?" Sargent said, and laughed. Isabel flushed.

"Shall we go on?" she said in a cold voice. The comedy was closed; but all the way back to the station that casual phrase of Sargent's echoed in her mind.

At the next tryst she was uneasy. When Skane tethered the ponies beside Old Two she asked, "Are you sure it's safe to leave them here? Mightn't they be seen from the north beach? After all there's quite a bit of travel now between Main and the stations down east."

Skane shook his head vigorously. "I've tested it, my dear. When you ride past on the beach you can look through the gap in the dunes for a moment and see the old gable sticking out, but it's just a quick glimpse, and you can't see the spot where we tether the ponies at all. Anyhow it's quite all right. Nobody's going to turn off the hard footing on the beach to ride up this way. Besides, like a good many other places on the island it's supposed to be haunted. The fellow who lived here last—the one who struggled so long with the dune— went off his rocker at last and cut his throat. None of the islanders would go inside as we did, even on a bet."

"I wish you'd told me that before I ventured into that chamber of horrors," Isabel said reproachfully.

"Oh, I'm just not superstitious. But can you see any of the others snooping about here? Giswell or Nightingale or any of those young savages of the lifesaving crew who believe so devoutly in the Fingerless Woman and the Singing Frenchman and the Thirteenth Sailor and all the other spooks and hobgoblins of Marina? My dear girl!"

She shrugged and walked on. There was always something delicious in the sensation of crossing over the dune and coming upon the hidden pond. It seemed so perfect a retreat. The cool green of its turf was balm to the eyes after the fierce glare of the sands and the dazzle on the sea. The still water that reflected their trysts and then erased all trace from its surface was like a tutelary spirit dedicated to their secret. But on this day as they dropped upon the turf Isabel said abruptly, "Sometimes I have a feeling that we're being watched."

"You're a bit queer today," Skane said. "What's the matter?"

He bent his head to kiss her but she turned her face away.

"Give me a cigarette, please. I want to talk, Greg. We can't go on like this—I can't anyway. It's different for you. But I'm still living with Matthew."

"Yes?" He frowned and shot her a quick glance.

"I daresay you've wondered—I ought to tell you that there hasn't been anything intimate between me and Matthew for a long time. Otherwise it would have been horrible."

"Yes." He lit the cigarettes. Isabel sucked in a long whiff of smoke and blew it out. Abruptly she tossed the cigarette into the pool.

"You must know how I feel, Greg. If I hated Matthew, if he were loathsome to me, or cruel, it would be different. But he isn't. He's kind, considerate, he's everything a husband ought to be—except that he's become so utterly distant since the winter began. There are times when he seems fairly happy but most of the time he seems depressed. He's strange. He seems to be miles away. I can't help feeling that soon after the autumn he began to regret the step he'd taken—me, I mean. I've asked him about it; I've said, 'Matthew, is it me?'—but he always puts me off and says it's nothing, that nothing's changed. Well, I know better. Everything's changed. You know how he's given up his walks, his shooting, his visits up and down the island, everything he used to love. His whole life's spoiled. And I know why. It's on account of me. If you only knew how terrible that is to me. It's bad enough to have been loved, and to feel that you're not loved any more; but to feel that you've ruined a man's whole life, and that he won't admit it and there's nothing you can do about it...."

Skane broke in angrily, "I wish you wouldn't go on like that, Isabel. Crying over spilt milk never did anybody any good. The important thing is that you love me now and I love you, I'm simply wild about you, and you know it. You're the only woman who's ever meant anything to me— and you're everything." He attempted to put his arm about her but she leaned away.

"I believe you, Greg. If I didn't I'd feel...soiled. But the fact remains that I'm living with Matthew and giving myself to you, and it's not fair to either of you, and it's not fair to me. That's what I wanted to say."

"What do you propose to do about it?"

She plucked at the grass. A minute passed before she spoke. "I can't leave Matthew, not while he's so kind to me. I owe him so much. I feel it's got to come from him. He's got to tell me that it's all over between us. Meanwhile," she went on slowly, "it seems to me you should do something yourself, Greg." Her tone hardened. "Greg, the boat is coming in a few days. I wish you'd go. Wireless to Hurd that you want leave, and after that go on to some other station. Don't say no, please! Hear me out. It seems the only way out of this frightful tangle. If you'll only go away and let me settle my thoughts a bit! After this boat there won't be another till August. That will give me three or four months to sort myself out."

"And what then, Isabel?"

She faced him. "When I'm certain Matthew doesn't love me any more, that he wants nothing but his old life back again—then, Greg, I'll leave Marina and come to you. That's the only decent thing. It's reasonable at any rate, and we haven't done much reasoning so far." She hesitated a moment. "There's something else, very important to me. I want you to go on leave, see your people, your friends, get the feel of civilized life again after all this time out here—and ask yourself in August if I still mean the same thing to you. I can't help thinking that, well, you'd been here two years or more, away from everyone and everything that a man normally wants; and then I came and you fell in love with me. I've got no illusions about myself, Greg. I'm not at all the sort of woman men go mad about when there are others to be had."

"That's where you're absolutely wrong," Skane said quickly. "I daresay you didn't know, you don't seem to realize even now, that quite apart from looks—and I can dispute with you on that—you've got something very few women have. It can't be described. It isn't anything physical. It's nothing that can be seen or touched or even suspected. I suppose a woman might have that quality and go all her life without knowing it unless some man made love to her and found her marvelous."

"Isn't that what every man tells a woman when he's making love?" she asked, with a sudden smile.

"I'm talking about what a man feels within himself," he answered impatiently, "and I know that here or anywhere I'd still feel the same about you. And that's why I won't leave Marina unless you leave at the same time. Isabel, darling, I'm thinking of your own happiness quite as much as mine. Marina's a tough place for any woman. It's no place at all for a sensitive woman like you, and Carney had no earthly right to bring you here. I knew that from the first. He knows it now. He's tried every way he knows to make you realize that, but he's too generous a soul to come right out and tell you to go. Don't you see that for the sake of all of us there's only one thing for you to do? You spoke of doing the decent thing. The decent thing for both of us is to go to Carney together and face it out, now, before the *Elgin* comes—for as you say, we can't go on like this."

He said this in a rapid eager tone, gesturing with his hand towards the west. Isabel remained in her defensive attitude, half turned away and staring at the pool.

"I still say you should go—and I must wait," she answered stubbornly. "The other day something happened that made me realize we'd been playing a very old and rather sordid little drama, and it hurt me to think that every beastly mind in the world had been laughing at it since time began. If we ran away together we wouldn't have to face it—but poor Matthew would. I can't do that to him. Please say you'll go, and let me stay till August."

"No! My dear girl, what do you take me for, an utter fool?"

She sprang to her feet. "Let's go back to the station. I can't let you make love to me today, Greg. I'm not in the mood." Skane rose and caught her shoulders. He felt her trembling. "Look here, darling, tell me the truth. Are you sure your mind's not made up already? Are you trying to send me away on a vague promise that you know you won't keep, simply because you can't bear to hurt me now, or Carney in August?"

Isabel refused to meet his eyes. The pool blazed at their feet in the downpour of sunshine; and as she turned her head away she saw a shadow falling down the slope and extending swiftly to the water. It was long and grotesque, the shape of a creature neither man nor beast. And there was a sound, a scuffle of sand, a rustle in the spire-grass on the crest of the hollow. They looked up, startled, and saw a pony poised on the rim above their heads, and Sara Giswell in the saddle.

CHAPTER 25

The girl and the pony made a picturesque statue seen thus from below, and against the sun. A brace of wild duck hung limp from the horn of the saddle. The reins were in her left hand and in the crook of her right elbow lay Giswell's old Mauser rifle. She had on a pair of faded blue denim trousers and a mackinaw shirt, and might have been any of the slim young men of the lifesaving station except for the long brown hair about her shoulders and the pout of breasts in the taut shirt. On her feet were a pair of seamen's rubber boots, the usual wear of the island men, with the tops turned out and folded to the ankles. Strapped about one of these was a rusty spur. The dark eyes glittered in her brown young face. She sat erect, looking down upon them with a mixture of triumph and contempt.

"So this is the place! I wondered where it was, after I seen the ponies tied outside Old Two a fortnight back. I crep' to the window an' listened but there wasn't a sound an' I was scar't to go inside..."

Skane cleared his throat. "Look here, Sara, Mrs. Carney and I..."

"Ho, yes! Miz Carney an' you! I seen Miz Carney an' you ridin' up this way every afternoon you could git away. I knowed what you was up to, too, on'y I couldn't find the place." The girl had a theatrical advantage, looking upon them from that height, and they felt curiously small. Skane stood tense and watchful but Isabel was furious. Her eyes met Sara's in a mutual instinctive hate. From that moment Skane was only a spectator. Isabel stepped away from him and clenched her fists. She cried, "How dare you talk to us like that!"

The girl threw back her head and laughed, showing a row of excellent white teeth. "Ho, I dare all right! Don't make no mistake about that! You ain't heard nothin' yit, Miz Carney. Too good for the likes of us, wasn't you? Wouldn't come down to see us people at Three, nor Four, nor East Light, would you?

Wouldn't let your men come, neither, would you? Wouldn't go nowhere but down to the Gov'nor's house, so Greg Skane could play his music for you. Ho yes, very high an' partic'lar, wasn't you? But you wasn't partic'lar with your men! Your husband, he wasn't enough. It had to be all three, an' Greg Skane for special!"

Isabel uttered an outraged gasp and swung away. "Come, Greg!"

"Wait!" Skane said in an odd voice. He had not moved. He was watching Sara with a most careful interest.

"If you think I'm going to stay here listening to that jealous little wildcat."

"I said wait!"

She paused, and Sara laughed triumphantly. "She'll stay all right. She'll listen, too. If she don't, Carney will, an' so will everyone from East Light down to West."

"Do you think, you vicious little fool, that my husband would believe you?"

"He'll hear me anyhow, an' I guess he can add two two's as good as anyone. I knowed there was somethin' queer about you from the day you come to Marina. I said you looked like a witch, with that white face an' those eyes all hollow an' burnin' like, an' showin' your legs to the men in that dress you wore. Ho yes! Pa told me to shut up, but I was right. You're a witch, all right. Carney never looked at a woman till you met him ashore somewheres an' put a spell on him. An' he ain't been the same man since. Vedder, he was smart, he lit out the day you come. But the others, they stayed an' got 'witched like Carney. You've had 'em all under your fingers, all winter, shut up in the station with you, makin' 'em do what you liked. I know. I wasn't born yesterday."

Sara paused for breath. She was working herself up to a fury and already she was shaking and panting with the stress of it. Her young voice was strident and she thrust out her face and spat the words like a bad-tempered child. Isabel was too angry to be concerned about the outcome of this discovery. It was awkward looking up against the sun and since Skane would not move she adopted an attitude of frigid contempt, staring at the reeds across the pool. She stood in a cold rage under the rain of words that fell from Sara's lips, making no effort to reply. And as it turned out, nothing that she could have said would have stung the bitter young creature on the pony more than her silence and apparent indifference.

The girl's voice cracked as she cried out oaths and obscenities that she must have heard from the young lifeboatmen in their hunts among the ponds, in their frequent brawls and during their severe labors on the beach when stores were being carried from the boats. Many were terms that Isabel had never heard, but she could guess their drift. Whole pages of Rabelais were being flung at her head, synonym by synonym, in the dialect of Marina and in the voice of a young girl.

In the midst of this she became aware that Skane was moving slowly up the slope, never taking his eyes from Sara's face, and calling to her softly whenever she paused for breath. "Sara! Sara!" He had exactly the air and movements of a man who approaches a restive horse with a halter clutched behind his back. Isabel looked up then and saw that the rifle lay no longer in the crook of Sara's arm. It was thrown across the saddle, with one brown hand grasping the barrel and the other behind the bolt, and the muzzle pointed down towards the pool.

Isabel was not alarmed. She knew very little of firearms and it was obvious that Sara's rage had reached a point where she was unaware of the rifle and only vaguely aware of Skane. The girl rose in the stirrups as if from this added height she could add force to the stream of vituperation that fell from her yelling mouth. Suddenly she paused. Without shifting that hateful gaze from Isabel she said hoarsely, "Don't come no further, Greg Skane. I know what you're thinkin' an' it ain't a-goin' to do you no good, nor her."

"Sara, don't be a little fool," Skane said, and began to run.

"Stay where you are!" the girl screamed. The pony reared.

The shot made a shocking sound in the hollow and it was followed by a shocking silence. Isabel felt a violent blow as if an invisible fist had struck her side. It staggered her for a moment but she recovered and turned her eyes slowly from Skane to the girl, and to the old seal-rifle falling from Sara's hands and slithering down the slope. She heard her own voice demanding in an amazed tone, "Why are you looking at me like that?"

"My God!" Skane said, and came towards her. Sara was sitting crouched on the pony with her hands spread over her face. Isabel looked down then, and saw a patter of red drops falling like dye from the edge of her scarlet jacket and splashing on her right boot and the sand. A wave of giddiness passed through her but she remained fully conscious, and she was saying in a bewildered voice, "I must sit down," when Skane caught her falling to the turf.

She lay very still while Skane wrenched open her clothes. The bullet had entered the right side near the lowermost rib and passed through her waist at a steep angle, emerging just above the flank. He tore her chemise in ragged strips, and as he tried to stop the gush of blood with hasty wads and bandages he called over his shoulder, "Were those soft-nosed bullets you were using?"

"I don't know."

"Did they have a bright metal jacket and a dark bit at the end?"

"Yes."

"Christ!"

Sara slid from the pony's back and came slowly down to the pool. She stopped some distance away from the prone form on the grass. The storm had gone from her face and there was now a naive and frightened curiosity.

"Is she dead?"

"No, but she's badly hurt. Go and bring our ponies here. You know where they are."

"I didn't do it," she whimpered, like a child whose ball has broken a window. "It was your fault, jumpin' at the pony's head. The gun went off."

"You had your finger on the trigger, didn't you? Go and get the ponies."

Isabel was still conscious when Skane lifted her into the saddle. She uttered a gasp of agony, and Skane gritted his teeth. He adjusted the pads and bandages.

"Come here and steady her while I get on my pony." Sara came reluctantly and held Isabel in a very gingerly way. Her mouth was drawn down in a child's grimace and the tears streamed. She watched Skane's grim face and cried out a babble of questions and entreaties that he did not trouble to answer.

"She ain't a-goin' to die, is she? 'Twasn't my fault. I didn't mean to hurt her, I just meant to call her names. You love her, don't you? What you goin' to tell Carney? You goin' to say I done it? Please, Greg, don't say it was me, I didn't want to do her no real harm an' Pa will take his belt an' whip me terrible. Greg! Oh Greg, I loved you so an' I couldn't bear to see you with her. I know I ain't good enough for you but she ain't neither. Is she hurt real bad?"

Skane rode in close to Isabel's pony and put his arm across her shoulders.

"Now give me those reins."

Sara put them in his left hand, looking up in his face. "What shall I say?" she cried.

"Nothing!"

"Can't I do something to help you?"

"Yes," he said savagely: "get out of my sight!"

He rode off slowly, heading across the island towards the lagoon and picking the way along the ravines where the going was easiest. It was awkward to keep the ponies together and hold Isabel as well. Several times he had to stop and adjust the bandages, and each time he was appalled by the amount of blood that soaked them and dripped down her leg and the pony's flank. Isabel sat dazed and wordless, clinging gallantly to her senses, knowing how difficult it would be for Skane to get her anywhere if she fainted. Fortunately she was riding the staid Lide-Jarge, but even so the pony was made uneasy by the dead-alive burden in the saddle which sat and swayed but did not grip with its knees. Skane had a continual dread that some further alarm, however slight, a sudden stir of wind in the marram, a ball of sea foam blown across the path, a pair of wild duck squattering away from one of the ponds, would cause the nervous beast to toss Isabel off and bolt.

There was good footing on the shore of the lagoon. The hard strand wound like a narrow road between the water and the dunes. The sun was far down towards the sea in the west and now that the sands no longer burned the mirage had dissolved.

Every object along the shore was very sharp and clear. When the wireless station came in sight Isabel's head began to loll.

"Just a bit more, darling," Skane begged. "Only a little way now."

When they turned off the lagoon shore and came up the easy undulating slope towards the station Carney and Sargent were outside, rolling a drum of gasoline to the intake pipe of the engine room. They did not notice the approach of the ponies for some time. Then Sargent exclaimed, Carney began to run first. He came in swift strides over the sand, shouting "My God, what's happened, Skane?" The sunset gave a coppery glint to his beard and hair. Skane did not reply at once but as they drew together he said in a flat voice, "She's been shot." In a profound silence they drew the ponies to the door and carried Isabel to the bedroom.

Carney turned to Sargent. "Get back to your watch," he said. "Phone McBain and tell him what's happened. Then crack off a message to the Department office at Halifax. Say my wife's been seriously injured and the *Elgin* must come at once. Mark it 'D' for urgent, and sign my name. Then see if you can raise the *Elgin*. She's up the coast somewhere."

Isabel swam in a dark sea, rising and falling with the waves. There were moments when she was acutely conscious of the careful hands of the two men as they cut her clothes away, and of the concerned murmur of their voices. She did not feel pain so much as exhaustion and a vast dull protest in her flesh that seemed to have no point of origin. Once she heard very plainly the click of the tin cover of the first-aid kit. Once, in reply to Carney, she heard Skane saying, "Some fool with a rifle I suppose, potting at ducks among the ponds." And again, "No, she didn't seem to know what had happened for a minute. She didn't cry out. She looked at me in a startled sort of way and then I saw the blood."

These interludes were brief. Most of the time she floated in darkness with the sound of a great surf in her ears. She did not hear the faint crunch of McBain's buggy wheels and she did not see Mrs. McBain come storming in, with a coat thrown over her apron and a moth-eaten Lily Langtry hat perched coquettishly on her gray head, crying, "Guns! Guns! Guns! Last year it was Jim Corrie with his arm blown half off, and the year before it was that Shelman child, playing with a loaded twenty-two. When are you going to learn, you dangerous idiots! Where's this poor girl?"

She took charge at once, drove Carney and Skane out of the apartment, shook up the fire in the stove, filled the kettle, and moved into the bedroom with her old carpetbag. For years she had been Marina's oracle in medical matters, a role that she sustained with homely remedies learned in her girlhood in a Nova Scotia fishing village, in the years when she went to sea with McBain and in her years on Marina and with a good deal of plain common sense.

For many hours Isabel lay unconscious, sometimes tossing in delirium, sometimes as still as if dead. There were fantastic dreams. Processions of hideous faces came and went on a bright red screen of whirling molecules. Weird hags that might have stepped out of Grimms' fairy tales sidled up to her, speaking softly, slyly, and suddenly struck her in the face. She was on the beach, fastened, unable to move, with the great ice pack thrusting towards her, the floes heaving, thundering, falling upon her. She was in the *Lord Elgin's* cabin again, feeling that sickening rise and fall of the ship, or being carried to the bathroom to retch. But chiefly she was back in the buried house at Old Two. The scene was repeated again and again, with the actors changing roles. Sometimes when she cried out in that horrible darkness it was Skane's voice she heard. Sometimes it was Matthew's, and when she screamed "Why don't you strike another match?" he answered, just as Skane had done, "I'm sorry, I haven't any more." But sometimes there was another match. She could hear the scrape of it in the dark, and when it flared she saw the face of Skane, dark and smiling in reassurance, or the face of Matthew, very calm and stern.

Once or twice the voice that cried was not her own, and she found the match in her fingers and struck it; and then the face was Matthew's, with a frightened and lost expression in his eyes.

On the second day she swam back to full consciousness, and Mrs. McBain fetched Matthew. "My dear," she said, "here's your husband. You mustn't try to talk to him. I don't know how far down the lung goes but the bullet may have touched it, though you seem to breathe all right. You talk to her, Matthew, while I put the dinner on." Isabel turned her eyes. There was pain now, intense pain, as if a red-hot iron had been thrust into her side and was being twisted without cease or mercy in the wound. She lay drenched in perspiration. She saw Matthew coming slowly to the bedside. He ignored the chair and dropped upon his knees.

"My dear, my dear, if you only knew how I wish to God it had been me."

Her eyes filled but she managed to twist her lips in a smile.

He turned his gaze to the wall and said with an assumed briskness, "You're going to be all right. We're going to take you off to hospital at Halifax. The Department's sent a message ordering O'Dell here at once. We're trying to get him now—so is Halifax. He's pottering about in some of those little harbors towards Canso, setting out buoys that were taken up for the winter, and of course there's no telegraph ashore and his wireless is blanked inside the hills and islands. We'll raise him the moment he sticks his masts outside. Thank God the weather's fair and the glass keeps high."

Mrs. McBain looked in the doorway and saw Isabel close her eyes, "That'll be enough," she said at once. "Don't talk any more. You can sit there with her if you like. You'll have to go out by and by when I change the dressings."

Isabel could hear the coughing of the engine exhaust, and presently the transmitter screamed. She knew Skane's hand at once. He was calling the *Lord Elgin* and she sensed in the long repeated signals the urgency of her lover. She could see his anxious face. And in the long silence that followed she could see him bent towards the tuner panel with his lean fingers on the dials, straining to hear the hoarse burr that was for all of them the voice of The Boat. There seemed to be no answer and she drifted into sleep. When she awoke again Matthew was gone, and Mrs. McBain was saying, "Ah! Now, lamb, before I touch those bandages do try to eat a little soup."

CHAPTER 26

The hours passed. Much of the time now she lay awake and feverish. The pain remained but she had grown familiar with it, and with the patience of women who are born to endure she lay quiet under the torture. She saw the next day's sunrise enter the window and brighten a strip of wall above the bed, and she watched it slowly move and fill the room. Mrs. McBain came in and went at once to draw the blind, but Isabel protested.

"Don't pull it down, Mrs. McBain, please, I love the sunshine. There hasn't been much in my life." Mrs. McBain looked at her curiously.

"You mustn't speak if it hurts, lamb. You haven't been happy on Marina, have you?"

"Yes and no."

"Well, it's not much of a life for a young woman like you that's been used to towns and such."

"It isn't that. But I don't want to talk about it. Where does Matthew sleep?"

Mrs. McBain pointed to the wall, "On the other side, in the cook's old room, so I could bang on the partition if you took a bad turn. Your voice sounds quite strong. You don't feel any bubbling inside or anything like that?"

"No."

"You look bad though, lamb. I suppose it's the shock and of course you lost an awful lot of blood. We're all praying for a calm sea, so McBain can get you off the beach all right, and then you'll have a good run to Halifax. Carney's going off with you, I suppose?"

"Oh no, he mustn't do that."

"I don't see why not."

"After this one there won't be another boat till August. He can't leave Skane and Sargent here to keep watch-and-watch all that time. Besides, he's so worried about the station, the engine and all that. The equipment is so old. He must stay. I won't hear of him leaving."

"You mustn't get excited, lamb. Well, I suppose you've got plenty of friends and relatives ashore."

"I shall be quite all right."

"Um. Well, I must go and get the men's dinner on. Your husband had the long watch last night and he turned in at eight this morning. He'll be up now, I expect. That man never sleeps more than four hours a day, it seems to me. After dinner I'll brush your hair and fix you up nice and he can talk to you. Would you like to see Skane and Sargent for a minute? They've been terrible anxious over you."

"That would be nice."

Mrs. McBain was an exact woman. Skane and Sargent had no more than her minute, standing in the doorway murmuring a few commonplaces and then being shooed off like importunate puppies. Then Matthew came, with a light of relief on his haggard face.

"My dear, Halifax raised the *Elgin* five minutes ago and we've just heard O'Dell's reply. He's heading for Marina at ten knots—should be off Marina tomorrow about the middle of the forenoon. There's a light westerly breeze and not much surf, and McBain thinks that will hold. He's fixed up a wagon with a mattress on top of some loose hay. Tomorrow after breakfast he'll hitch up his steadiest ponies and we'll take you along the north beach to the landing place. You must tell Mrs. McBain what things to pack up for you. I'll get my own duds later on."

Isabel licked her dry lips. "Matthew, will you close the door, please—gently, I don't want to offend Mrs. McBain. There's something I must tell you."

Carney arose and shut the door. He turned, drawing in a deep breath and squaring his shoulders. "Yes, my dear?"

"Please sit down, Matthew. I don't want you to come away with me."

"But I've made arrangements..."

"That doesn't matter. The station's what matters. You can't go off and leave two men to run the thing for so long. Don't argue—please! You must hear what I have to say. I've had a lot of time to think, lying here. My mind's been so muddled ever since I came to Marina, but now it's very clear. I'm going to be all right. I don't think I'm dangerously hurt. It's not even important, really. The important thing, Matthew, is that it offers me a way out of a nightmare. I think you know I've not been happy here. There were times when I was, when everything seemed wonderful, and I think you felt the same. But after the winter came everything changed. It did something to us. As if—as if we were both under a curse of some kind. There were times when I've felt that it was very close to me, that I could put out my hand and touch it, if only I knew what it was. But I don't know and it wasn't to be touched. It was like a darkness that you can sense but you can't feel. It seemed to shut us off from each other, you and me."

"Yes," he said. He was not looking at her. The massive blond head was bowed, the crisp beard against his chest. He sat hunched forward, contemplating his big clasped hands, and she saw that the knuckles were white.

"It's difficult to say this, Matthew. I realize now that I should never have come. It wasn't your fault. It was mine—all mine. I came to you in a moment of hysteria and threw myself at your head; and then I persuaded you to bring me here. That was the ultimate folly. I know that now. It's only brought unhappiness to you, to me—to all of us. I suppose we might have gone on like that, for how long it sickens me to think. Then this happened. It seemed a final judgment on my folly. But now I know it's the best thing that could have happened, for us all. It puts an end to this—this glum little play that we've all been acting here. At least it takes me off the scene and leaves you all as you were before, when you had what you considered the finest kind of life. I've never forgotten what you told me the day we met, that Marina was the only place that had any meaning for you. That's still true, isn't it?"

He remained bowed and silent. Then in a strained voice, almost a whisper:

"Yes."

"Then you'll promise to stay—and let me go?" Another silence; and again a hoarse "Yes." She saw a tear splash on the clenched hands, and her own eyes filled.

"Please leave me now," she said in a broken voice. "And tell Mrs. McBain that I want to be alone for a time."

She wept when he had gone; and in the morning, just before they came to take her away, she worked the wedding ring off her finger and slipped it under the pillow. It seemed the only way to mark the end of their relationship. Matthew would find it there when he returned from the beach, and he would understand.

Clothing the patient was a problem, for every movement was an agony; but this was solved by enclosing her carefully, just as she was, in an eiderdown sleeping bag from McBain's emergency stores. In this, securely buttoned from head to foot, they carried her on a stretcher to the wagon. It was Sargent's watch and she said good-by to him there, with a pale smile, and saw him turning away to hide his emotion. Mrs. McBain sat in the straw beside her, and McBain took the reins himself. They set off slowly over the dunes towards the north beach, with Carney walking on one side of the wagon and Skane on the other, to ease the sway of it as the ponies clambered over the slopes. For all that, it was a painful journey until they came out on the level footing of the beach.

There was a light breeze and the air was cool and fresh. The surf hissed on the shore and seemed at times to sweep about the ponies' feet but it did not sound like a bad sea. She noticed Mrs. McBain and the men glancing at it carefully from time to time. A flock of terns followed the wagon, darting, wheeling, soaring overhead, and filling the air with their outcry. The radio mast stood tall in the April sky, receding, sinking slowly into the dunes. Isabel watched it out of sight.

At the landing place the lifeboat crew were waiting with the station's best surfboat and a special stretcher with slings at both ends for hoisting aboard the ship. The Kahns were there, and the Lermonts had ridden down from Number Two.

"Is that thing safe?" demanded Mrs. McBain, eyeing the stretcher as the men eased the laden sleeping bag into it.

"I made it myself," said McBain rather indignantly. "She'll be strapped in. She can't fall out, even if one sling lets go."

"Well, you look to it sharp before they hoist her up. I won't have the poor girl slung aboard by the heels like a pony, John McBain. Are you all right, lamb?"

"Yes."

"Here's your husband to kiss you good-by."

Matthew's face appeared, bending over her. He looked very stern. His eyes were exactly the color of the spring sky, so different from the dark blue sea-tint of Skane's, and she saw in them now the strange "radio look" that she had so often remarked in all of them, the eyes unseeing and yet regarding things hidden and afar. There were no tears in them, as there were in hers. She felt the crisp hairs of the golden beard against her cheek and then a brief touch of his lips.

"I've written a letter to Hurd," he said in a measured voice. "He'll make all the hospital arrangements and see that you have everything you want."

He paused, and swallowed, looking off to sea. "Good-by, my dear, and God bless you. It's strange...that seems all there is to say." He turned away.

Mrs. McBain fussed about the buttons of the sleeping bag and kissed her.

"Good-by, lamb, and come back to us soon. Your suitcase and things are in the boat." And she added, "Don't cry, you mustn't cry," as if she were not weeping noisily herself.

Then Skane's face, gaunt and impersonal, but with an intimate message in his eyes. She blinked the tears away and said in a small cold voice, "It's good-by, Greg."

"We'll be seeing you," he said. She did not answer. In another moment McBain was saying, "All right, boys, shove off." He stood in the boat clasping the loom of the big steering oar in his seasoned hands. The crew, with Kahn, Lermont, Skane, Carney and the three island women, put their hands on the gunwales and waded out into the surf, thrusting the boat to sea. Isabel, in the boat bottom, could see nothing now but McBain's alert brown face and the sea birds wheeling in the cloudless sky. It was like that other boat journey when she had felt herself so lonely in the grip of the sea. The boat was water-borne now, dancing in the surf, and the crew jumped in and ran out the oars.

"Pull!" snapped McBain. "Lively now!" The rowers pulled violently. A sea ran along the gunwale and poured a thin lip over it. There was a sound of water trickling. Then the short quick chop of the inshore waves subsided. The boat moved up and down on slow glossy swells. McBain looked down and gave Isabel a grin.

"Nothin' to it, Ma'am. Janie's got us a good sea for her prayers."

Nevertheless there was concern in his eyes as they drew alongside the ship and looked up the swaying iron cliff of her side. O'Dell had his forward derrick boom swung out and the cargo hook came down to the boat like a predatory claw. One of the boatmen took the steering oar so that McBain could fasten the stretcher tackles himself. Then, easing one of the control lines through his hands and keeping a fierce eye on the man who held the other, he called, "H'ist away!"

Isabel heard O'Dell's high voice calling "Easy! Easy now!" to his donkey-man. It was done very well, without even a jerk as the stretcher left the boat. She had no fear, indeed despite her pain and weariness she found a twinge of humor in the thing. It was so like Little Eva going up to heaven on a rope from the flies of Acker's. For a time there was nothing in her view but the sky, the cargo hook and its wire, but as the boom swung slowly inboard the *Lord Elgin's* upper works came into sight, and the faces of O'Dell and his mate thrust over the canvas dodger on the bridge. The stretcher was lowered to the forward deck. Without warning Isabel was looking up into the smiling face of a woman.

"Hello," it said.

"Who are you?" said Isabel, astonished.

"Well, for one thing I'm a nurse. That's a bit of luck, isn't it? I was going up the coast to a sick woman at Kedge Rock lighthouse when Captain O'Dell got the order to come out here."

Then O'Dell's face, pale and sardonic, and his cold blue eyes. "Well, young woman, I s'pose you didn't know it was loaded?"

"No."

"They never do. We'll have you snug in a berth in a minute or two. How do you feel?"

"Rather mournful at the moment, I'm afraid."

"You'll be all right. Why didn't Carney come off with you?"

"I didn't want him to."

Captain O'Dell searched her eyes with his appraising stare, and found nothing but a challenge that defeated him. He shrugged and called seamen to carry the stretcher aft.

CHAPTER 27

The hospital was full and busy. Hurd had been unable to get a private room and Isabel found herself in a "semi," separated by a canvas screen from an elderly woman who groaned and fussed and made much trouble for the duty nurse. The nurse intimated to Isabel with whispers and a roll of eyes that old Mrs. Tappett was slowly dying of cancer and making rather a nuisance of herself in the process. It appeared that among other things she objected to drinking the city water. She came from a place in the suburbs where the people had their own wells and she had insisted that her son bring her a supply of water from home. He had driven up to the city with a large carboy of the authentic water and deposited it with the head nurse, who promptly poured it down the nearest sink. Then, carefully sterilized and refilled from a hospital tap, the carboy went up to the old lady's room.

At discreet intervals the nurse on duty whisked the carboy away and brought it back full, intimating that the son had sent up another supply by a friend. Whenever the patient demanded a drink the nurse would pour a glass full of the precious water and hold it to her lips; and Mrs. Tappett would drink with loud clucking sounds and then exclaim to Isabel on the other side of the screen, "Ah, my dear, what a difference! None of that horrid chlorine nor the iron taste off the pipes!"

The nurse would pop her head around the end of the screen with a quick grin and a wink, and Isabel would smile and murmur, "Yes, I'm sure."

With this innocent little farce, and occasional visits from another son, a bovine man of fifty very anxious to get away again, and from a young Anglican parson who believed in good cheer when visiting the sick and burst into the room crying "Hello! Hello! Hello!" like a parrot in holy orders, the long days were enlivened. Isabel's own visitors were of a somewhat different stamp. Hurd came once or twice. He was rather stiff. It was plain that he had not forgiven Miss Jardine for running off as she had. He had sent a wireless to

Carney saying that the wound while serious was not dangerous and that she was recovering nicely. He talked a lot of shop, in which Isabel was only faintly interested, and then mounted his hobbyhorse. Things in the wireless world were changing every day, everything was moving very fast, and he, Hurd, was hard put to keep up with it. Radio was developing new miracles and very soon the telegraphy would be just a petty side show. Broadcasting—now there was something big. Some people were laughing at it but they'd laugh on the other side of their faces before ten years were out, mark his words.

Hurd had started as an operator in what he called "this game." But he had soon got away from pounding brass and into management at the shore end. He spoke of that early experience aboard ship as a millionaire might speak of selling newspapers as a boy. Whenever a happy-go-lucky sea operator came under his notice he could not help thinking, "There but for the grace of God goes Rollo Hurd." He spoke appreciatively of Carney and Skane, but the note of condescension in his voice left no doubt that privately he considered Carney and others who served in such Godforsaken holes a lot of nincompoops. Isabel was glad when he left.

A visit from Miss Benson proved more entertaining. She came in wearing a chic spring ensemble including what must have been the shortest skirt in Halifax and what was known currently as a chase-me-Charlie hat. She put a bag of grapes on the bedside table, and sat on the chair crossing her greatest asset with a slither of taut silk.

"Well, my dear Mrs. Carney—it seems funny not to call you Miss Jardine— this isn't the way I expected to see you again. Shot, Mr. Hurd tells me, what an awful thing. But accidents will happen I always say and there's one thing you'll get a good long rest out of it. A bit of change never did anybody any harm either. That lonely place I mean and having to do all the cooking I mean and all that. By the way I've brought the check for your cooking wages—in my bag somewhere—ah! Here you are, four hundred dollars. It wasn't quite eight months—a day or so—but Hurd told me to make it out for the full amount. It's funny. I can't imagine you cooking for three men. But then I can't imagine you there at all, or being Carney's wife, or anything like that."

Isabel smiled. "Twelve months ago I couldn't have imagined anything like that myself. And now I wonder if any of it's really happened. Marina and Halifax just aren't in the same world. How are you getting along?"

"Oh, very well. It bothered me at first, especially not having you to show me the ropes, but I learned after a bit. I can't chin with the ops quite so much in the secretary's job and you know what a fuss Hurd makes about that anyway. But I get along. Fortunately he's out quite a bit now, making speeches to luncheon clubs and I don't know who all—'The Immeasurable Future of Radio'—and so on. Everybody's going crazy about this new broadcasting fad and they drink up everything Hurd or anybody else has to say about it. Must be deadly dull if he makes speeches the way he dictates letters. 'Dear Sir ...ahhh ... referring...ahhh...to your...ahhh...letter of...ahhh...the twenty-eighth ult...ahh.'"

It was a good imitation of Hurd in the throes of composition and Isabel laughed heartily. Miss Benson went on, "But the whole radio business is a bore if you ask me—barring the ops of course. All those fiddly things with crackjaw names to be sent to ships and shore stations as spare parts, or for repairs, or what-have-you. You can't find half of them in the dictionary, even. As for this new fad, these broadcast receiving sets, you sit hunched over a lot of tubes and coils and batteries and things with a pair of phones jammed over your hair, listening to somebody talking down in a barrel in Schenectady, New York, and saying 'Double-you Gee Why' in a slow solemn voice as if it was God pronouncing judgment on a wicked world. You just can't see a future in anything like that."

She rattled on for half an hour and then picked up her gloves and handbag.

"Well, so long, dear. I'll run out and see you when I can, but you mustn't expect me too often. You know how it is."

"Yes, I know how it is."

Miss Benson patted her marcelled blond coiffure and arranged her hat. She walked towards the door and turned. "You know you look changed."

"So would you if you'd got in front of a gun at the wrong moment."

"Oh no, I don't mean that. Perhaps it's because you haven't got your glasses on. Don't you wear them any more?"

"Never. I don't think I ever needed them much. Anyhow, once I got away from staring at letters and columns of figures all day long my eyes improved." Miss Benson gave her a shrewd glance. "You look better, anyway. It isn't just the glasses. There's something about you—I don't know how to put it. I used to think you looked a prude. Now you don't."

"You forget I've been married since I saw you last."

"Well, it isn't just that, either. If I was a man I'd say you looked interesting. That's not exactly the word I want but you know what I mean. Most of the married women I know just look married."

And away she went, a hat and a pair of legs, looking very unmarried indeed.

One day the house surgeon brought in a man with a bristle of iron-gray hair and the face of a benevolent bulldog.

"Mrs. Carney, this is Doctor McGrath, who did your operation, remember?"

"Oh, yes."

The bulldog smiled, and his eyes were lively. "How are you getting along?"

"Very well, I'm told. Doctor McGrath, you wouldn't tell me that morning how much I'd been damaged. Will you tell me now?"

"Of course. You're a very lucky young woman. A bit more to the center, or a bit higher, say, and you'd have come off that island in a box. As it was the bullet knocked some nasty splinters off your lower rib and then tore its way out without hitting anything important. Missed the liver very neatly, and I still can't see why it didn't tear the kidney to pieces. That was a dumdum bullet of some sort. You seem to play rough games out there. Fortunately it only mushroomed a little before it emerged. As it is, you'll have an interesting dimple in the top of your hip, something very few women can boast."

She laughed. "When shall I be able to leave?"

"Ah!" the house surgeon said. "There! We treat 'em nicely, we give 'em all the comforts of home, we even provide 'em with dimples, and what's the first question they ask? When can we go home! That's gratitude. That's women for you."

"Not long," Doctor McGrath said. "You picked a good time for your adventure. We know a lot more about gunshot wounds now than we did before the war. Say three more weeks if you behave yourself nicely. After that you'll have to go easy for a bit—no housework that involves much stooping, and so on. You've got a good healthy system and in two months' time you'll be as good as new. What's life like on Marina? Lots of excitement, all those shipwrecks, eh? But a bit tough, I should say."

"It's not as comfortable as this," she said. He nodded, peered around the screen at poor Mrs. Tappett, glanced at the carboy, chuckled—it was one of the stock jokes of the hospital—and went out.

The days in bed were interminable. It was an immense relief when she was allowed to get up and on fine days to spend several hours in an armchair on the ground-floor veranda. The May sunshine fell warmly on the stretch of lawn, where a troop of fat robins hopped after worms every morning and again late in the afternoon. The forsythia clumps about the hospital grounds were a yellow blaze but none of the other shrubs were in blossom, some were not even in full leaf, and the elm and ash trees along the driveway were still winter-bare. Along the street at the foot of the grounds, where the signs said HOSPITAL ZONE QUIET, an endless swarm of motorcars scuttled up and down. They observed the signs but at each end of the zone they broke into raucous sound, a medley of toots, whistles, squawks and bugle notes that reminded Isabel oddly of Marina. For a time she wondered why, and then she smiled. It was like the phones on a busy night.

May weather is a capricious thing in Nova Scotia, and these warm lazy morning and afternoon hours on the veranda were invaded frequently by fog, rolling up from the harbor in dank folds and driving everyone indoors; and there were days when the wind came out of the east and shot volleys of rain against the windows, when the bare trees along the driveway shone stark and black, and the traffic hissed along the roadway like an angry snake. Then most of the convalescents preferred to doze in bed and only the most restless went down to the reading room and lounge. Isabel was one of the restless. The idiosyncrasies of Mrs. Tappett had begun to get on her nerves. The water joke had become a bore; and when the house surgeon came in with his invariable "Well, and how's our pet gunshot wound today?" she felt that she could yell. She felt perfectly well, two of Doctor McGrath's weeks had passed and she could not see why she must drag out the hours of another.

She was reading by the fire in the lounge on a rainy afternoon when one of the nurses put her head in the doorway and said cheerfully, "Mrs. Carney? There's such a nice-looking young man to see you. A sailor. Shall I send him in?"

Isabel started violently. For a moment she could not speak. She got out of the chair and stood facing the door with her fingertips biting into the palms.

"No...Yes, send him in."

The nurse stepped back and beckoned to someone along the hall; and as he turned into the doorway Isabel breathed out a long sigh. It was Sargent. "Jim!" she said shakily, and relaxed in the chair. "What on earth are you doing here?"

He was wearing the sea uniform he had kept so carefully on Marina, with its bright merchant-navy buttons and the entwined gold sleeve braid. A wet blue raincoat was slung over his arm and he carried his cap in his hand. When she put out her hand he shook it in a gingerly way as if he were afraid she might fall to pieces at a single hearty touch.

"Well," he explained with a pleased look, "I got off Marina a fortnight ago. O'Dell was in quite a wax because he'd had to drop everything to take you off, and then turn round inside a month to make the regular trip out to Marina with supplies and mail. None too soon, I may say. The cupboards were getting pretty bare. Anyhow as you know my year was up and Hurd sent out a new chap, Battleford, to take my place. Three or four of the island people came off at the same time I did. One of 'em—you'd never guess—was Sara Giswell."

"Oh?"

"Ma Giswell's been trying to persuade her to go ashore and get some schooling for the past four years, but you know how potty Sara was about Skane. Well, apparently she's got over it at last. Going to live with Ma Giswell's people at Port Bickerton. So away we came, but not direct to Halifax. O'Dell wanted to go right on with his buoy work and he set us ashore at Canso and washed his hands of us. I had orders to join a tanker at North Sydney—Hurd had promised to get me a ship, you know—and I was in a bit of a stew because Carney and Skane had given me letters for you, with strict instructions to put them in your own hands. However I found the tanker was going to call at Halifax on her way south, so I carried 'em on to North Sydney. Hence the delay."

He fished in an inner pocket of his blue jacket and handed over the letters. Isabel put them in her lap without a glance but her hand shook.

"How are they—Matthew and Skane?"

"Oh, all right. We were all pretty blue after O'Dell took you off, and you can imagine the relief when we got Hurd's message saying you'd just come away from the operating room and everything was okay. It was pretty dull after that. The winter was nothing to it. Of course Carney and Skane are both the silent sort, and I was just counting the days. When I got aboard the *Elgin* I dropped on my knees and kissed the deck. Phew! What a relief! Give me life at sea."

"And now you're off to sea?"

"Yes, we dropped in here for stores and tomorrow we pullout for Talara."

"What a lovely name! Where's that?"

"It's not a very lovely place, I guess. It's in Peru. Oil, you know. It's a regular run. Panama Canal each way. The fellows aboard find it monotonous but it sounds like a pleasure cruise to me. And of course the grub and everything else aboard tankers are A-1 compared with the tramps and colliers I was in before. It's a bit quaint to be piping away with a half-kilowatt set again, after that roaring thing at Marina. The whole transmitter's stowed in a cabinet no bigger than your kitchen cupboard, and the spark's shut away behind thick doors—like a cat meowing in an icebox. But what a luxury to be able to throw a switch and let some bloke down in the engine room worry about the juice! The only gas engines I ever want to hear again are the kind they put in taxicabs."

His laugh was infectious and Isabel laughed with him. He chatted for another ten minutes and then went off with quick strides, with his cap cocked over one ear, with his gold braid gleaming in the corridor, like a new kind of Pizarro and as if Peru were just around the corner of Tower Road.

She opened Matthew's letter at once. The envelope was addressed in his huge scrawl. "Mrs. Isabel Carney. Personal. Care J. Sargent Esq." The letter read:

MY DEAR GIRL,

Sargent leaves tomorrow and I'm writing this in the night watch as it seems a good chance to get a letter off to you direct. We're getting along very well, as Sargent will tell you. Nightingale has sent down his oldest boy, eighteen, to do the cooking for us, and the new operator will be coming ashore in the first boat. It's always pleasant when a new man comes. You get the latest shop talk and of course a fresh lot of yarns.

I can't tell you how relieved we all were when we learned that you'd come through all right. Hurd says it's only a matter of time and rest and you are getting the best of care. Thank God for all that.

Now, my dear, I want to tell you what I couldn't find words for the day you went away. I knew from the first that you could never be happy with me on Marina, for several reasons, some of which you know. In a fit of selfishness at Halifax I forgot them all, even the one that was sharpest in my mind. I suppose we were both a bit delirious in those days but I think we both realized our mistake soon after we came to the island. You tried to make the best of it and I shall always be grateful for the joy you gave me then. But by the time winter came I knew much more than you what a frightful mistake it was. There didn't seem to be any way out of it. I felt like a man walking over a cliff and dragging someone else with me.

Then came your accident, a most unexpected and terrible turn in the affair. You can guess how I felt, thinking that I'd brought you here to die in such a way. And you must know how I felt when you rallied and I knew you had a chance to live. For a time I didn't realize the full meaning of it, but the moment you asked me to close the door on Mrs. McBain I knew. And I knew it was the only thing to do, for your sake and my own.

All this seems a maundering sort of way to tell you what is on my mind. You were always a direct sort of person and I know you're too sensible not to agree with what I have to say. It's simply this. As you know we were never married in the legal sense and you are free to live your own life as you choose. Live it then, my dear, and try to forget this sorry episode. You are young still and the world can be a very charming place. For my part the world is here. I shall never leave the island again. I have written a letter to my bankers, the Bank of Nova Scotia in Hollis Street, making over to Isabel Jardine the sum now lying to my credit there. It's something between eight and nine thousand dollars and will give you a good anchor to windward if you should ever be in need.

Do take it, my dear girl, for I won't need money anymore. Even if I did there's my pay, and I'm good for a long run yet. Try to think kindly of me. If I took advantage of your moment of weakness in Halifax it was because I was weak myself, catching at a kind of happiness that was new and wonderful to me. That I shall never forget. And now there seems nothing more to write but what I said to you on the beach as you left. Good-by my dear and God bless you and keep you always.

Yours sincerely,
MATTHEW CARNEY

The nurse came in. "Why, Mrs. Carney, you're crying! Was it that young man? And he looked so nice!"

"I'm quite all right."

A searching stare. "You don't look all right. You're as white as a ghost. I shouldn't have let him in. It isn't a regular visiting day but the convalescents are allowed visitors in the lounge in the afternoon and I didn't think...Hadn't you better go to bed? You can get up again tomorrow."

"Oh no, I'm quite well," Isabel protested.

But Nurse Thompson, obsessed with that fear of authority, that awe of the doctors, that abject worship of the rules which is the most tiresome characteristic of hospital attendants, would hear no argument. To bed Isabel went, clutching her letters and her self-command in the same forlorn fists. When Doctor Pelly came in with his fatuous cry she pretended to be asleep.

It was three days before she permitted herself to open the letter from Skane. It was written on the blue back of a long Press message form, and in the beautiful draftsman's script that flowed from Skane's hand as naturally as his dots and dashes and his music.

MY DARLING,

Sargent's off tomorrow and he's to put this in your hands himself. I don't know what they do with patients' mail in hospital but I have a vision of some snuffy female creature in a starched cap slitting the envelopes and reading everything aloud to you and anybody else who may be passing. What wonderful news that you weren't dangerously hurt. We were all smiles for days. Mrs. McBain has kept the telephone ringing every day since you went away and says everyone's been anxious about you from the Kahns right down east to Jude Shelman and his wife. Altogether it's been the greatest excitement on Marina since a schooner loaded with rum struck on the east bar and all the islanders went down with D.T.'s for a month.

Seriously, though, we were all terribly worried and for me it was hell. I'd tried in those afternoons by the pond to tell you what you meant to me but it wasn't till we were making that ghastly journey back to the station that I really knew, myself. I won't inflict it on you here. When spoken, love is so very fresh and original; you feel that nobody ever said these things before. But when written (judging from the books one reads) it's all so dismally trite and a lot of it looks damned silly. Yet actually those are the things one says and finds so marvelous. The moral is that you should speak of love but never write about it. Anyhow, I refuse to make love to you on paper, and this is chiefly to inform you that I've written to Hurd reminding him that I've been here nearly three years and that he must send a man to relieve me when O'Dell comes again in August. Then for a good long leave! You'll have left the hospital long before that, of course, so please keep Hurd informed of your whereabouts. When I get to Halifax I'll stop in the office long enough to pick up your address, and then my very dear I shall come to you with a D prefix demanding absolute priority.

All my love,
GREG

P.S. It's impossible to make plans until I see you. Hurd would give me a transfer to almost any station I wish. There are some snug ones up the Gulf and on the Great Lakes, in or near towns where we could live a civilized life and be completely happy. Or do you want to get away from the whole thing? I could quit pounding brass and go in for something else, anywhere you like. What about the West Coast— Vancouver, say?

Isabel read it through several times. And she walked over to the lounge fireplace, tore the sheet to small blue scraps and dropped them into the flames.

CHAPTER 28

Kingsbridge had sprung up about a crossroads and a river ferry in the time of William the Fourth; and in the course of several generations it had gathered a population of about five hundred, two churches, a large brick school, a hotel, a movie theater and a dozen shops. It called itself a town but in reality it was simply an overgrown village, with its shops and public buildings clustered about "The Corner" and its homes set well apart along the roads for a mile in each direction. It was the center of a farming district and a good many of the townsfolk were truck gardeners themselves. Apples were the chief crop. On all sides as far as the eye could reach the orchards marched in neat companies and battalions over the floor of the valley and into the lower slope of the hills.

Along the green floor the Annapolis River wound sluggishly between steep red clay banks as if a vast puncheon of sherry were leaking somewhere in the hills. The main valley highway, which was also the town's Main Street, dipped a little to the south past the Baptist church and leaped over this wine-stream on a black iron bridge. With the passage of time and fat crops a number of well-to-do farmers had moved into the town and built substantial white clapboard houses with deep verandas and red or green doors and window frames and shutters. There were trim lawns and gardens and shady maples and chestnuts. Main Street itself was lined with huge old elms that overhung the sidewalks and the road, and there was a constant battle between the residents and the telephone company about the mutilation of these trees in the name of progress.

In winter Kingsbridge went into hibernation like the bears on the mountainside. The townsfolk stayed close to their comfortable homes, stoking fires and stoves and furnaces with chunks of hardwood cut on the wooded sides of the valley. Those who owned motorcars stored them away in a shed when the fall rains turned the valley roads to red mud, and there they remained, jacked up on blocks to save strain on the tires, until the following April, when the frost had come out of the roads and the spring mud had begun to dry.

In summer there was a lot of travel through the town, and the dining room of the Trilby Hotel rang with the voices of American motorists on their way to the shrine of Evangeline at Grand Pre. Otherwise Kingsbridge was rather quiet all through the week, even in summer, except on Saturdays. It was a Saturday night town. On Saturdays when the farmers and their wives and families came in to shop and gossip and see the latest Western movie, Kingsbridge became another place altogether. Then the town's back yards and lanes were crammed with parked buggies and wagons and tethered horses, and Main Street itself was lined with the carefully polished cars of the new era. The shops were thronged, the Empire Theater was packed to the doors, and groups of girls and youths arrayed in their best mail-order finery strolled up and down the sidewalks under the elms. At eleven o'clock the crowd thinned away and vanished, and only the horse-droppings in the lanes and the scatter of gum wrappers and peanut shells outside the Empire remained to inform the Sunday morning churchgoers that another week's frivolity had come and gone.

Apart from the summer invasion of American tourists, whose cars stirred up clouds of red dust all along the valley from June to September, the chief traffic in and out of Kingsbridge was horse-drawn. Even the town's own motorists seldom drove farther than the next town to the east or west. If you wanted to go beyond that you went down to the small gray wooden railway station where Jim Farris, the agent, looked after your ticket and baggage; and you stood on the worn plank platform regarding the shining rails that led the eye and the mind towards the distant wonders of the world.

When Isabel got off the "up" train in the bright May sunshine everything looked exactly as it had eight years before, when she had cast off the career of a country school ma'am at the age of twenty-two and set out for the city a hundred miles away. Here was the station with its small freight shed, the red water tank and the big wooden warehouse of the fruit company, all set apart in the field outside the town; here were the rails, the cinders the very knots in the platform looked the same; and a few hundred yards away the familiar roofs and spires of Kingsbridge rose out of the surrounding orchards and the massive elms like half-tide rocks in an ocean of living green.

She had never lived in Kingsbridge but she knew it very well. It was the magic place of her childhood, to which her father and mother had taken her in the small riding-wagon every Saturday afternoon. She had grown up with a clear impression that the town was a center of civilization holding everything the heart could desire, and if she could have got a post in the Kingsbridge school she might have been there still. Unfortunately Kingsbridge folk had a profound faith in outside talent for the teaching of their offspring—except of course when the daughter of a leading merchant wanted a post at home—and anyone like the Jardine girl, herself a product of the small school at Scotch Springs, and with no more than a year's training at Normal School, had no chance at all.

Scotch Springs was one of the poorer hamlets of the countryside. It lay at the edge of the valley where the rich red soil gave place to coarse sands and gravels washed down from the rugged slopes of North Mountain. Its fields were stony, its orchards had a scrawny look. The farmhouses were kept in repair but seldom painted. A little group of Scots had settled there long after the good land in the valley had been taken up, and they had clung stubbornly to that grudging soil on the edge of the hills until the third generation. Then the young men began to drift away to the States and the Canadian West. There was a saying in Kingsbridge that the only worthwhile stuff they raised for home consumption in Scotch Springs was a fine tall crop of girls, and there was a good deal of truth in it.

Eight years is not a long time in the life of a country town in Nova Scotia but Isabel's absence included four years of war and nearly three of a post-war boom that had changed everything. In a town like Kingsbridge where the Victorian age had crept on undisturbed well into the twentieth century the impact of all this was immense. The scene that looked so familiar as she stepped off the train was an illusion. The first symptom of change was right at the station, where in place of the old Democrat wagon belonging to the Trilby Hotel which used to meet all the trains she found three shining cars, and three alert young men wearing war veterans' badges crying "Taxi, lady?" The second was at the rambling pine clapboard hotel, where she registered under her own name. It was in new hands, some of the rooms had private baths, the name had been changed to Boston House, and for the further attraction of American tourists a large Stars and Stripes waved slowly from a staff over the entrance.

The tourist season was not yet in full swing and she was given a very good room and bath facing upon an apple orchard at the side of the house. The trees were in full leaf and the buds were fat; in another week or two the whole valley would burst into blossom. The sun fell warm on the town and the air was quiet, indeed it was almost uncanny after the bustle of postwar Halifax and the eternal crash of surf on Marina.

As she unpacked she took stock of her resources. The trousseau she had bought so hastily on the way to Marina was almost intact. Mrs. McBain had put in everything with care. In Halifax she had cashed the four-hundred-dollar check for her "cooking wages." The hospital had refused to accept any money from her, saying that Mr. Hurd's office was taking care of all that, and she had not argued the point. She had not gone near Carney's bankers in Hollis Street. She had not even gone to see Hurd. All that was out of her life.

She found a small windfall in the second of her suitcases. Tucked away among the carefully folded underwear was a check for seventy dollars—the month's salary that Hurd had sent her by Carney on that hectic day of their departure for the island. With it was the wedding license. In the long months gone by she had forgotten both. There was something else. In the very bottom of the suitcase lay that Christmas gift of Skane's, the photograph of himself and Carney with the figurehead. She took it up and examined it curiously, seeing herself in Clélie's place between the two men, with Skane's face turned to hers in a whimsical smile and Matthew squinting against the sun. Skane had given it to her long before that revealing adventure of Old Two but she wondered now, seeing how perfectly the photograph set forth the living tableau from which she had fled, if Skane had known what must come of the silent little drama in the wireless station. She studied it profoundly for a time and then thrust the small lifebuoy frame away under the clothes in the suitcase. No more! It had never happened! A dream, everything, including the desk in Hurd's office and the room at Mrs. Paradee's. She told herself that she had never left the valley, and that now she had merely ventured into Kingsbridge looking for a job.

In prewar days the ideal of almost every girl in Scotch Springs was to teach school, but failing that the great thing was a job behind the counter of one of the Kingsbridge shops. There you saw life, you got money, a stuff seldom seen on the farm, and because of the money you were able to dress exactly like those languid creatures in the mail-order catalogues. This circumstance attracted beaux and in Kingsbridge you had a choice from all the country-side. The marriage rate among the shopgirls of Kingsbridge was very high, and for that reason there were frequent "vacancies." If you were young and strong and came of honest parents (and if you were willing to work for eight dollars a week) you got a chance to fill a vacancy, and in the next issue of the *Kingsbridge Courier* your parents could read with pride that Miss Maisie McCutcheon of Scotch Springs had "accepted a position" at Carson & Goble's Emporium. In Kingsbridge you could get board and lodging for five dollars a week (which you considered outrageous) and that left you more than a hundred and fifty dollars a year for clothes and amusement. And if you looked well in your clothes there were always young men eager to see that your amusement cost you nothing. It was marvelous.

Isabel walked along the street to the bank and deposited three hundred dollars and the seventy-dollar check. It was a very small anchor to windward but at least it was her own, and in Kingsbridge it would enable her to weather quite a storm. She made some discreet inquiries at the bank regarding "vacancies" and she walked up one side of Main Street and down the other, looking in the shops. There was not a single "Girl Wanted" sign. At the hotel she picked up a three-day-old copy of the *Courier* and found in the classified column a small advertisement for female help, with the blunt command "Apply Bon Ton." This was something new, a hat shop she supposed, but on application she found it to be a small restaurant off Main Street near the bridge, catering to farmers and other transient visitors who did not want to go to the hotel. It was not the sort of job she wanted but she went inside and inquired. A fresh-faced girl, obviously from an outlying farm and obviously delighted to be here, informed her at once that the position was filled. "I've got it," she said, and smiled.

"Do you happen to know if there are any other jobs likely to be open soon—girls getting married or anything like that?"

"Well," the girl said, "there are two girls getting married, one at old Markham's, the hardware merchant's, and the other in Olney's Dry Goods; but they're planning to keep their jobs. They're marrying town boys who've been out of work ever since they got back from the war."

"I see," Isabel walked out. Evidently the times and manners had changed a good deal since she went away to the city. In 1913 young men did not marry unless they had a farm or a good job. As for the girls, any girl who continued to work in a shop after marriage was regarded as an unfortunate. The phrase "She's keeping on with her job," went about the town and countryside and everybody condemned her for the poor little fool who had tied herself to that no-account fellow So-and-so.

But now that she had taken a careful look at the town Isabel realized that the Kingsbridge she had known had vanished. The war and the huge demand for foodstuffs of every sort had driven farm values into the sky and produced a flood of money beyond anybody's dreams in the frugal days of '13. The demand and the prices were still high. For almost seven years the valley had basked in this golden sunshine and there seemed no end to it. Shops were changing hands, farms were changing hands, everybody seemed to be on the move and prosperous except the young men home from the war, who hung about the Great War Veterans' rooms over Kerrigan's barbershop, talking of battles and beer.

Most of the veterans appeared to be farm boys and when Isabel asked the hotel manager why so many appeared to be out of work he simply shrugged and whistled the air of "How Ya Gonna Keep 'Em Down on the Farm Now That They've Seen Paree?" It seemed very strange. She wondered at all this outward prosperity when there were so many young men with nothing to do. Her acquaintances in Kingsbridge in '13 were young men and girls from Scotch Springs who had gone to work in the town. She inquired in the post office for them and found that everyone had disappeared. The girls had married and gone away. Some of the youths had been killed in the war; and the rest, unwilling to return to the prewar monotony of Scotch Springs, had taken their discharge money and passed on to Ontario or the West, or had crossed over the border towards the humming cities of the States.

Isabel had accepted the changes in city life without concern. In wartime Halifax was a city of strangers and a constant shift of faces was the normal thing. Even when it was shattered by the great disaster of '17 she had looked upon it as a natural result of a great war in which the port was of immense strategic importance. But it had not occurred to her that the war could so profoundly affect the life of the countryside. What was going on in her valley was happening all over the United States and Canada. It was as if some mighty hand had seized the land and given it a shake, so that all the human contents changed places, trades, amusements and ambitions. Kingsbridge looked the same but all the faces were strange and most of the old ways were as dead as William the Fourth. She thought of Matthew Carney. He had felt like "Rip Van What's-his-name" because he had come from ten lonely years on Marina and found every city a madhouse. She could understand that. But it was a shock to come back to the valley after eight years and find nothing familiar in what she had considered a scene and a way of life as fixed and eternal as the stars.

She walked back to the hotel thoughtfully. She was paying three dollars a day for her room and meals. This was the pre-tourist-season rate. In another three weeks the rate would jump to five. She could not afford anything like that. She had dinner and spent the evening reading in her room. When she put out the light and ran up the blind she saw the leaves of the apple trees gleaming faintly in the starlight. The night was warm and through the open window came a familiar smell of plowland, of fresh grass and the massed foliage of the orchard. The town's lights were out. In the darkness nothing moved. There was one word for it—peace. Whatever else had changed, this remained, the massive calm of the land itself, gravid, expectant, waiting to put forth blossom and fruit as it had waited every May since the first hopeful settler cleared a patch in the forest and planted seed. This is it, surely, she told herself. This is what I've wanted all this time. I was a fool to have left it, ever.

CHAPTER 29

Old Mr. Markham, the proprietor of Markham's Hardware Store, was chairman of the Kingsbridge school board. He was sitting in a cane chair on his veranda when Isabel came up the walk. It was a fine evening in midweek, and in the twilight stillness she could hear through the open door a faint rattle of dishes being put away. He made no attempt to arise when she came up the veranda steps, nor when she stood before him stating her errand. He was seventy-six, a tall man with neatly brushed gray hair, an aquiline nose and the eyes of a tired but watchful hawk. He motioned her to a chair.

"Jardine—You wouldn't be one of the Jardines from Scotch Springs?"

"Yes."

"Thought they were all dead or gone."

"I daresay they are, Mr. Markham. At least, my own parents are dead, and I've been away for the past eight years, working in Halifax."

"Schoolteaching?"

"No, I was a secretary in a city office."

He lifted his bushy gray brows. "Oh? What in thunder did you come back for?"

She ventured a nervous smile. "I wanted to live in Kingsbridge. I'd hoped to find a job in one of the shops or perhaps the bank or the post office, but there don't seem to be any vacancies. So I thought of my teaching experience, and somebody told me to see you."

"No vacancies there either." He pursed his thin lips. "Staff's fully engaged for next term. Might be something in one of the outside sections, come September. What's your experience?"

"I taught my home school at Scotch Springs two years, and I taught one term at Appleton." Both were poor sections. The most she had been paid was three hundred and sixty dollars for the term at Appleton. She could see what Mr. Markham was thinking.

"The money's not important so long as I've enough to live on," she said.

His eyes flicked over the smart city clothes. "The pay's a bit better in the back sections than it used to be, but I don't think you could live on what you'd get there, even now. Seems strange, giving up a good job in the city for something like that. Most girls head the other way."

"Yes, I know. I did myself. But I got tired of it."

"Married, by any chance?" He was trying to see the third finger on her left hand. She turned the hand casually.

"No."

"How old are you?"

"Thirty."

"Um. Good sensible age. Healthy?"

"Very." She did not know whether to be amused or annoyed. Mr. Markham was the shrewdest as well as the oldest merchant in Kingsbridge and he had made money in everything from hardware to real estate. He was inspecting her now as if she were a horse for sale.

"Supposing now," he announced, shutting one eye and staring at her keenly with the other, "supposing now I got you something—a school in one of the back districts say—how do I know you won't get tired of that and go off to the city and leave the trustees in the lurch? Girls have done that before."

"I told you I'd come back to stay," she said with spirit. "I meant it, Mr. Markham."

"Um. Suppose you can't get a job?"

"I've got some money in the bank here, enough to keep me several months. I intend to stay as long as it lasts. Surely something will turn up."

"Determined young woman, ain't you? Got a letter from your city employer?"

"No, but I can get one. Or I can give you his address and you can inquire yourself, if you'd like."

Again the squinted eye. "Would you prefer me to do that?"

"No," she said frankly. "Besides, I don't see what that's got to do with a job teaching school in the valley."

"Ah! Quite right. What sort of things did your city firm deal in?"

"Wireless telegraph apparatus," she said in a diffident voice.

"Electrical stuff, eh?"

"Yes, and parts for gasoline engines, and rope and wire rigging, lubricating oils, paints, provisions, all sorts of tools—a long list of things, everything from pumps to stationery."

"Ha! Well! And you were raised on a farm. Know a Baldwin apple from a Gravenstein?"

"Of course."

"Horses? Cattle? Fertilizers?"

"I know something about them, yes. But I don't see..."

"And of course you've done a lot of typing and shorthand and all that. Who looked after the office accounts?"

"I did. But you understand there wasn't much to that. The accounting was mostly done at the head office. Ours was just a port branch."

"Um."

Mr. Markham leaned back in the tall wicker chair. His eyes were closed. His fingers played a little jig on the chair arms. For two minutes he said nothing. Once or twice his eyes opened, shot her a quick glance and closed again. Isabel sat erect, with her hands in her lap. She was puzzled by this odd catechism and she had a suspicion that the old hawk in the chair had been indulging his curiosity at her expense. She wished now that she had got up and left when he uttered that blunt "No vacancies there either."

"Those Jardines," he said abruptly, without opening his eyes. "Good stock. Scotch. Proud lot. Hardworking. Honest. Moody, though. Minds up in the clouds half the time. Give the shirt off their backs for a whim. All of 'em gone now. Sad."

The wrinkled eyelids lifted. His slate-gray eyes had a look of decision.

"Tell you what. Got a girl in my store that's marrying one of these young fellers back from the war. Says she wants to keep her job."

Isabel spoke quickly. "I heard about that. But I won't put another girl out of a job, if that's what you mean."

He snorted. "You're a Jardine, no mistake. Jumping to conclusions. Proud as Lucifer. Come down off that high horse, girl. Didn't say I was letting her go, did I? She can have the job as long as she wants it but I know that kind of arrangement ain't going to last. Feller's got any gumption he'll get out of Kingsbridge. Find a job somewhere. If not, she'll find mighty quick that she can't keep herself and him on nine dollars a week. Fact is, I expect the pair of 'em to pull up stakes inside a month. Means I've got to get someone in there learning the business. Tricky business, hardware. Big stock, a thousand things, a thousand prices. Think you could do it?"

"I could try, Mr. Markham. But suppose..."

"Suppose nothing. I'll do that. Point is, I want more than a hardware clerk.

I'm into all sorts of things nowadays. Take real estate. Daresay I buy and sell more farms in a year than any other man 'tween Annapolis and Kentville. Take pulpwood. For the past five years I've been buying up those worthless farms in Scotch Springs and other places along the edge of the mountain, getting 'em for a song. People said I was crazy. Laughing on the other side of their faces now. Every one of those farms had a back lot of timber running up the mountain. Small stuff mostly but just the right size for pulpwood. Easy to log, easy to get out, railway handy, good price for all the pulpwood I can ship.

"Take vegetables and fruit. Nobody around here thought of canning 'em till I put up a factory here last year. Seen it? On the road west of the town, private railway siding, all that. Doing very well. Building a new piece on it right now. Next year I'm going into jam—strawberry, plum and so on. Wish I'd done it in time for the war—all that plum-and-apple jam they used to feed the troops. Um! Well, I suppose you're wondering what all this has got to do with you. Point is, I've been doing all my own letter-writing or getting one of the girls in the store to whack it out with two fingers on a typewriter. Won't do any more. Too slow. Letters don't look good. Point is, I need a secretary. No, that's too highfalutin. What I want's a good sensible girl that can look after my letters and answer the phone, and sell hardware—'specially on Saturdays, when the store's rushed. Girl that knows what's what. Girl that's dependable and won't go flying over the moon the first time some young fool waggles a finger at her. See what I mean?"

"I think so." But she looked her astonishment.

"What did they pay you down to Hal'fax?"

"Seventy dollars a month. I'd been promised a raise to eighty, this year."

Mr. Markham grimaced as if in pain. "That's a lot of money. Board's a lot cheaper here. Clothes—you won't need fancy clothes in Kingsbridge. Never paid a girl more than nine dollars a week in my life. Before the war it was eight. Tell you what I'll do. I'll give you fifty dollars a month and a half-day holiday once a week. Provided you prove out satisfactory, of course. All right?"

"Yes. Yes, I think so, Mr. Markham. I don't know if I can do all you want, but I can try." She was trying to keep down her elation and she did it very well. The old shrewd eyes observed her cool demeanor and approved.

"Um. Where you staying?"

"At the hotel."

His brows shot up again. "That's expensive."

"Oh yes, but I intend to get a boarding place somewhere in the town."

"Um. You do that tomorrow morning. Report to me at the store after dinner—half-past one, prompt. After that your working hours'll be half-past eight to noon, and one o'clock to half-past five. May have to work an evening now and again. I guess that's all. Good night."

He closed his eyes again and sat there rigid against the back of the chair, with his hands clasping the forward curve of the chair arms, impassive as a gray stone god in the growing dusk of the veranda. Isabel murmured "Good night," and passed down the gravel walk towards the street. She was still amazed when she got to her room. She looked at herself in the dressing table mirror.

"Those Jardines!" she said aloud, seeing for the first time a Jardine in luck.

Getting board and lodging outside the hotel proved a more difficult matter than she had expected. She remembered the Kingsbridge boardinghouse of prewar days, a big ramshackle unpainted house on a lane near The Corner, kept by a happy-go-lucky widow named Tess O'Donnell. But this, like so much else in the town, had changed hands and ways in the new flood of prosperity. The Widow O'Donnell had sold out and gone to live with a married daughter in Massachusetts, and the new owner had repaired and painted the house, installed another bathroom, and hung a "Tourists" sign over the door. Where the O'Donnell hens had stalked and scratched on the clay patch at the side of the house there was now a motor service station with two bright red gasoline pumps. And the house itself was full. There was not even room for a tourist.

In former days the big house had always been half empty and visitors of the more frugal sort used it as a second-rate hotel, staying a day or a week as they pleased; but now, with the increased staff of clerks at the bank, the additional teachers required by the enlarged Kingsbridge school, and sundry shopgirls and bookkeepers from the various stores, the place was full; and so were the three or four homes near The Corner that took in what used to be called "paying guests."

At last Isabel found a middle-aged couple willing to rent their spare room. The Halletts lived in a small white-shingled house on the edge of the town towards the east. It was almost a mile from The Corner, a long walk in rainy weather; but it was comfortable, simple and quiet, it had a nostalgic flavor of her old home at Scotch Springs, and Hallett's apple trees ran down to the river. From her bedroom there was a view of the orchard and the river and of a broad green stretch of meadows on the farther side. There were tall elms along the bank and the fields were broken here and there with copses of young ash and maple. In the distance arose the dark wooded shoulder of the hills known to all the valley folk as South Mountain.

Between the rows of Hallett's apple trees ran the furrows of his spring plowing, neat and exact as if they had been ruled and drawn with an ocher crayon, starting behind the barn where he kept his three cows and a horse, and extending to the clay bank of the stream. In front of the house Mrs. Hallett had her flower garden, and there were shrubs of japonica and lilac to screen it from the valley winds. Isabel's bedroom was a prim little chamber, redolent of paint, containing a small wooden bed, a chair, a chest of drawers and a washstand, all done in white. There was a cheerful flowered wallpaper. Two small oval rugs, made with hooked rags by Mrs. Hallett herself, lay on the painted softwood floor.

Altogether it was a pleasant place, a charming place, and Isabel was thankful that she had not been able to get a lodging among the huddled business houses of The Corner. The Halletts were much alike, a pair of tall gaunt people who had lost their only son in the war. They were descended from the Yankee pioneers who came to Nova Scotia after the old colonial wars and settled along the valley, and in manner, speech and appearance they might have stepped out of the hills of Vermont. Mrs. Hallett had been a schoolteacher when she married. She wore pince-nez and had about her the indefinable air of a school-ma'am in middle life, although for twenty-five years she had taught nothing more than a Sunday-school class at the Baptist church. She was a calm even-tempered person and she managed her house and Hallett with a calm and even hand.

Hallett was more volatile. He whistled about his chores and carried on lively monologues with his horse and the cows. He was full of dry little jokes and as Isabel departed after dinner to keep her appointment at the store he came part way down the gravel path towards the highway.

"We're a mite out of the way," he pointed out, "but you'll get used to that. When people twit me—and they're a great lot of twitters up to The Corner—when they twit me about living so far out, I just tell 'em, Ah but I'm well on the road to Paradise, friends, which is more'n you can say. That's the name of a village east o'here, see? But of course you've lived hereabout and you know. Well, that's what I say, I'm well on the road to Paradise. Anybody twits you about boarding so far out you tell 'em that. That'll set 'em back. That'll give 'em something to think about. 'Cause there's other towns besides Paradise on that road. Kentville, f'rinstance. Used to be called the Devil's Half Acre back in olden times. Can't help thinking of it when I see the tourists tearing off through Paradise in a cloud of dust so's to make the hotel in Kentville afore night. That's life for you, ain't it? Ain't that life?"

Isabel had to admit that it was.

CHAPTER 30

The *Courier* always referred to Mr. Markham as a pioneer, and so he was. He had been the first man in Kingsbridge to own an automobile and the first to install a gasoline electric plant for lighting his house. His bathroom had been the first in town, and so was the furnace that poured a gush of hot air through a grating in the floor and did away with a clutter of stoves. He had always been the most progressive businessman as well; and now, at an age when most men are thinking of the grave, he had launched forth with every dollar and every ounce of energy he had to take advantage of the postwar boom. Rumor said he was worth as much as three hundred thousand dollars, a fabulous sum in the valley, and there were people who predicted that he would be a millionaire before he died.

The hardware store from which his little empire had sprung was one of the best in the valley. He carried a stock of everything from shingle nails to the newfangled gasoline tractors. There was a busy plumbing and tinsmiths' workshop at the back. The office was a small coop with scant room for Mr. Markham's own desk, an immense old roll-top thing, and a small modern typewriter desk at which Isabel was soon installed. The staff consisted of three shopgirls and herself, a handy man and an errand boy. The girls looked upon her with suspicion at first, especially the girl who was about to marry; but when Isabel took over the typewriter and began to initiate Mr. Markham into the strange art of letter dictation their instinctive hostility vanished. It was a relief to see someone else struggling with the old man's correspondence.

In the next Saturday's rush, when she was able to help at the counters, they began to welcome her presence in the store. When the word passed around Kingsbridge that old Markham had brought in a typist from the city, the shopgirls were quick to point out that she was a home girl after all, a Jardine from Scotch Springs, and that she was "nice." This was confirmed by the Halletts, who were delighted with their quiet and sensible boarder; and when Isabel appeared in the Baptist tabernacle with them on Sunday morning her acceptance was complete. She was asked to join the choir but this she declined, saying that she hadn't a singing voice, which was not quite the truth. She wondered what her rigid Presbyterian father would have thought to see her there joining in the services of "those dunkers," and she salved her conscience with the fact that there was no church of her own faith nearer than Scotch Springs.

She liked Mr. Markham. He was really much more of a businessman than Hurd, who was so rigidly efficient in routine matters but whose mind too often drifted into the abstract realms of electrical science. Markham's only concern was business. He could see to the core of a problem at once and he dealt with each promptly as it arose and passed his attention to the next. He was one of those remarkable men who never hurry, who are never rattled or confused, who go through life without a wasted thought or movement getting things done. He had a profound reverence for the dollar but he did not let it interfere with his other religion. He was a devout Baptist, generous to the church, although he had that peculiarity of the pious well-to-do who give large sums each year to missions and will not bestow ten cents upon a wistful urchin outside a candy shop.

His scorn for "loafers" of whatever sort amounted to hatred.

He regarded the poolroom behind the barber's shop and the clubrooms of the Great War Veterans Association as dens of iniquity. He did not use tobacco and he had the quaint Victorian view that a man who chewed plug or smoked a pipe was merely a Christian with an amiable weakness, but that anyone who smoked a cigarette was bound for hell. Isabel found this a little wearing. There were times when she longed for a cigarette. Even in the privacy of her room at the Halletts' she could not indulge without risk of offending those good people, whose views were much the same. The shadow of the Puritan conscience, brought to the valley in colonial times, still lingered under many a roof in Kingsbridge, where in the more pious circles a pack of cards was still known as "the Devil's prayer book" and dancing (even of the old-fashioned "squares," heavily chaperoned in the Odd Fellows' Hall) was under the suspicion of the church and deacons.

As for the drinking of "rum," their general term for all alcoholic beverages, the Nova Scotia Temperance Act was for them a manifest act of God. But Isabel noted that even here the seeds of change had been cast by the winds of war. The young soldiers had brought back with them a scorn for Prohibition and a taste for "rum" that was not to be satisfied by the hard cider that even the most pious farmers made secretly and hid from their strait-laced women in the barns. And their free and easy manner with girls, especially their evening frolics with certain females in the long grass by the river, were things undreamed of in the Kingsbridge of '13. Their reluctance to go back to the old dull round was not due to laziness and foreign corruption, as Mr. Markham declared, so much as a deep dissatisfaction with things as they were and a longing for some zest in the lives that had been spared to them in the blood-baths of France and Belgium.

It was of no use for the Reverend Wilbert Palliser to belabor his Bible every Sabbath and set the tabernacle ringing with denunciation and warnings of hell-fire. The young men had seen hell-fire on the slopes of Vimy Ridge and in the bloody swamps of Ypres, where the devout had perished just as miserably as the damned, and they looked upon the preacher and Mr. Markham and the other tut-tutting elders as pious frauds or at best a flock of dignified ostriches with their heads plunged deep in the red valley soil. What was to come of all this no one could truly say; but Isabel perceived that the young men were the new generation, or what the war had left of it, and eventually theirs would be the only voices to be heard.

She was old-fashioned enough to feel some of Mr. Markham's concern; but she too had seen hell-fire, she had been in Halifax when the great disaster of '17 threw half the city in ruins and killed or maimed five thousand people at a stroke; and she had observed that it was not the rich or the worldly who bled and burned, but the poor folk of the north end of the city, the sort of people who according to the Scriptures were supposed to inherit the earth. There seemed to be something wrong, if not with the texts at any rate with the preachers' interpretation of them.

Moreover there was her own intimate case. In terms of what Mr. Markham constantly referred to as "the good old-time religion" she was doubly an adulteress, a creature to be scorned and rejected in this world and burned in the next. And she rebelled. Even when she sat under the rostrum with the kindly Halletts, conscious of these black and secret sins in the full tide of the Reverend Palliser's eloquence, she told herself that what he preached was not only wrong but a deliberate and monstrous injustice. She had been brought up with a deep sense of religion and until the age of twenty-nine she had walked the path of virtue with a sure and quiet step. Then, for no reason that she could see, she had been plunged into a fantasy of humiliation, frustration and pain that had no meaning or reward. Where was the justice in that? Where was the sense in it?

It was all very well for these people to talk. They could afford to be smug in the comfortable niches they had carved out for themselves in the little valley town. She tried to imagine Mr. Markham on Marina, where, whatever riches might be stored in Heaven, there was no hard money to be made or lost. She tried to picture the Reverend Palliser there with his bald white dome and his trombone voice, preaching his fiery gospel to a people who fully believed in hell and damnation but who believed no less devoutly in a ghostly Frenchman who roamed the dunes by night riding a great white horse and singing unintelligible songs, and in the spooks of drowned men and women wandering up and down the beaches—just as they believed with the utmost faith that a belt of tarred sennit worn next to the skin would cure the most stubborn case of lumbago, and that a salt herring split and wrapped about the throat under a bandage was God's own remedy for quinsy. It was easier to picture Matthew Carney counting dollars at Mr. Markham's roll-top desk; or Captain O'Dell, say, in the preacher's place in church.

Nevertheless she continued to attend church with the Halletts for the sake of good relations, and the congregation never suspected that they had an unrepentant and somewhat indignant Magdalen in their midst. During the rest of the week she plunged her mind into her work. She had a good memory and a knack for figures, and within a month she had grasped the workings of the hardware business in a way that astonished the other young women and drew even the cautious Markham's praise. But the real job lay in Markham's other enterprises and her duties as his secretary—that highfalutin word. It did not take the astute old man long to see that he had found a quick and precise tool for the dispatch of business. Before long Isabel was working two and sometimes three evenings a week in the effort to keep up with it. She had persuaded him to get some proper business stationery, and upon these crisp white sheets with their imposing letterhead, and with his grammar corrected and his country-merchant phrases rendered into city business jargon, he was able to admire the product of his own dictation and to wonder how he had ever got along without this cool and admirable creature.

She seemed actually to crave work, a quality that he had rarely encountered in the succession of young women who had passed through his employ in the course of the years; and he thrust work upon her with the eagerness of an Aladdin who has called forth a genie out of a lamp and is not sure at what moment it may vanish in thin air. The store accounting system consisted of a cashbook, a journal and a ledger which were in charge of the oldest counter girl. There was a bookkeeper at the canning factory. Another, in a shack on the mountain slope, looked after the logging accounts. Markham's real estate deals were jotted in a notebook, carried in his pocket. The bank passbooks and checkbooks he kept in the roll-top desk. All of these matters were assembled and reconciled more or less in his head, so that when he tackled the newfangled income tax (the worst disaster of the war) it was largely by a process of mental arithmetic.

With the present swift and complicated growth of his business activities this peculiar accounting would no longer serve. Apart from anything else there was now the prospect of inspection by some snooping income-tax official who undoubtedly would demand to see everything on paper and in order. He took his problem to the bank manager, and that useful man, anxious to please his busiest customer and largest depositor, came and held a long conference with Markham and Miss Jardine. The result was a new set of books for the office, with a master ledger containing what the man called "control accounts" for all the Markham activities. These and the bank accounts and checkbooks were placed in Isabel's charge. The new burden obliged her to hold daily telephone conferences with the cannery foreman and the logging boss, and frequently Markham drove her in his car to one place or the other so that she could straighten out some matter by a quick personal inspection.

From this he saw the advantage of taking her along with him when important real estate deals were in the making, so that she could jot down agreements in shorthand and turn them into indisputable type for signature before the matter had a chance to grow cold. Eventually he got one of the mechanics at Hemple's Garage to teach her how to drive the Markham car, so that she could run her own errands in connection with the business, leaving him free to tackle something else. In this way she soon came to know most of the people with whom Markham conducted his affairs, and they in turn came to recognize in her a competent person to whom they could refer a good many matters without troubling Markham himself. When the office phone rang it was usually for Miss Jardine. In the store, in the bank, on the street, even outside the church on Sunday morning, she was approached by persons anxious for her opinion or her intercession in everything from a mortgage on the farm to a job in the cannery.

This transition in her importance took about five months, and at the end of that time Mr. Markham recognized it by raising her salary to sixty-five dollars. In the meantime the summer had come and gone. Summer began officially at the end of May, when the orchards bloomed and for almost a hundred miles the valley lay in a pink and white snow to the very eaves of the farmhouses. This famous spectacle drew hordes of tourists, rolling along the red roads in dusty cars or peering from the windows of the trains. The Boston House and the Bon Ton Restaurant did a hustling business and so did the souvenir counter in the hardware shop. Even the inhabitants paused in their tasks to admire the annual miracle; at night Isabel, gazing from her window to the river, drank in the heavy scent of Hallett's trees.

The almost feverish devotion with which she had thrown herself into Markham's affairs did not prevent her from taking the promised half holiday once a week. She chose an afternoon when the weather was fine, borrowed Hallett's horse and buggy and set forth after dinner with a packet of sand-wiches and a Thermos flask full of cold milk in a basket under the seat. Her route lay towards Scotch Springs, where she visited the little churchyard and placed flowers on the graves of her father and mother. The old home was in the hands of strangers and was sadly changed. They had let the veranda go to rot and then torn it away. The barn was tottering. A group of ragged children played about the clay patch which had been her mother's flower garden. She did not go in.

Farther along the road she turned up an old familiar log road into the woods and drove a few hundred yards up the steep slope to a brook. Here she hitched the horse. She spread her blanket on the grass beside the water, undressed, and lay in the sunshine, reading, smoking, or merely dozing until five o'clock. She then ate a leisurely picnic meal and dressed, and towards dusk she appeared once more at the Hallett house, putting up the horse herself and trundling the buggy into the shed.

Her mysterious appearance from the city, the almost immediate job with Markham, the zeal with which she attended to his affairs, the fact that she got no mail, her general air of aloofness of which these weekly disappear-ances were part, all marked her down in Kingsbridge as "queer." Even good Mrs. Hallett, who knew her best, became worried about her lack of social life; and one evening with the somewhat breathless patter of an amateur conjurer she introduced into her parlor and Isabel's leisure a man. He was Brockhurst, the principal of the Kingsbridge school, an eligible male of about Isabel's own age. He was a dark stocky man whose tall brow and glasses gave him a proper schoolmasterly appearance, although he had fought in France with a regiment of Canadian infantry and still limped from a bad wound in the leg.

Like Isabel he saw through Mrs. Hallett's simple device at once, and they exchanged amused glances as they shook hands. Isabel was less amused when her hostess gathered up the garrulous Hallett on some paltry excuse and left her alone with the visitor. Her old trick of flushing made itself felt. She said in an exasperated tone, "I'm afraid Mrs. Hallett's trying her hand at matchmaking."

Brockhurst smiled. "I should have guessed that when she asked me here. She had that arch look of the female conspirator, and of course I'd seen and heard about you."

"What did you hear?" Isabel asked.

"Oh, that you came from these parts originally, and turned up again after a long time and become old Markham's right hand overnight. Frankly I'm glad to meet you. You sound like an interesting person—unusual, anyhow. That's refreshing in Kingsbridge."

"Don't you like it here?"

"Oh yes. I've always lived in towns, apart from a hitch in the army, and I find I like life in the country. What I meant by my remark was that social life here in many ways still follows a pretty definite pattern, laid down by the older women, and it's a change to see a young woman keeping herself out of the rut."

"You're quite wrong," Isabel said, leaning back in her chair and toying with a china dog on the side table. "I've merely got a rut of my own, and I happen to like it."

He gave her a whimsical grin. "That sounds rather hostile. Let me disarm any suspicion you may have by saying that I'm a bachelor who happens to like it. That doesn't mean I dislike women, especially intelligent ones like yourself. I'm not a bit romantic and I suspect you're not, either. That ought to give us a sound basis for an evening's conversation, don't you think?"

She regarded him, sprawling on the sofa where Mrs. Hallett had insisted on seating him, as if she hoped that Isabel would join him there once they were alone. His stiff leg was thrust out before him and he was engaged in filling his pipe.

"Tell me about the war. What did you do?" she said, with the too-obvious air of a woman determined to keep herself out of the conversation.

"Nothing much." He struck a match and puffed at the pipe. "I'd rather talk about things here and now. Apart from being principal of the school I'm president of the local branch of the G.W.V.A., which gives me a lot more trouble. The steadier veterans have gone back to work on the farms they came from, or cleared off to the States. The active membership consists of Kingsbridge lads and the more restless types from the farms, the How-ya-gonna-keep-'em boys. They attend the business meetings in the clubroom and I'm continually trying to talk them out of crackpot resolutions addressed to the government—demands for more gratuities, which they'd only spend on bootleg liquor; and demands for public works which presumably would provide 'em all with well-paid jobs—and actually would only provide new profits for smart operators like your boss."

"Mr. Markham?"

"Yes. That makes you sit up, doesn't it? Do you know what the war veterans call him? Old Dollars-and-Deuteronomy. To them he's the archetype of the profiteer, the man who made money out of their sweat and blood overseas, and is still making it, hand over fist, while they're out of work. Oh, he's a very holy gentleman, I admit. But you can see their point."

Isabel could not. But she was sitting up. Her back was one straight line of indignation. "What awful nonsense! Mr. Markham started his business long before you or any of your 'boys' were born, when Kingsbridge was nothing but a dozen houses and a ferry across the river. Everybody knows that, or should. He's been making money by hard work ever since, and he's got a reputation for honest dealing up and down the valley. Just now there's a good deal of money to be made by a man with energy and brains, and why should he sit back and do nothing about it? Would you, in his place?"

"Probably not. But I don't think I could be so smug about it."

"You sound very smug to me,'" she retorted.

"I'm merely giving you the viewpoint of the war veteran, the chap who made it possible for every Markham in the country to hang on to his money and add a lot more to it. In their eyes he's a very disreputable character."

"Indeed!"

Brockhurst enlarged his theme with the same air of cool indifference. There was nothing new in what he said. It was the reaction of the soldier to those who have lived snugly far from the noise of battle, and all over the world there were Brockhursts putting it into words. The Mr. Markhams of the world called them Bolsheviks. However, most of this was new to Isabel and she gasped at the schoolmaster's effrontery, knowing full well that she only had to repeat one or two of his more pungent phrases in Markham's ear to have the man discharged from his post as a menace to the innocent children of Kingsbridge, not to mention religion, law and order and the other foundations of government. In his recital of these heresies and her spirited rebuttals the evening passed very quickly. At eleven o'clock the schoolmaster caught up his hat and limped to the door.

"Have I bored you?"

"Of course not."

"Well then we must get together again. Half an hour after I'm gone you'll be able to think of all the brilliant things you might have said. You must let me have the benefit of them. Shall I come here, or would you prefer to take me on one of those buggy rides of yours? Some fine evening—Thursday, say?"

"I'm not sure I want to talk to you again," Isabel said.

"Ah, then you'd better give me at least another chance to offend you, so you can be sure. Say Thursday?"

"Very well. Thursday at seven."

The door closed. Isabel blew out the parlor lamp and passed into the hall on her way to bed. At the foot of the stairs she noticed a light in the kitchen, and going there perceived Mrs. Hallett knitting by the stove.

"How did you get along with Mr. Brockhurst?" Mrs. Hallett said. "You sounded sometimes as if you were quarreling."

"We were talking politics."

"Oh dear! What is he, Liberal or Conservative?"

"I'd call him a Progressive-Impossible."

Mrs. Hallett laid the knitting away in her sewing basket. "That," she said with a sniff, "sounds like one of those fancy new parties in Upper Canada, or is it in the West?"

CHAPTER 31

The apple blossoms shivered and fell, and the fat white candles dripped away from the horse chestnuts. Mrs. Hallett's lilac and japonica bloomed and faded. The hayfields were speckled with buttercup and daisy and the clover patches put forth their sweet perfume and drew a swarm of bees. Schoolboys caught tadpoles in the ponds, and the first crop of young robins learned to fly. In the green shade of the alders the violets bloomed, and in the woods there were lady's-slippers to be gathered, and in boggy places the pitcher plants put forth their tall Morocco-leather flowers. The young poplars made silver patches against the dark masses of spruce and fir on the hillsides. Suddenly the strawberries were ripe. And at night when the lamps shone forth into the orchard a fusillade of June bugs pattered against the panes like gleaming brown bullets.

July was a month of burning heat in which the wine-stream shrank in the river bed and many of the smaller brooks dried up. For days and nights on end there was not a stir of wind, not the whisper of a leaf. The air over miles of lush farmland quivered and the long ranges of hills to the north and south wavered gently in the sunshine as if stirred by the breath of Glooskap, the ancient Indian god whose habitat they were. Thunderstorms rolled up and down the valley, usually at night, sometimes with only a passing mutter in the sky and an occasional flash that tingled all the telephone bells and let it go at that, sometimes with drenching showers that set the hillsides streaming and brought the brooks to temporary life, with continuous eruptions of blue light that seemed to spring up from the earth instead of down from the sky, and a sound of powerful artillery rolling and echoing along the mountain slopes.

Farmers complained that the rains always came when they were haying, as they had complained ever since there were farms in the valley; but the crops grew tall and green and fat, and the apples formed well on the trees.

The cherries ripened early and (as if there were not enough fruit in the valley) boys and girls went up on the ridges to pick wild raspberries and blueberries in the old burns that showed like pale scars in the green flank of the forest.

The potatoes blossomed, and roses and dahlias and sweet peas bloomed in the posy gardens, and ramblers, white and crimson, hung their bunched finery over the verandas and the trellises. August brought a dry heat, more comfortable than the humidity of July, and now there were southwesterly winds blowing steadily along the valley and whirling clouds of red dust along the roads. The great tourist pilgrimage went on. The dining room of the Boston House rang with the gay accents of New England, of New York and Pennsylvania. Sometimes there were cars from as far away as Ontario or Illinois or Ohio; and once or twice there was a car with a California number plate, and when it stopped for gasoline the small boys gathered quickly, and the war veterans came out of their clubroom, and girls peered from the shop doors, because no one had ever known a car to come so far.

The corn ripened. The oats ripened and were mowed, and flocks of sparrows fed and chattered in the stubble, rising together at every petty alarm and settling down again. The apples ripened and the branches bent under their weight. Goldenrod began to bloom along the roadsides, the first hint of autumn. The swallows began to leave for the south. By the end of August they were gone, and the nighthawks followed them. In the swamps the blue petals of the iris had long since withered and gone, and now the seed pods stood on the stalks like small green sausages.

Isabel noted this passing show as she drove about the countryside on Markham's errands, on Sundays as she strolled with the Halletts to church, and on those precious weekly half days when she retired to her lair in the woods and lay naked to the sun. The doctors at the hospital had recommended sun-bathing and she had undertaken it as a rather embarrassing chore, but she soon came to look upon it with the utmost pleasure, an interlude of utter freedom in which she could give herself up to the golden light and the warm fir-scented air like a nymph enjoying the caresses of a sky-god—not here, not within a few miles of Kingsbridge and its prim society, but in some Mediterranean land where there were olive trees, and white temples hidden in cypress groves, and placid blue glimpses of the sea.

Actually her sunning place was a small patch of wild grass with a fringe of alders and then a dense mass of second-growth firs, and it was reached by the winding disused log road that she had known in her childhood. A stream rattled down the hillside past the ruins of a small sawmill, abandoned so long ago that the once tall heap of sawdust had rotted and shrunk to a gray scab on the turf. The haul-up chute had dropped into the grass and gone completely except for a few rusty bolts. The mill itself, no bigger than a country blacksmith's shop, tottered drunkenly over the dam, a crazy mass of weathered gray timber afflicted with sores of bright orange fungus; and the old wooden water gate had been carried away by a flood long since, so that the dam held only a shallow pool.

Here for hours she sat or lay, glistening with a protective lotion as if she had just arisen from that thin bright water, and watching the smoke of her cigarettes drifting in the sunshine. By mid August her entire skin had acquired the "nice genteel tan" that Skane had remarked on her face at Marina, and she took a sunworshiper's satisfaction in the new feel and appearance of her person, putting on her clothes with reluctance at the afternoon's end, and moving about afterwards with a sensation of confinement inside an uncomfortable husk.

Brockhurst called irregularly at the Hallett house. Sometimes he came every evening that she was free from business. Sometimes she did not see him for a fortnight. He had chosen to spend his summer holidays at Kingsbridge, making excursions about the valley on his motorcycle. When he called they spent the evening chatting on the veranda or wandering about the byroads in the Hallett buggy. Mrs. Hallett and most of Kingsbridge were convinced that it was a match.

Markham in his characteristic way demanded, "This Brockhurst—anything serious?"

"No."

"Odd sort of feller. What d'you find to talk about?"

"He does most of the talking," she answered lightly. "Oh, we talk about books, education, economics—mostly economics it seems to me."

"Sounds mighty dull. Like him?"—with one of his quick shrewd looks.

Isabel hesitated. "I don't know quite what to make of him, to tell you the truth. He's so very argumentative and so positive in all his statements that a good deal of the time he irritates me. But he's never a bore, I must admit. He can talk well about almost anything. When I went to school I found geology the dullest of subjects; but Brock can scratch up a handful of gravel and go on for an hour about the various kinds of stone and be quite fascinating. I think he must be a very good teacher."

"Umph. 'Brock.' Well, if you must ride about the countryside talking stuff like that why don't you take my car and do it comfortably? I've told you to take the car whenever you want it."

"For pleasure I prefer the horse and buggy. It's more leisurely."

"Ah!"

"And it reminds me of my childhood on the farm."

"I see. And do you remind yourself of your childhood when you go off alone once a week towards Scotch Springs? Or is that none of my business?"

Isabel gave him a level gray look and shrugged. She put it delicately. "It's just my weekly relief from business, Mr. Markham. I rather like to be alone sometimes."

"Um. Sure you're happy?"

"Oh yes, very."

"My wife says we should have you to tea more often. But I have a notion you don't care much for that kind of thing."

"I don't," Isabel said frankly.

The Markham household consisted of himself, his small myopic wife, and their daughter, a shriveled spinster who looked and talked exactly like her mother. Like Markham the two women were extremely pious but they lived a much more cloistered life. Isabel was horrified at their dull and sapless existence. Markham's drive for money seemed to her a reaction from the deadly monotony of his home, and she did not know whether to pity or despise the women who spent such drab lives almost entirely within the four walls of the Markham house, even in summer, having no outlet for their emotions but the religious ecstasies of the Sabbath.

"Um. Well, my dear, I must say you look a lot better than when you came. Nothing like the country air after being shut up in a city office for eight years. Enjoy yourself while you can. Harvest's almost upon us. Lot of work coming up—the apple crop to be gathered and barreled and shipped, and the cannery pack and so on. The Exhibition's coming up too. Have to drive you hard the next two months. Mind?"

"Not a bit."

She mentioned the first part of this conversation on her next evening ride with Brockhurst, and he grinned. He had a small black mustache of the sort developed by army officers during the war and when his mouth spread in a smile the mustache looked a mere pencil mark along his upper lip. His dark eyes twinkled behind the glasses.

"The old boy's terribly afraid of losing his new right hand," he observed. "Can't say I blame him, from a business point of view. You were the goddess from the machine. Just when his affairs were spreading like a grass fire in a gale you came along with your city-office experience and your knowledge of the local scene, and actually looking for a job. I bet he got you at a bargain, too. He wouldn't miss an opportunity like that. He's never missed an opportunity in his life and they've all come to his hands at exactly the right moment, just as you did. It's all right to talk about Markham's energy and brains—and his honesty if you insist—but what's pushed him so far on the road towards a million dollars is what pushes all men who make money in big chunks, the ability to cash in on his luck."

"You're spurring your hobbyhorse again," she said calmly. "I can tell you that Mr. Markham hasn't got anything like a million, even in property, and as for money in big chunks, that's nonsense. This is Kingsbridge, not New York or Montreal. But I've said all that before."

"So you have. And you've been properly reticent about the figures, as a confidential secretary should. Nevertheless I'm still mighty curious about your boss. He interests me as a sample of his type, the only one within my orbit, so to speak. Everywhere I've rambled this summer, talking to veterans here and there, I've come across Markham's trail. Apart from his pulpwood and cannery interests, and of course the store in Kingsbridge, he's been buying outright or buying options on farms all along the valley. The postwar boom is still shoving the price of farmland into the sky like everything else, and in another year or two at the present rate he'll be able to cash in for a very pretty sum. In the meantime the possession of so many orchards puts him into the apple business right up to his neck."

"Well, what's wrong with that?"

"As a student of history and economics—at ground level, so to speak—it seems to me there's plenty wrong. After all wars are old stuff in this world and the economic results are pretty much of a pattern. There's always inflation, which reaches its height, not at the end of the war as the ignorant expect, but a few years afterwards, depending on the length of the war and the money that's been printed to keep it going. Anyone in Europe could tell you that; but here in Canada and to a considerable extent the U.S. it's a new experience. In Europe they're pulling their horns in fast. Over here everyone, even canny people like Markham, have got the idea that the boom's permanent. There's a lot of nonsense being talked about 'the infinite resources of a new land,' and a 'permanent upward trend of development.'"

"You're such a pessimist," she said. "Haven't you any faith in Canada?"

"Of course I have. But new countries have to obey the law of economics the same as everyone else, and you can't pay for a war with a lot of undeveloped resources, however rich they may be. What counts is the cash you can put down on the barrelhead. In the case of this valley it's an apple barrelhead. And all those apples have to be sold across the sea in Britain because the home market's too small to absorb 'em. That's where the cash has to come from, finally. It's the same with Canadian wheat and a lot of other things. Call it a colonial economy if you like and you'd be pretty well right. It's been forced upon us by circumstances over which so far we've had no control. We can't sell to the U.S. because the Americans produce the same things. Agreed?"

"Go on."

"So our financial health depends on matters in Britain, on the other side of the Atlantic. That's too far away to bother people like your Mr. Markham, who can't see past the local bargains right under his nose, but it's bound to catch up with him and everyone else in Canada pretty soon. Don't forget the British bore the chief burden of the war. They were in there slugging away from the start, and after the Russians quit and the French and Italians were ready to fold up the British fought practically the whole war till the Yanks got there in force in the summer of '18. That was quite a contract. I well remember it because I got a bullet in my knee at Ypres, where we slugged it out with the Germans in the mud for months just to keep old Hindenburg's attention on us instead of the French, who were in a state of mutiny and strolling home by whole divisions.

"Look at the financial side of it. The British spent enormous sums on their own side of the show and lent as much to the French and Russians and others who'll never pay it back. Well, now that the postwar inflation's at its height they've got to face the facts, including a whacking big debt to the U.S.A. That means John Bull's got to take a big reef in his belt. The signs are plain if you read the English newspapers as you should—you and old Dollars-and-Deuteronomy. We're going to feel the squeeze ourselves and it's going to come hard."

"How soon?" asked Isabel, for the sake of conversation. She was used to his dialectics by now and she listened with the tolerance of one who has heard all this before and does not believe a word of it. Brockhurst had always refused to talk about his war experiences ("I won't play Othello to your blooming Desdemona") but she knew they had affected him powerfully, and in her opinion they had crippled his outlook no less than his knee.

"Ah, who knows? Within two years at most. Maybe this year. This could be the year that we'll all look back on as the Black Year '21, when the bottom dropped right out of the barrel."

"Poor Mr. Markham!" She smiled as she said it.

"Oh, he'll be all right, I don't doubt that. Probably got a lot of his war profits tucked away in tax-free Victory Bonds, like all his kind. It's the rest of us who'll be out of luck."

"You seem quite cheerful about it."

For answer he began to whistle "Pack Up Your Troubles in Your Old Kit Bag," and the horse, startled out of a somnolent amble, broke into a sudden trot.

Some days later as she lay in the sun beside the stream Isabel reflected idly upon these matters. Brockhurst talked a lot of nonsense but she enjoyed the vigor of his mind, and sometimes she wondered if she had any attraction for him apart from her role as listener and antagonist. He had never betrayed a trace of sentiment in their friendship. That was as she wanted it; but now and then in idle moments she felt a twinge of loneliness.

Rising on one elbow to get another cigarette from her hand-bag she contemplated the pale golden body stretched out upon the grass. She was conscious of a sense of waste. She had passed her thirtieth birthday, that ominous milepost on the way to withered age, and she wondered how many more years she could retain this physical perfection. She had never felt so much alive. In this orchard country amid the ceaseless talk of fruit in all its stages and values the similitude of women and apples came instinctively to mind. Some were best quite early in the season and these first fruits had the most potent attraction in the market. Others attained their ripeness later, and these usually were the ones that kept their quality longest. But all of them were made to be enjoyed in their time. After that they withered and were spoiled forever, Gravensteins, Pippins, Golden Russets—and Isabel Jardines.

In the rush of business through the week there was never time for such wistful introspections; and when on an occasional impulse she drew forth the photograph of Skane and Carney with poor shipwrecked Clélie it was only to face once more the enigma of her life on the island and to put it away once more unsolved. It was in these hours of self-contemplation, stretched beside the clear mountain water, that the future oppressed her. She wondered if it was because this place reminded her of that reedy pool amongst the dunes. Or was it merely that summer was passing, the warm and lovely time that seemed so like the best years of a woman's life? August was all but gone.

And then all self-examination perished in a single blinding thought. The end of August! With shaking fingers she caught up the newspaper that lay, half read, upon the grass. For their daily news the people of Kingsbridge, like everyone else in the valley, depended on a bundle of Halifax newspapers flung off the "up" train at each stop, and it was Isabel's custom to bring one of these to be read in the leisure of her sun bath. She flicked over the pages hurriedly and ran a swift glance down the Marine News column. And there it was. The letters seemed to jump out of the surrounding print.

"Arrived: *Lord Elgin*, O'Dell master, Marina Island, passengers."

CHAPTER 32

All the way back to Kingsbridge Isabel's thought ran furiously upon that scrap of news. "Passengers"! Among others Gregory Skane. No doubt of it. She could see him with that firm jaw and the hard blue challenge in his eyes, striding into Hurd's office and demanding the address of Mrs. Carney. She could see Miss Benson simpering, and Hurd putting on the quick glad smile and thrusting forth the quick glad hand that he reserved for crack shore-station operators. And she could hear Hurd murmuring that he was sorry, that Mrs. Carney had left the hospital without a forwarding address, that doubtless she was convalescing quietly somewhere, and how were things on Marina?

All those vague yearnings and speculations by the stream had perished. She was again Miss Jardine of Markham's office, the determined young woman who had set her future on a business career and would have no more of men. Skane would be angry and amazed, no doubt. But there was nothing he could say or do. She had disappeared and that was that. He would fume about Halifax for a day or two and then go off to see his people and spend his leave. She told herself (and admitted with a curious reluctance) that he would find other women charming and quite willing to meet his wants. It was silly to say that no woman could resist Greg Skane. The truth, she suspected, was that only a rare woman in good health and under forty could escape an impulse to throw herself into his arms, whether he wanted her or not. It was a strange gift, one of the sardonic jokes that life plays on its creatures here and there, for Skane was no Lothario. Lotharios are gay, they flash and whir like hummingbirds exploring every flower along the way, whereas Skane was a mixture of self-pride and self-contempt, he wanted to be whole master of himself and hated the need that could make him slave, even for an hour, to a woman; and there was a kind of fury in the passion that he expended in her flesh when at last he admitted, not her victory, but his own defeat.

Oh yes, that was Greg Skane. And she would have no more of him. She had never loved him, never!—any more than Skane had really loved her. They had both given way to something that sprang out of the emptiness of winter in the lonely gray station, a hot quick spark that leaped and flamed and trumpeted a message that had no beginning and no end and then was silent, leaving nothing but the tang of ozone and an echo down the dunes.

And now she was quite safe from that dangerous quality in him and in herself. She went over the points again and again. The hospital? She had told them nothing but that she was leaving the city. Hurd? Miss Benson? She had left without a word to them. There was no way that Skane could seek her out with that confident "D prefix" he had mentioned in his letter. She had never mentioned Kingsbridge or even the valley, not so much from reticence as because he had never been curious enough to ask her anything about her background before she met Carney.

Nevertheless for several weeks she started whenever a quick new step came through the shop towards the office, whenever the telephone rang and a man's voice demanded "Miss Jardine?" At evening when Brockhurst came on one of his erratic visits and Mrs. Hallett let him in and called, "Here's a man to see you, Miss Jardine," in the arch way she had, there was always a tense moment until Isabel heard his voice. Brockhurst himself remarked that she seemed "jumpy"; and on one of their buggy wanderings he paused in the midst of a scathing denunciation of the capital system and remarked with his wise grin, "You're not listening. Am I slipping or are you? I can't get a rise out of you any more."

"I'm sorry. I was thinking of something else."

"Something important, I hope."

"In a way, yes."

"May I ask what it was? Or is that impertinent? I'd like to know what could be more important than the rule of Canada by a handful of bloated capitalists in Toronto and Montreal."

"You're forgetting the one in Kingsbridge."

"Just ignoring him for the moment. What's the trouble? Business, I suppose, you poor weak tool of the capitalist class. Old Markham must be worrying about the fall in pulp and paper prices in the States. All his wood goes to pulp mills over the border, and the price of groundwood pulp over there has dropped from something over a hundred dollars a ton to something under forty—or does he know that yet? He never reads anything but his Bible and the *Courier*."

"He knows."

"Ah, then he's begun to taste the pickle his greed has got him into. I happen to know that the mills have stopped buying wood—presto!—like that. They've all got big stocks on hand, and they're carrying 'em on their books at values that don't exist any more. The mills won't get their breath back till they've ground up the wood on hand and got it off their inventories.

That means a year at least, from all I can learn. In the meantime there's old Dollars-and-Deuteronomy left with at least ten thousand cords of spruce and fir, cut and piled in the woods or stacked at sidings all the way from Windsor to Karsdale. In the round! With the bark on! Do you see the pretty picture? Wood left like that will rot within twelve months and then the mills won't take it as a gift. So there's our local Midas stuck for ninety thousand dollars at the very least, unless he can sell the stuff for firewood. Even at that it's almost a dead loss. Why are you turning the horse?"

Isabel's mouth was set in an angry line. "We're going back to Kingsbridge. And there I'm dropping you, Brock, not just for this evening but for keeps. I've had enough of you and your everlasting sneering at my boss."

She gave the horse a smart flick of the whip and they rattled off towards town. For a time Brockhurst said nothing, watching her frigid profile and the vexed set of her lips.

"Look here, I didn't mean to upset you," he said seriously at last. She did not reply.

"After all I'm just a student of economics and Markham only interests me as a specimen of his type."

"You've said that before," she exclaimed scornfully. "You've been repeating yourself all summer. 'Specimen of his type'! Brock, you're a specimen of your own type. The man who got hurt in the war and feels he owes the world a grudge. I met your type once before; only he didn't go about preaching a backwoods version of Marx; he went off to sulk on a desert island. There seem to be a good many others—all this talk about a 'lost generation'! And you're all alike, the lot of you. All you've lost is your sense of decency. Sooner or later you hurt other people. Not always in the same way, but they suffer just as much."

"But,'" he protested, "you used to take all I said as a lark. Why the sudden change?"

"I just couldn't stand any more."

Isabel flung out these remarks without looking at him, without relaxing for a moment that fixed stare on the road ahead. The buggy clattered into Main

Street at the same brisk pace. When Isabel pulled up at the sidewalk the horse turned its head reproachfully, no doubt wondering like the schoolmaster what had so changed the peaceful evening ramble. Brockhurst limped down and put his hands on thy side of the buggy, looking up at her. There were people strolling under the elms and he waited for a group to pass before he spoke.

"You don't mean what you said about dropping me for keeps?"

Isabel turned her head and met his eyes firmly. "Yes, Brock."

"Surely you know that on that night we first met, when you were so annoyed with poor Mrs. Hallett and so much on your guard with me, I deliberately threw out some remarks that would sting—as a kind of challenge—because you seemed to me a mysterious and rather attractive personality that I wanted to know better? And, well, it worked."

A youth and a girl passed arm in arm, and Brockhurst waited again. He went on in a low voice, "I'm not trying to imply that I didn't mean all I said then or since, I meant a good deal of it, the basic things, the principles in which I believe. But I stuck in some fireworks here and there because it seemed to stimulate you, because I enjoyed hearing your retort. Have I misjudged you all this time? Is it possible that you haven't a sense of humor?"

"I daresay not," she said acidly, and turned to jerk the reins.

"One moment!" he begged quickly. "You're determined to have no more to do with me, I can see that in your face. And I'm quite sure it's not entirely due to things I've said. There's something else. You've been queer for the past few days. Won't you tell me what it is? You see, I'm afraid I'm in love with you and I can't let you drop me without knowing fully why."

Isabel gave him a startled look. For several moments she was speechless. It was the last thing she had expected to hear him say. And far from being mollified she was outraged by this calm confession. She was disturbed by the news of Skane's return, by all those poignant memories of Marina, and with her thoughts so full of the two men who had loved her this voice of a prospective third seemed utterly indecent. She drew away as if from some lewd proposal.

"Brock," she said in a rapid and breathless voice, "you're mad. What right have you to say such a thing to me?" And with that she drove off. Brockhurst stood on the edge of the sidewalk and watched the buggy flit away into the dusk.

She went no more to the old mill. She told herself that the sun had lost its value now that September was far gone, that the cool winds had begun to blow, that in any case there was too much work to do. There was some truth in all this, but she would not admit that she was afraid to give herself a chance to think of Skane, and of that future which had seemed so peaceful and so satisfying and was now so empty and so bleak. Even in her few leisure evenings she fixed her mind on the past day's business and the problems of tomorrow with all the fervor of Markham himself.

There was much to ponder. The inquisitive Brockhurst had been right. The market for pulpwood had collapsed, and Markham was left with nearly one hundred thousand dollars stacked in neat wooden heaps along the valley slopes. Most of the wood had been cut during the previous winter. The autumn rains would soon begin, and then would come another winter's frost and snow. When the hot sun of another springtime fell upon the sodden stuff it would ferment and rot. The woodsmen had an old English word for it, handed down from colonial times. Unless Markham got rid of his wood before another winter, they said, the damned stuff would *dote*.

Markham knew it as well as they. He was making desperate efforts to sell it, offering bargain prices by wire to every pulp mill on the seaboard and hunting up the owners of small lath and stave mills all along the valley. But now another problem loomed. The apple market was going the same way. Through his speculations in farmland the old man had the crops of twenty-eight orchards on his hands—crops on which he had advanced money for spraying and general nurture through the year. Already the bank had called him into agitated conference. There were conferences with other growers and shippers; and twice in a month he joined a deputation to the government at Halifax.

It must have gratified the sardonic Brockhurst to see how far his guess had been correct; but it would have surprised him to see how old Dollars-and-Deuteronomy was taking it. The man who worshiped money only a little less than God met the prospect of ruin with all the cool philosophy of those sinful men who play for big stakes with cards. And with a stubborn courage that Isabel admired he persisted in running the cannery at full production, finding somehow the money to pay his hands for their labor and the farmers for their fruit and vegetables.

"The bank calls this a 'dubious experiment,'" he told her with a thin smile. "So it is, I suppose. But it looks to me the only real solution of the market problem in the valley, done on a proper scale. Don't expect I'll live long enough to see a cannery or a jam factory in every town and village but at least I've made a start. Hate to see it shut before it has a chance to prove itself. Trouble is, I'm living thirty years ahead of my time. They call me old. Good gracious, I'm too young for my boots."

"Things look very bad, don't they?" Isabel said.

"'Course they do. They'll look a lot worse by-and-by, the way the world's going. But it's natural, mind you. Progress ain't a thing that goes straight up like a flight of stairs. Got to be dips and hollers and thank-ye-ma'ams along the way. This is one. We'll come out of it all right unless every tomfool loses his head. What worries me is that later on, when we've pulled out of this one, the valley'll go on in the same old way, packing apples in barrels when every-one else is using fancy boxes, growing special types for the English market instead of shifting, gradual of course, to kinds that'll sell here at home with a bit of push; and then some day there'll come another flop that'll really knock it flat. Thank God—and I say it in all reverence, Miss Jardine—I won't be living then. All I hope is that someone then will remember old Jase Markham and say, By gosh, the old boy showed us where the bear crossed the brook."

The valley had never yielded such a harvest as it did in that golden autumn of '21. For a hundred miles the orchards bent under the weight of gleaming fruit. There was never such a crop of corn, of potatoes, of turnips and beets. The pumpkins had never been so fat or such a deep golden hue. The plums were never so juicy nor the pears so firm and sweet. The weather held fine. The west wind trailed white mares'-tails across the lightest of blue skies, blew thistledown across the fields, waved the tassels of the corn stalks, flapped the Union Jack on the post office and the Stars and Stripes over the porch of the Boston House, set up dizzy whirls and capers in the dust of Main Street and blew away the last brown rags of the rambler roses.

Cattle moved slowly by the river in the rich green aftergrass of the hayfields. In the orchards an army of men and larking boys and giggling girls moved among the branches, picking the fruit into baskets and turning each basket-ful with care into the waiting barrels. The barrels were new and clean, the pale yellow staves gleamed in the sun, and they stood in orderly ranks along the roadsides and were posted like sentinels among the trees. Frequently along the highways came a hay wagon filled and piled high with barrels fresh from the cooperage and drawn by a pair of immense oxen. The oxen wore a heavy yoke strapped to their horns, and the yoke was painted a bright red or blue, and studded with brass ornaments. The last wandering tourists swung their cars aside to let them pass, and smiled and said how quaint it was to find such things in Canada in the twentieth century, and the ox-bells tinkled and the cameras clicked.

Along the lanes and beside the paths and ditches through the fields the goldenrod blazed like a fire in grass, and the celandine was butter-yellow and the Michaelmas daisies came to the knee, and the wild white asters were tall. By the pasture walls the red hips of the wild rose gleamed like cherries, and the withe-rod berries hung in their clusters pink and black. On the hardwood ridges a few red maples had put on their autumn dress before the rest and made rich spots of color in the green. Underneath the trees the ferns already had turned the tint of rust and made a dry swish against the legs of the partridge hunters, and the huckleberry leaves were freckled with the bright fall stain that soon would turn them all to blood.

The noons were hot. A blue haze transformed the more distant ridges of South Mountain to waves of a giant sea that heaved in the warm shimmer off the valley floor. But the evenings, as the farm folk said, were drawing in. By the end of September they found the sun going down as they sat down to the evening meal; and by the time the dishes were washed and put away the twilight was getting dim. The nights were chill and sometimes in the starlight the heavy dewfall looked like frost. For some time now the northern lights had been making experimental flickers in the sky, and by the end of the month they were putting on their autumn show with sheaves of glittering spears, with single beams that crept sometimes to the zenith and then fell back, with sheets of pale fire that shivered, that ran in ripples along the top of North Mountain as if twitched by the frost giants of the Micmac tales.

The first week in October brought to full tide that change of color in the autumn leaves which is the special miracle of North America and is seen at its best in New England and the Maritime Provinces of Canada. Between the long hills the valley unrolled its length in a quilt of patches, green and brown, very square and exact when you looked upon them from a height; and the river, the wine-stream, wandered through the pattern in lazy curves as if in contempt of such old-maidery. When you stood in the valley the fields and orchards on either hand ran flat or in mild undulations to the edge of the hills, and there the modest tints of the farmland gave way abruptly to a riot of gaudy forest rising sheer toward the sky and extending its length as far as the eye could reach. If you had an eye for trees you could pick out the bright scarlet, the salmon pink and the delicate yellow of the maple clumps, the purple of the ash, the yellow torches of the poplars flaming in the breeze along the slope, the gold of beech and birch, the wine of the young oaks, the clearings where huckleberry bushes made a solid red like a dress parade of the Royal Mounted, and the somber green of pine and spruce and fir that served for contrast and background to the rest.

One night in mid-October Isabel lay awake and heard a familiar cry far up in the dark, the honking of wild geese on their way south. It was the old warning of winter on the way. But it was also the old Indian promise that before the real snows there would come a spell of summer, one last glow of warmth before the cold. She smiled in the darkness. It was the best time of year. All the months led up to October, and afterwards there was only a waiting for the miracle to come again. And again she told herself, These are the things that matter. All these lovely things that I've missed so long. Nothing else. Nothing!

CHAPTER 33

The great public event of autumn in Kingsbridge was the County Exhibition, held in what were known as the Fair Grounds at the western edge of the town. Like all fall fairs in country towns it was a simple affair that brought everyone together, for the space of a week, in a holiday atmosphere in which they could gaze upon the champion cattle, horses, swine and poultry, the prize fruits and grain and vegetables, the finest homemade pickles and jams of their own district. The exhibits were housed in four long barrack-like structures of wood, arranged about an open rectangular space, and the whole surrounded by a fence of tall weatherbeaten boards so that everyone but active and impecunious small boys must buy a ticket at the central gate before passing inside.

The Exhibition was arranged and governed by a committee of farmers and merchants, of whom Mr. Markham had been Director as long as anyone could remember. This meant that Markham undertook the whole burden of the Fair, without remuneration or thanks, year after year, and was blamed for everything that went wrong, from the theft of Mrs. Hodge's prize mustard pickles to the leaky roof on the pig shed.

All through the summer there had been a desultory correspondence in connection with the Fair; and from the first of September onward Isabel waded in a rising stream of letters, manufacturers' pamphlets, telephone calls and visitors, all with the one object in view. Her employer had thrown himself and his secretary into the Fair with all the ruthless energy and thoroughness that he gave to his own affairs. Indeed Isabel found that the month of October was devoted to the Fair as if there were nothing else to do, as if the shadow of bankruptcy were not blackening the old man's mental sky with the speed of a thunderstorm rolling over the mountain from the Bay of Fundy.

As October drew toward a close the rickety sheds in the Fair Grounds received their annual coat of whitewash, the interior walls were lined and draped with faded bunting stowed away last year; and then the exhibits began to arrive in trucks, in carts, or pattering along on four feet. The horse shed resounded with stampings and neighings, the cowshed with indignant moos and the clangor of bells, the poultry shed with cluckings and crowings, the pig shed with its customary squeals and grunts.

The concessionaire of Faker's Row appeared by rail with his mysterious punctuality and his raucous men and women; the Ferris wheel appeared overnight like an enormous metal fungus strung with electric lights; the merry-go-round set up its calliope and its worn but spirited steeds; and along the rest of the central space appeared the brown tents and booths of the wheels of fortune, the housie-housie games, the ring games, the shooting gallery, Jo-Jo the Dogfaced Boy, and the hootchy-kootchy dancing girls.

Isabel found a little comedy in the inner workings of this show. There was a sheepish and comical air of custom in the debate of the committee, which she attended as Markham's secretary, regarding certain features of the Row. It was pointed out that the gambling devices were highly immoral, and what was of more importance they took a great sum of money out of the town. As for the dancing girls, there was sure to be complaint from the church elders, and the Reverend Palliser would certainly devote a scathing sermon to the subject on the Sunday following Fair Week. When all the other committee voices had been heard, together with an almost audible tucking of tongues into cheeks, Mr. Markham said the final word.

He did not approve of things like this himself. As a deacon of the church he was opposed to all such vanities. But, he went on dryly, as Director of the Fair he was bound to point out the business side of it. It was true that Faker's Row took a lot of money away, but it paid a big fee for the privilege and most of the Exhibition prize money came from that fee. Without cash prizes, friends, what sort of Exhibition could you have? Apart from that there was no use denying that the people liked the fun of Faker's Row. It gave 'em a bit of excitement after the toils of harvest time. The young men and women had to be considered. They were not like us folk who were brought up in the good oldtime religion. They wanted a little fling. And that applied also, he regretted to say, to the matter of the dancing girls. He had observed (still more dryly) that the young ladies in the grass skirts never seemed to have any difficulty in filling their tent. And there seemed to be a surprising number of the older farmers and other good church members in the throng. It was the most profitable side show in Faker's Row and the concessionaire stressed that point when the annual fee was being discussed. Well, gentlemen, the matter had been threshed out in former years, and it had been found that the best procedure was to let the dancing show stay open for the first three days and nights and then to inform the concessionaire sternly that the thing was immoral and must be closed and removed. It was, he admitted, a compromise, and as the Reverend Palliser pointed out a compromise with the Devil was a sin committed; but you had to be practical, it was a worldly age, especially since the young men got back from the war, and it was the only way to please the farmers and satisfy the concessionaire. He hoped there would be no difficulty on that point.

There was no difficulty on any point. The fortune wheels clicked merrily, the housie-housie games collected a shower of dollars and gave out cheap Indian blankets and aluminum ware, a game of Crown-and-Anchor did a roaring business with the war veterans; and the Hawaiian young ladies twanged their ukuleles, waggled their bosoms and bottoms, and shivered in the air of three frosty Canadian nights.

It would have been entertaining to hear Brockhurst's comment on these matters. Isabel saw and spoke to him several times in connection with the school art exhibit. She was friendly but distant and he did not attempt to close the gap. He had his old satirical manner. As they went over bundles of drawings and water colors she had a clear impression that he regretted ever having made that confession of bourgeois sentiment.

Fair Week reached its climax on Saturday when the entire population of miles of farmland came to town to do its weekly shopping, to see the prizes awarded, to take a last look at the exhibits, to submit to a final fleecing in Faker's Row, and to watch and applaud the fireworks that brought the show to its brilliant end. It was a busy day for everyone, especially the Ladies' Aid of the church, who had set up a dining room in a shed near the gate. The profits were for church funds and the ladies did a tremendous business from noon until late in the evening. Mrs. Hallett as a zealous member of the Aid was there all day. Hallett himself was in charge of the field crop exhibits in the main building. He turned up at the farm to milk his cows just as Isabel was making a lone meal in the kitchen.

He looked in the kitchen doorway. "Goin' up to see the fireworks, ain't you? Want a ride in the buggy? I'll be off again as soon's I'm done milkin'."

"Don't bother about me," she said, pouring tea. "I've got to change my clothes. Besides the walk will do me good." She made a leisurely meal of it and washed up the chinaware and put it away. It was a relief merely to be able to do something slowly after the long rush; and the quiet of the empty house was balm for the past week's clamor of voices, the furious clatter of the typewriter and the constant jangle of the telephone bell.

She went upstairs, washed, and changed into a new tweed suit, with a pair of warm stockings and her walking brogues. She had decided lately to do her hair in a new way, with two thick plaits drawn forward like a gleaming brown coronet, and like every woman who clung to long hair in this postwar era she had found it very difficult to get a hat to fit over it. The craze for bobbed hair was almost universal and the millinery trade was turning out a tight felt helmet that made any gathering of women look like a parade of the Amazons. She put on her brown tam and wondered if she should take a coat.

Hallett had finished his chores and she heard him washing up in the kitchen. On her way along the upper hall towards the stairs she heard his voice at the front door, shouting, "Man to see you, Miss Jardine!" The door slammed. As she came down the stairs she heard his retreating steps on the gravel walk. She was smiling to herself and wondering what she should say to Brockhurst when she saw a tall figure in the light of the lower hall. She stopped sharply. She gasped. It was Skane. Skane in a well-tailored blue suit, in a crisp white shirt and a smart winecolored tie. Skane tossing his hat and topcoat on the hall rack and turning, smiling up at her with his teeth very white in the dark face. Skane with his black hair neatly trimmed and parted and brushed. A handsome and urbane and incredible Skane standing there in the Hallett hall as if it were the most natural thing in the world, and as if he had known that she would be coming down the stairs at that moment and must walk straight into his arms.

Isabel's knees felt weak. She put a hand on the rail. She could not bring herself to move further or to speak. In the painful silence the clock in the parlor made the loud hacking strokes of an axman in the woods.

"It's been years," Skane said.

Isabel came down another two steps and halted again, breathing deeply and quickly as if the effort had been violent. She could not take her eyes from that eager upturned face. Skane moved to the foot of the stairs and put a hand on the polished oak ball of the post. The staircase was steep and narrow in the style of country houses and she was suddenly conscious of the shortness of her skirt. She was in what Brockhurst in one of his military humors would have called an exposed and untenable position and she must either advance or retreat. She came down swiftly to the third step from the bottom and paused again with a hand stretched back on the stair rail, as if she were ready to fly at a touch.

Skane gave his head a quick short toss and chuckled. He had always understood her better than anyone she had known and she saw in the whimsical set of his lips a recognition of her dismay and a promise of forbearance on his part.

"Well, Isabel?"

"Greg!" She poured out her breath on the word, so that it was not a name at all but a long-drawn cry of reproach. "How did you get here?"

He shrugged his elegant blue shoulders and grinned. "That's quite a story. As good as Sherlock Holmes." He cast a significant glance along the lower hall and then up the stairs behind her. "Are we ...er ...is there anyone else around who might be interested?"

"I'm alone, if that's what you mean," she answered reluctantly.

"Then suppose we sit down somewhere like civilized people." There was a note of the lordly male in that and she felt a little indignant, as if she were a child being delicately reproved for sulking on the stairs.

"Very well," she replied haughtily, and walked down the remaining steps and past him into the parlor. "Will you sit there?" She indicated a chair and took another well removed on the farther side of the room. Skane sat, with his hands in his trousers pockets and stretching out his long legs. He still wore that curious smile, and his eyes had a look that she remembered too well for the dignified calm that she so desperately wanted now. Hallett had lit the tall brass lamp on the parlor table before going out, and its shade cast a warm yellow glow upon the lower part of the room. Through the west window as Isabel walked to her chair she could see the distant glow of the fair.

"I'll tell you how I found you," Skane said crisply, "and then perhaps you'll tell me, darling, why I had to look so long for you, which is much more important. I'll begin at the beginning and state that I left Marina in the *Elgin* on August thirtieth—a detective story must be precise—and arrived in Halifax on the following evening full of joyous anticipation, as you may suppose. In the morning I bought a suit of hand-me-downs and slicked up a bit, and then I made straight for the office. Hurd gave me the full treatment—the right hand of fellowship and the keys more or less of the city. I had to give him a full account of things on Marina and then listen to a long discourse on modern trends in radio before I could get to my point. Please don't look so alarmed—I was very discreet. I said quite casually that I'd an important message for Mrs. Carney and if Hurd would let me have her address I'd be on my way."

He paused and put his head back, gazing at the ceiling. "I should have known what the answer would be. It was in the way you'd said good-by to me. It was in your face and manner that afternoon by the pond when you refused to face the issue between Carney and me, when you asked me to leave the island. Still, I couldn't believe it. And when Hurd said he didn't know where you'd gone, that you'd disappeared from the hospital without a trace, I thought he was lying. It was a temptation to slam my fist into that smug face of his. But that wouldn't do, of course. On the way out I stopped to speak to his secretary—that blond creature, you must know the one I mean, she has a come-hither look—and I told her what I'd told the boss, that I'd an important message for you, that sooner or later you'd get in touch with the office, and she must let me know at once. I said I was going to spend part of my leave with my father in Cape Breton and I left the address.

"Before I left the city I phoned all the hotels asking for a Mrs. Matthew Carney or a Miss Isabel Jardine, and I drew a blank. Then I got from the city directory a list of boardinghouses and I waded through it. Where there wasn't a phone I called in person. It took me nearly a week and made me the friend for life of half a dozen taxi drivers. The only thing I got out of it was at a place on the shabby end of Hollis Street..."

"Ah!"

"...where a woman with the face of a third-rate Lady MacBeth told me that a Miss Jardine used to rent one of her rooms."

"What else did she say?"

"Nothing, except that you'd left almost exactly a year ago.

Then she slammed the door. I played with a notion that you might be there and had told her what to say, but something in her manner..."

"I see," Isabel said coldly. "And what then?"

"As a last resort I went to the hospital and talked to the nurses you'd had, but they knew no more than Hurd. So I shoved off for Cape Breton. I spent a week with my father, and visited a number of old friends and relatives. Father lives a quiet life—he's a retired parson, I think I told you that. Most of the time he's fathoms deep in books, translating Gaelic poetry and that kind of thing. He's been preparing for years a collection of verse and folklore of the early Highland immigrants into Nova Scotia. A good many people up there still speak Gaelic, I suppose you know that. Well, after a week I couldn't stick it any more. I'd been away too long. Everyone seemed a bit strange. The place was as lonely to me as Marina before you came. There was no word from Halifax. I had two months' leave and a quarter of it was gone. I'd told Hurd I wasn't going back to Marina and he'd offered to get me a station up the Gulf— as O-in-C, you understand. But the more I thought of it the less I liked it.

"There's a lot of sense in Hurd's raving about the future of radio. I couldn't help feeling that there might be something in it. And I didn't want to end my life like Carney, pounding brass in some Godforsaken hole for the rest of my days. Anyhow I went to Montreal and hunted up a fellow I used to know, a former op named Hartigan. He'd quit the sea and gone into some sort of electrical business, selling toasters and irons and fancy lamps and that kind of thing; and there was a sort of workshop at the back where he had two men busy putting radio sets together, from his own design. It was a cluttered little place; the back windows were shut in by high buildings, there wasn't much daylight, and among all that radio apparatus the two chaps looked like gnomes in a wizard's cave. But Hartigan was enthusiastic. His sets were selling like hot cakes and the craze was spreading all the time. He said there was a fortune in it.

"He talked about getting in on the ground floor and using our technical know-how and so on, and it didn't take him long to convince me I should quit pounding brass and go into the business with him. There's one thing about service in a place like Marina, you can't spend money and you gather a bit of good green moss in the bank. I had nearly thirty-four hundred dollars and I put it into the firm. I put myself in, too, working away with the others. It's interesting stuff—it's pure H. G. Wells compared with that antiquated gear on Marina—and the basic principles are the same as in radiotelegraphy. We got another shop right away, with a better show window and a good-sized place at the back where we can put the sets together. We've got three men working there now besides ourselves, and we've got a couple of girls in learning to do the soldering."

During this recital Isabel sat erect and tense, gripping the chair arms and pressing her knees together, the picture of a woman surprised and cornered and watching warily for some chance to escape. But the old revealing flush was on her face and it seemed to envelop her whole flesh; she had a dismaying sensation of defeat from within, and of Skane's complete awareness of the fact. He talked on easily and pleasantly, meeting her gaze now and then, as if he had merely dropped in for a chat. And between them, all but visible, hung those passionate memories of Marina which were so much more real than anything else in the room.

"It isn't all work," Skane went on lightly. "There's quite a bit of fun in the game. If you want to sell radio sets you've got to give the public something to listen to. Of course the Americans are going strong with WGY and KDKA and there are a good many smaller outfits that you can pick up here, but you've got to have something local for the benefit of the little crystal-set listeners. So Hartigan had got together with two or three other people in the business, and they'd fixed up a small broadcasting outfit on the top of an office building and got a government license. It's not much of a thing, mostly built around an experimental army radiotelephone transmitter that they got cheap from surplus war stores, but it works. There's no paid staff. They broadcast in the evenings, impromptu stuff, phonograph records, talks, news, that sort of thing. One or two girls come in, and I play the piano and we sing 'Alouette' and 'En Roulant Ma Boule' and 'Shenandoah'—all sorts of things like that, that haven't any copyright. It's a great lark. You'd enjoy it—like one of those evenings at McBain's. By the way, you don't seem to be quite enjoying this. I'm not boring you?"

Isabel stirred. "No, it's all very interesting. But none of this explains how you found out I was here." Skane waved a hand.

"All in good time. But I'll get on towards the point. You were constantly in my thoughts. It was maddening not to know where you'd gone. There was a picture on the wall of my bedroom, a cheap reproduction of a painting of Rossetti's; you've studied art, you must know it—a thing called Manna Pomona. A young woman with a pale face, rather striking but not a bit pretty, wearing a green thing. A basket of flowers in the offing and one or two roses in her lap. Her left hand toys with her necklace and underneath her right hand she's holding an apple in an odd sort of way, as if she's trying to keep it out of sight. Monna Pomona caught my eye every time I came into the room and she fascinated me. I couldn't think why, at first. And then it struck me that she was rather like you. There were times when she looked exactly like you—as you're sitting now, for instance, with your face turned partly away, and that chin of yours so firmly lifted. "Well, I needed nothing to remind me of you but there it was anyhow. Meanwhile time was getting on. Hurd would soon expect me back from leave. I sat down and wrote out my resignation, and posted it the same night. Some days after that a brilliant idea occurred to me—old Sherlock Skane. I knew the *Elgin* would be making her autumn trip to Marina about the end of October, and that any mail for Carney would be coming into the office to be forwarded. I was certain that you'd slipped away because, well, because you were torn between your loyalty to Carney and your love for me." He paused, and asked suddenly, "That was it, wasn't it?"

CHAPTER 34

Isabel broke her rigid pose and walked to the empty fireplace, looking down at the polished brass knobs of the andirons. With her left hand she plucked off her tam and let the arm drop full length at her side. She rested the other hand on the mantel.

"Suppose it was," she murmured.

"I knew you hated the island, and I felt sure you'd be writing Carney to say you weren't coming back. All I required was one look at the postmark on any letter in your hand. Simple, wasn't it?"

"But there was no letter, I've written nothing!" Isabel cried.

"So I found," he smiled. "I got a quaint reception from Hurd. I expected him to be peeved. You know how he hates losing useful personnel. When he read my quitting notice I could feel his anguish all the way up there in Montreal. Well, he was a bit stuffy all right, but when I told him what I was quitting for his face lit up like a Chinese lantern. He went right into one of his long spiels on the future of radio broadcasting and at the end of it he told me something that absolutely flabbergasted me. 'I'm quitting myself in a month,'" he said, like a pleased kid. 'For some time I've had the standing offer of a very good job in the States, in the technical end of a radio business, and by Jove I've decided to take it!' Grinning all over his face, imagine that! Hurd! He's leaving for New York at the end of November and can hardly wait. Shook hands with me and slapped me on the back as if we'd both struck oil right under the office floor. I was still a bit dazed when I shut the door and bumped into his secretary, the blonde."

"Miss Benson."

"Right. She told me her name. In fact she told me a lot about herself before I was through. I was still playing my hunch and she swam right into it. She had that chase-me-Charlie look so I invited her out to dinner and a show. You may not believe this, but she told me in the course of the evening that

I was a fascinating man, and that she couldn't help hearing what I'd said to Mr. Hurd. She said I was smart to be getting into business. 'After all,' she said 'what future has an operator got?'—and she thought it must be wonderful to live in Montreal. She'd been seriously thinking of going there herself, because Halifax seemed dead now that the shipping slump had set in, and after all a girl had her future to consider. And what was my advice?"

Isabel smiled faintly. She could hear Miss Benson saying it, and she could see the wide-eyed look and the careless crossing of Miss Benson's luscious legs.

"Well," Skane went on, "there was quite a bit of that. It took me a long time and some very careful conversation to get around to you. I said it was rather urgent that I know Mrs. Carney's whereabouts, because I had to convey that important message before I went back to Montreal. 'Look here,' I said, 'Mrs. Carney must have received a check from Hurd after she got ashore from Marina. She wouldn't cash it while she was in hospital because Hurd was looking after everything and charging the bills to Carney's pay account. Now where was that check cashed?' Miss Benson said she didn't know, but she'd find out."

"It was cashed in Halifax right after I left the hospital," Isabel said tartly.

"True, my dear. But in going over the canceled checks in the office next morning La Benson discovered another, an old one for seventy dollars dated in August last year. She'd noticed that it was outstanding every month when she made up the bank reconciliation statement, and then suddenly last June or late in May it had been cashed. She dug the thing out and phoned my hotel. I went down at once. Fortunately Hurd was out. She showed me the check and when I looked at the endorsements..."

"Ah! How very clever!"

"Elementary, my dear, quite elementary. There was your signature under my hand—it was like touching you—and there was the rubber stamp of the bank branch in Kingsbridge. I caught the morning train and took a room at the Boston House. The bank was closed for the Saturday half holiday and everybody seemed to be going to the fair. I got somebody to point out one of the bank clerks in the street and I asked the chap if a Mrs. Matthew Carney did any business at his place. He thought a minute and said No. But you can't fool old Sherlock Skane. I asked if by any chance there was a Miss Isabel Jardine—and of course there was. I gathered that you're the right hand and both feet of the local Rockefeller. Monna Pomona! I might have known I'd find you right in the middle of the apple belt!"

He laughed. In the downcast glow of the lamp his teeth gleamed in the keen dark face.

"I wish you didn't sound so—satisfied," she said resentfully. It was very easy to picture him with Miss Benson. Skane arose from the pool of yellow light and came to the fireplace, leaning his tall figure against it, with one hand thrust in a trousers pocket and the other stretched along the mantel, almost but not quite touching hers. Isabel's head remained bent, staring thoughtfully at the hearth, but she did not miss the delicacy of that inch between their finger tips. She thought again of the old snapshot album and those torn-out chapters in his life when he had learned the art of estimating women.

"You're very sure of me, aren't you?" she added in the same tone.

"No," he replied quickly. "I wish I were. You're a strange creature, Isabel. Do you know what you really want, yourself?"

She did not reply. She remained absorbed in her study of the hearth, and there was a certain melancholy in the drooping pose of the slender figure in the dusk thrown by the lampshade. From the westward came a sharp hiss and a report high over the town, and the night outside was lit by a cascade of falling stars. They heard the distant drawn-out *ahhh* of the crowd enjoying the first of the evening's fireworks.

"Do you?" Skane demanded.

"Tell me about Marina—about Matthew," she said in a subdued voice.

Skane turned away and walked across the room. He remained there, staring out of a window, "What is there to tell?" he said over his shoulder.

"Did he know about—about us?"

He turned and came several steps towards her. "Who can say? Matt's not a suspicious sort of man. In any case he wouldn't say anything. Matt and I were very close, we were like brothers in those days before you came. And you know how he felt about you. It was a mistake to bring you there. He came to realize that and so did you. In his own way and for his own reasons he became just as unhappy as you were in yours. If he suspected what was passing between you and me, that we'd found happiness together there in that desolate hole, he must have decided that silence was his only course. In any case he said nothing. He was always very reserved and I saw no change whatever in his manner. When I told him early in August that I was putting in for leave in time to catch the August boat he accepted it almost with indifference. Murmured something about three years being a long time, and that I was young."

He turned and walked to the window again, paused a moment and came back restlessly. He dropped upon the sofa and lit a cigarette. The blue fumes curled about the lamp. He studied the pensive figure at the fireplace.

"I don't think Matt realizes how the world's changed," he said in his former conversational tone. "He caught a glimpse when he was ashore last year and fled from it. But he can't avoid seeing some of it, even on Marina. The radio traffic's falling off at a great rate. The big liners are all fitted with continuous-wave sets now, and they get off the old six-hundred-meter channel and buzz their stuff direct to New York. Even the tramps nowadays can raise the mainland direct instead of retransmitting through stations like Marina. The old system, the old stations—the whole outfit's obsolete. Do you realize that Matt's station was built in 1905? In the radio game that's as old as Noah."

"What do you think will happen?" she asked.

"I don't think—I know. Hurd told me that within another year Marina is to cease handling commercial traffic altogether. That's why he's refused to install anything really new and ignored Matt's demands for a stand-by engine. The Marina station's quite good enough, just as it stands, for all future needs."

"And what are they?"

"It will continue to exist merely for communication between the island and the mainland. That means the staff will be cut to one man—Matt himself. He doesn't know that yet. He won't know till the thing is done. What's more the whole setup on Marina is due for a change. That elaborate chain of lifesaving posts along the island was all right back in the days of sailing ships when there were wrecks galore. Nowadays they never see a wreck except an occasional fishing schooner taking a chance on the west bar, and then usually the crew put over their dories and row ashore. The old establishment's been going on since the days of Victoria and nobody's given it much thought; but the war's changed everything and now that a postwar slump is setting in there'll be some sharp economies in all the government services. Somebody's bound to take a cold look at that ancient setup. Of course there'll always have to be a boat's crew to handle stores and to do the odd job of rescue work. The two lighthouses naturally will be maintained. And there'll be Matt to operate the wireless outfit and to report barometer readings and so forth to the weather people. The rest will be washed up. You see what it means?"

"What?"

"It was lonely before. What'll it be like in a few more years?"

She considered his question gravely.

"'Why are you telling me all this?" she asked.

Skane drew in smoke and blew it out slowly. "You asked me about Matt. I'm telling you. And now it seems to me time you said, something about yourself, darling. And won't you sit down? That attitude is charming but it's awfully distant. You look like one of the brooding Fates."

Obediently she came towards him. Skane arose and took the tam from her hand and laid it aside. He gestured towards a chair near the sofa.

"I promise!" he said ironically. She sank into the chair. Her eyes were no longer wary. She looked at Skane in the low broad cone of lamplight with a thoughtful gaze but she did not resemble Monna Pomona in the least. Rossetti's woman was too bloodless and her features too masculine and ascetic. Skane saw a face warm and golden-tanned and wholly feminine, even a little weak, with the appealing weakness of a woman dreaming of old loves.

"Well?" he said. Isabel lowered her eyes and regarded the hands clasped in her lap.

"I wish you hadn't come," she said in a disturbed tone. "'You bring everything back, all the things I wanted to forget. It was you who hurt me, you and Matthew, not the bullet, not that silly girl with the rifle. Oh I know you couldn't help it, either of you. I don't blame anyone but myself. You've always thought that Matthew seduced me in some way—got me on his island under false pretenses. Well, you're wrong. You should have known him better than that. It was the other way round. Does that shock you? It should. Because I didn't really love Matthew when I persuaded him to take me to Marina. I was lonely. I was nearly thirty and I had no one in the world. The only time I'd ever been in love I was jilted. And then one day something frightened me, I was desperate—and Matthew happened to be there. That was the way it came about. Within forty-eight hours I regretted it. But then it was too late. When I landed on Marina I was sick to death of Matthew, of myself, of everything."

Skane sat motionless, as if he were afraid to disturb this low voiced confession. After a pause she went on, "I felt quite sure that Matthew was in love with me, and after a time I resolved to make the best of it. I made love to him. I gave myself to him absolutely. For a month or so we were happy together. It was perfect. I found that I really loved him and I was utterly content. And then—this is the irony of it—he began to draw away from me, in little ways, in the trifles that mean everything. I couldn't understand—I couldn't believe it. And when I taxed him with it and he said that nothing was changed I knew that he was only being kind. You see? Before the winter was half gone our positions were reversed—it was he who was sick of me. There was no explanation except that he wanted his old life back again. There was no quarrel, you understand? We simply drifted into a mental state as dreary as those long Marina nights, with the wind sobbing in the aerials, when there was no relief, not even sleep. We were haunted. I came to believe all the ghastly tales of the island in those winter nights. That air of mystery! Something melancholy, something heart-rending and very close. It seemed to affect us all, even you and Sargent. Surely you felt it?"

"Yes," Skane said.

She leaned forward quickly.

"Then what was it? That mystery! You must know!"

It startled him, the abrupt question and the change in her from a woman in a mournful trance to this creature, tense and alive, her whole attitude one fierce demand. Her large gray eyes stared into his with a furious curiosity. Instinctively he drew back a little.

"Mystery?" he repeated. And then in a more assured tone, "Oh! Well, the mystery was simply that we three men were all in love with you in our separate ways and in various degrees. That was what you felt. How could you help it? Because it set us all apart from one another, each nursing his own emotions and wondering what the end was to be. For it had to come to a head before the winter passed. By Christmas we all knew that."

Isabel sat back in the chair. Her eyes closed. "And that was it? There was nothing else? It seems strange. After all, Matthew had ceased to love me by then. And Sargent—Sargent just had a sort of calf love, not the sort of thing that disturbs a woman's dreams. You were the only one really in love with me, Greg. Why should that distress me so? Why was I so frightened and so sad?"

She got up and looked out of the west window. The firework display was now at its height. The whole sky over the Fair Grounds was in eruption with explosive stars, with balls of fire, red, blue and green, that arose and sank in. beautiful parabolas and suddenly perished, with fountains and falling curtains of glittering tinsel. Against this blaze the roofs and treetops of Kingsbridge were in sharp black silhouette.

Skane lit another cigarette. "My dear girl," he said vigorously, "take a look at yourself as you were then; a hypersensitive young woman, used to the matter-of-fact bustle of the city, suddenly dumped into that weird environment of sand and sea and spooks; you were lonely, you felt that you weren't loved, that you'd ruined your life and there was no escape. Why wouldn't you feel scared? Why wouldn't you feel some sort of doom closing in? Eh? But my dear Isabel you're not on Marina now. You've got away from all that. You're in the midst of good sane things and people and you've nothing but your own happiness to think about. Why spoil it with a lot of morbid speculation about what's past?"

He tossed the cigarette into one of Mrs. Hallett's best vases and crossed the carpet swiftly to the brooding figure at the window. Isabel felt his arms slipped about her waist from behind, his lips against her ear.

"Look here, darling, when you think of Marina think of those very sweet afternoons we had together, those rides when we put the station behind us and could be ourselves, in love. Surely you can't forget all that?"

"No."

"Then come to Montreal with me—let me take care of you, amuse you, make love to you. We're not a pair of silly kids, you and I. We're old enough to know our own minds and to realize that life is short. We're in the thirties— the best time of life. Let's make the most of it. Surely you don't want to go on trying to be a career woman in a tank town in the apple belt?"

"Why not?" she said in a hard voice, gazing into the night. "It's all very well to talk in that romantic fashion, Greg. All I know about love is that it made me miserable. And I've been quite happy without it, here in this tank town, as you call it."

Skane tightened his grasp and kissed her cheek. She turned her face away; but her heart was a small quick drum beating the retreat, she felt the old insidious languor, the familiar urge to have done with thinking and give in. Skane really loved her, he had come all this way to find her, why deny him any longer? Outside the pane there was a stir of the night wind in the orchard branches. A dead leaf blew against the glass. The fireworks had ceased and now she noticed that the glow of the Fair itself had subsided. Intuitively she looked towards the road and saw the small yellow flicker of a buggy lamp.

"Let me go," she said quickly. "Here come the Halletts, and the blinds are up."

"Damn!"

Skane released her and they moved to widely separated chairs with a swift and guilty air. It was a little ridiculous and Skane laughed. But his laugh could not conceal his chagrin and Isabel could not resist a mischievous glance. She said in a shaking voice, "Please remember that I'm Miss Jardine and I've never been further than Halifax in my life."

"And that's where I met you?"

"Yes. And you mustn't stay after Mr. Hallett's put up the horse. They'll want to go to bed, and so shall I." Skane gave her a comical look of reproach.

"When may I see you again?"

She considered a moment. "I always go to church with them on Sunday mornings. I'll ask Mrs. Hallett if you may come to tea in the afternoon, and I'll phone you at the hotel."

The front door opened and Mrs. Hallett bustled in, throwing a naive inquisitive glance at Skane and crying, "Why didn't you make a fire? That young man looks chilled. It's quite frosty tonight. And you missed the fireworks. My dear, they were wonderful."

CHAPTER 35

The Sunday morning service was remarkable for two things. The Reverend Palliser, contrary to all precedent, said not a word about the vanities and indecencies of the Fair, and instead devoted his sermon to the joys of a bountiful harvest and the beauties of the countryside, clear evidence of God's smile on a people who while not deserving it could at least appreciate its magnificence. He quoted from the Scriptures and the poets and was very eloquent.

The other phenomenon was the appearance of a tall and handsome stranger, walking down the aisle to the Hallett pew and saying "Do you mind?" in a clear voice to that odd person Miss Jardine. Her face had turned scarlet but she appeared to know him, she had moved over to make a place for him, and they had shared a hymnbook and sung together very nicely. When the collection was taken he had placed a five-dollar banknote in the plate beside Miss Jardine's modest envelope. They made a good-looking couple when they stood together for the hymns, and after the service everyone asked everyone else who he was.

Isabel, surprised by his uninvited presence but accepting it with all the nonchalance she could muster, knowing how the tongues would wag, had not forgiven Skane when he came on Mrs. Hallett's own invitation to the Hallett house for tea that afternoon. But he carried off the tea as he had carried off the visit to church, with a pleasant assurance that disarmed her and enraptured the Halletts. There was no denying Gregory Skane's charm. He talked with animation to Mrs. Hallett about the legends of the valley and especially of Kingsbridge, which he had studied apparently in a copy of the *History at Duke County* at the hotel. He talked to Hallett about the problems of an orchardist as if he had lived in the valley all his life. And when they asked him about himself, as they had been itching to do, he entranced them with tales of his life at sea, the pleasant side of it, with excellent word-sketches of queer out-of-the-way ports, and the humors and problems of his radio business in Montreal.

He included Isabel in these conversations with remarks given particularly to her, and with a swift and intimate smile. The evening flew. The Halletts sat lost in these glimpses of a world unknown to them. When Skane left at eleven o'clock, long past the bedtime of that well-ordered house, Mrs. Hallett turned to Isabel and sighed gustily.

"What an interesting man! So polite and nice—and so goodlooking. He seems quite fond of you."

"Yes."

Mrs. Hallett gave her a quizzical look. "Is he staying long?"

"I really don't know."

"It seems to me," Mrs. Hallett said slyly, "that he's come to Kingsbridge a-purpose to see you. Confess now, aren't you a bit fond of him too?"

"Yes."

"I could tell by the way you looked at each other, and the way you blushed in church. I hope you won't mind me saying this, but it looks to me as if you two'd had a tiff and that's why you came back to Kingsbridge. Isn't that it? Well, I understand. A woman's got to keep her pride where a man's concerned. And you've made him come to you. That's as it should be. And now I suppose..."

Isabel was moving towards the stairs. She called over her shoulder, "You mustn't suppose too much, Mrs. Hallett. I'm not nearly so romantic as you think." The romantic Mrs. Hallett said no more. It seemed to her that beneath the sensible Miss Jardine was a rather willful minx, and she was indignant. You expected a girl of thirty to be womanly. And at thirty, when a charming and prosperous suitor like this appeared upon the scene, you expected her to be very womanly indeed.

On the following morning the fine fall weather broke. A hurricane had crept out of the Gulf of Mexico, leaped upon Florida, scourged the Bahamas, frightened the tourists of Bermuda, and now followed the Gulf Stream into northern latitudes, giving New England and Nova Scotia a lash of its tail. It began with a gray scud moving up the sky and then a drizzle of rain. An uncertain wind stirred out of the southeast and set up a shudder in the autumn leaves. The rain changed to heavy drops, to a torrent that drummed on the roofs and set all the eaves-spouts gushing. Then in the midst of this downpour a mighty wind rushed along the valley. The orchards, the woods along the mountain slopes, bent before the thrust of it like so much grass. The brooks, already raised by the first autumn rains, became red cataracts surging through the fields. The air was thick with flying leaves of all colors, like drops of paint flicked from an enormous brush. Shingles took wings, apples showered, chimneys toppled, sheds collapsed, half a dozen fine old elms that had stood for generations went down before the blast, tearing up lawns and taking with them a tangle of telephone wires.

Isabel was blown and drenched when she reached Markham's store, and she found the girl clerks huddled together about the stove and twittering like wet sparrows. She took off her hat and raincoat and stood for a time with the others, warming her wet legs. When she entered the little office Mr. Markham greeted her with his usual crisp good morning, and he arose and shut the door.

"Well," he announced dourly, "the wind's in the east."

"Yes, and very wet."

"I don't mean the weather," Markham said, coming slowly to her desk. "I mean the wind up the street. The bank. They've clamped right down. No more money for anything. I must close up the cannery tomorrow."

"I see." She thought for a moment or two. "That means laying off all the hands, doesn't it?"

She flicked over the leaves of her cashbook to see if there was money to pay them.

"Got enough?"

"Yes. They were paid on Saturday, of course. It means two days' wages."

The old man fiddled with a letter basket on her desk. "Seems a pity, all those people out of work. No use dwelling on that, I suppose. If only I could sell the pulpwood! That's all cash outlay. With that turned back to money I could handle the apple crop and keep the cannery going and settle with the bank—I could do everything! Trouble is, everything's happening at once. I'm caught like one of those old-time sailing ships—in a hurricane with all my canvas up. Too eager! Too eager! But how was I—how was anybody to know that a storm like this would come up out of nowhere?"

Isabel thought of Brockhurst and his quip about the Bible and the *Courier*.

"You know what it means?" Markham added.

"I'm afraid so, yes."

"I think I can salvage the store out of the mess," the old tired voice went on, "but that's about all. That and my house. Think of it! Right back where I started fifty years ago. Don't seem possible."

"I'm awfully sorry, Mr. Markham."

"My dear, the Lord giveth and the Lord taketh away. Blest be the name of the Lord. I wish I could say the same for the bank. I guess the bank's got its own troubles though. You can close up that control ledger. There won't be any more entries—there's nothing left to control. Just the store books from now on." He looked up at her earnest face. "I want you to know, Miss Jardine, that whatever happens you'll have your job. You're a good girl. Faithful. Hardworking. Smart head on your shoulders. This'll all blow over, by and by. The valley's still here. Soil's as good as ever. Pulp mills'll want wood after another year. World's got to have food and newspapers. Um!" He walked over to his own desk and sat down heavily.

Isabel blinked back tears. "Mr. Markham," she said without turning her head.

"Yes?"

"What I'd be doing for you after this, any girl in the store could do, couldn't she?"

"I suppose so. But look here..."

"You're awfully kind, Mr. Markham. But, you see, something's happened to me, too. A man wants to marry me."

"Gracious, girl, you make it sound like a calamity. It's not that schoolmaster?"

"No, an old friend—from Montreal. You must have noticed him in church on Sunday, morning."

"Ah! So I did. Nice clean-looking chap."

"Mr. Markham, if I decide to marry him he'll want me to go back to Montreal with him. And if I do—you won't feel that I'm running away just when things are bad?"

She turned and met the gaze of the old gray eyes. Mr. Markham smiled in a weary fashion, as if she were talking about teacups during an earthquake. He made a gesture. "My dear, if you think the chap's good enough for you, take him. Be sure, that's all. We'd all miss you very much—goes without saying— but nothing here's half as important as a husband. When will you know?"

She considered, as if it were a matter of careful calculation.

"By tomorrow night."

The storm blew itself away, leaving a drenched and tousled valley in its wake. Towards noon on Tuesday the overcast broke in the west and within an hour a pallid sunshine fell upon the countryside. The "late" orchards, still unpicked, had been stripped of their fruit; but the great change in the landscape was the face of the long hills, where the gaudy autumn foliage had been erased by the great wind like so much colored chalk from a blackboard. Isabel phoned Skane at the hotel, and at two o'clock she picked him up with the Markham car. She wore her tweeds and tam, for there was a damp chill in the air in spite of the sun. Skane got in beside her murmuring, "Nice car. Yours?"

"Of course not. It's Mr. Markham's. I use it a lot for business errands but this is the first time I've ever taken it for pleasure."

"Thank you, Ma'am. It's very nice of you to say so. But why didn't you phone me yesterday? I thought I'd go wacky sitting about the hotel parlor, smoking myself blue in the face and looking out at the rain."

Isabel turned off the main highway towards Scotch Springs. "All the wires were down—you ought to have known that. Besides, there was nothing to do. I'd thought we might go to the movies but of course there was no electricity. When the Kingsbridge movie man can't put on a show for any reason he always says he's got a dark house. Last night he really had one."

Skane watched her as she drove. "I like your suit. Nice fit. Lovely figure. Seems to me I've told you that before somewhere. Where are we going? Looks to me as if you're heading straight for the North Mountain—which, I may say, we'd consider just a good steep ridge in Cape Breton."

She went on for a time without answering. Then she said quietly, "I thought it was time we finished what we were talking about the night you came."

"Aha!"

"You sound like the villain in the play. I'm taking you to a place where we can talk freely without being watched or over-heard by anybody, and you mustn't presume on the fact. Is that agreed?"

"It's all very cold and businesslike. Why don't you just drive around in the car?"

"Because I can't drive and look you in the face at the same time.

"Okay. Anything to please."

They left the car at the roadside beyond Scotch Springs and walked up the log road to the old mill. The stream was a shouting torrent. The pool above the crazy dam had spread and flooded the grass where Isabel had lain, and upon its surface a thick mat of colored leaves eddied slowly like a great painted wheel. Around the mill itself the stripped maples had a wintry look. The firs, dense and dripping still, remained triumphant and untouched after the great wind.

"I used to come here a lot during the summer," Isabel explained. "It was quiet and sunny, a good place to lie and smoke."

Skane glanced about the sodden edges of the stream, "You couldn't say that now. Rum sort of spot. That sawmill looks like something Champlain left behind. Where shall we sit? That log over there?"

He produced cigarettes and they smoked for a time in silence, sitting well apart, each waiting for the other to speak.

"Well?" Skane exclaimed impatiently at last. He regarded the flooded grass with a wry expression. He was bareheaded and wearing a gray suit with a smart blue polka-dot tie. He looked no more like the shabby and savage Skane of Marina than this torrent in the woods resembled the quiet pool amongst the dunes. He might have stepped out of an office in St. James Street.

"You want me to come with you to Montreal," Isabel said. "I suppose that means you'll marry me?"

"Of course, as soon as you're free. Carney will give you a divorce all right. We'll get a lawyer in Halifax to draw up the necessary papers and send 'em to Marina for him to sign. The *Elgin* sails in two days' time—I phoned to make sure. You'll have to write a formal letter to Carney saying you don't intend to return to him, and that should be all the evidence required. If desertion isn't sufficient grounds for divorce in the Nova Scotia courts we'll take the papers some place where it is. In the meantime, well, after all we've been to each other I suggest that we go on right where we left off. Why waste any more of our lives over some legal fiddlesticks?"

"Greg," she said carefully, "suppose I told you that Matthew and I weren't married?"

He looked up sharply. "You don't mean it!"

"I do. We got a license and a wedding ring, but we discovered that you have to wait three days—and we had to catch the boat. So we dashed off just as we were, without benefit of clergy or even a justice of the peace."

"Well I'm damned! Why didn't you tell me that before?"

"Does it make any difference?" Isabel said bluntly.

"No—not at all. It—simplifies things, doesn't it?" He was still amazed.

"So you see, you can really make an honest woman of me," she went on in a composed voice. "That's rather important, isn't it? At least it's important for a woman to know if a man wants a wife and companion or if he just wants to go to bed with her."

Skane uttered a short laugh. "You're very frank, aren't you?"

"Shouldn't I be? We're considering a frank relationship."

Skane looked at the stream again, sucking hard on his cigarette and blowing out the smoke through his nostrils slowly. For a time he seemed lost in thought. His jaw tightened. He turned to face her with the old hot blue blaze in his eyes.

"I don't care. Say anything you like. It doesn't matter. Nothing matters except that I'm mad about you and I've got to have you. You've been frank. I'll be frank with you. When I left Halifax after that empty search I cursed you thoroughly. I convinced myself that our affair on the island was just one of those things, that you'd seemed attractive there for lack of any comparison, and that anyway the whole thing was a shabby trick on Carney, who trusted me, who'd trusted both of us. It seemed to me that you'd run away and hid because you felt guilty. Well, so should I. For a man running away from anything I can recommend Montreal. Prohibition doesn't trouble them up there. You don't have to sneak behind a fence and drink hard cider and furniture polish. And there are droves of pretty women ready to amuse a lonely man.

"I don't mean that I behaved like a sailor on a spree. There was too much work, too many interesting things to learn about Hartigan's business, to leave time for much foolery. But at certain times I tried very hard to confirm the notion that you meant absolutely nothing to me. Well, it didn't work. Every time I came back to my room Monna Pomona was there to remind me of that idyll on Marina. If I'd thrown the picture out of the window it wouldn't have made any difference. The whole truth was that there was something about you no other woman had, and it spoiled me for anyone else. When I told you that on the island you thought I was just swinging the lead. Well, I was stating a simple fact. One woman in a thousand has what you've got and none of the rest are worth a damn. Isabel, I don't know what else I can say. There isn't anything to say. That's everything."

He tossed the cigarette into the stream with the gesture of a man throwing everything to the wind. With this rush of words he had brought his emotions to a sudden pitch. He was visibly excited. He regarded Isabel with an almost arrogant impatience. She ground out her own cigarette on the log, very slowly and carefully.

"And Matthew?" she asked deliberately. "Surely Matthew found that quality in me, whatever it is? You must remember that for a time we were very much in love. He was passionate in my arms. Don't look so incredulous. He was my lover and I know. I was the first woman in his life. And having had me after all those lonely years do you think he can forget so easily?"

"Matthew!" Skane snapped. "For God's sake put Carney out of your mind, Isabel. Carney hadn't an earthly right to you. He deliberately swindled you. He was going blind and he damned well knew it."

CHAPTER 36

Isabel gazed at the crushed cigarette stub lying on the log between them. She said in a small voice, "Please say that again—that last."

"He's going blind," Skane repeated contemptuously. "He made me promise not to tell anyone, but there it is. He noticed it first in the spring before he went to the mainland. He was a great reader—always had his nose in a book or a magazine or anything else in print that he could get his hands on. And one graveyard watch, after a winter's reading by the light of oil lamps, suddenly he couldn't see. He told me everything went green. For several hours he sat there at the instruments doing everything by touch. After a day or so his sight cleared again. But he found that when he walked the beach at night, as he liked to do, things weren't as distinct as before. He could always see like a cat in the dark. Suddenly he couldn't. And it worried him. He decided to go ashore on the spring boat and see an oculist, and at the same time to hunt up his mother, whom he hadn't seen since he was a boy. A business-and-pleasure sort of thing.

"He went to an oculist in Halifax, who told him that in a year, or two at the outside, he'd be stone blind, and that nothing could be done about it. It seems that years before, on a voyage to the West Indies, Carney's ship had gone into a port where there was an epidemic of malignant ophthalmia, and he caught it. He had the devil of a time in some miserable port hospital but eventually he recovered and shipped north again. His eyes seemed to be all right and he didn't give it another thought. But apparently after all this time the thing's caught up with him. Some sort of optical atrophy—I think that's the term—has set in, aggravated no doubt by all those years in the sun-blaze of Marina, and all that poring over books in the winter nights.

"Well, Carney went to Newfoundland to see his mother but apparently she'd died a good many years before. So he went on to Montreal. He saw oculists there. Then to Toronto—more oculists, and always the same story. They told him he'd see all right by daylight for a time; the weakness would manifest itself at night or in a dim light of any sort. He could see movies or anything like that, but walking in starlight, say, he'd notice it. Then he'd become completely night-blind. Then he'd find his daylight vision shrinking. Nothing sudden, you understand, but day by day, a bit at a time. He'd notice it especially when winter came, when the days got very short and the sunlight was weak or shut off by clouds most of the time.

"It was like a sentence of death. Carney refused to believe it. After all, he'd recovered after that West Indian affair, and that spell at Marina had passed off all right. A bit of weakness at night, that was all. The doctors didn't know what they were talking about. So back he came to Marina—with you. It was still summer and the light was strong. His eyes were all right, by Jingo—you know the way he talks. But he found he couldn't walk the beaches at night any more. That's why he objected when you insisted on walking back from Main Station in the dark. But he got away with that all right. You didn't notice. He memorized the lagoon shore, where nothing ever changes much and the going's pretty smooth. He couldn't have done it on the seashore because a high tide or a big surf always shifts the raffle about. But it's a wonder you didn't notice how clumsy he was at evening before the lamps were lit.

"When the cloudy autumn days began he noticed a change in his vision by day. That's why he quit duck-hunting. A flying duck's a small object and it moves very fast. He couldn't spot 'em coming till they were right down to the decoys—and that's much too late. And he noticed it at his work. His handwriting got bigger and bigger all the time. And at night, even by the light of a good lamp, he had to take a magnifying glass to read the smaller print. You didn't notice that of course, because he wouldn't try to read anything like that when you were around. He cut out his walks. For a time he'd go for pony rides and even gallop about the dunes—because he could trust the pony's eyes. But then he had to give that up as well.

"I'll say this for him—he put up a wonderful bluff. He knew where everything was, about the station, and he'd go straight to it, day or night, and do whatever had to be done. He'd hear a bird in the grass, or see a pony vaguely at a distance, and tell you all about it just as if he could see every detail of the thing. And he cultivated his sense of touch. I've seen him close his eyes and go all over the receiving apparatus with his fingers, adjusting this and changing that, and then checking everything with his eyes open and if necessary with his magnifying glass. He persisted in his notion that all this was just a sudden case of shortsightedness and that he'd never go really blind. He deceived himself just as willfully as he'd deceived you in the first place.

"By November, when the weather shut in and the long winter nights began, he had to face the truth. He knew by the end of that month that the oculists were right—he knew the worst. He was very upset. Especially about you. We were chums, remember, and he told me everything. He felt that he'd swindled you—which was the truth—and that by another year you'd find yourself tied hopelessly to a man as blind as a bat. He didn't seem to care so much about himself. But he felt—he still feels that he can keep on running the station, sight or no sight. The old apparatus he knows like the palm of his hand. He can take the engine or the generator apart and put it together again blind-folded. The same with the other gear. He could depend on the loyalty of the ops—and on their eyes—for everything else. He told me again and again, 'I'm good for several years yet.' He'd always said that when it came time to retire he'd build himself a small shack in the dunes to the east of the station and live out his days there. And I suppose that's what he had in mind ultimately when he found he was going blind. The only problem was you."

Isabel spoke. "How true!" And she asked in the same low voice, "Did anyone else know this?"

Skane waved a hand. "I think O'Dell suspected something wrong—he's known Carney longer than any of us, although not so closely of course. Nobody else knew except Sargent, not even McBain. Sargent was a shrewd young chap behind that innocent face of his. You couldn't fool him very long about anything. I rather think he knew what was afoot between you and me. He used to come out with some odd sayings from time to time—you could take 'em any way you liked. But he was a nice kid, a happy-go-lucky sort. He was in love with you and he felt sorry for Carney, but after all that was Carney's worry. When he left the island he was like a dog with two tails—he didn't know which to wag first. He was crazy to be off to sea again.

"I felt like that once. It's a wonderful feeling while it lasts. Then one day you find yourself hating the sight of blue water and it's all over. It never comes back. All you want after that is to be ashore. You steam along a coast at night and you lean on the rail and look at the lights of towns, and you think of all the pleasures of life that shore people enjoy and you don't—like a caged tiger in a circus parade passing all the butcher's shops. Some sailors marry and they're worse off than ever. They only get to see their wives and kids a few times a year. In every port they moon about the ship, watching the young chaps go ashore for fun. All they can afford themselves is a pint of beer at the pub outside the dock gates or a bottle of some foul South American wine. Poor devils, I used to laugh at them, and why not? They were fools. Only young men and fools go to sea—or to places like Marina—and the smart ones quit before it's too late. I've been talking an awful lot, haven't I? Wandering all over the map! But surely you see my point now?"

Isabel arose and sauntered to the edge of the mill pool, stretching a foot to the slowly turning carpet of bright leaves.

"What's going to happen next year, when the staff is cut?"

"Carney will find himself alone on the station. He'll bluff it out as long as he can. There won't be any traffic to handle except a message to or from the island and sending out weather reports and ice warnings and that kind of thing for the benefit of passing ships. Chiefly it'll be a case of keeping watch at certain hours during the day and the evening, listening for distress calls and so on. It'll be quite simple. The end will come when he can't see to put the messages on paper any more—not even to write up his fifteen-minute log entries. Then the authorities will catch on, and he'll have to quit."

"And what then?"

Skane shrugged. "The little shack in the dunes, I suppose, or more likely a room at McBain's. Carney's got quite a bit of money in the bank ashore, I daresay you know that. Anyhow the island people will look after him all right. It's his own wish, after all. Marina's his home. He's got no people anywhere and he'd perish very quickly in an institution for the blind."

"And that's the whole story, Greg?"

"Every word."

He was lighting another cigarette, with his hands cupped against the cool draft blowing down the little glen. It had gone against his principles to play that forbidden trump. He had thrown it out without thinking. But he did not regret it now. She had taken it quietly, even casually. She had to know the truth sooner or later and it might as well be now, before she wasted any more of her life in silly regrets and recriminations. After all she wasn't the first woman who'd lost her head over a man and then found herself cheated. He blew out the match with a whiff of smoke and looked up. He was startled to see Isabel standing close to him with her slender brown fists gripped at her sides. She was looking down upon him, a bitter anger in her eyes, and her face was contorted to the point of ugliness. She was in a passion of rage.

"So that was it!" she exclaimed in a harsh whispering voice. "That was the mystery! That was the secret you all knew! That was what I felt about me all that frightful winter! Something I could reach out and touch. Of course! What a fool I was not to have seen! I even noticed the strangeness of his eyes, but I thought it was just the faraway look you all had at times, the look you got from sheer habit at the phones. He was going blind. Blind! Oh, you cowards—you and Sargent—you utter cowards! Why didn't you tell me?"

She turned away again, shaking. Skane sprang to his feet. He put out his hands in a futile gesture. "My dear girl, don't take it so hard. Probably I shouldn't have mentioned it. But there was nothing Sargent or I could have said or done. He swore us to silence. After that we could only wonder how long Carney could conceal it from you. He should have told you himself but he wouldn't face it. Why should we?"

Isabel swung about, and the cigarette fell from Skane's fingers. He had expected to see her weeping, and she was; but he was stunned by the look which had replaced the anger in her face. It was one of happiness, an almost delirious happiness that shocked him. For a moment he thought she had lost her mind. And in that strange tone, like the swift rush of feet in dry grass, she cried, "You're wrong! He did face it! He concealed his blindness because he didn't want to hurt me. Don't you understand? He loved me—he loved me all the time! And he forced himself to conceal that, too. He forced himself to draw away from me, to let me think he'd grown sick of me in those dreary winter months. For my sake he was willing to part with the only joy he'd ever had in his life—for my sake, just for that! Which of you others would have done it? Which of you had half his courage or his love for me?"

"Oh come!" Skane protested. "It's not fair to make a comparison like that. I love you as much as Carney ever did—more! I'm absolutely mad about you and you know it."

"Blind!" she exclaimed in that crushed voice, as if she had not heard, as if Skane were not there at all. "I was the blind one—I! Not to have seen! Not to have known! And all those things so plain to anyone but me!"

Skane regarded her carefully. Her lit face puzzled him. A bit of sentimental hysteria at the full knowledge of Carney's misfortune was feminine and natural, he supposed, but he could not understand the look of wild delight that now transfigured her.

"After all," he said reasonably, "there's nothing you can do about it. You've got your own life to live. And what about me?"

"I'm going back to Marina."

He started violently, as if she had announced that she were going to cut her throat. "My God, Isabel, pull yourself together. You can't go back there."

"Oh yes, I can, Greg. And I'm going. The *Elgin* leaves in two days, didn't you say? Don't you see how wonderful it all is—as if everything had been ordained in some way? It was so strange, the way Matthew and I came together in the first place. And then the whim that led me to Marina. And the urge for some-thing to do—'something to do'—that set me learning the code and practicing at the instruments. Do you remember the day we persuaded him to let me take a watch? Don't you see the meaning of it all?"

Skane stared at her. "Look here, you don't mean you'd chuck everything that's good in life to go back to that barren heap and be a—a lamp for Carney?"

She threw back her head and smiled. "Yes—yes, that's it. A lamp for Carney! I've always dreamed of being loved by some man utterly—completely—abso-lutely—as Matthew has loved me. But love by itself wasn't enough. All my life I've wanted—I've craved to have someone need me absolutely and completely. To feel that I was doing something that mattered, that nobody else could do. To feel that my life had a purpose. And not to feel lonely any more. Those are the things I've really wanted. They've been vague and separate things. I never saw them clearly and together until now. And now they're waiting for me on Marina, in spite of all my folly and stupidity!"

Skane took his amazed eyes from the radiant face. He kicked a twig into the stream, watched it drift aimlessly on the skirt of the eddy and then dash over the sill of the old dam towards the valley and the sea. From the moment that Isabel had brought him here he had debated the exact point at which he should take her in his arms and put an end to her doubts and questions with his kisses. He was confident that his own keen long-ing must pass to her with actual contact like so much electricity. But the moment had never come, and now her face confounded him. He regarded her with sidelong glances, incredulous and appalled, as a savage who has come upon a lunatic in the woods might regard a creature touched by the gods.

"Come!" she said imperiously, and she began to run down the rough trail towards the car.

When she stopped to let him out at the hotel Skane closed the car door carefully and paused with his hands upon it. The exalted look had gone out of her face and to the glances of passers-by she was once more the composed young woman who worked for old Dollars-and-Deuteronomy. But in the clear gray eyes Skane perceived a deep and shining happiness that he had never seen before. It nettled him. It was as if he had never existed.

"Tell me," he said. "If I'd managed to hold my tongue, if I hadn't solved the riddle of Carney for you, would it have made a difference?"

She gave him her hand and a brilliant smile. "Good-by, Greg. I shall always be grateful."

"Would it?" he repeated, with her hand in his grasp. She drew it free with a firm little tug and turned with a brisk air to the steering wheel. Her lips twitched. A mysterious expression played over them.

In that moment she seemed to Skane the image of Eve incarnate, at once weak and resolute, wise and foolish, prim and bold, a creature of impulse with a strangely rational mind, the natural prey of man's deceptions and desires and yet his master in these and all things, world without end, amen. His kisses, his embraces, all those hot intimacies by the island pool, had passed over her like a summer storm on the dunes. They had not left a trace.

"That, Greg," she said, slipping the clutch into gear, "is a riddle that you'll have to solve for yourself."

The car fled away towards the Hallett house and left him standing in the puddled clay before the hotel, among the fallen leaves.

CHAPTER 37

The train clicked along the valley, passing towns exactly like Kingsbridge, and the small red chalets of way stations, and farmhouses with white shingles or clapboards glinting in the sun, and mile on mile of orchards marching through the fields. Most of the trees stood bare, and they and the shrubs along the roadsides had a scrubbed look after the storm. The autumn sunshine gave an amber tint to everything but the air was very clear and the long hills looked close enough to hit with a pebble.

At Windsor the train rumbled over a deep chasm of red mud and poured smoke along the main street of the town. Here the orchard country ended. The engine uttered a mournful howl and dived into somber woods of spruce and fir. There were sudden gaps where small streams flashed beneath the bare branches of maples, and sometimes a stony clearing and a ramshackle cottage shot into view and disappeared. Sometimes the rails emerged from the woods and ran beside the motor highway, and then there were fields and wayside farmhouses, and an occasional crossroads hamlet with a store, a red gasoline pump and a church, or a small sawmill with its yellow heap and its tall stack belching the smoke of burning slabs.

When the conductor came through the cars announcing "Bedford next! Bedford!" Isabel sat up with a flutter in her breast. The first sight of salt water after months in the country was always exciting, and now—now it meant everything. The train rushed beside a small river, past the rifle ranges of the garrison troops, and suddenly there it was, the placid water of Bedford Basin pink in the sunset, and far across its polished surface the outskirts and the smoky pall of Halifax. She remembered the time when this great anchorage was alive with ships awaiting convoy, and from the transports came the music of military bands playing Lancelot towards the wars. It was empty now except for a few pleasure craft, and enclosed as it was by the bowl of hills it seemed no part of the harbor or the sea.

The engine trailed its smoke around the curving shore. Then it howled again and rushed between steep rock faces that shut out the evening light and left the passengers with nothing to see but each other, gathering coats and hats and hand-baggage in a sudden dusk. Wreaths of mingled smoke and steam sailed past the windows. Daylight again, the last light of an autumn evening, and the red and green lights of switch points going past, and the train slowing down in a multitude of tracks that ran off like the delta of a steel Mississippi spreading and flowing to the sea. Isabel could see the masts of ships. Then the final plunge into the vast sooty cavern of the Halifax station, with electric lights glowing in the smoky vapor overhead like rows of small moons, the clatter of baggage trucks, newsboys shouting, people running, exclaiming, clutching and kissing, the iron ring of garrison boots, and best of all the familiar sight of seamen laden with duffel bags, laughing and whistling along the platforms.

When the taxi driver said, "Where to, Miss?" she hesitated. She had always stayed in boardinghouses or private lodgings and it appalled her to realize that her only acquaintance with hotels was the Boston House at Kingsbridge and that one night in the dingy Travelers' Arms. On this last fateful journey she determined to have nothing but the best. The Queen Hotel was where most of the government members stayed when the legislature was in session, and she had heard that there was a telephone in every room. It seemed to her the height of respectability and luxury. "The Queen," she said.

Half an hour later she was dining in her best frock in the heart of Nova Scotia politics. When she returned to her room she went to the telephone, and paused. Hurd's office was closed, of course. She considered calling him at his home, but she remembered how he hated being disturbed after office hours and after a mental wrestle she gave it up. Nevertheless she burned with impatience. She had a morbid fear that Skane was mistaken about the date of O'Dell's sailing for Marina. Suppose the *Lord Elgin* had gone? She would have to wait until next spring for another chance. Frightful! A dozen times she went to the phone determined to call Hurd out of his evening diversions, out of his bed if necessary, and each time she came away.

She had brought nothing to read and she rejected the notion of going to a show. Nothing on stage or screen could approach her own small drama in importance. Indeed when she thought of the island far off in the night, with its living and its dead, all gripped and imprisoned by the sea, then the lights and noise and human scramble of the city became obscene. How selfish and how petty all these creatures seemed. They lived off the sea, they admitted that in the very motto of the port, and yet each day they scurried away from their shops and offices, their docks and wharves, and never gave a thought to what passed beyond the harbor heads. Sometimes they saw in their newspapers that a steamer had rammed another in a fog, that a schooner had foundered in a gale, that fishermen had gone adrift in a dory on the Banks or that a lobster smack had been blown off the coast to oblivion; and always there were men dead or missing who only a few nights back had been whistling along Water Street and winking at the girls. But nobody cared.

Isabel knew none of the phrases that were to become so worn and shabby in the time to come, and it did not occur to her even vaguely as she looked from the hotel window that she was gazing upon the brave new world, the world fit for heroes to live in, the world of the lost generation, the world made safe for democracy in terms of jazz and bootleg whiskey and money, that grew on the bushes, the era of wonderful nonsense that could ignore the slump of '21 and go on to the crash of '29. Along the sidewalks passed the bobbing heads, male and female, intent upon an evening's pleasure after the day's pursuit of cash, and she looked upon them with resentment and contempt. And she saw again the figure of Carney wandering these streets, the blond bearded man from the sea with his simple dignity, his strength, his faith in duty, his honest heart, a lost and lonely figure in the rush. She could see him now, standing outside the post office, looking sternly at that preposterous soldier on the South Africa monument, and waiting for the pale young woman from Hurd's office. And she could smile now at the memory of herself slipping up to him, hoping that no one she knew would see her with this outlandish character, and praying for a quick end to the evening.

With recollections of that embarrassed friendship and its climax she filled the wakeful spaces of the night, for she was too excited to sleep properly. The port's small yellow tramcars clanged and droned past the hotel, the arc lights cast a blue-white glare into the room, the voices of passers-by floated up to her window until the small hours. When at last the city lay dead under its lights like a great corpse in state she could think of nothing but the morning, and she lay full length on her back in the big hotel bed praying devoutly that the *Lord Elgin* was where it ought to be, loading stores at the Dartmouth wharf. At a quarter to nine in the morning she was part of the daily throng, walking quickly to the office as if the events of the past fourteen months had not happened at all and she were simply on her way to work like all the others. When she entered she found the anteroom and the stenographers' room deserted. Evidently Miss Benson and the new girl had stopped at the post office to pick up the mail. There was a sound of movement in Hurd's sanctum. She rapped on the door and went in, and found him hanging his bowler hat and black topcoat on the tree behind his desk. He looked up casually and his eyes went very wide.

"Miss Jardine—Mrs. Carney, I mean! It was so natural to see you standing there that for a minute I was taken quite aback. Where on earth have you been?"

"Convalescing in the country," Isabel replied coolly. He adjusted his pince-nez and looked her up and down.

"You look very well. You've fully recovered?"

"Oh yes, and now I'm on my way back to Marina." She said it glibly but she held her breath until he spoke.

"I see. Well, there's no rush. The *Elgin's* just begun to load the winter stores for the island, and it'll take two more days—all that coal and so on. There's some mail for the operators; do you want to take it or shall I put it in the mailbag? There are one or two mail-order parcels."

"In that case you'd better put it in the mailbag—all but Matthew's. I'll take that. I've got some shopping to do. Will you send word to Captain O'Dell and arrange about my berth?"

"Yes, of course." Hurd sat at his desk and adjusted his tie.

"You really intend to stay this time? I mean of course you really like the life out there?"

"I'd much rather live there than here."

"Did you see that chap Skane? He had a message for you and seemed quite anxious about it."

"Yes. It wasn't important after all."

She heard Miss Benson come in, and she withdrew to the outer office, closing Hurd's door behind her. The new typist, a petite brunette with a skirt as short as Miss Benson's, was talking vivaciously to a brass-bound young sea op in the anteroom. Miss Benson was at her desk, looking a little drawn.

"Hello!" she said in an astonished voice, like Hurd. "You're going back to Marina? Really?"

"Really."

"How do you feel?"

"Wonderful."

out with sailing ships. Marina's long and low, with shallow bars out from both ends. You can't see it until you're right on top of it. The windjammers used to get caught on a lee shore and there was nothing they could do to save themselves. With steamers it's altogether different."

"But in fog—you have a lot of fog out there, don't you?"

"Oh, there's always some danger, of course. But most ships nowadays have modern sounding equipment. And since the war they can get cross bearings any time they want them, from the radio direction-finding stations on the mainland. A lot of the passenger liners now have their own D.F. equipment, and my husband says it won't be long before everything down to the smallest tramps will carry it. There's no guesswork in navigation any more."

He regarded Isabel with interest. This brisk nautical talk fell from her lips with fluent ease. She did not look or talk the least bit like a former school ma'am.

"Then what on earth do the islanders find to do?"

"Ah, that's my point. They attend to the lighthouses and they patrol the beaches in thick weather. They practice with the lifeboat and the breeches-buoy equipment—just in case. But most of the time they just exist, in stations miles apart, month after month, summer and winter, watching the sea, waiting for something that almost never happens. And yet they must be there in case it does. Don't you see? The monotony! The monotony! Nowhere to go, nothing to do, nothing to read—a lot of them can't read—nothing to see but their own strip of dunes and the surf breaking miles out on the bars. The utter dreariness of life in such a place—neither land nor sea, a foothold you might say in the midst of the Flood, with an Ark that turns up three or four times a year with supplies!"

"The people," he asked, "What are they like?"

She thought before replying. "The lifeboat crew are all sorts, mostly single men, or men without women anyhow. They come and go. The others are the real islanders, most of them born there. In some cases the post has been handed down from father to son or to daughter's husband for generations. They're very superstitious, as you may readily understand; but they're good people, they do their duty faithfully, and they're always ready to risk their lives if an occasion should arise. Marina's their home and they don't look upon it as anything else. They don't get much pay, but of course money doesn't mean very much out there, They're housed and supplied with food and fuel—none of the ordinary worries of existence. It satisfies them. And that's the trouble, that's their actual danger—the inertia of a life in which nothing ever happens but a duck shoot or a pony ride. That's what I've come to talk to you about. The older people are settled in their ways and nothing can be done about it. For them it's an ideal existence. But I think the children ought to have a chance."

He tapped a pencil on the desk. "What you propose, as I understand it, is to hold classes for the children on certain days of the week, from April to November—the fine months of the year. How could the youngsters get there? You say the stations are scattered from east to west and the island's twenty-odd miles long."

"On pony-back. It will be a long ride for those from the east end. But in case of a sudden storm they could stay overnight with us or at Main Station—a mile away. The McBains would be very glad to help in that way."

"Any children of your own?"

"None—yet."

"I see. Of course you understand this is very unusual. You say you can't guarantee to hold school more than two or three times a week, and none at all in the winter months. I'm afraid the Board wouldn't approve paying a teacher on that basis."

"Oh, I don't want pay!" she exclaimed. "All I want is a set of school-books, pencils, scribbling paper—all that kind of thing— for about a dozen youngsters."

"I see." There was a friendly gleam in the eyes behind the desk. "Well, we can do that all right. I'll see that the stuff is sent down to the ship in time for sailing." He arose and put out his hand. "May I say that this is not only an unusual but a very heart-warming experience. It's splendid!"

Isabel flushed. "I'm thinking purely of myself," she explained. "I'll have my household duties—I've got a very good husband to look after—but there will be times when like everybody else on Marina I shall need something else to do."

She walked out with her own words ringing in her ears on a gentle note of mockery. That awful phrase!

CHAPTER 38

The *Lord Elgin* cast off her lines and drew away from the wharf on a gray November afternoon, in a drizzle of cold rain. Captain O'Dell invited Isabel to the bridge to watch the departure, and she stood in the starboard wing in her plain khaki raincoat and brown tam. The city's smoke hung low over the rooftops and the long waterfront slid past, a succession of dingy wharf ends and the fat round sterns of ships, like a caricature of the horse stalls at the Kingsbridge Fair.

"Depressing, eh?" said O'Dell's voice at her side. "I like Halifax, mind you, but when you're pulling out on a day like this it looks like the city that God forgot. The war, I suppose. The big explosion of '17 played skittles with the wharves and warehouses, and they were just patched up on a make-do basis. Now there's a shipping slump and I suppose there won't be a lick of paint or a new nail driven on Water Street for years. But all ports look the same, by and large. The citizens see towards the water and everything town-side is fixed up pretty well. Nobody cares a hoot what Jack thinks, coming in at the back door. That's the way the world lives, when you stop to think of it; all paint and plate glass where the street goes by, and the garbage and the dead cats at the back. How do you like that starboard cabin? Are you comfortable?"

"Oh yes, it's very nice."

"Sorry I couldn't let you have the one you had before. It was booked for an inspector of lighthouses, making the round."

She laughed. "I wouldn't want it for anything. The memories are too powerful. I was awfully sick in there—do you remember? I hope to behave better this time."

"You keep your chin up and you'll be all right. The sea's been down for days—one of these oily fall calms. And we'll be out of the rain in a few hours. I got the weather probs just before we pulled out. A spell of Indian summer moving up from the sou'west. In Boston they're sweltering. There'll be some hot work at Marina, getting all this stuff ashore and up the beach, especially the coal."

"When shall we be there?" Isabel said eagerly.

"We'll be rounding the west bar at first light tomorrow if all goes well. That'll give McBain a full ten hours of daylight for the job. Are you happy to be going back?"

"Very."

"You keep clear of guns after this. That was a nasty accident you had. I hear Carney's given up duck-hunting." The cold blue eyes bored into hers. "He getting squeamish about his feathered friends?"

"He's getting civilized," Isabel said calmly. "It's the result of having a squeamish wife. I'm starting a Society for the Prevention of Cruelty to Ponies, too."

"Good! Can't you do something about the Prevention of Going to Sea for poor old chaps like McIntyre and me?"

An incoming steamer loomed in the rain ahead, and O'Dell moved away towards the helmsman, speaking in his high voice.

A yacht club appeared to starboard with all its craft hauled up and snugged under tarpaulins for the winter. Then the long stone breakwater and the dark pines of Point Pleasant. Isabel watched eagerly for the place where so often she had brooded alone, and where she had kept that first involuntary tryst with Carney; but it was shrouded in rain and only the sea wall of the old battery showed against the gloomy mass of the pines. The entrance to Northwest Arm gaped beyond, a wet doorway leading nowhere and screened by gray portieres that thinned and gathered mysteriously with the uncertain easterly breeze. Then the tall mass of York Hill, with the steep road, and the white church halfway up, and the low gun-casements of the fort on top. A foghorn blared from the port side, where the squat round tower of the lighthouse showed very close and clear with the long wooded bulk of McNab's Island running on beyond.

The ship began to lift and settle gracefully on the easy swell running in past Chebucto Head. Soon to starboard Isabel could make out the low hill of Camperdown, with the old army signal tower on its crest and the gray wooden bungalow of the wireless station on the shoulder below. Within a few moments she heard the hoarse spark of the *Lord Elgin's* wireless sounding through the bulkhead. At once in the inner mechanism of her brain the sound became a spoken and familiar tongue, without effort, without even conscious thought. O'Dell's operator was calling VCS, that gray box on the hillside, and asking QRU?—"Have you anything for me?"

Apparently VCS had nothing, for in a moment or two the ship's spark uttered a couple of dots, the operators' casual way of saying All Right or 'Nough Said, and she heard the dying whine of a switched-off motor. She was reassured to find that this scrap of code talk came so pat to her mind, that she had forgotten nothing of those patient lessons nor those long hours at the Marina phones. And she summoned up Carney's deep voice repeating, "Once you've stood a busy watch or two the code is yours for keeps. After that it's simply a language that you know, that you can't forget if you tried. By Jingo, you'll think in dots and dashes for the rest of your life." And she heard Skane adding, with his dark grin, "Horrible, isn't it?"

The rich essence of the valley, the after-harvest smell of the fields and the wet pungency of the mountain woods, had faded in the stuffy varnish and coal fumes of the train; and that had given way to the city smell, that compost of soot and sweat and gasoline, of cloth and scent and paper, of hot food and warm flesh and stale human breath which hung in the streets and poured from the doorways of shops and offices. And now all that was gone, too. Now there was only the breath of the sea, the sharp clean reek of salt and kelp, rich in its own way, distilled from thousands of square miles of untainted ocean for the ventilation of the world.

The North Atlantic was in one of its tranquil moods. Under the weeping veils of rain its mild swell rose and sank with a majestic regularity, the breast of a stormy woman gone to sleep and gathering fresh strength for the passions of tomorrow. All that was evil and cruel about her, all that was bright and beautiful, lay concealed now beneath that enormous breathing skin. There was no sky and no horizon. The ship, weary and old like O'Dell himself, pushed forward in a gray murk dragging a white train that spread and was lost in the murk astern. She had good lines, she was shapely in her fashion, and she had a fine sheer forward and an old-fashioned clipper bow that always gave dockside loafers an impression of great speed. But at best she did ten knots, usually it was much less, and here in the thick weather she seemed to crawl, uttering a tremulous *moo* from time to time.

Yet she moved, and as she moved the dim bulk of the land slipped away behind the rain like a shadow, an illusion after all. With it went all those other illusions: the scrabble for cash that could not buy security, the frantic pleasures that could not give content, the pulpit-thumpings that could not summon virtue, the Temperance Acts that killed temperance, the syncopated noise that was not music, the imbecile daubs that were not art, the lavatory scrawls that were not literature, the flickering Californications that were not drama, the fortunes that grew upon ticker tapes, the statesmanship that was only politics, the peace that led only towards more bloody war, the whole brave new world of '21 that was only old evil with a mad new face. Like an aging empress quitting with dignity a palace given over to the *Jacquerie* the old ship departed from the continent and trailed her long white gown across the green fields of the sea.

Towards the end of the afternoon the rain ceased. There was a stir of air, warm and delightful, from the starboard hand; and in another half hour the overcast broke in the west and revealed the sun poised on the edge of the sea, a fat red ball that cast a ruddy shimmer widespread on that gently heaving skin. In a few moments it rolled over the edge of the world and was gone, but the whole of the west was drenched with the scarlet splash of that plunge and there were streaks of bloody gold along the horizons to north and south. For a long time afterwards in the new high western sky that display remained when all the rest was dusk, except that towards the east, towards Marina, where the night already was far up the sky, there hung in reflection a wonderful purple stain slowly fading into the dark.

Isabel left this splendid show reluctantly to bath and change her dress before dinner (a meal known in the *Lord Elgin* with simple honesty as supper) and when the steward rang his bell along the deck it was night. In the saloon once more she was the only woman at the board. O'Dell was there in his best uniform and with the eager preoccupied look that always came upon him at the prospect of food, and in their places stood the chief officer, handsome and severe; the gloomy McIntyre; the purser and his dissipated gray features, strange in so young a man; and the bluntly healthy second mate. The other passenger, the inspector of lighthouses, a Mr. Forbes, came in at Isabel's heels, and there were introductions as they all sat down and the steward began to pass the soup.

As before the wife of the fabulous Carney was the center of interest, but with an added glamor of her own; she had overheard a seaman saying as she came on board, "Here's the Marina woman, the dame that came off in a sling." She bore the concentrated attention of the table with *sang-froid* and there was a respectful admiration in their glances, as if the ability to get shot and carry it off well were a mark of the greatest distinction. For a time the talk was slow and awkward but before long Isabel discovered that Mr. Forbes, like so many others whose profession dragged them up and down the coast, dreamed of a day when he could retire to a snug little farm inland. He was a tall and heavily built man nearing sixty, with thick gray hair and a pair of hazel eyes that sparkled behind his steel-rimmed glasses when Isabel, at his urging, gave an account of harvest time in the valley.

He was enraptured. He paid no attention to his food. He had the air of a man listening to celestial music. At length he said to her with a curious lift of his brows, "I don't see how you can tear yourself away from all that to face a winter on Marina. What a contrast!"

"You forget my husband's there."

"Why don't you make him take you ashore and buy a good house in the country?" Isabel knew what he thought; it was a common illusion on the coast that wireless operators, especially O-in-C's like Carney, got fantastic salaries and that after a few years in some isolated spot they could retire in comfort for the rest of their lives.

"Some day perhaps," she answered deliberately. "In the meantime I shall be entirely happy on Marina. Once you know what a place is like, you know what to do about it. Life anywhere's what you make it—and life on Marina can be wonderful." Forbes glanced up expecting to see the patient look that belonged to such words about such a place, and saw the radiance that had so astonished Skane, and that made her plain face beautiful.

Afterwards, when the officers had gone and the steward had cleared the table, she sat with Forbes and O'Dell on the red plush cushions of the settee. Forbes produced cigars, and Isabel lit a cigarette. The steward turned on the phonograph. It was a very good machine securely fastened to a special shelf beside the sideboard. The tune of the latest fox trot crashed in the silence of the saloon. The warm wind from the southwest, still blowing in the dark, had changed the direction of the swell, and as the *Lord Elgin* swayed with a long easy motion the needle arm occasionally jumped out of the groove and slid across the record, producing discords even wilder than the African strains of the band. At last the steward moved beside it, steadying the needle arm with his hand.

O'Dell turned to Isabel. "D'you like this modern stuff? I can't call it music."

"No."

He gestured to the steward. "Belay that thing." The jazz notes perished.

"Do you want me for anything else, sir?"

"No, you may go."

The trio on the settee talked in a desultory fashion for a time and then Forbes arose, stifling a yawn and murmuring something about a long day tomorrow and all those confounded steps to climb. He bade the others good night and walked away with his solid tread to bed. The porthole curtains swayed gently and the glasses on the sideboard clicked together in their fiddleholes.

"Still feel all right?" Captain O'Dell asked.

"Perfectly all right. On that first trip I was rather upset from the start—we'd come away in such a rush; and of course the weather wasn't anything as mild as this."

O'Dell nodded absently. "There'll be a bit of a slop on the beach in the morning, though. You'd better stay aboard till we've got some of the heavy stores ashore. A surfboat with a light load rides up on the beach better."

He studied the gray wisp arising from the cigar in his delicate fingers.

"There's something I want to speak to you about, now that we're alone, and I don't quite know how to say it. About Carney. I've known him a long time. I think a lot of him. It's always seemed to me that Carney measured closer to God's standard of a man than anyone else I knew. Lately, ever since he came off the island in the spring of '20 in fact, there's been something about him I couldn't fathom. Men who didn't know him very well used to say that Carney lived in a shell, but I could never see it. Till now. The shell's there all right. And he's right down inside."

"Yes?" Isabel kept her gaze on the sideboard and its polished brass rail.

"I suppose you're wondering why I've brought this up. Partly it's because I've a notion that something went adrift between Carney and you. That's none of my business, I know, but I might as well say what I think. However there's something else. When I went to the island last spring and again in August he didn't come off to the ship. That was strange. He always steered one of the surfboats when they were unloading stores. The rougher the sea the better he liked it. With some of the wilder young lifesavers he'd take a boat off the beach in a surf that would scare McBain—and Mac's a good little man. Now all of a sudden Carney's lost his delight in that kind of thing.

"When I went on the beach in August he was there backing stuff up the shore from the boats. Didn't seem to want to talk. Wouldn't look me in the eye—just kept lugging things back and forth. I stayed to the last, talking to the other people, and when we were about to shove off he spoke to me, gazing over my shoulder somewhere. He said in a dull sort of way, 'There was no other passenger?' I said 'No.' Then he asked, 'Was there any personal mail for me?' And again the answer was no. He turned away. He looked mighty tired—he'd been working like a slave all day, of course—and I noticed then a small gold ring slung by a cord about his neck. I'd often seen him stripped to the waist like that when the work was hot, but I'd never noticed the ring before. I didn't think much about it, but that night, lying in my berth, one or two things occurred to me and set me wondering.

"The third mate had gone ashore with me that morning. We stepped out of the boat on opposite sides and walked up the beach towards Carney. I suppose we were ten or twelve feet apart. We were both in uniform and about the same height; otherwise we're not a bit alike. Carney was at the beachhead checking stores with one of his operators and I sang out Hello. He straightened up and gazed down the beach, turning his head slowly from me to the Third. And he addressed himself to the Third, calling out something about empty gas drums to be shipped off, and that they were coming up by wagon from the wireless station and mustn't be left behind, and so on. I thought it kind of funny that he should be saying all this to the Third and ignoring me. He was still talking when we got within ten feet of him, and then he stopped, with an odd look on his face, and turned his eyes to me. For a moment he was silent. Then he went on with what he had to say—you know, as if he'd been addressing me all the time.

"After that, as I've said, he didn't seem to have anything more to say, not a personal word, none of the old chummy gam we used to have together on the beach. After a time another boat came in, and out jumped one of the lifesavers who'd gone to Halifax with us in the spring. Chap named Blackburn. He sang out 'Carney boy!'—you know, the way they all do when they see him—and walked up the beach towards him just as we'd done. Carney merely answered hello in a noncommittal sort of way, but when the fellow got about ten feet away—I was watching the distance this time to make sure—Carney suddenly grinned and exclaimed 'Blackie!' You know, as if the name had just slipped his mind until that moment. Afterwards, in my berth aboard the ship, these things rang a little bell in my mind. Do they ring anything in yours?"

Isabel turned and met his sunken eyes, the small blue eyes that were so keen and alive in that weary cynical face.

"Yes. You mean Matthew's losing his sight. The doctors say he will be blind in another year at most."

"So you knew! I wondered."

"I know now. I didn't when you took me off last spring. He concealed it from me. For some months he wouldn't believe what the oculists said. He thought it was just a sudden case of shortsightedness. It wasn't until last winter that he knew they were right. When I last rode along the island with him, last spring, in the bright sunlight, he could still distinguish people at quite a distance. But that was nearly seven months ago."

"Ah!" O'Dell nodded slowly. "That explains a good deal." He ground out his cigar in the ash tray before him. "Do you know, when you failed to turn up in August I thought you'd had enough of it—that you'd left the island for good. I used to phone the hospital from time to time when we were in port, to see how you were getting along; and so I knew that you could have come back on the August trip if you'd wished. And Carney knew it. I could see it in his manner there on the beach, when he asked about the passengers and mail. He looked very lonely. And later on, when I realized he was losing his sight—and how fast it was going—I got a double shock. For I remembered something he'd told me long before.

"You know what a reader he was—always quoting Byron and so on. Always after me for any old books or magazines that might be lying about the ship. Some time in '17 or '18, when all sorts of navy people were going about the coast with us, someone left behind a book about the old Norse kings. In English of course. I'd picked it up from time to time and read a bit of it. Well, I gave it to Carney, and you can imagine how he ate it up. When I came, next trip, he was full of it, and he sent off for a book on Norse mythology. You know, he looks like a Viking himself. I don't mean just that he's big and blond but his manner, the way he carries himself, something noble and fearless about him, like one of those old sea kings. I used to kid him about it. I told him once he was living proof that the Norsemen came to Newfoundland. He didn't like that, I remember, and went on to talk about something else.

"Well, one day on the beach he got talking about the old Norse beliefs. This must have been in the spring of '20—the time he went off to see the eye doctors. Told me about Ran, the sea goddess. She had caves at the bottom of the ocean, a sort of Fiddler's Green, where drowned sailors were entertained with food and drink and each found a nymph waiting for him shaped in the image of the woman he'd most desired on earth. It sounded pretty swell. But there was a bit of a catch. It seems that the Lady Ran's a rather mercenary creature. No sailor could get in unless he had a bit of gold to pay for the accommodation. A bit of the real yellow stuff—nothing else would do. That's why those old Norse rovers used to wear a gold bracelet or a ring or an amulet or something of that sort whenever they shoved off to sea. Just in case. A kind of life-hereafter insurance. Carney told me all this and we both laughed. But then he said, quite seriously, 'It's all bosh, of course, but the idea's sort of splendid. When the ship went down or the fight was lost, when there was no hope left, a man could let himself sink and feel that all would be well.' And he threw out that big right arm of his towards the breakers on the outer shoals, where he often used to swim."

Isabel was rising from her seat and staring with eyes that seemed to him enormous. "What do you mean?"

"I'm just trying to explain," O'Dell said quietly, "why I couldn't find words to say when you came up the gangway this morning. My dear, you were the finest sight in the world."

CHAPTER 39

She was awake long before daylight. When the *Lord Elgin* rounded the west bar she had washed and dressed and was busy packing her things and checking over the multitude of parcels which seemed to fill half the cabin. As she tucked away her nightdress her fingers encountered a piece of paper. She drew forth the old wedding license and stood for a moment in profound thought. It had no value here. She had kept it out of sentiment and a notion that it made her relations with Carney quite respectable. Absurd! Her union with him was ordained and complete in itself. Life had thrown them together on a desolate shore where none of the old rules applied. A marriage of castaways. As for this patch of print and scrawled ink, the license had lost its meaning along with the world of which it was part, the mad world they had put behind. Slowly and firmly she tore the thing to shreds and let them flutter from her fingers out of the porthole.

She appeared at breakfast with a tranquil face; and afterwards, watching the hatches taken off, the boats arriving alongside, the cargo booms sweeping back and forth, the flicker of white surf on the distant shore, she seemed to the glances of the crew no more than a composed wife returning from a holiday on the main. The heavy stores went first, the drums of gasoline and kerosene and lubricating oil, the coal sewn up in hundred-pound bags for ready handling in the boats, the deceptive little cylinders containing mercury that looked so insignificant and weighed so mightily, the bales of pressed hay, the barrels of salt beef and pork, of flour and sugar and molasses, the bags of salt, the machinery parts.

It was well on towards noon when she said good-by to the officers and went down the Jacob's ladder to the boat. Forbes came with her, and O'Dell. The captain, awaiting this moment, had delayed his customary state visit to the shore. He was burning with curiosity. All the way to the beach he watched with sidelong glances the calm face of the young woman in the stern. There was, as he had prophesied, a bit of a slop on the beach. Nothing to be alarmed about, but he regarded Isabel's smart costume and silken legs with some concern. He leaned over to her.

"When we run in, you'd better let one of the boatmen carry you out of the surf."

"I shall be all right."

"You should have worn boots and trousers," he said severely.

The steersman watched his chance. He chose the crest of a long green swell and cried to his oarsmen fiercely. The boat rode in. It was very neatly done. Almost as well, O'Dell thought, as Carney himself could have done it when his eyes were at their best. Not a drop came over the gunwales until the boat's keel touched the sand and the wave broke. There was a rush of island figures about the boat, clutching the gunwales or snatching up the most perishable packages. O'Dell turned swiftly to the steersman, commanding him to lift Mrs. Carney to dry footing. But his breath was wasted with the thought.

Before the words were out of his mouth Isabel stepped upon the thwart and poised a foot on the gunwale. In another moment she was in the water to her knees and wading swiftly to the shore. The captain sprang out and followed her, but at the edge of the dry and trampled sand he stopped. The air on the beach, where the sun was falling now with the full stroke of noon, made a grateful contrast to the cold nip of the water. The spell of Indian summer, which comes to the north country after the first hard frosts, had awakened an almost tropical heat in the sands of Marina. The dunes wavered as if it were July. In the mirage towards the east the tip of the wireless mast sagged in a drunken bow, the surf breaking on the long curved sands past Number Two seemed to spring straight in the air like the spouts of great whales; and the west lighthouse was going up and down like an insane phallic monument.

The brown men on the beach stared at the slender figure coming out of the sea with a wet dress clinging to her legs. But Captain O'Dell was looking past her. Carney stood at the beachhead by the pile of stores, where the little group of island women had gathered after their custom. Like most of the island men he had stripped to trousers and sea boots for the work and his skin gleamed like new bronze after the summer's exposure. Beside the figures of the women he seemed to tower, a sculptor's study posed before the lesser figures of a symbolic group. From the girl running up the beach came a single cry.

"Matthew!"

O'Dell saw Carney start, and throw up a hand to shield his eyes from the water glare. And in that attitude, with the clipped golden beard and hair gleaming in the sun, he looked—yes, by Jove, he looked like one of those Norse kings, right out of the *Heimskringla!* You sought for the winged helmet and the long war ax and saw nothing but the bit of gold, Ran's tribute, slung by the cord upon his breast. He gazed blankly towards the swiftly approaching figure of the woman. When she was almost up to him suddenly the frown dissolved and became a look of wonder, of incredulous delight. Then she was sobbing against his breast, held in those great bronze arms as if he feared the sea might take her back again.

"A fathom's length," muttered Captain O'Dell, "and not another inch," as if it were a matter of great moment, something that ought to be marked on the chart. "And noon—full light." He turned away, swallowing. He was a man who abhorred emotion and he summoned all his cynicism for a final judgment on this affair. Women! What strange creatures! All outward passion, all tears and kisses, all craving ease and pleasure and yet all morbid readiness for sacrifice and martyrdom. And yet—and yet who knew what lay at the bottom of their secret hearts?

Isabel Carney was not what you'd call pretty but she was rather nicely made. She had the ripe attractiveness which comes to slender women in their early thirties, she was at her best, you might say, and she knew it. And could she fail to know, this intelligent young woman, that in the days to come when Carney could see her no more he would go on thinking of her as he saw her now? Could she fail to realize that for Carney she would always be young, her hair would never be anything but that softly shining brown, her skin always fair, her eyes that clear gray, her figure that of a nymph running out of the sea? By Jove, what woman wouldn't chuck up the world for love in a desert on terms like that?

And having satisfied himself with this pronouncement Captain O'Dell startled the gaping boatmen with a shout.

"Look alive, there! D'ye think I've got all winter to drag my hook off this beach?"